# The Disappeared

ALSO BY KRISTINA OHLSSON
FROM CLIPPER LARGE PRINT

Unwanted
Silenced

# The Disappeared

## Kristina Ohlsson

Translated by Marlaine Delargy

W F HOWES LTD

This large print edition published in 2014 by
W F Howes Ltd
Unit 4, Rearsby Business Park, Gaddesby Lane,
Rearsby, Leicester LE7 4YH

1  3  5  7  9  10  8  6  4  2

First published in the United Kingdom in 2011
by Simon & Schuster UK Ltd

A CIP catalogue record for this book is available
from the British Library

ISBN 978 1 47126 109 1

Typeset by Palimpsest Book Production Limited,
Falkirk, Stirlingshire
Printed and bound by
www.printondemand-worldwide.com of Peterborough, England

*For Pia*

'In films murders are always very clean. I show how difficult it is and what a messy thing it is to kill a man.'

ALFRED HITCHCOCK

# PAST

# PREMIERE

When the film begins she has no idea what she is about to see. Nor does she realise what devastating consequences this film and the decisions she then makes will have on the rest of her life.

She has placed the projector on the coffee table, and the film is showing on a screen which she hastily dug out of the storeroom and set up in the middle of the floor. To get the angle right, she has propped the projector up on a book: Ira Levin's *A Kiss Before Dying*. A friend gave it to her for Christmas, and she hasn't yet plucked up the courage to read it.

The sound of the projector as it feeds the film through sounds like hail tapping against a window pane. The room is in darkness and she is alone in the house. She can't explain why she was curious about the film right from the start. Perhaps it's because she can't remember having seen it before. Or because she feels there is a reason why it has been kept hidden from her.

The first frame shows a room; she is sure it looks familiar. The picture is gloomy, the focus slightly

3

blurred. Someone has covered all the windows with sheets, but the daylight still finds its way in. There are a lot of windows; they seem to go all the way up to the ceiling. The film continues, the picture grows sharper. A door opens and a young woman appears. She hesitates in the doorway; she seems to be saying something. She looks towards the camera with a tentative smile. The picture bobs up and down and it becomes obvious that the camera is not fixed to a tripod; someone is holding it.

The woman walks into the room and closes the door behind her.

When she sees the door closing she realises where the film was made: in the summerhouse in her parents' garden. Without knowing why, she suddenly feels afraid. She wants to switch off the projector, but cannot bring herself to do it.

The door of the summerhouse opens once more and a masked man walks in. He has an axe in his hand. When the young woman sees him, she cries out and begins to back away. She bumps into one of the sheets and the man grabs hold of her to stop her from falling through the window and into the garden. He pulls her towards the middle of the room; the camera is shaking slightly.

The scenes which follow are difficult to comprehend. The man swings his axe at the woman's chest. Once, twice. Then at her head. He switches to a knife and – *oh, God* – soon she lies dead on the floor. One, two, three seconds elapse, and the film is over. The projector rattles impatiently, waiting for her to switch it off and rewind the film.

She is incapable of doing anything. She gazes blankly at the screen. What has she just seen? Eventually, she switches off the projector with stiff fingers. Rewinds the film. Runs it again. And again.

She isn't certain that it's real, but that doesn't actually matter. The content is disgusting, and the second time she watches the film she recognises the man in the mask. When was it made? Who is the young woman? And where were her parents when someone took over their summerhouse, covered all the windows and made a violent film inside it?

It is evening before she decides what to do. There are still more questions than answers, but that doesn't affect her ability to act. By the time he puts his key in the door and calls out 'Hi darling!' she has already made up her mind.

She will never be anyone's darling again.

And her child will never have a father.

# PRESENT

## 2009

## QUOTATION FROM INTERVIEW WITH ALEX RECHT, 01-05-2009

'I have worked as a police officer for more than half my life. This is without doubt the most revolting case I have ever encountered. It is a nightmare, an inferno of evil. A tale with absolutely no chance of a happy ending.'

# TUESDAY

# CHAPTER 1

The sun had been up for less than an hour when Jörgen saw a dead person for the first time. The frequent snowfalls of the winter followed by the spring rain had softened the ground and made the water levels rise. The combined forces of wind and weather had worked through layer after layer of the earth covering the body, and eventually a huge crater had opened up in the ground between the rocks and the trees.

However, the dead woman still wasn't fully visible. It was the dog that dug her up. Jörgen was standing among the trees, somewhat at a loss.

'Come on now, Svante.'

He had always found it difficult to make his voice heard, to gain the respect of others. His boss had pointed this out in countless appraisal interviews, and his wife had left him for that very reason.

'You take up so little room that you're practically bloody invisible,' she had said on the night she moved out.

And now here he was, standing in an unfamiliar forest with a dog that didn't even belong to him. His sister had insisted that he move into their house while he was looking after Svante. It was only for a week, after all, and surely it didn't make any difference to Jörgen where he lived for such a short time?

She was wrong; Jörgen could feel it in every fibre of his body. It made a huge difference where a person lived. Neither he nor Svante were particularly happy with this arrangement.

Weak rays of sunshine filtered down through the trees, making the glade glow softly in a golden light. Silent and peaceful. The only disturbing element was Svante's constant scrabbling in the pile of earth, his front paws thumping out a drumbeat on the ground. Soil was flying in all directions.

'Svante, come here,' Jörgen ventured, with a little more authority this time. But the dog was deaf to his plea and started to whimper with excitement and frustration. Jörgen sighed. He walked wearily over to the dog and clumsily patted his back.

'Listen, it's time we went home. I mean, we were here yesterday too. We can come back tomorrow.'

He could hear the way he sounded: as if he were talking to a small child. But Svante was not a child. He was a German Shepherd who weighed something in the region of thirty kilos, and he had picked up the scent of something that was a lot more interesting than his owner's weary brother, standing there on a mossy mound banging his feet up and down.

'You need to show him who's boss,' Jörgen's sister had said. 'Give clear commands.'

A burst of birdsong made Jörgen glance around anxiously. He was overcome by a sudden fear that someone else was nearby.

With one click he attached Svante's lead, and was about to embark on the final battle to get the dog home when he saw the plastic sack that had been exposed by Svante's efforts. The dog's jaws were locked, his teeth biting through the plastic; he tore away a large piece of the sack.

A body?

A dead person buried in the ground?

'Svante, come away!' Jörgen roared.

The dog froze in mid-movement and backed away. For the first and only time he obeyed his temporary master.

# INTERVIEW WITH FREDRIKA BERGMAN,
## 02-05-2009,
### 13.15 (tape recording)

Present: Urban S, Roger M (interrogators one and two). Fredrika Bergman (witness).

Urban: Could you tell us about the events which took place out on the island of Storholmen on April 30th, late in the afternoon?
Fredrika: No.
(The witness looks annoyed.)
Urban: No? OK, why not?
Fredrika: I wasn't there.
Roger: But you should be able to tell us about the background.
(Silence.)
Urban: It's an offence if you don't co-operate with us in this situation, Fredrika.
(Silence.)
Roger: After all, we already know everything. At least we think we do.
Fredrika: So why do you need me?
Urban: Well, the thing is, thinking we know something isn't really what police work is all about. And Peder Rydh is a colleague of all three of us. If there are any mitigating circumstances,

we would really like to hear about them. Right now.

(The witness looks tired.)

Roger: You've had a pretty rough time over the last few weeks, we're well aware of that. Your husband has been held in custody and your daughter . . .

Fredrika: We're not married.

Roger: Sorry?

Fredrika: Spencer and I are not married.

Urban: That's irrelevant; this case has been incredibly difficult and . . .

Fredrika: You're out of your bloody minds. Mitigating circumstances . . . how many do you need? Jimmy, his own brother, is dead. Dead. Do you get that?

(Pause.)

Roger: We know that Peder's brother is dead. We know that Peder was in a dangerous situation. But back-up was on the way, and there is nothing to indicate that he didn't have the situation under control. So why did he fire his gun?

(The witness is crying.)

Roger: Can't you just tell us the whole story, from start to finish?

Fredrika: But you already know everything.

Urban: Not everything, Fredrika. Otherwise, we wouldn't be sitting here.

Fredrika: Where do you want me to start?

Urban: From the beginning.

Fredrika: From the discovery of Rebecca Trolle's body?

Urban: Yes, I think that would be a good place to start.

(Silence.)

Fredrika: OK. I'll start there.

# CHAPTER 2

Inspector Torbjörn Ross was standing motionless among the trees in the forest glade. Straight-backed, his feet kept warm by lined Wellington boots. A chilly spring breeze crept by as the sunlight filtered down through the trees. It would soon be time to put the boat back out on the water.

Torbjörn gazed at the macabre discovery that had come to light when the two sacks unearthed by the dog an hour ago were slit open. The lower part of a body, and the torso.

'How long has she been lying there?' he asked the forensic pathologist.

'It's impossible to be precise out here, but I'd guess at around two years.'

Torbjörn let out a whistle.

'Two years!'

'I'm guessing, Ross.'

A constable coughed to attract Torbjörn's attention.

'We can't find the hands or the head.'

Torbjörn muttered to himself, then said, 'This is an old crime scene. I want a detailed examination of the entire area to see if the missing body parts are nearby. Use the dogs, and dig carefully.'

He didn't expect to find either the hands or the head, but he wanted to be sure. Cases like this always attracted a great deal of media attention. There was a limited margin for error. He turned back to the pathologist.

'How old do you think she is?'

'Unfortunately all I can say at this stage is that she's young.'

'And there's no sign of any clothing.'

'No, I can't find any traces of rotted fabric.'

'A sex crime.'

'Or a murder where it was vital that the victim couldn't be identified.'

Torbjörn nodded thoughtfully.

'You could be right.'

The pathologist held out a small object.

'Look at this.'

'What is it?'

'A navel piercing.'

'Bloody hell.'

The piece of jewellery rested between his thumb and forefinger: a silver ring with a tiny disc. Torbjörn rubbed it on his sleeve.

'There's something engraved on it.'

He peered at it, turning away from the bright sunshine.

'I think it says "Freedom".'

It slipped out of his hand and disappeared in the soil as he spoke.

'Damn.'

The pathologist looked distressed.

Torbjörn retrieved the item and went to fetch an evidence bag to put it in. Identification shouldn't be a problem now. Strange that a murderer who had been so meticulous otherwise should have missed such a crucial detail.

The body parts were lifted onto a stretcher with great care; they were then covered and taken away. Torbjörn stayed behind and made a call.

'Alex,' he said. 'Sorry to disturb you so early, but I wanted to warn you about a case which is bound to end up on your desk.'


It would soon be time for lunch. Spencer Lagergren wasn't really hungry, but as he had a meeting at one o'clock and didn't know how long it would take, he wanted to make sure he had something to eat beforehand.

He ordered chicken and rice at Kung Krål restaurant in the Old Square in Uppsala, and after his meal he walked quickly through the town, up towards Carolina Rediviva, past the majestic library and on towards the English Park where the Department of Literature was based. How many times had he taken this route? Sometimes he almost believed he could do it with his eyes shut.

His leg and hip began to ache when he was only about halfway there. The doctors had promised him a return to full mobility after the car accident, if only he would be patient. In spite of this it had been difficult to remain optimistic at first. It had been such a close thing. How ironic it would have been if he had died just when everything was starting to come right. After decades of unhappiness, Spencer was about to pull himself together and do the right thing. And that led to even more unhappiness.

He had been off sick for several months. When he became a father for the first time, he had just started learning to walk again. During the birth he didn't know whether to sit or stand; the midwife offered to wheel in a bed so that he could lie down. He declined, politely but firmly.

With the baby came fresh energy and an ability to recover. The split from Eva was nowhere near as dramatic as he had imagined it would be. His departure was overshadowed by the car accident that almost cost him his life, and the woman who was now his ex-wife didn't say a word as the removal men emptied their home of his belongings in just a few hours. Spencer was there to make sure everything went smoothly, keeping an eye on proceedings from his favourite armchair. When the van was loaded it felt almost symbolic as he rose from the chair and allowed it to be carried out as the very last item.

'Look after yourself,' he said as he stood in the doorway.

'You too,' Eva said.

'I'll be in touch.'

He raised his hand in a hesitant gesture of farewell.

'Good.'

She smiled as she spoke, but her eyes shone with unshed tears. Just as he was about to close the door he heard her whisper:

'Things were good between us for some of the time, weren't they?'

He nodded to show his agreement, but the lump in his throat prevented him from speaking. He closed the door of the house that had been their shared home for almost thirty years, and one of the removal men helped him down the steps.

That was almost nine months ago, and so far he hadn't been back.

However, life had been full of other, more trivial steps on the road to recovery. His return to work was one example. Rumours spread like wildfire through the faculty that the esteemed professor had left his wife and home to live with a young woman in Stockholm who had just had his baby. Spencer realised with a wry smile that people couldn't decide whether it was appropriate to offer their congratulations when he became a father.

The only thing he found difficult about his new life, apart from his restricted mobility, was the move to Stockholm. All of a sudden he felt spiritually lost. When the train pulled into the station in Uppsala, he didn't want to go back. This town was a big part of his identity, not only professionally but privately too. The rhythm of life in Stockholm didn't really suit him, and he missed Uppsala more than he was prepared to admit.

He had reached the university. The head of the Department of Literature was Erland Malm, and he and Spencer had known each other ever since they were both newly employed graduates working towards their doctorates. They had never been close, but nor had they been enemies, or even rivals. Their relationship could be described as good, but nothing more.

'Sit down, Spencer,' said Erland.

'Thanks.'

It was nice to rest his leg and hip after the walk. He leaned his stick against the arm of the chair.

'I'm afraid I've received some rather distressing information,' Erland went on.

*Distressing?*

'Do you remember Tova Eriksson?'

Spencer thought for a moment.

'I was her supervisor last autumn, along with Malin, the new tutor. I'd just started working part time.'

'What are your recollections of your work with Tova?'

A sound from the corridor reminded them that Erland's office door was open; he got up and closed it.

'I don't remember there being any problems.' Spencer spread his hands wide, wishing he'd been offered a cup of coffee.

'She wasn't particularly conscientious, and both Malin and I wondered why she'd chosen such a tricky topic for her dissertation. It wasn't easy to

24

set her on the right track. As far as I recall, her dissertation wasn't approved at the final seminar.'

'Did you have many meetings with her?'

'No, only a couple; Malin took care of the rest. I think that annoyed Tova; she didn't really want to be supervised by a tutor rather than a professor.'

Spencer's stick slid to one side, and he propped it against Erland's desk.

'What's this actually about?'

Erland cleared his throat.

'Tova Eriksson claims that you put obstacles in her way from start to finish. That you said you wouldn't help her unless she . . .'

'Unless she what?'

'Carried out sexual favours for you.'

'I'm sorry?'

Spencer laughed out loud before the anger kicked in.

'*I'm sorry*, but surely you're not taking this seriously? I hardly had anything to do with her! Have you spoken to Malin?'

'We have, and she backs you up. But at the same time she acknowledges that she wasn't present at your meetings with Tova.'

The last sentence was left dangling in the air.

'Erland, for God's sake! The girl must be out of her mind. I've never overstepped the mark with my students, you know that.'

Erland looked embarrassed.

'You had a child with one of your former students. Several members of the department find that

25

rather strange. Not me, of course, you know that, but some people.'

'Like who?'

'Now let's not get upset . . .'

'*Like who?*'

'Er . . . Barbro and Manne, for example.'

'Barbro and Manne! Bloody hell, Manne lives with his own stepdaughter, and . . .'

Erland slammed his hand down on the desk in sheer frustration.

'It's you we're talking about, Spencer! Manne was a bad example – I take that back.'

He sighed heavily.

'Another student saw you giving Tova a hug on one occasion.'

Spencer ransacked his overheated brain.

'She said her father had had a heart attack, and that was why she was finding it difficult to concentrate. She said she was spending a lot of time at the hospital.'

'Her father is dead, Spencer. He was a town councillor; he died of leukaemia several years ago.'

The stick slid to the floor and Spencer didn't bother to pick it up.

'Are you sure that's why you gave her a hug?'

Spencer looked at him, and Erland tried again.

'I mean, a hug isn't necessarily a bad thing, just as long as you know what's behind it.'

'She said her father was ill, Erland. That's what she told me.'

Erland shuffled uncomfortably.

'I'm afraid this will need to be taken further, Spencer.'

The April sunlight found its way into the room, making the shadows of the flowers in the window dance on the floor. Soon it would be the festival of Valborg, 30 April, and the students were getting ready to party. Picnics in the parks, raft racing on the river Fyris.

'Spencer, are you listening to me? This is serious. Tova's best friend has just been elected chair of the student union's equality committee; it doesn't look good if we don't pay attention to what she is saying.'

'But what about me?'

His heart ached for Fredrika.

'You've had a tough year; take some time off.'

'If that's your final word on the matter, there's a risk that I won't come back at all.'

Consternation on the other side of the desk.

'Listen to me, Spencer. This will all be sorted out by the summer. Girls like Tova are always caught out if they're not telling the truth.'

'*If* they're not telling the truth?'

Spencer snorted and got to his feet.

'I would have expected more of you, Erland.'

Erland Malm walked silently around the desk and picked up Spencer's stick.

'Say hello to Fredrika from me.'

Spencer left the room without bothering to reply. He was furious and anxious at the same time. How the hell was he going to get out of this?

\*　　\*　　\*

27

'Rebecca Trolle,' said Alex Recht.

'How do you know?' asked Torbjörn Ross.

'Because I was in charge of the investigation when she disappeared almost two years ago.'

'And you never found her?'

Alex stared at his colleague.

'Obviously not.'

'The hands and head are missing and the body is in a very poor condition. Identification will be difficult, but of course it will be possible using DNA if we have something to compare it with.'

'Which we do. But you can regard the official identification as a formality; I know it's Rebecca Trolle.'

Alex could feel his colleague's gaze; he had encountered more looks like that than he could count over the past six months. Curious eyes that pretended to convey sympathy, but in fact held only doubt.

Is he going to make it? they seemed to be wondering. Can he cut it now he's lost his wife?

Margareta Berlin, head of Human Resources, had been a refreshing exception to the rule.

'I'm trusting you to give me the signals I need,' she had said. 'Don't hesitate to ask for help. And don't doubt that I'm behind you, because I am. One hundred per cent.'

It was only then that Alex had lowered his guard and asked for some leave.

'Do you want me to sign you off on the grounds of ill health? I can sort that out.'

'No, I just want some leave. I'm going to do some travelling.'

To Baghdad, he could have added, but it sounded far too exotic to say it out loud.

Alex held up the item of jewellery from the navel piercing.

'Her mother gave her this when she passed her final exams at school. That's why I know it's her.'

'That's a hell of a present.'

'She was also given twenty-five thousand kronor to help her with her studies. Rebecca was the first person in the family to go on to higher education, and her mother was incredibly proud of her.'

'Has anyone contacted her? The mother?'

Alex looked up.

'Not yet. I thought I'd do it tomorrow.'

'Not today?'

'No, I want to see if we find the victim's head and hands today. There's no reason to act quickly. Her mother has already waited for such a long time; one more day won't make any difference.

It was only when he had spoken the words that he realised how painful they were. One day could be a lifetime. He would have given ten years of his life for one more day with Lena. Just one day.

*It hurt so much to be without her.*

His hand trembling slightly, Alex slipped the piece of jewellery back into the bag.

'What's the staffing situation as far as your team goes? Can you take on such a big case?' Torbjörn wanted to know.

29

'I think so.'

Torbjörn looked dubious.

'Is Rydh still on the team?'

'He is. And Bergman. But she's still on maternity leave with her daughter.'

'Ah, yes.'

His colleague smirked.

'She ended up with a bun in the oven from some old professor, didn't she?'

He stopped smirking when he saw the expression on Alex's face.

'Talk to somebody else if you're going to come out with that kind of crap, Torbjörn. I'm not interested.'

Torbjörn changed the subject.

'But she'll be back soon, won't she?'

'I think so. Otherwise, I have other investigators I can bring in. But it would be excellent if Fredrika came back very soon. Tomorrow, for example.'

Alex gave a wan smile.

'You never know,' Torbjörn replied. 'Perhaps she's tired of being at home.'

'Perhaps,' said Alex.

# CHAPTER 3

'Tomorrow?' said Fredrika Bergman.

'Why not?' Spencer replied.

Fredrika sat down at the kitchen table, completely taken aback.

'Has something happened?'

'No.'

'Oh, come on, Spencer.'

There was a click as he switched on the kettle. His back told her everything she needed to know. There was something wrong.

She had been perfectly happy with their decision not to share parental leave equally. The future had been crystal clear: Spencer would stay married to Eva, and Fredrika would be the main carer for the child they were expecting. But then everything had changed. Spencer had chosen to tell his story little by little. A father-in-law with a hold over his son-in-law. A wife who demanded a lifestyle he couldn't afford. A mistake in his youth that ended up shaping his entire life. And then – from nowhere – the strength to break free.

'If you want to,' he had said when she went to visit him in hospital after the car accident last winter.

31

'If I want to what?'

'If you want to live with me. Properly.'

For various reasons, she had found it difficult to answer right away. She and Spencer had been an unofficial couple for more than ten years; it would take time to get used to the idea that he could be hers for real.

Is that what I want? she had asked herself. Do I really want to live with him, or did I just think that was what I wanted when he was unattainable?

The question made her heart race. I do want to. *I do I do I do.*

His disability following the accident had frightened her. She couldn't bear the idea of him ageing any more quickly than he was already doing. She couldn't cope with him becoming a burden at the same time as she was taking care of a newborn baby. Perhaps he sensed her fear, because he worked furiously to get better. He was still using a walking stick, but not for much longer.

The baby woke from her lunchtime nap, and they could hear noises from the nursery. Spencer beat Fredrika to it, and went to fetch Saga. She rarely cried when she woke up, but would lie there talking to herself. Or rather babbling, blowing little bubbles of saliva. She looked so much like Fredrika it was almost spooky.

Spencer came back into the kitchen with a smiling Saga in his arms.

'You did say you'd want to go back to work.'

'I know, but these things need planning. How long were you thinking of staying at home?'

'A couple of months,' Spencer replied. 'No more than two.'

'And then?'

'Then she can go to nursery.'

'We've got a nursery place from August, Spencer.'

'Exactly. And before that we've got time for a holiday. It would work out perfectly if I stayed at home until the summer.'

Fredrika fell silent, gazing at his lined face. She had seen the way his love for Saga had taken him by surprise, how amazed he had been at the strength of his feelings for the child. But at no point had he shown any interest in taking paternity leave.

'What's happened, Spencer?'

'Nothing.'

'Don't lie to me.'

His pupils dilated.

'The department's in a hell of a mess,' he said.

Fredrika frowned, recalling that he had mentioned two colleagues who had fallen out. She hadn't realised that he was involved.

'Same arguments as before?'

'Yes, except it's worse this time. The atmosphere is terrible, and I feel it's affecting the students.'

He pulled a face and put Saga down on the floor. Fredrika could see that the movement caused him pain.

'Can you cope with Saga on your own all day

every day? I could go back part time to begin with.'

He nodded. 'That's a good idea. I'll still need to go over to Uppsala to attend meetings and so on.'

His eyes flickered to one side, unable to meet her gaze. He was keeping something from her. She could feel it.

'OK,' she said.

'OK?'

'I'll talk to Alex. I'll call in at work this afternoon and see what he says. He might be working on something new.'

A dismembered body in two plastic bags. Rebecca Trolle, according to Alex. Peder Rydh stared sceptically at the pictures of the body parts. The head and hands were still missing, but Alex recognised the navel piercing. DNA tests would either confirm or disprove his theory. Peder had his doubts. Admittedly, the piece of jewellery was unusual, particularly in view of the disc with the word 'Freedom' on it, but they couldn't base the identification on that alone.

The damp earth and the plastic bags had played their part in preserving the body, but judging by the photographs it was difficult to imagine what the woman had looked like when she was alive. Had she been fat or slim? Straight-backed, or the kind of person who always lifted her shoulders a fraction too much, giving a hunched impression?

Peder opened the file Alex had given him and took out a photograph of Rebecca Trolle, taken just before she disappeared. Pretty. Healthy. A freckled face, smiling broadly into the camera. A plum-coloured top that brought out the blue of her eyes. Dark blonde hair caught up in a ponytail. Confident.

And now she was dead.

She had had many strings to her bow. Twenty-three years old, and working towards a degree in the history of literature at the University of Stockholm. She had spent a year in France after leaving school, and was a member of a French reading group. She sang in the church choir, and ran a swimming class for babies one evening a week.

It made Peder feel tired. How could young people cope with doing so many different things at the same bloody time? He didn't recall living that way himself, with so many irons in the fire, always on the way to a different activity.

She had been single at the time of her disappearance. There was an ex-girlfriend who had been interviewed by the police on several occasions, and there were rumours of a new love, but no one had come forward and the police hadn't managed to extract a name. She had had a lot of friends, all of whom seemed to have been interviewed at least once. The same applied to her tutors at the university, her colleagues at the swimming baths and the members of the choir.

Peder realised that the investigation had got absolutely nowhere. He was relieved that he hadn't been involved in such a depressing case. He read through Alex's notes in the margins of the documentation, and could see that the situation must have been desperate. In the end the police had started to wonder whether Rebecca Trolle might simply have decided to disappear. She had been upset by a quarrel with her mother, and this might have made her firm up her plan to spend some time studying abroad. Her father no longer lived in Stockholm: he had moved to Gothenburg when Rebecca was twelve. The police had spoken to him as well.

Rebecca had disappeared on a perfectly ordinary evening when she was on her way to a so-called mentors' social event at the university. She had called her mother at about six o'clock and told her about the party. Then she had received a call from a mobile with an unregistered pay-as-you-go card. At seven o'clock her neighbour had met her in the corridor of the student hostel on Körsbärsvägen where she lived, dressed up and obviously stressed. There were witnesses who had seen her on the number four bus at quarter past seven, heading towards Radiohuset, the headquarters of Swedish Radio. This had puzzled the police, because it was in completely the opposite direction from the university. The friends who had been waiting for her at the party said that she never arrived. And nobody knew where she might have been going on the number four bus.

Just before seven thirty, she had been seen getting off the bus and walking towards Gärdet. There were no more witness statements from that point; it was as if Rebecca had been swallowed up by the earth.

Peder took out a map that had been used in the original investigation. All the people who had featured in the case in any way and who lived in the vicinity of Radiohuset had been marked on it; none had seemed more suspect than any other. There were only a handful of individuals, and they all had a viable alibi. None of them had arranged to meet Rebecca that evening. No one had seen her. Until now – if it was Rebecca's body in those plastic bags.

The discovery had been made on the outskirts of Midsommarkransen. Was there anyone in the original investigation who had a connection with that part of the city? It was a long shot, but worth checking.

The case had been short on suspects. The analysis of Rebecca's mobile phone traffic had been of no help; the last link to a mast merely confirmed that she had been in the vicinity of Radiohuset, after which all activity ceased. They hadn't managed to find any enemies, but that didn't necessarily mean they didn't exist. Rebecca's mother had mentioned a dispute with a colleague at the swimming baths, but that particular trail had quickly gone cold. The colleague had reacted with surprise, referring to the argument as nothing more than a trifle. In addition, he had had an alibi for the evening when Rebecca was reported missing.

Peder stopped in his tracks. Who misses a single girl the same evening she disappears? The first report showed that a male friend had called the police at eleven o'clock that night. Rebecca hadn't turned up at the party as agreed, and she wasn't answering her phone. The reaction from the police had been cool to begin with. Her parents were contacted as a matter of routine, but they hadn't heard from her either. Her mother hadn't been worried at first; her daughter was perfectly capable of taking care of herself. By two o'clock, the situation had changed. According to her mother, Rebecca still hadn't been in touch with any of her friends, and her phone was switched off. Early in the morning, she was officially logged as missing, and the investigation was under way.

The person who had first called the police was one Håkan Nilsson. Why the police rather than Rebecca's parents? Perhaps he didn't know them. But why didn't he wait? Why was he worried? Peder flicked through one document after another. Håkan Nilsson had gone out of his way to assist the police throughout the investigation: a friend who thought her disappearance was terrible, and wanted to help out. But why had Nilsson been more helpful than any of Rebecca's other friends? He had printed posters, given an interview to the student newspaper. He kept on saying that 'we' were concerned, but there was no indication as to who 'we' might be.

Peder decided to mention it to Alex. He opened the database of residential addresses on the computer and ran a quick check on Håkan Nilsson. He had previously lived in the same student hostel as Rebecca, and his current address was Tellusgatan. In Hägersten. Which was in Midsommarkransen.

Peder stared at the screen. If it really was Rebecca Trolle in those plastic bags, then Håkan Nilsson had some explaining to do.

When Fredrika Bergman knocked on Alex's door, he was slumped in his chair, his brow deeply furrowed. Fredrika had seen him only a few times since he was widowed, and she could have wept when she saw how much he had aged in just a few months. Although it went against the grain to admit it, she had noticed the same thing with Spencer. Both men had recently gone through difficult times, which had left their mark. She forced herself to smile.

'Fredrika,' Alex said as soon as he saw her.

His face broke into a warm smile that put her at ease. After a brief hesitation he got up and came around the desk to give her a hug. Strong arms around her body; she felt herself blushing.

'How's it going?' she asked.

Alex shrugged. 'Not too bad,' he replied.

They sat down.

'How's your daughter?'

'Saga's fantastic. She's almost walking.'

'That's early, isn't it?'

'Not really; she'll soon be one.'

Fredrika glanced around the room. He had several photographs on the wall behind him. Photographs of his family. Of the wife who no longer existed.

Life's a bitch and then you die.

'We were talking about you earlier on today,' Alex said.

'Really?'

Alex immediately looked brighter, cautiously optimistic.

'We miss you. We were hoping you'd be ready to come back soon, perhaps in the summer?'

Fredrika felt ridiculous.

'Well actually . . . I could come back before then.'

'Wonderful. When were you thinking of?'

Should she tell him? Should she explain that her partner had suddenly announced that he wanted to spend some time at home with Saga after all? That things were difficult at work, and he couldn't face going in?

Suddenly she asked herself if she even *wanted* to come back to work. The days with Saga had been wonderful. Fredrika had been pregnant at the same time as several of her friends, and they had met up almost every week during her maternity leave. They would think she had lost her mind if she rang and told them she had started work so suddenly.

'I could start off working part time – say seventy-five per cent?'

'From when?'

She hesitated.

'Tomorrow . . .?'


Margareta Berlin, head of Human Resources, had a meeting with Fredrika a little while later. She didn't normally concern herself with routine matters, but when she realised it was to do with the staffing of Alex Recht's team, she sent for Fredrika.

'Thank you for coming.'

Fredrika smiled and sat down.

'I was just on my way home, so I hope this won't take too long . . .'

'No, of course not.'

Margareta gathered up some papers and placed them in the filing cabinet behind her. She was tall and strong, or rather powerfully built. Fredrika didn't want to describe her as fat, but she gave an impression of sturdiness.

'How are you?' she asked.

The question gave Fredrika a bad feeling.

'Fine. Thank you.'

Margareta nodded.

'You look well. I just wanted confirmation, really. How's Alex?'

'You'll have to ask Alex about that.'

'But I'm asking you.'

There was a brief silence as Fredrika considered the question.

'I think he seems OK. Better, anyway.'

'I think so too. But I have to admit that things weren't too good for a while.'

She leaned across the desk.

'I've known Alex for over twenty years, and I want nothing but the best for him.'

She paused.

'But if he's guilty of misconduct, if he turns out not to be up to the job, then I will have to act.'

'Who says he's not up to the job?' Fredrika asked, sounding more confused than she would have wished.

'Nobody, so far. But I've been told on the quiet that he's been unnecessarily hard on certain colleagues. You could say he's been doing my job.'

She laughed softly.

Fredrika wasn't laughing. She had the greatest respect for Margareta Berlin, not least because she had finally put a stop to Peder Rydh's nonsense. But Fredrika's loyalty lay with Alex, not with the head of HR. She hadn't expected this to cause any kind of conflict.

'Anyway,' Margareta said in conclusion. 'I just wanted to give you an opening in case you feel you need to talk at some point in the future.'

'About Alex?'

'Or anything else.'

The meeting was over, and Fredrika got ready to leave.

'This new case,' Margareta said as she stood in the doorway.

'Yes?'

'I remember what Alex was like when he led the investigation into Rebecca Trolle's disappearance.'

Fredrika waited.

'He was like a man possessed. It was the last case he dealt with before he was given the chance to form his own team, the one you and Peder belong to. He took the fact that we didn't find her very badly.'

'And you're afraid things will be too much for him now she's finally turned up?'

'Something like that.'

Fredrika hesitated, her hand resting on the door handle.

'I'll keep an eye on him,' she said.

# WEDNESDAY

# CHAPTER 4

It was a fantastic spring, Malena Bremberg thought, as she dealt with the flowers that one of the residents in the care home had received from her son. All those hours of sunshine after a long winter.

She returned to the old lady's room with a vase.

'Aren't they lovely?' she said.

The old lady leaned forward to inspect the flowers.

'I don't like the yellow ones,' she said firmly.

Malena found it difficult to suppress her laughter at the emphasis on the word *don't*.

'Oh, dear,' she said. 'I'm sorry to hear that. What would you like me to do with them?'

'Chuck the lot.'

'Oh, no, they're so pretty! And from such an elegant young man.'

'Stuff and nonsense, he's only after my money. Take the flowers away – give them to Egon. He never has any visitors.'

The glass vase was cool against her palms as Malena carried it into the kitchen.

'Doesn't she want them today either?' asked her colleague, who was busy emptying the dishwasher.

They both laughed.

'She told me to chuck the lot.'

Malena's colleague shook her head.

'I don't know why he keeps on turning up week after week, when she's so unpleasant.'

'She says it's because of his inheritance.'

'And I say it's love.'

Malena put down the vase on one of the tables.

'Do you think she'll recognise the flowers by dinnertime?' she asked.

'No chance. Her memory seems to be getting worse and worse. It's almost time to see if they've got room for her upstairs.'

Upstairs. The abstract paraphrase for the secure unit on the upper floor where those suffering from dementia were cared for. Many residents seemed to end up there sooner or later. The heavy doors of the unit frightened Malena. She hoped to God that she would never be affected by some form of dementia.

The television was on in the kitchen. Malena's attention was caught by a news item about a woman's body that had been found in an area of forest in Midsommarkransen. The police hadn't released many details, but the man who had found the body was happy to be interviewed.

'It was the dog that found her,' he said, standing up very straight. 'Unfortunately, I'm not allowed to tell you any more than that.'

'But what did she look like?' the reporter asked.
The man looked confused.

'I'm not allowed to say.'

'Can't you tell us if she was wearing any clothes?'

The man's earlier self-confidence had completely disappeared.

'I've got to go,' he said. 'Come along, Svante.'

He walked away from the cameras, dragging the dog behind him.

Malena's mobile rang in the pocket of her overalls. The ugly uniform with which the care home provided its employees had just one advantage: the big pockets where you could keep a mobile phone, throat lozenges and other unnecessary items.

She stiffened when she saw who was calling. So long ago, and yet the memory hadn't faded at all. He just kept on ringing, making his demands. Threatening and saying those foul things.

'Hello.'

'Hi, Malena. How are you?'

She left the kitchen and moved down the corridor, hoping her colleague wouldn't overhear the conversation.

'What do you want?'

'The same as before.'

'We had an agreement.'

'Yes, and we still do. I can only apologise if you thought otherwise.'

She was breathing heavily; she could feel the panic rising like the bubbles in a bottle of cola.

'Nobody has been here.'

'Nobody?'

'Not a soul.'

'Good. I'll be in touch when I need more information.'

She remained standing in the corridor for a long time after the conversation was over. She would never be free. Certain debts could never be paid off, it was that simple.

# CHAPTER 5

'Aren't we meeting in the Lions' Den?'
Peder stopped dead when he heard Fredrika's question.

'We can't use it at the moment; the air conditioning system broke down and the whole corridor smelled of shit. We're borrowing the others' room for the time being.'

The others, Fredrika thought. An interesting way of describing the colleagues who were on the same corridor, but who didn't belong to Alex's team.

Peder glanced at her.

'You came back a bit bloody fast,' he said. 'Overnight, in fact.'

When Fredrika didn't reply immediately he added hurriedly:

'It's good to have you here, of course.'

'Thank you,' said Fredrika. 'Things changed at home, so I ended up coming back to work a bit sooner than I'd intended.'

Peder still looked surprised, but Fredrika couldn't help him. She was confused herself. The step from beginning to miss her job and thinking it might be nice to go back part time to actually starting work had been rather shorter than she had expected. Astonishingly short, in fact. And she wasn't really back, not properly. She would be working part time for the next three weeks, and then . . . She would just have to wait and see what felt right.

Alex was waiting for them in the conference room, which looked almost exactly the same as the Den. The memory of her conversation with Margareta Berlin was bothering Fredrika. She had promised to report back if Alex's leadership seemed unsatisfactory, out of the ordinary in some way. Few things were worse than volunteering to be a spy for the head of HR. But it wasn't entirely voluntary.

*It's because I care about you, Alex.*

Fredrika had heard about his trip to Iraq, and wept when she was told why he had gone. There were no words to describe how she felt when she thought about the kindness of what Alex had done, travelling halfway around the world to return an engagement ring to a woman who had lost the man she loved without knowing how or why.

*I nearly lost you, Spencer.*

They sat down around the table: Fredrika, Alex, Peder, and a number of faces Fredrika didn't recognise. These were additional colleagues on loan to the team because of the dismembered body in the plastic bags.

Rebecca Trolle. Initial tests using DNA from

a body in an advanced state of decay had proven her identity. The process had been speeded up because of the unusual circumstances, given priority at SKL, the National Forensics Laboratory in Linköping, and everywhere else as necessary.

Alex, who had never been in any doubt about the identity of the corpse, was keen to get started.

'We heard from SKL less than an hour ago, and we won't be releasing any information to the media until Rebecca's mother has been informed.'

'Are we telling her that her daughter's dead?' Peder asked.

Is that the right term when you're informing someone that a person who has been missing for two years has been found dead? Fredrika wondered. She decided it probably was. Even if death was the only logical assumption, there was no reason to give up hope. Not if you really loved the person who was missing, not if you needed that hope. If Saga disappeared, how many years would it be before Fredrika gave up? A hundred? A thousand?

'We will be informing her that her daughter has been found dead,' Alex said. 'I'm going to do it myself when the meeting is over. Fredrika can come with me.'

'But there's something I wanted to ask her,' Peder objected. 'The mother, I mean.'

'There will be plenty of opportunities to speak to her, Peder. I've kept in touch with her since

Rebecca disappeared, and I think this news will bring her peace of mind. She already suspects that her daughter is dead, but she wants that confirmation. And of course she'll want to know what happened.'

Alex took a deep breath.

'It's difficult to establish the exact cause of death because the body has been lying there for such a long time. There is nothing to indicate bullet wounds or other physical trauma – broken ribs as a result of a struggle, for example. She might have been strangled, but we can't be sure.'

He opened a folder and took out a number of photographs.

'However, the pathologist was able to establish that she was pregnant at the time of her death.'

Fredrika looked up in surprise.

'Did we know that?'

'No, it didn't come to light in any of the interviews during the course of the original investigation. And we spoke to every single person Rebecca knew. We went through everyone she'd been in touch with on the telephone, we checked out every friend listed as a contact in her email address book, but nobody mentioned the fact that she was pregnant.'

'So no one knew?' Fredrika said.

'It looks that way,' Alex replied. 'In which case we have to ask why. Why doesn't a young girl tell anyone she's four months pregnant?'

'Four months,' Peder echoed. 'Wouldn't it have shown?'

'If it had, somebody would have told us,' Alex said.

'She must have confided in someone,' Fredrika insisted.

'The father, perhaps?' said Peder. 'Who wasn't very pleased to hear the news, and killed her?'

'Then chopped up the body,' said Alex.

He pointed to the photographs.

'There are two main reasons why a perpetrator dismembers the body of his victim. One: to make identification more difficult. Two: because he's a sick bastard who enjoys sadistic activities. But in that case he would probably bury the whole lot in one place.'

'Perhaps both reasons apply,' Fredrika suggested.

Alex looked at her.

'Maybe. In which case we're in real trouble. Because Rebecca might not be the only victim.'

'But if we bring the pregnancy into our hypothesis, that makes it personal,' Peder said.

'Absolutely, which is why we're going to start from there,' Alex said. 'Who was the child's father, and why did nobody know she was pregnant?'

'What happened in the original investigation?' Fredrika asked. 'Did you manage to narrow down a list of suspects?'

'There was talk of a new boyfriend, and we threw everything into looking for him, but we never found him. It was a peculiar story from

start to finish. We couldn't find any trace of him
– not in phone calls or in her emails. Nobody
knew his name, but several people claimed they
had "heard about him". He hovered over the
entire investigation like an evil spirit, but we never
saw him. We didn't find any other credible
suspects.'

Peder frowned.

'There was also an ex-girlfriend.'

'Daniella.'

'Exactly, so how come Rebecca suddenly had a
boyfriend?'

Alex looked weary.

'How the hell should I know? Her mother
described her as a seeker. She'd had several
boyfriends, but only one girlfriend.'

'Was this Daniella ever a suspect?' Fredrika
asked.

'We considered that as a working hypothesis for
a while,' Alex replied. 'But she had an alibi, and
we couldn't really come up with a motive.'

'And what about Håkan Nilsson?' Peder
wondered.

A smile flitted across Alex's face, got lost among
the lines and disappeared. That short-lived smile
had become the characteristic sign of his grief.

'We looked very carefully at Håkan. Not at first,
but later on when we had no other leads to follow.
His eagerness to help, his campaign to make sure
she was found at any price – it all seemed to
indicate rather more than friendship. It was

almost manic. When her other friends just couldn't go on any longer, Håkan was still there all on his own, still searching.'

'The person who has the most to hide . . .'

'. . . is the most keen to show he cares. I know. But in Håkan's case, I don't think that was true.'

When Alex paused, Peder spoke up.

'He lives in Midsommarkransen, Alex. We need to take another look at him.'

Alex straightened up. That was something he hadn't been aware of.

'Absolutely,' he said. 'We have to look at everyone again, but particularly Håkan. Put him under surveillance and see where he goes.'

Alex glanced at Fredrika.

'And you and I will go and see Diana Trolle, Rebecca's mother.'

They hardly spoke on the way to Diana Trolle's house. Alex could feel Fredrika's questions hanging in the air – how were things, was he lonely, how did it feel to be back at work? He had questions of his own – how was Saga? Did she sleep through the night, or did she keep her parents awake? Was she eating well, was she teething? But he couldn't get a word out. It was as if he had been transformed into a mussel that was impossible to prise open. The kind of mussel that was easily disposed of.

It wasn't far to Spånga, where Diana lived. He had often been there in the past, but it was a long time ago. He remembered that he had liked her, found her attractive. An artistic soul, lost in a boring job at County Hall.

To begin with, she had been optimistic as they searched for Rebecca. Alex had been honest with her: the first few days were critical. If her daughter was not found at that point, the prospect of finding her alive at a later stage was minimal. She had accepted his words calmly, not because her daughter was an insignificant part of her life, but because she had decided not to meet trouble halfway. She had stuck to that point of view for a long time.

'As long as she's not dead, she's alive,' she had said, giving Alex a phrase he could use in similar situations.

But now there was no avoiding the truth. Rebecca was dead, desecrated and buried. The piece of jewellery from her navel was in his jacket pocket. There was nothing merciful about the news Alex and Fredrika must now deliver. Perhaps there might be a chance of closure, but only if they could also explain what had led to Rebecca's death. And they weren't there yet.

Diana opened the door before they had time to ring the bell. It was Alex who told her when they sitting in the living room. Diana wept as she sat alone in a big armchair.

'How did she die?'

'We don't know, Diana. But I promise you we'll find out.'

Alex looked around. Rebecca lived on in this room, in photographs with her brother and in a picture her mother had painted when she was confirmed.

'I knew as soon as I saw you getting out of the car. But I still hoped you might have come to tell me something else.'

Fredrika got to her feet.

'I could make us all a drink, as long as you don't mind me rummaging around in your kitchen?'

Diana nodded silently, and Alex caught himself wondering if he had ever heard Fredrika offer to do something like that. He didn't think so.

They could hear the sound of the kettle and the clatter of cups being set out on a tray. Alex chose his words with care.

'We'll be giving this investigation top priority from now on; I hope you don't think otherwise.'

Diana smiled through her tears, the droplets shining on her high cheekbones. Dark eyes, hair slightly too long. Had the sorrow over her missing daughter aged her? He didn't think so.

'You didn't find the person who did it,' she reminded him.

'No, we didn't,' Alex said. 'But the situation is different now.'

'In what way?'

'We have a crime scene, a geographical location to which we can link the perpetrator. We're hoping to be able to secure evidence of the person who did this, but . . .'

'But it's been such a long time,' Diana supplied. 'We can still do it.'

His voice was tense with fury and conviction. It was always painful to abandon the hope that preceded despair; nobody knew that better than Alex.

*We can still do it. Because anything else is unacceptable.*

He had said those words to Lena more times than she wanted to hear them. In the end he had spent so much time trying to find a way of saving her that he could no longer see that she was getting worse.

'Mum is dying,' his daughter said. 'And you're missing the end, Dad.'

The memories were so painful. So agonisingly painful.

His vision was clouded by tears. Fredrika came back with a tray of coffee, rescuing him without realising it.

'Here we are,' she said. 'Milk?'

They drank in silence, allowing the absence of words to bring peace.

So far, Alex had not commented on the circumstances surrounding the discovery of Rebecca's body; he had not told Diana that it had been dismembered and buried in two plastic bags. He hesitated before he spoke; he hated this part of his job.

Diana listened, wide-eyed.

'I don't understand.'

'Nor do we, but we're doing everything we can to find out what happened.'

'Who would be sick enough to . . .?'

'Don't think about that.'

Alex swallowed.

'There's one more thing I need to tell you. Well, two in fact. I don't want you to hear this through the press.'

He told her about the missing head and hands, calmly and in plain words. Then he gave her the piece of jewellery. Diana took it without speaking, then after a moment she said:

'You said there were two things?'

Her voice was hoarse with tension, the tears pouring down her face.

'She was pregnant.'

'What?'

'You didn't know?'

She shook her head, her whole body trembling.

'We're very keen to identify the child's father,' Fredrika said. 'I know you weren't aware of a specific boyfriend, but had Rebecca ever said she wanted a child?'

'Of course she did, but not until she was older. We spoke openly about that kind of thing. She was on the pill; she was very careful about contraception.'

'How long had she been on the pill?'

'Let me think; how old was she when the subject

first came up? Seventeen, I think. I drove her to the clinic.'

A model parent, in Fredrika's eyes.

Alex took over, not wanting the first meeting with Diana since the discovery of Rebecca's body to go on for too long.

'It's quite a while since Rebecca disappeared,' he said. 'Has anything new occurred to you during that time?'

How long was two years? Two years was the difference between being single and having a family, between having a family and losing it.

Diana cleared her throat.

'A friend of mine said something horrible a while ago, but I didn't really attach any importance to it. It was just too stupid.'

Fredrika and Alex waited.

'My friend has a daughter who was on the same course as Rebecca, and she hinted that the person who took her could have been someone she met on the internet.'

'That doesn't sound too unlikely,' Fredrika said tentatively. 'These days a lot of people meet their partners that way.'

'Not like that,' Diana said. 'She meant . . . Her daughter had said that my Rebecca was selling certain things on the Internet.'

'Things?' Alex said.

'Herself.'

Alex stiffened.

'Where the hell did she get that from?'

'She said there was a rumour going around after Rebecca disappeared. But in my wildest imagination I can't believe . . .'

Her voice died away.

'Was Rebecca insecure?' Fredrika asked.

'God, no.'

'Lonely?'

'She had loads of friends.'

'Was she short of money?'

'She would have come to me. She always did.'

Not always. That was something Alex had learned over the years. 'Always' was a word construed by parents when 'usually' was more accurate.

'We'd really like to speak to your friend and her daughter,' Fredrika said.

Diana nodded.

'I must ring Rebecca's brother,' she said.

'Of course,' Alex replied. 'And if you like we can arrange some counselling for you.'

'That won't be necessary.'

They headed for the door, passing several photographs of Rebecca on the walls. Don't take them down, Alex thought. You would bitterly regret it.

'What happened to her things?' Fredrika asked.

'It's all in storage,' Diana said. 'Her brother and I emptied her room in the student hostel once the investigators had taken what they wanted, and we put it all in my sister's garage. If you want to have a look I can give you directions.'

'That would be kind,' Fredrika said.

'Just one more thing,' Alex said.

They stopped.

'Do you remember Håkan Nilsson?'

'Of course. We're still in touch; he was very fond of Rebecca.'

'They'd been friends since school, hadn't they?'

'That's right. And Rebecca helped him when his father died; that was in their last year at school.'

As the front door opened, the spring sunshine flooded the hallway.

'Did Rebecca ever say anything to indicate that he might be a problem?' Fredrika asked.

Diana looked past her, out into the street. A whole world was waiting on the other side of the door. She would have to think about when she might be ready to face it again.

'I remember her telling me that he was upset when she decided to study in France. I suppose he had expected her to stay in Stockholm.'

'Did he have any reason to expect that? Were they a couple.'

'Definitely not. He wasn't her type at all.'

Alex thought for a moment.

'But they became friends again when she came home?'

'I know they got back in touch, but it was only afterwards I realised they were close friends.'

'What made you realise that?'

'It was the only logical explanation. Why else would he have got so involved after her disappearance?'

# CHAPTER 6

The news that Rebecca Trolle had been found in Midsommarkransen eclipsed every other news story that afternoon. In his role as the officer in charge of the investigation, Alex Recht held a brief press conference. He chose to omit the macabre details – the fact that the body had been dismembered and that certain parts were missing.

There were plenty of questions from the journalists, but his answers were limited.

No, he couldn't say what progress the investigation had made; it was much too early.

No, he did not wish to comment on whether they had any suspects.

No, he did not wish to explain how they had been able to identify the body so quickly, in spite of the fact that Rebecca had been lying in the ground for so long that there was no possibility of recognising her.

He brought the press conference to an end and went back to his office. His daughter Viktoria called him on his mobile.

'Are you coming over for something to eat tonight, Dad? It would be really nice to see you.'

'I don't know; I'm in the middle of a new investigation and . . .'

'I saw you on TV; your jumper looked great!'

The jumper he had been given for Christmas. The worst Christmas in living memory.

'Are you coming?'

'Mmm, if I can fit it in. You know how it is, these cases take time, and . . .'

'Dad.'

'Yes?'

'Just come over. OK?'

She was so much like her mother. The same voice, the same drive, the same stubbornness. She would do well in life.

He ambled past Fredrika's office; she was absorbed in the documents from the investigation into Rebecca's disappearance. When she heard his footsteps, she looked up with a smile.

'I thought you were supposed to be working part time,' Alex said.

Half joking, half serious.

*Don't be like the rest of us – don't forget your family as soon as you come back to work after your maternity leave.*

'I am,' Fredrika replied. 'I just wanted to read for a while before I go home. What an active person she must have been.'

'Rebecca? Indeed she was, to say the least. The investigation was a mass of dead ends. Part time jobs, student life, the church choir, friends, the world and his wife.'

'We need to speak to that friend of Diana's, and her daughter, about the rumour that Rebecca was selling herself on the internet.'

'We do.' Alex smiled. 'But not you, Fredrika. It's time you went home.'

She returned his smile.

'In a minute. One question before I go: What was she studying when she disappeared?'

'The history of literature, as far as I remember.'

'What level? How far had she got?'

'I'm not really sure. I think she was writing her dissertation. We spoke to her supervisor; he was a bit odd, but hardly her new boyfriend, and definitely not a murderer.'

'Alibi?'

'Just like everyone else we spoke to.'

Fredrika leafed through the papers in front of her.

'I wonder who he was, this new boyfriend. I mean, it could be someone she met on the internet.'

Alex nodded in agreement.

'You're right. But in that case, why didn't one single person tell us she was meeting men online? Girls talk about that kind of thing, don't they?'

'They do.'

Fredrika looked pensive.

'The child,' she said. 'Someone must have know she was expecting. She must have contacted a pregnancy advisory centre.'

'Must she? By the fourth month?'

Fredrika rummaged through the piles of paper.

'I've looked very carefully at the list of items the police took away,' she said. 'You turned her student room upside down, made a note of which fluoride tablets she used, her preferred brand of tampons. There's nothing about contraceptive pills.'

Alex came into the room, walked behind Fredrika and read over her shoulder.

'They made a note of every item of medication found in Rebecca's room.'

'Cough medicine, Alvedon, Panodil,' Fredrika read. 'Believe me, none of them work as a contraceptive.'

'Perhaps she'd run out?' Alex suggested. 'And because she wasn't in a relationship, she didn't renew the prescription?'

'And when she did have sex after all, they didn't use any protection. That sounds odd to me, given how careful she had been in the past.'

Fredrika turned to face Alex.

'I'd like to speak to Diana Trolle again. Ask if she knew where her daughter got her prescription for the pill.'

'OK. Hopefully, that will enable us to find out when she stopped taking it.'

'Exactly. And it should give us more information about her pregnancy, at least if she usually had her prescription filled at a clinic. There's no reason to think that she would go somewhere completely different to discuss her pregnancy.'

'If she did actually discuss it with anyone.'

Fredrika gathered up the documents on her desk and handed them to Alex.

'I'll ring Diana straight away. Then I'm going home. Have you heard anything about Håkan Nilsson from the surveillance team?'

Alex clutched the folders to his chest.

'Nothing so far. He's still at work. Peder and I will probably bring him in for a chat this evening.'

Fredrika nodding, trying to remember what Håkan Nilsson had looked like in the pictures she had seen in the files. Pale, thin, a lost look in his eyes. His expression seemed angry in some of the photographs. How angry do you have to be to kill someone, then dismember their body? Put the pieces in plastic bags and bury them? She shuddered. Death was never pretty, but sometimes it was so ugly that it was completely incomprehensible.

Diana Trolle knew exactly where her daughter got her contraceptive pills from: first of all from the youth clinic in Spånga, then later on – when she was too old to go there any more – from the Serafen clinic opposite City Hall.

'She said a lot of positive things about that place,' Diana recalled. 'But I've never been there myself.'

Fredrika decided to call in at the clinic on her way home, partly because she felt like a walk, and partly because she was curious.

She tried to phone Spencer as she was leaving work. They had already spoken twice during the day. She could hear from his voice that he was tense, and she wondered if he had taken on too much. If that was the case, she would have to stay at home for a while longer, that was all there was to it. At the same time, she was frightened by the direction her thoughts were taking.

What would happen to Saga if Fredrika died, and Spencer was unable to look after his daughter? Would she go and live with Fredrika's brother?

No chance. Spencer would never abandon his only daughter, Fredrika was sure of that.

Spencer interrupted her brooding when he finally answered his mobile. Saga was asleep, he informed Fredrika. It was fine if she came home a bit later than they had agreed.

The walk from police headquarters in Kronoberg to the clinic opposite City Hall was short but invigorating. Fredrika decided to go via Hantverkargatan, and enjoyed breathing in the fresh spring air. It always seemed lighter and cleaner than the air at any other time of year. Good for the soul.

The clinic was located on the first floor of the magnificent building that resembled a British stately home; it was right by the water. Fredrika gazed at all the mothers-to-be, sitting in the waiting room with their big bellies, several of them with older children in buggies. How could people cope with more than one child? She just didn't get it. Neither she nor Spencer wanted any more children; at least that was how they felt at the moment.

'One is more than enough,' Spencer had muttered one night when Saga had a cold and kept on waking up over and over again.

Fredrika showed her ID to the nurse on

reception and explained why she was there. The nurse hesitated when she asked to see any notes they might have on Rebecca.

'I'll be back in a moment,' she said, and returned after a short while with an older colleague.

Fredrika explained the situation again, and the midwife listened attentively. With long fingers she searched through the suspension files in the filing cabinet. She nodded silently to herself as she took one out.

'I was the one who saw her the last time she was here,' she said, pointing to a note in the margin. She screwed up her eyes.

'I see so many women every day, it's difficult to remember them all.'

You don't have to remember them all, Fredrika thought. Only this one.

'But I think I know who you mean,' the midwife said, much to Fredrika's relief. 'She was here to renew her prescription for the pill, but suspected she might be pregnant. She was terribly upset, if I remember rightly.'

'So what happened?'

'She was pregnant, of course. I think we worked out she was probably in the third month. She was terrified.'

'Then what?'

'She left, saying she was going to get rid of the baby. I have no idea whether she did or not; she never came back.'

Fredrika glanced through the notes.

'Is there anything else you recall from your meeting with Rebecca?'

'Only that she seemed anxious. And she asked me whether it was possible to have a termination even if the child's father might want to keep it.'

Fredrika put down the file.

'Did she, indeed?'

'Yes. I thought it was a stupid question. It's obvious that it's the woman who decides whether or not she wants to be a mother.'

But it wasn't obvious, and both Fredrika and the midwife knew it. Fredrika began to feel concerned. Why had Rebecca felt the need to ask the question? Who was the man she suspected would want to keep the child?

'Håkan Nilsson,' Alex said when she called him.

'That's what I thought.'

'But?'

'But that would be too easy.'

'He's been in touch with Diana, expressed his condolences and so on. Asked if he could come over.'

'What did she say?'

'She said no.'

They ended the call, and Alex carried on going through the previous investigation. There was a wealth of material, but hardly any leads.

A young woman, expected at a party at the university, leaves home and gets on a bus travelling in completely the opposite direction. Secretly four months pregnant, possibly afraid that a termination will antagonise the child's father. Did that mean she had told him about the baby?

*Where were you going that evening, Rebecca?*

Peder appeared in the doorway; he came in and sat down. He had spent a considerable amount of time speaking to Rebecca's closest friends on the phone, and to her father and brother.

'I've given Ellen a list of the people you highlighted in the investigation into Rebecca's disappearance,' Peder said. 'I've asked her to check the names against our records to see if they've been mixed up in anything suspect since then.'

'Good,' Alex said. 'And what about the interviews you and the other investigators have conducted so far – anything there?'

'Maybe,' Peder replied, chewing on a fingernail.

Alex gave him an encouraging look.

'Not long after Rebecca went missing, there was a rumour that she had been selling sexual services on the Internet.'

'We heard the same thing from her mother,' Alex said. 'A friend had told her.'

'We'll have to follow it up, but I don't believe it.'

'Me neither.'

'I also heard something else that sounded more credible. Did you speak to her ex-girlfriend?'

'Several times. Why?'

'According to the gossip, she never got over the fact that Rebecca had dumped her, or that Rebecca regarded her as an experiment.'

Alex rubbed his hands together; it was something he often did when he was distracted, or when he was thinking. Scarred hands that had been burned, then healed. A constant memory of a case that ended in chaos, a case that had troubled their consciences for a long time.

'There were certain indications that the ex wasn't quite as she should be,' Alex said. 'She'd been in a youth psychiatric unit when she was younger; I think she'd been diagnosed as bi-polar.'

'Any violent tendencies?'

'Not as far as we know.'

'We ought to check her out anyway.'

'I agree,' Alex said. 'However, there is one thing I think we can be absolutely sure of.'

Peder waited.

'She can't possibly be the father of the child Rebecca was expecting.'

Peder grinned.

'No, but Håkan Nilsson could have been.'

'Absolutely.'

'One of Rebecca's female friends had some fairly unpleasant things to say about him. Apparently, Rebecca thought he was a real nuisance; he didn't seem to realise they weren't such close friends any more.'

'In that case I think we need to have a chat with him,' Alex said.

Peder worked late that day. He called home to let Ylva know he would be missing dinner. It was a conversation that would have triggered a huge row two years ago, but now she accepted it calmly. He and Ylva had sorted all that out when they decided not to get a divorce, but to move back in together and try again. Perhaps 'sorted out' was putting it too simply; the road back had been long, with many painful upsets along the way. Ylva needed time to forgive, to learn to trust him again. He also needed time to forgive himself. For all the damage he had caused. All the responsibility he had failed to accept.

The counsellor said they had to stop arguing about problems that couldn't be solved. Peder's job was never going to change, unless he went and did something else. However, he could try to negotiate with his employer for better terms when it came to time off in lieu, which he had done.

The reconciliation with Ylva had done him good. He had slowly begun to find his way back to the feeling of fulfilment he had enjoyed during the early years with her, when he had just joined the police and everything was going well. The birth of his twin boys had ruined everything, wrecked any attempt at a normal family life, because Ylva had suffered from serious postnatal depression. Her longing for children had turned into despair and insecurity. Peder had been unfaithful to his wife for the first time, and from then on he was caught in a downward spiral with no apparent end.

The fact that the end was not apparent did not mean it didn't exist. It came the day he was called

76

in to see the head of HR, and was sent on an equality course and for a programme of counselling. He had hated that old witch, punishing him for things he hadn't done. He had hated her until the news about Alex's wife and how ill she was became common knowledge at work, and at the same time Fredrika's lover was involved in a serious car accident. It was as if Peder was able to gain some perspective on his own troubles, and at some point things turned around. And they had got better and better.

Peder and Alex wondered whether to bring in Håkan Nilsson right away, or wait until the following day. The prosecutor made it clear that they would be unable to hold him; the evidence was too weak and mostly circumstantial. However, they could certainly bring him in for questioning.

Peder went with a uniformed patrol to pick him up. It was almost half past five, and he was hungry. They stopped off briefly at a fast food kiosk, then carried on.

Håkan Nilsson opened the door after the second ring. It was obvious that he had been crying, and Peder felt something akin to contempt.

'Håkan Nilsson? May we come in?'

Peder briefly outlined the reason for their visit. No doubt Håkan had heard that Rebecca's body had been found; would he mind coming along to the police station for a short interview? Oh, no, he was no more of a suspect than anyone else, but they would like a chat with him, mainly so that they could eliminate him from their inquiries; he had been so helpful in the past.

Håkan wasn't as easily manipulated as Peder had expected. He asked a number of questions, mainly about what had happened when they found Rebecca. What had she looked like? How had she died? He didn't get any answers.

Eventually he agreed to accompany them, and they drove back to Kungsholmen. Alex and Peder conducted the interview together.

'Could you tell us how you and Rebecca knew each other?'

'You know that already.'

Alex looked amused.

'I do,' he said, 'but Peder doesn't. He's not as familiar with Rebecca's case as I am.'

'We were at school together, that's how we became friends.'

'Were you more than friends?'

Håkan blushed.

'No.'

'But you would have liked to have been?'

'No.'

'OK,' Peder said. 'What did you usually do when you met up?'

Håkan shrugged his narrow shoulders.

'We just used to hang out. Have a coffee, watch TV.'

'How often did you see each other?'

'Now and again.'

'Could you be more precise?'

'Once a week, maybe. Sometimes less often.'

Peder glanced down at his notebook.

'How did you feel when she went off to study in France?'

Håkan looked tired.

'I was disappointed.'

'Why?'

'I thought we were closer friends than that. It wasn't so much that she went away, but that she didn't tell me beforehand.'

Alex looked surprised.

'She left without saying a word?'

'No, no. Well, almost. She told me a week before she went, something like that.'

Håkan shifted on his chair.

'But we sorted all that out,' he went on. 'There was no animosity between us.'

Alex gazed at him, frowning.

'You were a great support to the police when she went missing.'

'It was important to me to help out,' Håkan said.

'Did she mean a lot to you?' Peder asked.

Håkan nodded. 'I didn't have all that many friends.'

Peder leaned across the table, his posture more relaxed.

'She was a pretty girl,' he said.

'She was,' Håkan agreed. 'She was lovely.'

'Did you sleep with her?'

Håkan looked dismayed, and Peder held up his hands in a defensive gesture.

'I don't mean any harm,' he assured Håkan. 'I'm just saying that you were friends, she was pretty, and you might just have fancied her. There's nothing strange about that, I'm well aware of how these things can happen.'

Alex gave him a sideways glance, but said nothing. He would rather not hear any more about Peder's lifestyle than Margareta Berlin had already told him.

Håkan picked at a cuticle without speaking.

'What Peder is trying to say is that perhaps you just got together one night even though you weren't a couple,' Alex said. 'As Peder said, these things happen, and it's not the end of the world.'

'It was only the once,' Håkan said without looking at them.

'Why didn't you tell us this before?' Alex asked.

Håkan looked at him as if he had lost his mind.

'Because it was nothing to do with you. Why do you think, for fuck's sake?'

Peder interrupted him.

'When was this?'

'A while before she went missing.'

'How long?'

'Three or four months.'

'Did you use protection?'

Håkan squirmed. 'I didn't, but she did. She was on the pill.'

'So she didn't get pregnant?' Alex asked.

'No.'

Håkan refused to meet Alex's gaze as he answered.

*Was he lying?*

'Are you sure?'

A silent nod. Still no eye contact.

'From a purely hypothetical point of view,' Alex went on, 'if she had got pregnant, what would you have done?'

At last, Håkan raised his head.

'We'd have kept it, of course.'

'Of course?' Peder repeated. 'You were both very young; no one would have blamed you if you'd decided on a termination.'

'Out of the question,' Håkan said. 'It would never have happened. Abortion is murder if the child has been created within a loving relationship. I despise people who think differently.'

'Did you and Rebecca agree on that?'

'Of course we did.'

Håkan's expression darkened and his voice grew hoarse.

'We would have been excellent parents, if she'd lived.'

# INTERVIEW WITH FREDRIKA BERGMAN,
## 02-05-2009,
### 15.30 (tape recording)

Present: Urban S, Roger M (interrogators one and two). Fredrika Bergman (witness).

Urban: So at that point you believed Håkan Nilsson to be the guilty party?

Fredrika: There were a number of indications to support that view. He had a motive and the personality traits that led us to believe he was capable of murder.

Roger: Had you discovered the link with the writer Thea Aldrin at that stage?

Fredrika: At that stage we barely knew who Thea Aldrin was; she still hadn't come up in the investigation.

Urban: So you hadn't identified the film club?

Fredrika: Absolutely not.

Roger: OK, back to Håkan Nilsson. What about his alibi?

Fredrika: It had been checked during the previous investigation and deemed valid. We reached the same conclusion. He had spent the whole evening at a social event for mentors and students, and witness statements confirmed that he had been there from five o'clock until midnight.

Urban: But you didn't write him off completely?

Fredrika: No, definitely not. No alibi is one hundred per cent reliable.

Roger: How was Peder Rydh at this point?

Fredrika: I don't understand the question.

Urban: Was he stable?

Fredrika: Yes. He was feeling better than he had for a long time.

Urban: So you're saying that there were occasions when Peder Rydh had been feeling under par and had acted injudiciously?

(Silence.)

Roger: You must answer our questions, Fredrika.

Fredrika: Yes, there have been times when he was unstable.

Urban: And acted injudiciously?

Fredrika: And acted injudiciously. But as I said, he was in a good place throughout the investigation, and . . .

Roger: We're not there yet. It's too soon to talk about the investigation as a whole. We've only got as far as Håkan Nilsson.

(Silence.)

Urban: What happened next?

Fredrika: Next?

Urban: What happened after that first interview with Håkan Nilsson?

Fredrika: The team who were working on the scene of the crime called Alex. They'd found something else.

# THURSDAY

# CHAPTER 7

As usual, morning coffee was served in a blue mug with her name on it. She couldn't decide whether she found it childish or humiliating, or both. The nurse padded discreetly around her, setting out bread, butter and marmalade. A soft-boiled egg, a plain yoghurt. The nurse was new; she stuck out like a sore thumb. The new ones were always so stressed around Thea; sometimes, she would hear them whispering in the tiny kitchen area.

'They say she hasn't said a single word for nearly thirty years. She must be completely barking.'

As time went by it had become increasingly easy to ignore that kind of talk. It wasn't the young people's fault that they didn't understand. They had no mechanism for understanding Thea's story, nor were they under any obligation to do so. Thea wasn't so old that she had forgotten her own youth. The years preceding those that she had decided to kill with silence had largely been good. She recalled her teens, so full of happiness that it hurt to think about it. She could remember falling in love for the first time, the first book she wrote, and the way her heart leapt when the press praised her children's books to the skies, predicting the most astonishing success. Everything had been smashed to pieces and taken away from her. She had nothing left.

The new nurse bustled around behind her back, stopping to look at the vase of flowers. An auxiliary came in and started changing the sheets on Thea's bed. Unpleasant, Thea thought. It could easily have waited until she'd finished breakfast.

'What lovely flowers,' said the nurse.

Not to Thea, but to the auxiliary.

'She gets a fresh bouquet every week.'

'Who from?'

'We don't know. They're delivered by someone from the florist's; we usually hand them over and she arranges them herself.'

Thea contemplated the nurse's back view, knowing that she was reading the card that accompanied the flowers.

'It says "Thanks",' Thea heard her say. 'Thanks for what?'

'No idea,' the auxiliary replied. 'There are so many odd things about all this that . . .'

She broke off when she realised that Thea was watching them. They never seemed to grasp the fact that her hearing was excellent. They assumed she was an idiot, just because she had chosen not to speak.

The auxiliary moved closer to the nurse and lowered her voice.

'We don't know how much she grasps of what's going on around her,' she said. 'But sometimes I think she's listening. I mean, she's fully mobile. There's nothing to indicate that she doesn't understand what we say.'

Thea almost burst out laughing. The yoghurt tasted disgusting, and the bread was dry. She ate it anyway. There was no more conversation between the nurse and the auxiliary, and after a little while she was left alone. When the door closed behind them, Thea felt nothing but relief.

She got up from the table and switched on the television. She gripped the remote firmly and went back to her seat. The stroke she had suffered a few years earlier had caused enough long-term damage to prevent her from living alone, but on the whole she coped relatively well with everyday life. She would go mad if the staff interfered with her life any more than they already did.

The morning news had just started.

'The police confirmed yesterday that the body found in Midsommarkransen was that of Rebecca Trolle, a young student who went missing one evening almost two years ago. They have not released any further details, and have stated that they do not have a particular suspect in mind at this stage.'

Thea stared blankly at the television. She had followed every single news broadcast since she heard that it was Rebecca Trolle's body that had been found. Her heart was beating slightly faster. Now it would begin, she was certain of that. She had been waiting for the conclusion for almost thirty years, and now it was coming.

# CHAPTER 8

Alex Recht walked up to the crater and stared down into the damp earth. The men standing at the edge of the excavated area were surrounded by trees. Peder moved closer, leaning forward to get a better view.

'How did you find him?' Alex asked.

'We dug around the area where Rebecca Trolle was buried, and we found a man's shoe that looked as if it had been lying in the ground for a long time. We expanded the search area and dug deeper, and there he was.'

The man who had answered Alex's question pointed out exactly where the second body had been found.

'How long had he been there?'

'The pathologist said he couldn't be sure until the body was brought in, but probably several decades.'

Alex breathed in the fresh air; in spite of everything, it was good to see the rays of the sun caressing the trees and the ground, still wet with dew. Spring was his favourite time of year, and he was definitely a morning person. It was still only seven o'clock, and he was pleased that

90

Peder had been able to join him at such an early hour.

'How can you be sure it's a man?' Peder asked.

'The height,' replied a female officer who had been involved in investigating the scene. 'The pathologist estimated that the deceased was over six feet; not many women are that tall.'

'That should make the identification easier,' Peder said. 'If we can get an idea of how long the body has been in the ground, and an approximate height and age, we ought to be able to match the profile with people who disappeared around that time.'

Alex crouched down, studying both graves.

'There's not a cat in hell's chance that this was a coincidence.'

'What do you mean?'

'The fact that Rebecca was buried in this particular spot.'

Alex squinted into the sun.

'The person or persons who buried Rebecca here had buried someone else here in the past.'

'Although he or she must have felt safer last time,' said the female officer.

'In what way?'

'The man we found last night still had his head and hands.'

Alex thought for a moment.

'The perpetrator was younger the first time,' he said. 'Which means he might well have been both naive and careless.'

Peder zipped up his jacket as if he had suddenly realised he was cold.

'How do we know it was the first time?' he asked.

Fredrika Bergman had just got up when Alex called to tell her that he and Peder were on their way to the place where Rebecca Trolle had been found, and that a second body had been discovered the previous night.

'See you at HQ,' Alex said.

Fredrika hurried into the kitchen for breakfast.

Spencer was sitting at the table reading the paper. She kissed his forehead and stroked his cheek. She poured herself a cup of coffee and cut two slices of bread. She gazed at the love of her life in silence.

*Talk to me, Spencer. I've known you for over ten years; I know what you look like when you're unhappy.*

He didn't say a word, refusing to let her in.

'What are you two going to do today?' Fredrika asked.

'I don't know; I expect we'll go for a walk.'

Spencer put down the newspaper.

'I could do with going to Uppsala this afternoon, and I'd prefer to go without Saga.'

'That's fine,' Fredrika said, even though she suspected it could be a long day at work. 'I'll come home when you need to go.'

She took a bite of her sandwich, chewed and swallowed. Her friends had taken the news that she had gone back to work much better than she had expected. Several of them had even hinted that it wasn't a complete surprise.

'Are you going to the department?' she asked Spencer.

'Yes, to a meeting.'

A meeting. No more, no less. When had they started talking in half-sentences? Fredrika thought about Alex, about the previous winter when his wife had found out she was ill and hadn't told him. Suddenly she went cold.

'Spencer, you're not ill, are you?'

He looked at her in surprise. Grey eyes, like stones shot through with more shades than she could count.

'Why would I be ill?'

'I can tell there's something wrong. Something more than an argument at work.'

Spencer shook his head.

'It's nothing, believe me. The only thing I might have left out is . . .'

He hesitated, and she waited.

'Apparently, one of my students wasn't happy with her supervision last autumn.'

'For goodness' sake, you were still off sick most of the time!'

'That was the problem,' Spencer said. 'I had to share the supervision with a graduate tutor who had only just started in the department, and it wasn't a popular move.'

Fredrika could feel the relief flooding through her body.

'I thought you were dying or something!'

Spencer gave her the crooked smile that always made her melt.

'I wouldn't leave you now we're living together at long last.'

Fredrika leaned forward to kiss him, but was interrupted by the unmistakable sound of Saga waking up in the room next door. She followed Spencer with her eyes as he limped out of the kitchen.

'Now what?' said Peder when they were back at HQ.

'We wait for more precise details from the forensic pathologist, and we continue to pursue the investigation into the murder of Rebecca Trolle,' Alex replied. 'I spoke to the pathologist on the phone; he thinks the man has been lying there for at least twenty-five years, possibly more.'

'A serial killer?'

'Who kills at random? Such disparate victims, three decades apart?' Alex shook his head grimly. 'I don't think so. Besides which, serial killers are few and far between. This is something different.'

He cursed his own shortcomings, even though he knew it was pointless. At the time of Rebecca's disappearance there had been nothing whatsoever to indicate that she might have been one of several victims; the investigation had been based on the premise that this was an isolated incident. Were there more victims? Alex wondered. He hadn't hesitated to order the complete excavation of the site where the bodies had been found, expanding the parameters of the search area. It would take several days to complete the task, but if there were more bodies in the ground, Alex wanted them found.

'If we think the same person killed Rebecca and the man we found yesterday, then it can hardly have been Håkan Nilsson,' Peder said. 'He wasn't even born when the man was murdered.'

'That's what I was thinking,' Alex said. 'But we know too little about all this to eliminate him completely. He might have a connection with the first killer that we're unaware of. I want to run a DNA check on him and compare it with Rebecca's unborn child, if that's possible. If he's the father, we've got enough to bring him in.'

'What if he refuses to co-operate?'

'If he refuses to supply us with a DNA sample voluntarily, then we'll go to the prosecutor. We know that Rebecca was pregnant, and that she'd expressed concern about the fact that the father would want to keep the child, even though she was keen to have a termination. We also know that Rebecca and Håkan had slept together, and that Håkan would have wanted to keep the child if she had got pregnant. That's enough. More than enough. Even though I have to admit that I don't really see Håkan as our killer.'

'Any other leads?'

'In the light of the fact that we've found another body, the rumours about Rebecca selling sex over the Internet have become more interesting than

95

her pregnancy. See what you can find out; there might be more history to it; the older body might fit in somehow.'

Peder glanced at his notebook.

'There's the ex-girlfriend too,' he said.'

'I thought Fredrika could take care of her when she comes in.'

At that moment Fredrika appeared in the doorway.

'Who am I taking care of?'

'Rebecca Trolle's ex-girlfriend, Daniella. Good morning, by the way.'

'Good morning.'

Fredrika was fiddling with a pale blue scarf draped over the shoulders of her jacket.

'We need to go through her things as well.'

Alex looked unsure.

'Why? We already have copies of everything that was considered interesting when we went through the material two years ago.'

Fredrika frowned.

'It struck me yesterday that it looks as if a significant amount was weeded out. For example, I can't find any information about text books, or copies of her notes.'

'Why would you want those?' Peder asked.

'She was a student when she went missing. That means she spent a large proportion of her waking hours studying, attending lectures, hanging out with friends. According to Alex, she was in the middle of writing her dissertation when she died. I can't find any indication of what her topic was.'

Alex ran a hand through his hair, choosing his words with care.

'As I said yesterday, we spoke to her supervisor. He told us about the topic, but to be honest we didn't think it was relevant. I think she was writing about a children's author: Thea Aldrin, if you remember her.'

He shrugged.

'The topic itself didn't suggest any exciting theories, so we left it at that.'

'Do you mind if I take another look?' Fredrika asked. 'Thea Aldrin was a controversial figure, to say the least.'

Alex suppressed a sigh. How many times had he had a similar conversation with Fredrika?

'If you have time,' he said. 'I want you to talk to the ex-girlfriend first; you can look at the other stuff tomorrow.'

Fredrika went back to her office; Peder stayed with Alex.

'I'll start with Håkan's DNA sample, then I'll look into the sex rumours.'

'Good,' said Alex. 'I hope we hear from the pathologist pretty bloody quickly; I want an ID for the second victim as soon as possible.'

Håkan Nilsson was very annoyed when Peder rang his doorbell, accompanied by a colleague. Peder introduced his fellow officer and explained why they were there.

'Why do you want my DNA?' Håkan asked.

'Rebecca was pregnant when she died, and we want to establish who the father was.'

The colour drained from Håkan's face.

'Pregnant? You didn't mention that yesterday.'

His voice was weak, his eyes open wide.

'Didn't you know?'

Peder's tone was harsher than it had been the previous day.

'No.'

It was difficult to know whether he was telling the truth.

'Do you think I did it?'

Håkan was trying to look tough, but the uncertainty shone on his face like newly polished shoes.

'We don't think anything,' Peder replied. 'And we want to keep it that way as far as you're concerned. That's why we want to run a DNA check, so that we can eliminate you from our inquiries.'

'I've got to go to work – can I come in later?'

'No, we'd like you to come now. Make a phone call and tell them you'll be late for work.'

He tilted his head to one side and added in a gentler tone of voice: 'Tell them you're helping the police with their inquiries. That usually impresses an employer.'

Håkan gave him a long look, then went to fetch his keys and wallet.

'It doesn't matter whether I'm the child's father or not,' he said. 'You've already checked my alibi, and you know I couldn't have done it.'

'If I remember rightly, you were at a big party

the night Rebecca disappeared. Would anyone have noticed if you'd slipped away for a couple of hours?'

When Håkan didn't reply, Peder looked more closely at him. He looked upset. Hurt.

'It wasn't a party,' he said. 'It was more of a dinner for the mentoring network. It was an all day event. Rebecca was supposed to be there too, but she didn't turn up.'

Peder frowned.

'Had you fallen out? Was that why she didn't come?'

'I answered those questions yesterday.'

Håkan grabbed his jacket.

'You think this is all about me,' he snapped. 'You'll be embarrassed when you find out how wrong you are.'

'I'm sure we will,' said Peder.


Fredrika was accompanied by a new colleague when she went to see Rebecca's ex-girlfriend – DC Cecilia Torsson was driving, with Fredrika in the passenger seat.

'You've just come back to work, haven't you?' Cecilia asked.

'Yesterday,' Fredrika replied.

They were covering the short distance between HQ and Tegnérlunden, where Rebecca's ex-girlfriend rented an apartment. The city looked beautiful beneath a clear blue sky; Stockholm at its very best.

'Are you the one who's had a baby by a married man?'

Fredrika stiffened. What kind of a question was that, for God's sake?

'No,' she replied. 'And if you have any more questions about my private life, I suggest you keep them to yourself.'

'Oh, God, I'm so sorry, I had no idea it was such a sensitive issue.'

Silenced descended inside the car. Fredrika breathed deeply to stop herself from boiling over. Obviously, she realised that her private life aroused a certain amount of curiosity, but surely people could be tactful? She would have been. At least she thought she would.

'This is where she lives.'

Cecilia pulled up by the kerb.

'We can't park here,' Fredrika said, pointing to a sign.

Cecilia stuck a note on the windscreen to indicate that this was a police vehicle.

'We can now.'

That wasn't true, but Fredrika couldn't face making herself even more unpopular than she already was. The note could be used only when officers were involved in an operation, which was hardly the case at the moment.

Daniella lived on the second floor, and there was no lift. Fredrika had checked up on her before leaving the station. Rebecca's ex had a colourful past. While she was still at secondary school she had spent time in both child and youth psychiatric units on a number of occasions. She also had a criminal record and had been a suspect in other cases, but these involved only minor offences such as theft and vandalism. After leaving school, she had spent a term at college, and since then she had either been working or signed off due to ill health.

Rebecca and Daniella had got together when Rebecca returned from studying in France. Fredrika found it difficult to imagine what the two girls would have had in common, apart from the desire to experiment. Rebecca was a sensible girl who lived a structured life and had clear-cut ambitions – at least on paper. Although that might have been the problem, of course. When structure and ambition become too suffocating, a desire to push the boundaries often grows stronger.

Cecilia rang the doorbell.

No reply. She tried again. They heard the sound of running feet from inside the apartment, heavy footsteps heading for the hallway. The latch clicked and the door opened.

'Daniella?'

Fredrika edged in front of Cecilia and showed her ID.

'Police – we'd like to speak to you.'

Daniella backed away from the door and Fredrika and Cecilia stepped inside.

'Coffee?'

They both refused. 'We won't keep you for long,' Cecilia said.

'That doesn't mean you can't have a cup of coffee, does it?'

Daniella led the way into the kitchen, where she flopped down on one of the mismatched chairs. The apartment was sparsely furnished; it was obviously a sublet. The bare walls were covered in photographs, all showing the same person: a young boy staring into the camera with a defiant expression.

'Who's this?' Fredrika asked, pointing to one of the photos.

'My brother.'

'It looks as if you're the same age.'

'Wrong. He was ten years older than me. He's dead.'

Fredrika sat down at the table, well aware of Cecilia's triumphant expression as she gloated over Fredrika's faux pas.

'I'm very sorry,' she said quietly.

'Me too.'

Daniella didn't look the way Fredrika had expected. She was more powerfully built, bordering on fat. Her hair was spiky and as black as coal, contrasting sharply with the pale eyes.

'I presume this is about Rebecca?'

'Yes, we've found her.'

'I saw it on TV.'

'Are you glad she's been found?' Cecilia asked.

Daniella shrugged indifferently.

'I didn't care at the time and I don't care now. She was a complete fucking bitch.'

The language was far removed from anything Fredrika would normally use.

'Why do you say that?'

'She was just playing with me, making me think what we had was real.'

'When was this?'

'A few years ago, when she got back from France.'

A few years ago. And she was still a fucking bitch.

'You must have really loved her,' Cecilia said gently.

Instead of replying, Daniella got up to fetch a glass of water. This time she didn't bother asking them if they wanted a drink.

'How did it end?' Fredrika asked.

'She rang and told me it was over.'

'That's low, not telling you face to face,' Cecilia said.

'Too bloody right,' Daniella agreed. 'And then she came back.'

'You got back together?'

'Not properly, just the odd snog. She was at the university – she was too good for me. I think she was ashamed of me.'

Fredrika looked at a photograph on top of the fridge: Daniella's brother again. He was everywhere.

'When did you break off contact?'

Daniella shuffled uncomfortably.

'We didn't. I didn't want to let go completely, if you know what I mean.'

'Not really.'

'If you like a person, you want to keep in touch. You don't want them to disappear.'

*Like your brother did.*

'And what did Rebecca think about that? Did

she call you sometimes, or was it always you who called her?'

'It was mostly me. She was always so fucking busy. Swimming lessons for babies and the church choir and God knows what. And then there was bloody Håkan as well.'

Fredrika straightened up.

'Håkan?'

'He kept on poking his nose in, saying I shouldn't ring Rebecca. He was off his head – he couldn't see that she didn't want him to ring her either.'

'Did Rebecca regard Håkan as a problem?'

Daniella gave a short, barking laugh.

'He followed her around like a puppy. He seemed to think they were best friends, or something.'

'But they weren't?'

'No fucking chance. In the end she couldn't stand him.'

And could she stand you? Fredrika wondered.

'When did you last speak to Rebecca?' Cecilia asked.

'The day before she went missing; I rang her, but she didn't have time to chat. She was on her way to see that toffee-nosed mentor of hers. She was supposed to call me later, but she never did.'

Fredrika noted the mention of Rebecca's mentor; it had come up several times, and she still didn't know what it meant.

'One last question,' she said. 'Do you know whether Rebecca was involved in internet dating?'

'Everybody knew that.'

'OK, but do you remember hearing her talk about it?'

'No, I don't think so.'

'We've heard rumours that she was selling sex on the internet; do you know anything about that?'

Daniella's cheeks were burning as she looked at Fredrika.

'No.'

Her voice was subdued, almost a whisper.

'Daniella, it's extremely important that you don't keep any information from us at this stage,' Cecilia said.

Daniella cleared her throat and looked Cecilia in the eye.

'I'm not keeping anything from you, because I don't know anything. OK?'

Fredrika and Cecilia glanced at one another and reached a mutual decision to bring the interview to an end.

'She's lying,' Cecilia said as they were getting in the car.

'You're right,' Fredrika said. 'The question is why? And what about?'

# CHAPTER 9

Alex was trying to persuade the pathologist to work faster. He was keen to get on, to move a step closer to a definite identification of the second body discovered in the forest.

'I'm doing the best I can,' said the pathologist. 'I can't work any faster when the body is this old.'

Alex was ashamed of himself, but thanked his lucky stars that they had known each other for such a long time. Their relationship was purely professional; over the years any personal exchanges had been few and far between. If the pathologist knew that Alex had been widowed, then it was because someone else had told him. Alex himself had never mentioned it.

*It's not because I've forgotten you, Lena.*

He gathered the team in their temporary meeting room. Fredrika was still there.

'What hours are you actually working? I thought you were supposed to be doing seventy-five per cent?'

He was trying to sound caring rather than annoyed.

'I'm working approximately seventy-five per cent,' Fredrika replied. 'I was actually supposed to be somewhere else after lunch, but it all sorted itself out.'

An evasive tone, indicating that her working arrangements were negotiable. Alex didn't know what to think. Apparently, the child's father was about the same age as Alex; he wondered how that was possible. He certainly wouldn't want to start all over again with a baby. Dirty nappies and sleepless nights, snotty noses and potty training. The thought made him feel a little sad. He hadn't taken paternity leave, and to be honest he hadn't actually wiped very many snotty noses. For a long time he had convinced himself that he wasn't missing anything, that he could make up for it with the children later on.

Few lies in the history of the world have become more prevalent than the idea that you can somehow compensate at a later stage for not spending time with your children when they are little. When Alex was faced with the horrendous task of burying his wife, the mother of his children, it was very clear which parent was closest to those children. His son had come back from South America during the summer and stayed until it was all over. In every gesture he made, every word he said, Alex recognised Lena. He couldn't see himself anywhere at all.

'The pathologist is hoping to get back to us with further information tomorrow,' he said, 'but we shouldn't get our hopes up. The second body has been in the ground for a long time, and key evidence is no longer available.'

He got up and began to write on the whiteboard at one end of the room.

'As far as Rebecca Trolle is concerned, this is what we know. She went missing on her way to a party. She was seen on a bus heading in the opposite direction from the party; we don't know why she was on the bus. She was expecting a child she didn't want, and might well have been afraid that the child's father would want to keep it. At the time of her disappearance she wasn't in a steady relationship, as far as we are aware, but we do know that she had had sexual intercourse with a friend, Håkan Nilsson, whom she has referred to as a nuisance when speaking to other friends. And Håkan would have loved to be a father.'

Alex fell silent.

'We also know that after her disappearance there were rumours that she had been selling sex on the Internet, but we seem to have hit a brick wall there,' Peder said. 'No one can give us the name of the website where she was allegedly active, and no one can tell us exactly how long she was supposed to have been doing this. Nor can anyone remember when the rumour started, or where it came from.'

'What happened with Diana Trolle's friend?' Alex asked. 'Did you speak to her and her daughter?'

'I'm seeing them in an hour.'

'This sounds like nonsense to me,' Fredrika said. 'We have nothing that would explain why Rebecca would do such a thing. Selling your body isn't exactly something you do because it's fun – you do it because you have to, or because you're sick and you don't know any better.'

'I agree,' Alex said. 'Let's see where we are after Peder has spoken to Diana's friend and her daughter.'

He stepped back and looked at his notes.

'Håkan Nilsson is still the most interesting character. Unless the DNA test shows that someone else was the child's father; if that's the case, we need to prioritise the search for the secret boyfriend.'

'Håkan could still be of interest, even if he isn't the father,' Fredrika said. 'That might even make him more interesting. He was obviously keener on Rebecca than she was on him. He might have found out she was pregnant and confronted her, gone crazy with jealousy.'

'And killed her,' Peder chipped in.

Alex looked at him.

'Not just killed her,' he said. 'Dismembered her body as well.'

He left his words hanging in the air.

'It could have happened,' Peder said. 'He's an odd bugger. Unpleasant.'

'I'm not saying you're wrong,' Alex said. 'What I'm saying is the fact that her body was desecrated in that way tells us something important about the murderer. He must have had the time and the opportunity to dismember the body, then to transport the sacks to the place where she was buried.'

'Can we tell whether he knew what he was doing when he cut up the body?' Fredrika asked.

Alex paused for a moment before replying.

'I received some information on that point just before the meeting. According to the pathologist, the body was dismembered using a chainsaw, which definitely does not indicate that the murderer knew what he was doing.'

No one said a word. Alex allowed them time to digest what they had just heard.

'The use of a chainsaw proves that the murderer must have had access to a remote and probably isolated venue which belonged to him. You can't go into a friend's garage and start chopping up a body with a chainsaw; it would be too messy and too difficult to clean up.'

'What does this mean in terms of the killer's profile?' Fredrika asked. 'Using such extreme violence . . . it's sick. This has to be personal. The murderer seems to have wanted to debase Rebecca, even after her death.'

Alex nodded.

'Which is why we have to be careful. Under no circumstances must this information be leaked to the media. For one thing, the attention would create problems for us, and for another it would be difficult to question suspects. No one would dare to speak to us.'

He looked worried; he turned to Fredrika.

'What about Daniella, the ex-girlfriend; can we eliminate her from our inquiries?'

Fredrika considered her response.

'Not entirely. She reacted oddly when we mentioned the rumours about Rebecca selling sex on the internet. I got the feeling that she was lying, or keeping something from us.'

'OK, we'll keep her on the books for now. Do you think she could have been the source of the rumour?'

'I don't know. It did cross my mind.'

Fredrika decided to carry on talking while she had the opportunity.

'That party Rebecca didn't turn up at, the mentors' party – what's that all about?'

'Rebecca was part of a so-called mentoring programme,' Alex explained. 'To put it briefly, the students who were selected for the programme were given a personal mentor, who would provide advice and regular contact. The mentors were a wide range of different people: high flyers in industry, priests, authors, a couple of politicians.'

'Who was Rebecca's mentor?'

'Let me think . . . Valter Lund.'

Fredrika was surprised.

'Valter Lund? The boss of Axbergers?'

'Exactly.'

'But why was he her mentor if she was studying the history of literature? Did they just allocate these mentors in a completely random way?'

'I've no idea,' Alex said. 'I remember we spoke

to him, but we were able to eliminate him more or less straight away.'

Peder spoke up.

'I went through Rebecca's diary this morning. It was bloody hard to make out.'

Alex nodded, looking less than happy.

'Thanks for the reminder, Peder.'

'What do you mean, hard to make out?' Fredrika asked.

'She had her own system for noting things down,' Alex said. 'For example, she never wrote the name of the person she'd arranged to see, just the initials. We managed to identify most of them, but we had to give up on some. We made a list of everyone who appeared in her diary in the months leading up to her disappearance.'

'Two weeks before she went missing she met a "TA",' Peder said. 'Who was that?'

Alex frowned, trying to remember.

'I think it was something to do with her dissertation. Completely irrelevant.'

'And who was she seeing on the day she disappeared?' Fredrika asked.

'Nobody at all. We mapped out her final days as best we could with the help of the diary, but we didn't find anything earth-shattering.'

'Could I have a copy?'

'You can have mine,' Peder offered. 'I don't need it at the moment.'

Fredrika looked pleased, and started gathering her things together.

Alex felt a sudden pang in his chest. Of course she was going home; she had a family to think of. He thought back to dinner with his daughter the previous evening. He was a grandfather now; earlier than he had expected, perhaps, but it felt good.

*But Lena never knew what it was like to be a grandmother.*

'See you tomorrow,' he said to Fredrika.

The rest of them stayed on for a while, talking over a number of points. The officers who had been brought in to supplement the team had remained silent during the early part of the meeting, but now felt able to air their views and ideas. Alex caught himself not listening. Instead, he was thinking of Diana Trolle, whose daughter's body had been dismembered using a chainsaw. He would solve this case if it was the last thing he did.

# CHAPTER 10

The meeting took place in Erland Malm's office, the room Spencer Lagergren had visited just a few days earlier. Apart from Spencer and Erland, there was a representative from the student body and a member of the university board. Spencer had naively assumed that the meeting would put a stop to his miserable plight, and was looking forward to informing his employer that he had no intention of returning to work at present, but wished to remain on paternity leave. Fredrika had been unable to come home and look after Saga this afternoon as she had promised, so Spencer had brought the child with him to the meeting.

He hated lying to Fredrika. To be fair, he wasn't exactly lying, but he was deliberately withholding information which he really should have passed on to her. He couldn't bring himself to tell her what had happened, besides which he assumed the matter would soon be resolved.

He immediately realised that he had made a series of errors. Bringing Saga with him didn't look good; she lay there asleep in her buggy, the very personification of his sinful life. Nor did the meeting appear to have the aim of putting an end to a regrettable misunderstanding. Spencer very quickly became aware that in fact the opposite was true.

'Spencer, we have conducted a significant number of lengthy interviews on the situation with which we are faced,' Erland Malm began. 'And believe me, it hasn't been an easy exercise.'

He paused and looked at Spencer as if to check that he was really listening. Which he was.

'Tova's accusations are so serious that we feel we have no alternative but to take the matter further, so that any uncertainty can be removed once and for all.'

Erland appealed silently to his colleagues, hoping that someone else would feel able to carry on. No one spoke.

'What uncertainty?' said Spencer.

'I'm sorry?

'You said you wanted to remove any uncertainty, but I don't understand what you mean.'

Erland pursed his lips and glanced at the woman representing the university board, who took over: 'When a student comes forward to report the kind of experiences Tova has outlined, it is our duty to take that person seriously,' she said. 'Otherwise, our reputation would be damaged, and student confidence in us would be eroded. The matter has been raised within the student body, and we are under considerable pressure to act.'

'For God's sake,' Spencer said. 'I've said it's all nonsense. You've spoke to Malin, who was also Tova's supervisor. She can confirm that Tova is lying.'

'Unfortunately, that is not the case,' Erland said. 'Malin doesn't know what happened when you were alone with Tova. In addition, other points have emerged which we must now take into account.'

'Like what?'

'Like your emails to Tova, for example.'

Spencer blinked.

'Emails?'

Erland removed a sheet of paper from a plastic folder and pushed it across to Spencer, who read through it with mounting astonishment.

'What the hell . . .?'

The woman from the board agreed.

'That's exactly what I said. What the hell has got into Professor Lagergren? You just can't take liberties like that!'

Spencer looked in disbelief at the printed messages.

'I didn't send these,' he said, pushing the sheet of paper away. 'For a start, I don't communicate with my students by email, and secondly I would never express myself in that way.'

'They come from your email account, Spencer.'

'Bloody hell, anybody could have sneaked into my office and sent them! This isn't the CIA; my computer is open for anyone to use if I forget to lock my door when I leave!'

'Let's just calm down,' Erland said in a desperate attempt to assert his authority. 'You have to understand that we cannot simply assume that someone else sent these messages. And given the gravity of the content and the concrete nature of the accusations, we have decided to advise Tova to make a formal complaint to the police.'

Spencer felt the colour drain from his face.

He looked at the messages again. Three of them.

'Tova, it's unfortunate that you have chosen not to accede to my demands. Sadly, it looks as if your dissertation will suffer if you do not do what I have asked you to do. Come up to my office after 7 p.m. tomorrow and I'm sure we can reach an agreement. Spencer.'

In spite of himself, he laughed out loud.

'This is absolutely ridiculous. I've never seen these messages, and I certainly didn't write them. I . . .'

He broke off.

'Let's go to my office and check my messages,' he said. 'If they really did come from my computer, they should be in the "Sent" folder.'

'And if they're not?' said the board member. 'That could simply mean that you've deleted them.'

Spencer was already on his way out of the room, heading towards his own office down the corridor. The rest of the group followed hesitantly. Spencer was limping, because he had left Saga behind in her buggy; without a stick or the buggy to lean on, his leg ached more than usual.

It took a couple of minutes to log in, but it was

117

long enough for him to start feeling extremely nervous. He used email far too infrequently to bother organising his folders. The messages someone else had sent could easily be sitting there in the 'Sent' folder waiting to be discovered, he realised as he clicked through the menus with a trembling hand.

But they weren't there. There wasn't a trace of the messages that had been sent to Tova, and nor were they in the 'Trash' folder.

'This doesn't prove anything,' Erland said.

Spencer swallowed hard.

'What do you actually want? What can I do to get out of this mess?'

'Prove that none of this ever happened,' Erland said. 'But to be honest, I think that's going to be very difficult.'


Once, when Peder was a child, a classmate had started a rumour about him.

'Peder sucks up to Miss, that's why she always gives him a gold star for his Maths tests.'

It made no difference that Peder could show he had got all the answers right in the tests; the other children still chose to believe the boy who said the stars were a result of Peder sucking up to the teacher. That was the first time Peder realised how soul-destroying the battle against a rumour can be. It is impossible to shake off certain things; they acquire a life of their own and cannot be suppressed.

The suggestion that Rebecca Trolle had been selling sex over the Internet seemed to be just such a rumour. All her friends had heard it, but none of them knew where the information had come from. And when the police started asking questions, they became evasive. No one wanted to be held responsible for passing on the gossip, no one was prepared to admit that he or she had started it.

The interesting thing was that the rumour had begun *after* Rebecca's disappearance. As if it were an answer to the question why. Why did she disappear? Because she was selling sex over the internet, and one of her clients killed her.

Peder met Diana Trolle's friend and the friend's daughter in reception.

'We'd like to speak to you separately,' he explained.

Diana's friend went off with another officer while Peder took the daughter, Elin. She looked scared when he opened the door of one of the bright interview rooms; she hesitated, and for a moment he thought he might have to chase her along the corridors of HQ.

'Please sit down.'

They sat down on opposite sides of the table. He considered how best to tackle the conversation. On the one hand, he would quite like to give the girl a good shake, pin her up against the wall and ask her how the hell she could say such a stupid thing about a dead classmate. On the other hand, he didn't really think this would achieve the desired effect. Elin looked as if she was on the verge of

119

tears, more like a fourteen-year-old girl than a woman of twenty-five.

'It wasn't me,' she said before Peder had even opened his mouth.

'What do you mean?'

'It wasn't me that made up all that stuff.'

'OK. So who was it, in that case?'

'I don't know.'

Peder tried to shuffle down in his seat, to look more relaxed.

'So when did this rumour actually start?'

'After she went missing, I think. My friends and I hadn't heard it before.'

Peder thought for a moment.

'Why do you think someone would make up something like this?'

Elin shrugged.

'Everyone was so scared when she disappeared; I think the gossip became a kind of protection for us. If that was why she went missing, then it couldn't happen to the rest of us.'

'Because you weren't selling sex over the Internet?'

'Exactly.'

She looked as if she were telling the truth; she also looked relieved.

'Were you a close friend of Rebecca's?'

'I wouldn't say that. We just happened to be on the same course, and we went to the same parties. We hardly ever met up on our own.'

'Was that why you helped to spread the rumours about her? Because you weren't really friends?'

'Hang on a minute, I didn't "help", as you put it.'

'Oh, but you did. It was through you that the gossip got as far as Rebecca's mother. I'm sure you realise that was unfortunate.'

Elin's voice was trembling now.

'I didn't tell anyone except my mum; I didn't think she would go to Diana with gossip. I didn't tell anyone else. And even if I had, it wouldn't have made any difference.'

'Because everyone knew anyway?'

'Yes.'

Peder decided to keep pushing.

'So who started it?'

'*I told you, I don't know!*'

'Oh, come on, Elin. You must be able to tell me about the first time you heard someone mention that Rebecca was selling sex over the Internet.'

His voice was harsh and implacable. A voice he would never use to Ylva or his sons. The boys were almost three – still too young to be held responsible for their actions. And he had too much respect for Ylva.

'I can't remember exactly; I think I heard it at a party a few months after she disappeared. Some people were talking; they said she'd been seen on one of those websites. But when we looked at it, we couldn't find her. The gossip died away eventually.'

'Just a minute, you're telling me someone had seen her on a website? What website?'

'I don't know.'

'For God's sake, Elin! You just told me you had a look!"
Elin sighed.
'I think it might have been called "Dreams Come True", or something equally cheap. I haven't looked at it since, and I don't think the others have either.'
*Right.*
'The person who found her on this website – are they in the habit of buying sex there?'
'No, no, I don't think so. Definitely not.'
'He or she just happened to end up on that website, and just happened to spot a friend?'
'He. He's a law student and he was writing an assignment about the new law relating to prostitution, so he was checking out a load of websites where girls were selling themselves.'
*At last.*
'And what's the name of your friend?'
'He's not my friend. Nobody likes him. And I think he regretted talking about what he'd seen; he kind of tried to take it all back. But by then it was too late; people were already talking. Not that we thought it was true, but . . .'
'But?'
'He had seen her on the website, after all.'
Silence.
'I need a name.'
'His name is Håkan Nilsson.'

# CHAPTER 11

Malena Bremberg's expression was anxious as she watched the lunchtime news on the flickering TV screen. She didn't normally bother with the news, but today's newspaper headlines had driven her back to the sofa. She thanked her lucky stars that she wasn't working; sometimes it was difficult to find time to sit down in front of the TV in the care home.

There were lots of different stories. An earthquake in a country she'd never been to, unrest in the car industry, new proposals regarding legislation to make things easier for small businesses. She couldn't have cared less. The only thing she wanted to know more about was the woman whose body had been found in Midsommarkransen. After fifteen minutes her prayers were answered.

'The police are still refusing to release further details surrounding the discovery of the body of Rebecca Trolle,' the newsreader reported. 'A murder investigation is well under way, and a significant number of additional officers have been placed at the disposal of the Senior Investigating Officer. Rebecca Trolle was twenty-three years old when she disappeared; she was last seen in the vicinity of Gärdet in Stockholm . . .'

Terror clutched at Malena's heart. She recognised Rebecca Trolle as soon as her picture appeared on the screen. The bright smile, the freckled face. She had never understood what made the girl so important. She had visited the home on only one occasion, and hadn't come back.

The following day he had phoned.

'Has anyone been in?'

And for the first time, she answered yes. Yes, someone had been in. A young woman. She'd stayed for half an hour. She'd had coffee with Thea Aldrin, the writer, then left. He had demanded the name and telephone number of the person in question, said he had to get hold of her. Malena had hesitated, agonised, wished she was a million miles away.

*Rebecca Trolle. That was her name.*

A week passed. Then another. Then came the headlines. Rebecca Trolle, who had visited the home, was missing. After a week Malena was a wreck, and went off sick. He rang every day, patiently explaining that she would regret it forever if she told anyone about their work together.

'We don't work together!' she yelled.

Hurled the telephone at the wall.

Didn't dare to set foot outside for several days.

He was waiting for her the first time she left the apartment. Materialised behind her out of nowhere, forced her back inside. He stayed for a whole day, after which she never considered defying him again.

She still felt sick when she remembered how he had looked when he left, having kept her prisoner for twenty-four hours. Noticeably pleased with himself and what he had achieved. His final words drove her crazy:

'You're beautiful in real life, Malena. But you're even more beautiful on film.'

# CHAPTER 12

T he list of matches against the database came through just as Peder Rydh was starting to think about going home for the day. Ellen Lind, the team's administrator, knocked on his door.

'I've run a check on all the main characters who came up in the original investigation,' she said.

'Anything interesting?'

'There are a few points, but two are definitely worth looking at: her supervisor at the university, and the leader of the church choir.'

Peder suddenly felt stressed. Two new names. They already had more than enough to do.

Ellen placed the lists on his desk and left. Peder thought she was starting to fill out; could she be pregnant? Best not to offer congratulations until she mentioned it herself.

A quick glance at the clock, and Peder decided he would stay a while longer. Just a little while. He could hear Alex talking in the corridor, his voice loud and agitated. Alex worked day and night. On several occasions, Peder had thought about inviting his boss round for dinner, but the words stuck in his throat every time. What would be the point?

The list of names was practically burning his fingers. He didn't know what to think any more. Håkan Nilsson was beginning to look more and more suspect. Elin's words echoed in his mind:

*He's not my friend. Nobody likes him.*

Peder found it difficult to understand Håkan's behaviour. If he was the killer, why would he start a rumour about having seen Rebecca on a website selling sex? In order to divert attention from himself? And if he wasn't the killer, why hadn't he told the police what he had seen, when he had spent so much time helping them? Peder had discussed the matter with Alex, and they had decided not to confront Håkan until they had the results of the DNA test. Meanwhile, he was still under surveillance, and the prosecutor had also given Alex permission to tap his telephone. With a bit of luck, that would be in place later in the day.

Peder glanced through the results of Ellen's checks. The leader of the church choir of which Rebecca had been a member had been reported for violence against his partner on two occasions during the past eighteen months. The accusations had not led to charges, as there was no proof. According to the register, the couple were still living together.

During the original investigation the choirmaster had been dismissed as being of no interest. Since he was relatively young, the question of whether he might be Rebecca's new boyfriend had come up, but there was nothing to suggest that this was the case. He already had a partner, and the analysis of telephone traffic to and from Rebecca's mobile showed that they had been in contact only once during the weeks before her disappearance. He did not feature in her emails, on her Facebook page or in her cryptic diary entries. Peder therefore concluded that these more recent accusations of violence did not alter the situation as far as the police were concerned; the man would still remain outside the inquiry.

The supervisor, however, was another matter. Gustav Sjöö, a man approaching sixty, who had been reported for attempted rape by a female acquaintance less than a year ago. The report indicated that she had described him as controlling, jealous and unstable. The woman had obvious injuries that were difficult to explain away, and the case had gone to the magistrates' court. Gustav Sjöö was not convicted, but the woman had appealed to the crown court. The hearing had not yet taken place.

Peder's interest was caught by the information that had emerged during the first hearing. The prosecution had called two female students to testify that Sjöö had made inappropriate advances, and that he had threatened them with dire consequences if they told anyone. For this reason he was suspended from his post at the university until further notice; Peder suspected that he was unlikely to be reinstated even if he was acquitted.

He went back to the original material. Sjöö had

been in touch with Rebecca by telephone on a number of occasions during the months before her disappearance, but this had seemed perfectly natural since he was her supervisor. Peder remembered that he had also appeared as 'GS' in her diary.

Could Gustav Sjöö be the new man in Rebecca's life? Peder had his doubts when he looked at pictures of Sjöö, just as Alex had done. An elderly, grey man without any hint of a spark in his eyes. Then again, everyone's taste was different; perhaps Sjöö had attributes which were not apparent in a photograph, and which Rebecca had found attractive.

He checked records and saw that Sjöö lived on Mariatorget in Södermalm. He seemed to have moved there about a year ago; before that he had lived on Karlavägen. Peder searched for the address on the internet and saw that it wasn't far from Gyllenstiernsgatan. Close to Radiohuset. He went back to the old telephone records. Rebecca had spoken to Sjöö the day before she went missing. And he had been living near Radiohuset at the time, which was the final destination of the number four bus.

Sjöö had been interviewed, of course, and had an alibi for that evening. He was at a conference elsewhere, and didn't get back until the following evening. But he lived alone, Peder thought. There was no one to confirm that he got home when he said he did. And while his colleagues could state that he really had been at the conference in Västerås, the distance from Stockholm was negligible if he had a car, which he did. Peder decided to take a closer look at the conference programme. Rebecca had disappeared some time after seven thirty in the evening; it could be that she had arranged to meet Sjöö.

The property register provided Peder with more information: Gustav Sjöö owned a summer cottage in Nyköping.

*Was that where you took her to dismember the body?*

Peder felt his pulse rate increasing. Gustav Sjöö must be interviewed at the earliest opportunity. Perhaps he had raped Rebecca and forced her to keep quiet about it? Peder's vision clouded over, his palms felt sweaty. A young woman's body, hacked in half with a chainsaw. Stuffed into plastic sacks and buried in south Stockholm.

Håkan Nilsson or Gustav Sjöö. Or a person or persons as yet unknown.

*Who did you cross, Rebecca?*


The evening came, and the night came, and it was time for Alex to go home. The night was far too long, in spite of the fact that the dark time of the year had been left behind. He sat alone in his living room, a glass of whisky in his hand. He had sworn that he wouldn't turn into a tragic figure when he was alone; he had promised both Lena and the children.

'You're not to turn into one of those B-movie cops on TV,' his son had said. 'Sitting at home drinking, then going to work to beat up the bad guys.'

Alex looked at the whisky glass. Lena would have understood; she would have trusted him enough not to begrudge him a drop of the hard stuff. It helped to calm him, allowed him to relax. The road to a good night's sleep was long; the road to a warm smile was endless.

*I will never be happy again.*

Nor would Diana Trolle.

He put down the glass, realising that he couldn't push aside thoughts of Diana. What was she doing right now? Was she also sitting at home alone? She must be paralysed with grief. And shock.

Alex thought back to when Rebecca had first been reported missing. It had started off as a routine inquiry. People didn't realise how many individuals of Rebecca's age went missing in Sweden every year – and turned up safe and well. But Rebecca didn't turn up safe and well. She had disappeared without a trace. Sometimes the leads were so vague that Alex began to wonder if she had ever existed. When he spoke to her family and friends he felt closer to her, got an impression of her character, the essence of her. After two weeks, he was absolutely convinced that Rebecca had not disappeared of her own free will. And that she was probably dead.

He had had many conversations with Diana. Sometimes she would call him in the middle of the night.

'Tell me you're going to find her, Alex. Promise me that, otherwise I won't be able to sleep.'

He had promised. Over and over again. However,

he was always careful not to promise that Rebecca would be found alive. Diana must have known, because she had never demanded that assurance.

'There has to be closure,' she had said. 'A grave to visit, a breathing space in this purgatory of speculation.'

And now, two years later, she would have her closure and her grave.

Alex had given so many people a grave to visit over the years.

Too many.

Lena had pointed it out.

'Sometimes, Alex, I think it would have done you good to work with the living as well, so that you could dilute all that black grief with something more life-affirming.'

She had thought he couldn't cope with it on his own; sometimes she had seen that he was on the brink of going under, and had helped him to rediscover a balance in life. Fear clutched at his heart. Who would help him now?

Fredrika Bergman couldn't stop thinking about Rebecca Trolle. When she closed her eyes to go to sleep, she could see the young woman in her mind's eye, running for her life with a madman chasing after her with a chainsaw in his hand. But it couldn't have been like that, surely? She couldn't have been alive when he cut her body in two, could she?

Fredrika felt sick. Shortly before midnight she gave up, got out of bed and went into the kitchen.

She made some coffee and read the previous day's newspaper without taking in what she was reading. Restlessness drove her to the nursery; she had to check that Saga was asleep, that she was all right. She was fine. Through talking to the mothers in the parents' group – which was actually a mothers' group – she had realised that Saga's ability to sleep soundly was a blessing. She went down after she had been fed in the evening, and didn't wake until half past six in the morning. At the earliest.

As she stood there in her daughter's bedroom, Fredrika could hardly believe that it was only a few days since she had been on full time maternity leave. Had it gone too fast, she asked herself? Would Saga be damaged by Fredrika's abrupt disappearance from her life? She didn't think so. It wasn't as if she had put Saga into day care; she was at home with her father.

Fredrika couldn't help smiling. Spencer as a father. She would never have believed it that first time she and Spencer met outside the university, and he went home with her. Not then and not later on. She had loved him, but she had never counted on him. Not until now.

The last year had been unimaginably turbulent. Spencer had taken the step from being her secret lover to becoming her partner with astonishing ease. After some initial hesitation, her parents had understood how important he was to her, and had accepted him. On one occasion when Fredrika had gone away for the weekend to visit a friend in Malmö, Spencer had actually gone to dinner at her parents' on his own.

'Why not?' Fredrika had said. 'You're the same age, after all.'

Age wasn't an issue for Fredrika, but she knew perfectly well that few people shared that view. The mothers in the group looked horrified when Fredrika talked about Saga's daddy. They smiled, but their eyes betrayed sheer panic. They found her life choices challenging; she made them feel insecure about what they had.

Fredrika went back to the kitchen. The mothers' group was the last thing to provide her with peace of mind. If she wanted to sleep, she needed to think about something else.

But not Rebecca Trolle.

Those pictures again, almost like a film. The chainsaw raised in the air, cutting and slicing and hacking. Fredrika covered her eyes with her hands; wanting the images to disappear. *Think about something else, think about something else.*

If Rebecca Trolle had lived and had chosen to carry her baby to full term, she would have been a young mother in Stockholm. More than ten years younger than Fredrika. Rebecca hadn't wanted to keep the child; Fredrika could feel it in every fibre of her body. She had gone to the clinic, discussed a termination. She hadn't told a single friend. Was she so lonely, or was there another reason why she kept quiet about such an important matter?

Peder and the other officers had asked around

among Rebecca's circle of friends, reminding each one that this was a confidential matter. They didn't want the media to find out about the pregnancy yet. No one had heard that Rebecca was pregnant, but several had heard that she was selling sex over the Internet. How was that possible?

The answer was simple: it wasn't possible.

The two were incompatible. A person with secrets of that magnitude would not be so involved in their studies, the church choir, friends, the mentoring network, teaching babies to swim.

The pregnancy was indisputable; it was a medical fact. But the rumour that Rebecca had been selling sex was not. It was an alien concept; it just didn't fit.

Her mind full of anxious thoughts, Fredrika returned to the bedroom and lay down next to Spencer.

'Can't you sleep?' he murmured.

She didn't answer, but crept closer and laid her head on his arm.

She was thinking about Rebecca Trolle.

About the body in the plastic sacks.

About the violence to which she had been subjected.

The chainsaw. It said something about the murderer, something Fredrika just couldn't grasp. She was struck by a sudden, unstoppable thought: *routine*. He kills as a matter of routine.

# INTERVIEW WITH FREDRIKA BERGMAN,
## 02-05-2009,
### 17.30 (tape recording)

Present: Urban S, Roger M (interrogators one and two). Fredrika Bergman (witness).

Urban: In spite of the fact that you found a second victim, you still subscribed to the theory that Håkan Nilsson was the killer?

Fredrika: We didn't subscribe to any particular theory; we were keeping an open mind.

Roger: And the second victim, what happened there?

Fredrika: It took time to secure an identification.

Urban: Because you made mistakes.

Fredrika: Because we stuck to facts.

Roger: And Peder Rydh? Did he stick to the rules?

Fredrika: All the time.

Urban: And Alex Recht?

Fredrika: He stuck to the rules as well.

Urban: I was thinking more in terms of his mental state.

Fredrika: He was fine throughout.

Roger: And what about you?

Fredrika: I was fine too.

Urban: We were thinking more of the issue of sticking to the rules.

(Silence.)

Fredrika: I don't understand the question.

Urban: We're wonder if you followed the letter of the law and stuck to the rules when you were carrying out your work.

Fredrika: Of course.

Roger: You didn't suppress any evidence?

(Silence.)

Urban: Not when you went through Rebecca's things in the garage?

Fredrika: No.

(Silence.)

Roger: So what about Thea Aldrin? You must have found her by this stage?

Fredrika: No, we hadn't.

Urban: Isn't that a bit odd?

Fredrika: The investigation was complicated by the fact that the victims had been in the ground for such a long time. We were constantly waiting for test results and analyses. It took a while.

Urban: That's obviously a downside of being meticulous; everything is so slow.

Roger: What happened next? You were about to bring in both Håkan Nilsson and Gustav Sjöö. But you went off on a tangent of your own as usual. Isn't that correct?

(Silence.)

Urban: It was your idea to go through Rebecca's belongings in the garage, wasn't it?

Fredrika: Yes.

Roger: And what did you find?

137

(Silence.)

Urban: Answer the question, please.

(Silence.)

Roger: That was when you found Spencer, wasn't it?

Fredrika (whispering): Yes.

# FRIDAY

# CHAPTER 13

A second body buried next to the first one. Thea drank her coffee out of the same stupid mug as always, then banged it down on the table. The shock was making her chest feel tight. Who was the man who had been laid to rest just a few metres away from Rebecca Trolle? The police were refusing to comment; they had merely stated that the deceased was a man, and that he had probably been lying there for at least two decades, possibly three.

Two decades. That was a long time to be missing.

Thea reached for the morning paper. The discovery of the two bodies was a major story. The editorial team dealt with a lot of news, but rarely anything as exciting as a double murder. The press were asking if there might be a link, in spite of the time that had elapsed between the deaths. And the police were saying nothing.

They were saying nothing because they knew nothing.

Thea's father had been a police officer, which was why she believed she knew how the police thought. He had visited her in prison just once. She couldn't make up her mind whether the number of visits was a measure of his inadequacy as a father or a judgement on her.

'You have to start speaking, Thea,' he had said. 'If there's anything you want to put forward in your defence, you must speak now. *Now.* Otherwise it will be too late.'

Her silence had provoked him.

'The evidence is overwhelming. There is *nothing* to suggest that you are innocent. I just don't understand. How did you become so . . . disturbed?'

*Darling Daddy, children become what you make them.*

'I've told your mother I don't want her to visit you. Not while you're behaving like this. Do you understand what I'm saying, Thea? You're going to be horribly lonely.'

*I have been lonely for as long as I can remember.*

Eventually, he had got to his feet, looked at her for the last time.

'I'm ashamed of you,' he had whispered. 'I'm ashamed because my daughter is a murderer.'

*And I am ashamed because my father is an idiot and my mother is a milksop.*

Thea's hands shook, making the newspaper rustle. She thought she knew who the dead man was. The man who could have made a difference, but who had vanished when she needed him the most. The police had believed he had disappeared because he wanted to, but Thea had always known that he was dead. She had longed for him to return, been unable to understand why no one could find him. How deep do you have to bury a man so that no one will find his grave? About two metres, according to the police. That was how far down he had been lying. How many feet had walked over him, unaware of what lay hidden beneath the moss and the fallen branches?

She closed her eyes, wishing her thoughts would leave her in peace. The police would need more time to work out who he was, and what his connection with Rebecca Trolle was. And with Thea.

She wondered if they realised that they would find more bodies in that accursed grave.

# CHAPTER 14

'We're digging day and night, but it's difficult to keep all the bloody journalists away,' said the DS.

Alex listened, along with his colleague Torbjörn Ross, who had been first on the scene when Rebecca's body was found.

'Do you need more manpower?'

'At least another five, if we're going to get anywhere. We daren't use mechanical diggers; we're doing everything by hand. But it's starting to feel unsustainable. The lads can't carry on much longer.'

Torbjörn thought for a moment.

'Could we get some help from the Local Defence Volunteers?'

'Check out the possibilities,' Alex said. 'If there are any more bodies in there waiting to be discovered, I want them out over the weekend.'

The DS headed back to the site, which was growing steadily. He promised to do his best; if there were more bodies, they would see the light of day before Sunday night.

It was Friday now; Alex didn't know where the time had gone. He had been lost in a maelstrom of interviews and meetings, and a never-ending flow of thoughts and speculation.

'Are you working over the weekend?' Torbjörn asked.

'Looks that way.'

'My wife and I are going to our cottage from Saturday until Sunday; we'd be very pleased if you could join us.'

Alex didn't quite know what to say. Peder appeared in the doorway of the meeting room.

'Are we in here today?'

Alex nodded and turned to Torbjörn as Peder walked in and sat down.

'We've got a meeting; the forensic pathologist is coming over to speak to us.'

More people came in; chairs scraped against the floor as the team settled down around the table.

'Thanks for your offer . . .' Alex hesitated. 'It's very kind of you, but I don't know if I'll be able to get away; I'm probably going to end up working all weekend.'

A firm hand on his shoulder, Torbjörn's eyes fixed on his.

'In that case, I suggest you give it some thought and let me know if you can make it. Sonja and I would be very happy to see you, and I'd love to take you fishing on Sunday morning.'

'Fishing?'

'Think about it, Alex.'

The hand disappeared, but the offer lingered as Torbjörn left the room.

Fredrika was the last to arrive, just after the pathologist. The team seemed to have grown overnight; there wasn't room for everyone around the table, and some had to sit over by the wall.

Birger Rosvall, the forensic pathologist, sat down in the corner just to one side behind Alex, but Alex waved him forward and moved his chair to make room at the head of the table.

'Birger has been kind enough to come over and pass on his conclusions verbally on this occasion. I would like to remind everyone that any information which emerges during this meeting is confidential and is not to be passed on. Not under any circumstances.'

There was complete silence in the room; some people glanced away when Alex looked at them.

'We can't afford mistakes in this investigation,' he said. 'Given the level of media interest, we need to be particularly careful about what we say and what steps we take. Does everyone understand that?'

Some people nodded, others murmured their assent. No one objected; nor had he expected them to. Without further ado he handed over to the pathologist.

'We'll start with the woman,' Birger said in his characteristic voice, both nasal and hoarse at the same time. 'The head has been separated from the body immediately below the chin, if you can imagine a line just here.'

He ran his finger under his own chin from ear to ear.

'Damage to the trachea suggests that she might have been strangled, but I am unable to establish a definite cause of death. The hands were removed from the body by the same method as the head, using a chainsaw.'

The pathologist's words bounced off the walls in the meeting room and settled over those present like a sodden blanket. Not everyone had known about the use of the chainsaw.

'The severed surfaces of the bones are the main indication that a chainsaw was used rather than an ordinary blade. In addition, traces of a particular oil which could be used to grease the chain itself have been found where the amputations took place.'

'What do you mean by a particular oil?'

'Most chainsaw oil on sale today is biodegradable. The person who dismembered Rebecca's body didn't use that kind, which would have been cleverer; he used an older product which takes longer to break down. The damage to the skeleton, together with the discovery of traces of this oil or grease, leads me to conclude that the body was dismembered with a chainsaw.'

The door opened and a colleague looked in; when he saw that there was a meeting in progress, he apologised and quickly withdrew.

'Can you tell what kind of chainsaw was used?' Alex asked.

'That's impossible,' Birger replied. 'All I can say, given the choice of oil, is that it could well be an

147

older model. However, I will be able to tell you exactly what kind of oil or grease was used.'

Unpleasant images of what the process of dismemberment might have looked like came into Alex's mind. He shook his head; he didn't need pictures, just words. Facts.

'Birger, how messy would this kind of thing be? I'm sure we're all imagining horrific scenes.'

The pathologist leaned back on his chair.

'That depends on the circumstances. If the heart is still beating, even if the victim is unconscious, there will be a considerable amount of blood. However, if she is dead and no longer has a pulse, then the process will be neater. If you spread out enough plastic under the body, it shouldn't be too difficult to clear up afterwards.'

Fredrika coughed discreetly.

'And what about Rebecca?'

'What do you mean?'

She shuffled uncomfortably.

'I'm wondering if she was dead or alive when she was dismembered.'

'I can't say for certain, but I would guess that she was dead. Otherwise I am unable to explain the damage to the larynx.'

Everyone present felt like letting out a sigh of relief, but the pathologist's words brought no real comfort. Rebecca Trolle had probably been dead, but she *could* have been alive. *Could* was a taboo word.

Alex interrupted the low hum of conversation that had broken out.

'Did she have any other injuries?'

'As I mentioned in my previous report, she did not. There was no damage to the ribs or any other bones. The only injuries I managed to document were those to the larynx.'

Warm hands around the young woman's throat, pressing and pressing until it was all over.

Alex moved on.

'What can you tell us about the male?'

'As I'm sure you have already seen from the photographs, the man was found with bound ankles and his hands tied behind his back. He was lying on his side in the grave, and there was damage to his hipbone and collarbone which could have occurred as a result of being thrown down into the hole.'

The pathologist consulted his notes.

'The man has a number of injuries which suggest that he was subjected to violence before he died: a crack in the jawbone, two broken ribs, one of the nasal bones broken off.'

'How long had he been in the ground?'

'Difficult to establish with any precision; somewhere between twenty-five and thirty years.'

*Thirty years. Such a long time.*

'And the actual cause of death?'

'I believe he was strangled.'

Alex raised his eyebrows.

'Like Rebecca?'

'Yes. But it's hardly a unique way of killing another person. It's not sufficient grounds to conclude that it was the same murderer.'

How many reasons were there to assume they were dealing with two different killers, Alex thought. It was beyond unlikely that two people had been killed in the same way and buried in the same place by two different perpetrators. Unless of course there were a number of perpetrators working together. The very thought made Alex feel stressed. If that was the case, things were going to get even more complicated.

'How old was he?'

'My estimate would be between forty and fifty; I haven't been able to verify that as yet.'

'Is there anything else you think we need to be aware of?'

'Not really, apart from the obvious,' Birger said. 'First of all: the perpetrator is strong. It's impossible to drive all the way to the place where the bodies were buried, and the man was tall – one metre eighty-five. Either he walked to the grave himself and was killed in situ, or the killer would have found it very difficult to get him there. If he was really strong he might have dragged the body; otherwise, I think he must have had help. Second: the killer has used extreme violence, particularly in the case of the woman. There has to be more to it than an attempt to make identification more difficult. And third: if it's the same perpetrator, he must be at least fifty years old today. Perhaps that could go some way to explaining why the woman's body was dismembered: he wasn't strong enough to carry her in one piece.'

Once again, the meeting was disturbed as a colleague opened the door by mistake. One of the team took the opportunity to slip out to the toilet.

'How far do you have to walk to get to the grave?' Alex asked the officers who had been working on site.

'About four hundred metres.'

Four hundred metres. That was a long way to carry a dead body. Could there have been two people involved? Once again, Alex pushed away the thought; please God no.

There was one killer. Anything else was unthinkable.

Once Birger had left, the meeting continued under Alex's leadership.

'I want an answer to this question today: how many men matching the height and age profile of the male victim went missing between, let's say, 1975 and 1985? We need to try to limit the number of possible victims, and given his height that shouldn't be a problem. I want a definite ID by the beginning of next week at the latest.'

He looked at his colleagues.

'Some of you are going to have to work over the weekend; I hope that won't be a problem.'

A few glanced away, not wanting to volunteer, but the vast majority nodded. They would be able to gather a team. Alex could see the prospect of going fishing with Torbjörn fading fast. Some other time, perhaps.

'Rebecca Trolle,' he said. 'Where are we up to there?'

'I want to speak to her supervisor, Gustav Sjöö,' Peder said.

Surprise around the room; another name to take into account.

Peder briefly explained what he had found out the previous day.

'And Håkan Nilsson?'

'We're still waiting for DNA results; SKL said they would get back to me this morning. But I'd like to speak to Sjöö, anyway.'

Fredrika spoke up.

'We need to get to the bottom of these rumours about Rebecca selling sex over the internet. I've got a strong feeling they're not a part of this. I agree that we need to interview the supervisor, but Håkan Nilsson has some explaining to do if he started the rumours about Rebecca.'

'We have two interesting lines of inquiry when it comes to Rebecca,' Alex summarised. 'There's the pregnancy, and the rumour that she was selling sex. It would make life simpler if we could eliminate one of them.'

'The problem with the pregnancy is that it's personal,' Peder said. 'And if Rebecca's death is connected to the man who was buried in the same place, then it seems highly unlikely that the pregnancy had anything to do with it.'

'That leaves the issue of selling sex,' Alex said. 'Anything else?'

'Gustav Sjöö,' Peder said.

'How come the supervisor is interesting if we've decided the pregnancy isn't?'

'He could be a pervert, that's all.'

The odd burst of laughter around the room made Peder feel embarrassed.

'You mean both murders are connected with sex?' Fredrika said.

'Exactly. He's old enough to have killed the man as well. And he's fairly tall; he might have been stronger when he was younger.'

Strong enough to carry a dead man four hundred metres? Maybe, Alex thought.

'I don't think we can afford to eliminate any lines of inquiry when it comes to Rebecca Trolle,' he said. 'Not one, not in the current situation. OK?'

Nobody looked as if they wanted to disagree, and Alex was more than tired of the dry air in the conference room. He brought the meeting to a close and his colleagues returned to their offices and their assigned tasks. Fredrika lingered for a moment.

'I'm going over to Diana Trolle's sister's house today; I want to go through Rebecca's things.'

Alex heard his own words echoing in his head; they couldn't afford to eliminate any lines of inquiry.

'Fine.'

He wanted to say something else, to reprimand her for thinking that Alex had missed something two years ago, but he knew that would be the wrong thing to do.

They could have missed virtually anything.

Fredrika met Peder in the doorway as she was leaving.

'SKL just called. They confirmed that Håkan Nilsson was the father of Rebecca's child.'

# CHAPTER 15

There had never been a better April as far as the weather was concerned. Not that Peder Rydh could remember. The sun found its way down between the buildings, warming the air and making everyone slip off jackets and jumpers. Peder strolled out of HQ in his shirtsleeves, followed by two colleagues.

'What about the car?' said one of them. 'Surely we're not bloody walking to Midsommarkransen to pick him up?'

'The car's there,' Peder said, pointing to a dark-coloured Saab parked further down the street. 'And we're going to Kista, not Midsommarkransen. We're picking him up from work this time.'

For the third time within a relatively short period, Peder was on his way to see Håkan Nilsson. The prosecutor felt that they now had enough to arrest him, but Alex was dubious. If they arrested him, they would have three days to elicit a confession or other evidence to strengthen their case; otherwise, they wouldn't be able to charge him. Since the police were working on several different suspects at the same time, Alex wasn't convinced it was a good idea to arrest Nilsson at this delicate stage of the investigation.

And Peder was still curious about Rebecca's supervisor, Gustav Sjöö.

Alex had decided that Nilsson was definitely to be brought in for questioning. They needed to talk to him about the child, and about the assertion that he was the one who had started the rumours about Rebecca selling sex.

Peder parked outside the firm where Håkan worked, then went inside with one of his colleagues while the other remained outside, keeping an eye on the door. Brightly coloured signs directed them to Reception on the second floor. Peder and his colleague took the stairs two at a time, strong and agile after many hours in the gym and out running. Black shoes, blue jeans. To the trained eye it wasn't difficult to see that they were police officers.

However, the receptionist failed to spot it.

'How may I help you?' she asked in a friendly tone of voice.

Peder and his colleague showed their ID and quietly explained why they were there. The receptionist went pale and directed them to Håkan's desk in the open-plan office. He was sitting with his back to them wearing headphones, and was busy writing a report, his eyes glued to the screen. He didn't hear them approaching from behind.

Håkan gave a start when Peder placed a hand on his shoulder.

'Could you come with us, please? We'd like to talk to you again.'

The interview room was too small – at least that was how it felt. Peder called Ylva before he went in.

'Hi,' she said. 'Has something happened?'

The anxiety in her voice was testament to how rarely Peder contacted her during working hours.

'No, no, I just wanted to ring and say hello. Hear your voice.'

He could sense her smile on the other end of the line.

'That's sweet!'

*Don't underestimate the simple things, the gestures that cost nothing.*

The therapist Peder had been seeing the previous year had told him that.

'It's the little things that go to build up the whole, and that's what will save you when you have to work late or over the weekend.'

In the end, Peder had started listening to the therapist, realising where he had gone wrong.

'I can't become a completely different person,' he had said.

'Nobody wants you to do that. However, you can improve on the things that you're screwing up at the moment. Like your close relationships, for example.'

Peder's stomach hurt as he recalled the time when he had lived apart from Ylva, and had found it difficult to fill his days. But he had made a real effort, and they were back on track; they had started to rediscover a balance in their lives.

'By the way, Jimmy rang,' Ylva said. 'He wants to come over at the weekend; I said that was fine.'

Jimmy was Peder's brother; because of a childhood accident, he would never be an independent adult. Sometimes, Peder felt that he actually envied some aspects of his brother's life. The ability to be totally carefree that epitomised Jimmy's approach could make anyone consider what was important in life. Jimmy's world was limited to the assisted living complex, and it suited him perfectly. Peder knew for certain that in Jimmy's world there were no young women who had been chopped in half with a chainsaw. He ended the conversation with Ylva and went into the interview room with Alex.

Håkan Nilsson was waiting with a legal representative who had been brought in on his behalf. His expression was nervous; he looked tired. It was obvious that he had slept badly for several nights in succession. His hands twitched like the wings of a wounded bird, sometimes resting on the table, sometimes in his lap. Sometimes he sat there picking at his face.

Alex took the lead, outlining the specific issues which led the police to suspect him.

'I don't understand,' said Håkan. 'I mean, I've been in here several times. I've always co-operated fully. Why would I do that if I was the one who killed her?'

'That's exactly what we're wondering,' Alex replied. 'And that's what I'd like to clarify right now. Perhaps the whole thing is a misunderstanding, in which case it would be good to get it all sorted out.'

Alex's expression didn't change as he spoke; he was implacable and utterly focused.

*You're not leaving here until you've told us the truth, Håkan.*

'Tell us about the child,' said Peder.

'What child?'

'The child you and Rebecca were expecting. Were you happy?'

'I've already told you, I didn't know she was pregnant! And if she was, it definitely wasn't mine.'

Initially, he sounded very sure of himself, then suddenly the doubt crept in.

'Was it mine?'

'The child was yours, Håkan. When did she tell you she was pregnant?'

Håkan began to cry.

'Would you like some water?'

Peder poured a glass of water from the jug on the table and pushed it across to Håkan. Waited. They had plenty of time, which was essential if they were to get a result. Most criminals could cope with a short interrogation, but the longer it went on, the more uncertain they became, and sooner or later they would make a mistake.

'Why are you crying?'

Alex's tone was matter-of-fact without being cold.

When Håkan didn't reply, Peder spoke:

'Do you miss her?'

Håkan nodded.

'I always believed she'd come back.'

*Not if you strangled her and hid her in the forest, Håkan.*

He snivelled and wiped his nose on his sleeve.

'How come?'

'It just didn't seem possible that she could be gone forever, that she would never come back. I didn't think that could happen. Not really.'

The tears had turned Håkan into a child. A little boy, talking as if he had the same grasp of reality as a nine-year-old.

'Oh, come on, Håkan,' Alex said. 'She'd been gone for two years. Where did you think she'd gone?'

'She might have gone away.'

He dried his tears, took a sip of the water.

'Where to?'

'France.'

Had that been the issue all along? The trip to France that Håkan had never been able to forgive her for?

'Did she say anything about taking off like that?'

'No, but you never know.'

Alex straightened up and looked deep into Håkan's eyes.

'Yes, you do,' he said. 'There are certain things that you do know.'

Håkan swallowed. Drank some more water.

'Now tell us about the child.'

'I didn't know anything about the child!'

His voice grew louder in the little room.

'She didn't tell me she was pregnant! She never mentioned it!'

A lie has many faces, both Alex and Peder knew that. But it was impossible to work out what secrets Håkan was hiding.

'Tell us about the time you slept together.'

Håkan blushed.

'Like I said before, it wasn't planned. I think she'd been seeing someone else, and she was upset because he'd dumped her. She came round to mine one evening and I opened a bottle of wine. Then we started on some vodka that I'd bought in Finland. And . . . it just happened.'

'How did you feel afterwards?'

Håkan's eyes shone as if he had a temperature.

'I felt as if we were much closer.'

'Did Rebecca feel the same?' Peder asked.

'I think so.'

'Did she actually say it?'

'No, but I could tell just by looking at her. She tried to play it down afterwards, but I knew what was really going on. She thought it was too early to have found the right person before she had even turned twenty-five.'

All at once, Håkan looked much more confident.

'That was what I liked about her, the fact that

she was clever. And mature. Not like other girls who mess around.'

Peder looked blank.

'Did you meet up and have sex on any further occasions?'

'No, because she wanted to wait. Just like I said.'

'Wait?'

'Until it felt right to go all the way.'

He laughed and spread his hands wide. Alex and Peder stared at him for a long time.

'You don't think you might have misinterpreted the situation?' said Alex.

The light in Håkan's eyes died as if someone had switched off a light.

'What do you mean?'

'I'm just wondering if the reason that you didn't have sex again was actually because Rebecca wasn't interested in you.'

'That's not the way it was. She liked me, I was important to her. The fact that she needed more time . . . I thought that was a positive sign. I mean, I wasn't ready to live with someone, or to get married.'

'Or to have a child?'

Håkan's eyes flashed and he raised his voice.

'There was no child, for fuck's sake!'

When Alex and Peder remained silent, he went on:

'Don't you think she would have told me something like that? She loved me! Do you hear me? *She loved me!*'

The roar died away, disappearing in a heavy

exhalation as the legal representative laid a hand on his arm.

'She loved me.'

A whisper, as if he believed that if he said it enough times, it would become the truth.

Alex adopted a more conciliatory tone.

'She pushed you away, Håkan. That must have been very upsetting for you.'

Håkan was weeping again.

'She didn't. She just needed a bit more time. And then she disappeared and she never came back.'

He buried his face in his hands.

Alex leaned forward.

'What about those pictures you said you'd seen on the internet, Håkan? The pictures on a website where girls were selling sex?'

Håkan looked up.

'You mustn't show them to anyone.'

'We haven't got them; we don't know how to get hold of them.'

'They weren't real; she should never have been on there. Someone must have put her on the website. One minute she was there, then she was gone.'

Alex frowned.

'When did you first see these pictures?'

'A few weeks after she went missing.'

'And you didn't mention it to the police?'

Anxiety appeared to be making Håkan's skin crawl; he looked like a little boy once more.

'She disappeared from the website; I thought I might have made a mistake.'

'Did you tell anyone about the website?'

'Not at first. Then I asked one of her friends, which was the wrong thing to do. After that, the rumour just took off, and I couldn't stop it.'

Alex could just imagine the rumour spreading like wildfire through Rebecca's circle of acquaintances until one day, much later, it reached Diana. Shameful.

'We need to know exactly which website it was, and the date when you visited it, if you have that information.'

Håkan nodded.

'I made a note of everything.'

'So who do you think could have put her on there, if she didn't do it herself?'

'Someone who was seriously pissed off with her.'

'Can you think of anyone who might have felt like that?'

*Apart from you.*

'Maybe that fat cow Daniella.'

'The ex-girlfriend?'

Håkan pulled a face and nodded.

Peder rested his elbows on the table and leaned forward.

'Did you kill Rebecca?'

Håkan blinked and wiped a solitary tear from his cheek.

'I want to go home now.'

# CHAPTER 16

The swing was really meant for older children, but Spencer Lagergren tried sliding his daughter into the seat anyway. She gurgled with glee as he began to push. There were several parents in the park, all younger than Spencer. Much younger, in fact. He was old enough to be their father, every single one of them.

Spencer's own father had always maintained that everyone should be allowed to do things at their own speed and in their own way. Spencer had appreciated this aspect of his upbringing, and had adopted the same attitude. He had never thought he would have a child of his own as he approached the age of sixty. He gazed at Saga, unable to grasp that she was his. At the same time, there was absolutely no doubt about it. In spite of the fact that the child was so like her mother that it sometimes brought tears to his eyes when he looked at her, it was also possible to see that she had inherited some of her father's features: the shape of the forehead, the lines around the mouth, the well-defined point of the chin.

A woman was coming towards Spencer holding an older child by the hand.

'Look, Tova, there's an empty swing next to this little girl.'

*Tova.*

Spencer forced himself to smile at the mother and gave Saga's swing another push. He wondered whether he ought to get in touch with Tova, the student who had decided to make life so difficult for him. Perhaps he could get her to see reason, sort out the conflict that must have arisen between them, even though he hadn't realised it.

He had tried to think back to the autumn. How had it begun? He had been working part time, and had been asked if he could supervise one of the students on the C-course. It always looked good if one of the professors was able to get involved in a dissertation, and the others didn't have time. Spencer didn't really have time either, which was why Malin had been asked to assist. By the end of term, she had virtually taken over full responsibility for the supervision, and Spencer hadn't seen Tova after the final seminar.

Tova hadn't exactly been one of the more highly motivated students. She was tired of studying, the topic she had chosen was far too advanced, and she always tried to take short cuts.

How had the supervision worked out? Badly. Spencer had had to postpone their meetings on two occasions, but he didn't recall Tova being

166

particularly upset about it. She had always seemed perfectly obliging when they spoke on the phone, agreeing to rearrange the date and time without raising any objections.

Perhaps she had been *too* obliging?

She had always been nicely dressed when they met. On one occasion, she had brought along a home-made cake. He remembered being embarrassed by the cake; he had forced himself to go and fetch some coffee. And when he turned around to go back to his office . . . she was standing right behind him.

*Fuck.*

The thought had occurred to him – just once – following that particular incident. He had wondered if she might have a crush on him. He could picture the scene; he swung around with the coffee cups and gave a start when he saw her standing just a few centimetres away from him. Smiling, with her hair loose.

'Is there anything I can do for you?'

*Bloody hell.*

What had he said? Probably nothing; he had just smiled foolishly and handed her one of the cups.

'It's fine, thanks.'

Was that when he had signed his own death warrant?

*Is there anything I can do for you?*

He remembered the hug to which Erland Malm had referred. A wordless, meaningless embrace intended to provide solace. She had been finding things difficult; she had burst into tears and told him how ill her father was.

Spencer's mouth went dry. Erland Malm insisted that Tova's father was dead, and had been for many years. Could his memory be playing tricks on him? After all, he had been taking quite strong painkillers during the autumn and winter. But Spencer knew that wasn't the problem. He knew exactly what had led him to give Tova a hug. Quite openly, in the corridor and in front of other people. There was no bloody way she could have misinterpreted the gesture.

Spencer shuddered. Saga was tired of the swing and wanted to be picked up.

'Haven't you got a lovely granddad?' the woman standing beside them said, smiling at Saga as Spencer picked her up.

He forced a smile in return and carried Saga back to the buggy. The fact that he still hadn't told Fredrika about the hell he was going through was making him feel more and more guilty by the minute. He would have to start talking very soon.

Spencer had dismissed the idea that Tova might be interested in him, told himself he was being a silly old fool. He had thought he was doing the right thing, when in fact he couldn't have done anything more wrong.

The garage was bigger than Fredrika Bergman had expected. A broken ceiling light, an undisturbed layer of dust. The place hadn't been used for a long time. Diana Trolle's sister confirmed this as she handed Fredrika a torch.

'We use the garage as a storage room. I don't know how many times we've said we ought to sort it out, get rid of all the old stuff. But we never quite get around to it somehow . . .'

She sighed.

'I suppose it will be easier to throw it all away now we know she's dead.'

Fredrika could understand the logic. The beam of the torch swept across boxes piled on top of one another. A few black bin bags, stuffed to the brim, had been pushed into one corner. A sofa was standing on end in the middle of the room, next to some chairs and a dining table that had been dismantled.

'She didn't have much furniture; it was mainly clothes and bits and pieces. It's all in these boxes.'

'What's in the bin bags?'

'Bedding, that kind of thing.'

Fredrika looked around. The garage door leading to the street was closed; they had come in through a door leading from the house. All the windows had been covered with cardboard; hardly any light found its way inside.

'Give me a shout if you need any help.'

Diana's sister disappeared back indoors, leaving Fredrika alone. The relatively meagre pile of belongings made her feel sad; Rebecca hadn't acquired very much during her life.

Resolutely, she marched over to the pile of boxes

and opened the top one. Dust and grime stuck to her hands as she began to rummage. She propped the torch on another box to give her some light. The box contained books. Fredrika pulled out one after another; they were all children's books, titles that she too had read: The Famous Five, Anne of Green Gables, the story of Kulla-Gulla the little orphan girl, Whitenose the pony. She closed the box, lifted it down onto the floor and opened the next one.

More books.

The third box contained what looked like textbooks. She recognised several of them from her own degree course. She took them out one at a time, flicked through them, read the back cover, put them back. She carried on searching even though she didn't actually know what she was looking for.

Another box, more books. Right at the bottom, a magazine rack full of newspapers and journals. Fredrika noted that Rebecca Trolle had been very organised; everything had its allotted place. On closer inspection she had noticed that several piles of books were arranged in alphabetical order according to the author's surname. She couldn't imagine that whoever had packed the boxes would have bothered to do that, so they must have been in order on Rebecca's bookshelves. Fredrika, who had always read a great deal, felt an intuitive affinity with Rebecca.

She moved on to the next pile of boxes, wishing they were marked in some way. The top box contained household items, the next one shoes.

The torch fell to the floor; Fredrika shook it anxiously as it flickered. It would be impossible to carry on without light. She was relieved to discover that it had survived, and she resumed the search. The sight of all those shoes almost made her feel ill, as if they brought her too close to Rebecca. Shoes seemed somehow private; it was obvious that they had been worn. Hesitantly, she picked one up: pink, with high heels. When did you wear that kind of shoe? She dropped it back in the box and moved on.

Notes. Fredrika's heart beat a little faster and she picked up the torch so that she could see better. Files and folders and a hardbacked notebook. Fredrika grabbed the box and with a sweeping movement she tipped everything out on the floor. Then she sat down cross-legged and started to leaf through all the papers. The garage floor was cold; Fredrika dug out a book and sat on it.

Two of the files were full of what she presumed were lecture notes. Page after page of neatly written phrases, snatched from their context to the uninitiated reader. Weighty words on the significance of Selma Lagerlöf for Swedish women writers, summarised in a few simple sentences.

Fredrika put the files to one side and opened the notebook. On the first page, Rebecca had written 'Thea Aldrin and the lost Nobel Prize'.

Thea Aldrin. The name evoked memories that washed over Fredrika like warm waves. Thea Aldrin's books about an angel called Dysia had

171

been Fredrika's absolute favourites when she was a little girl. She had been surprised when she found out that the publisher had stopped reprinting them, on the basis that there was no demand. Anyone who wanted to read Thea's books had to seek them out in a library or a second-hand book shop.

Fredrika thought this was ridiculous, and suspected that the publisher's lack of interest in new editions was more than likely due to the fact that they didn't want anything to do with the author. Fredrika knew only the salient points about Thea Aldrin's life story; from time to time, she would appear in a double-page spread in one of the tabloids under the headline 'Unforgettable Crimes'. She knew that Thea had been sentenced to life imprisonment for the murder of her ex-husband, and that the police had also suspected her of the murder of her teenage son, who had been missing since the early 1980s. There was also a suggestion that she was the author behind two extremely vulgar works that had been published under a pseudonym in the seventies. Fredrika had no idea what Thea was doing today; she only knew that she had been released in the nineties.

But Rebecca had found out a great deal more. From her notes Fredrika could see that she had got quite a long way in her research into Thea's life. How had Alex put it? He had said that Rebecca was writing her dissertation about a children's author. An author who, according to many critics in days gone by, was likely to be the first children's writer to be awarded the Nobel Prize for Literature. Fredrika flicked quickly through the notebook. She decided to take it with her and read it properly later.

The folders contained a plethora of photocopied articles on the fate of Thea Aldrin, covering every possible angle. There were feminist critics, insisting that the interest in Thea's books would never have faded if she had been a man. More traditional researchers claimed that Thea's writing would not have attracted so much attention if she hadn't been such a controversial figure, challenging the basic values prevalent in the 1960s.

Fredrika found a carrier bag and started packing up the files and notes. She couldn't find a draft of the dissertation, which annoyed her. The dissertation had obviously not been completed, which meant that the likelihood of the university having a copy was increasingly unlikely.

She went through the last two boxes. One contained ornaments and photo albums. Fredrika assumed the albums had already been checked and dismissed as being of no interest, but she couldn't resist opening them. There were pictures of lots of different places and people she didn't recognise. She must remember to mention the albums to Rebecca's aunt; the pictures would mean a lot to the family.

She put them back and opened the last box. Even more papers, and – right at the bottom – two floppy disks, which indicated that Rebecca had owned an old computer. Fredrika was surprised that the police hadn't taken the disks; then again, perhaps they had been checked and returned to the family. She picked them up and turned them over; one was labelled 'DISSERTATION' and the other 'THE GUARDIAN ANGELS'.

She put them both in her bag.

Among all the papers there was a mass of administrative information relating to her course. One of the brochures was entitled 'Welcome to your studies in the History of Literature'. Fredrika felt quite nostalgic as she turned the pages and read about how the department worked. Somewhere in the middle she stopped as one particular sentence caught her eye:

'Not sure what to do after graduation? Come and find out more about Alpha, our mentoring network!'

The exhortation was signed by the president of the students' union.

The mentoring network again. Now it had a name: Alpha. Fredrika knew something about the process, and she was aware that by no means all students who showed an interest were allocated a mentor. An assessment was made based on the student's profile and ambitions. According to Alex, the financier Valter Lund had been Rebecca's mentor; he was a man who had climbed rapidly within Axbergers, a major company. He was originally from Norway. But how had this come about?

How did a girl who was studying the history of literature end up with Valter Lund as her mentor? Fredrika decided to take a closer look at Alpha.

On the last page of the brochure, she found a list of those who worked in the department, together with their contact details. Gustav Sjöö, Rebecca's supervisor, was circled in red ink.

And next to his name, written by hand in the same red ink,

'SPENCER LAGERGREN, DEPARTMENT OF THE HISTORY OF LITERATURE, UNIVERSITY OF UPPSALA'.

The red ink seemed to glow, and Fredrika suddenly felt weak at the knees.

Without thinking, she folded the brochure in half and slipped it into her pocket. She put everything else she wanted to take with her into the carrier bag, then switched off the torch and went back into the house.

'I've finished now, thank you,' she said to Rebecca's aunt. 'I'd like to take this with me, if that's OK.'

She held up the carrier bag, the brochure burning a hole in her pocket. She could hardly breathe.

*Spencer.*

The man who had once promised he would never lie to her again. Who had suddenly decided he wanted to go on paternity leave.

*What are you hiding from me, my love?*

# CHAPTER 17

Alex Recht couldn't decide how to proceed. Håkan Nilsson had been allowed to go home, but he was still being kept under surveillance, and both his mobile and landline were being monitored.

Fredrika had come back from her visit to Rebecca's aunt, and was closeted in her office with the material she had brought in. She had given him a brief verbal report, suggesting that they should look more closely at the mentoring network. Alex didn't really agree with her, but since none of their other lines of inquiry were entirely satisfactory, he didn't raise any objections.

*We need to keep every line of inquiry alive.*

He glanced at the clock. Fredrika would probably leave in a few hours, and she wouldn't be back until Monday morning. He hoped she would be able to balance work and home life successfully; the team didn't need another Peder.

Alex decided to call Torbjörn Ross and thank him for the invitation to go fishing at the weekend. Unfortunately, he would have to say no; he had far too much on at work. Far too much to think about. Far too much to . . .

'Torbjörn Ross.'

'Hi, it's Alex. I just wanted to let you know that I'd really like to come over this weekend.'

*Would I?*

His palms suddenly felt sweaty. Had he taken leave of his senses?

'That's great,' said Torbjörn. 'I thought you'd say no.'

*So did I.*

'It was the fishing trip that persuaded me.'

'Thought so. I'll ring Sonja and tell her you're coming with us.'

'Hang on. I think it's best if I bring my own car; I have to work tomorrow, and I'd like to join you a bit later, if that's OK.'

Of course it was OK. There was nothing that couldn't be sorted out. The important thing was that Alex was coming to the cottage, getting away from the city for a while. Fresh air and a glass or two of cognac with Torbjörn.

When he had ended the call, Alex rang his daughter to tell her about his plans for the weekend. He could hear how pleased she was, and knew that he was sending out signals that she found very welcome. Look, I've got a life. Friends, leisure interests. Everything I need.

His chest contracted with pain. The loss of Lena had proved that there are very few things people

177

actually need. In the end, there hadn't been a single thing he wouldn't have given up to get her back. Not a single thing.

His mobile rang, providing a welcome distraction. Something to focus on.

'It's Diana Trolle. Am I disturbing you?'

'Of course not. How are you?'

What would she say? What could he cope with? What if she said that her life was meaningless, that she could hardly bring herself to get out of bed in the mornings? She spared him the worst; it was understood.

'I'm getting there. I just wanted to know how things were going.'

Alex closed his eyes for a second, wishing he could say that things were going really well, that they had identified the killer who was now under arrest in Kronoberg. Instead, he said:

'Do you recognise the name Gustav Sjöö?'

'No. Or . . . hang on. Yes, I do. He was Rebecca's supervisor at the university.'

'What was his relationship with Rebecca like?'

'There was no relationship, as far as I know.'

'I mean did they get on well on a professional basis?'

'No, I don't think they did. She wasn't satisfied with him.'

'What was the problem?'

'He never seemed to have time for her. I remember she felt frustrated; she thought he could have done a better job. She even tried to change to another supervisor, but the university wouldn't let her. Why are you asking about him? Is he a suspect?'

A question Alex didn't want to answer.

'We're looking at a number of different people.'

Evasive, not warm and confiding as he had wanted to be.

'Do you know who the father of her child was?'

There was only one possible answer to that question.

'I can't comment on that.'

There was silence at the other end of the line, and he could hear the sound of pain and loss.

'Sometimes, I think I can hear her. All those little noises she used to make, and I never even noticed. I hear her, Alex. Does that sound crazy?'

When Alex tried to reply, the words stuck in his throat.

'Not at all. I think it's quite common to experience that kind of phenomenon in your situation. Losing someone you love can be like losing an essential part of your body. You're aware of it all the time, even though it isn't there any more.'

'Phantom sounds.'

He smiled, blinked to clear his vision.

'You hear them virtually all the time.'

'Even though they're not there.'

Her voice had faded to a whisper, and Alex rested his head against the receiver. He realised that he liked hearing her voice. It breathed life, even though it spoke of death.

When he had ended the call he went to look for Peder.

'I want Gustav Sjöö brought in before the weekend.'

'Me too,' said Peder. 'I've made a few calls, checked his alibi. It's weak. He could easily have driven into Stockholm, picked up Rebecca and driven back to Västerås.'

'Bring him in. Now.'

The view from her window was depressing; there was no point in looking out. How could anyone possibly have given planning permission to construct buildings as ugly as police HQ in Kungsholmen? One monstrosity after another. Small windows and poky offices.

There was no air, Fredrika decided. They assumed everyone had somewhere else to be where they could breathe more easily.

She rang home, checked that everything was OK. She sensed some imbalance in Spencer, but decided not to mention it on the phone. She couldn't explain why, and that scared her. She could hear Saga in the background, and felt her heart swell. She had never imagined that it would be possible to feel such love. It was so pure, so self-evident and so unconditional; sometimes it left her speechless. She would catch herself watching the child and would suddenly realise she was on the verge of tears. If any harm came to Saga, she would lose her mind. Her very soul would be damaged.

*Take my child and I would have nothing left.*

She wondered if that feeling would weaken over time, if she would start to take Saga for granted or love her less. Didn't Diana Trolle look like a woman who could learn to live again? After two years in the limbo of uncertainty she had finally found out what had happened to her daughter, and with that knowledge came a much longed-for peace. Fredrika was struck by a depressing thought: Diana had another child. Did that make any difference? Was the grief easier to bear if you still had one child left?

*Take my child and I would have none left.*

She tried to shake off the sense of unease that had crept up on her. Spencer didn't want any more children, and she was almost forty. It was the right decision, not to have any more. For the whole family.

She unfolded the brochure she had slipped into her pocket earlier, and stared at Spencer's name. It didn't mean anything, she told herself, which was why she would ignore it. But she would keep the brochure.

Keep it and keep it to herself. A breach of the rules, but what could she do? There was obviously some logical explanation for the fact that Spencer's name had come up.

The mentoring network, on the other hand, looked interesting. She checked on the website of Stockholm University's students' union and discovered that the scheme still existed. With a mentor by his or her side, the student was promised a guide, a greater sense of security and better preparation for life after graduation.

'Have you decided what you want to be when you grow up?' the website asked.

I haven't, actually, Fredrika thought wearily.

All students were welcome to join the network. There were lectures and social events, a range of opportunities to develop contacts in different branches of industry. According to the website, a number of students would be selected on the basis of merit and education, and would be allocated a personal mentor. The mentors themselves had a variety of backgrounds, but were united by a desire to help ambitious young people progress in their chosen career.

But had Rebecca, a conscientious student with literature as her main subject, really been heading for such a career?

Valter Lund, the man who was predicted to be the next Swede to be invited to join the legendary Bilderberg Group – why had he been chosen to mentor Rebecca? Fredrika had read a number of articles about him, the financial superstar who came out of nowhere and eclipsed all the other stars in the sky. If she remembered correctly, he was about forty-five, and came originally from Norway. He looked pleasant; he was tall and slim. A much sought-after member of the most important company boards; a man who could reputedly turn cold ashes into gold. For Valter Lund, there was no such thing as poor soil or bad luck, simply an underlying belief in competence and ability.

How could he even find the time to be a mentor?

Fredrika found the number of the president of the students' union on the website; he answered on the third ring.

'Mårten, right in the middle of a meeting.'

'Fredrika Bergman, police.'

Always equally effective; why did people have this innate respect for an organisation that aimed to manage society's monopoly on violence?

'OK, give me two seconds to finish off what I'm doing.'

He was back a moment later.

'Police, you said?'

'I'm calling about your mentoring network.'

'Oh?'

A hesitant response, full of suspicion. Why would the police be calling about a network that could take the individual student to heights he or she couldn't even dream of?

'I'm investigating the murder of Rebecca Trolle, and your mentoring network has come up. I'd appreciate it if you could answer a few questions.'

'OK. Although I wasn't president when she was here.'

'But you remember her being part of the network?'

'Oh, yes, I was one of the people who set the whole thing up.'

A hint of pride in the voice, mixed with a distinctly less appealing smugness.

'Valter Lund was Rebecca's mentor.'

'I remember that; a lot of people wanted him.'

'Wasn't it a bit strange that he ended up with Rebecca? Given that she was studying literature, I mean. She doesn't seem to have been aiming for a high-flying career in industry.'

Fredrika was striving to maintain a neutral tone, trying to pretend that this question was just one of many that she was pondering.

'It was different back then,' said Mårten.

'In what way?'

'That was the year we set up the mentoring network. We thought the mentor's role should be to coach and inspire, to be a kind of general guide. When we paired up the students and mentors, we disregarded what course they were following and their future plans, and tried to find a combination that was as exciting as possible. That meant we avoided pairing up men with men and women with women, business people with students of economics, artists with art students.'

'That was daring.'

'And stupid. It didn't work at all, because it turned out that everyone thought the same as you. The students wanted a role model, and the mentors wanted a carbon copy.'

She heard him sigh.

'So the following year we revamped the whole system.'

'By which time Rebecca wasn't there.'

'No, and if she had been, she definitely wouldn't have kept Valter Lund as her mentor.'

'Did you know Rebecca?'

'No, I can't say I did. I saw her now and again through the network, exchanged a few words here and there. She seemed nice. Incredibly busy.'

'Did you ever talk about her work with Valter Lund?'

'That was the only thing we talked about.'

*Of course it was.*

'Did she say how it was going? Do you know how often they met?'

'He once invited her to lunch somewhere really expensive. And he came to listen to the choir; he does go to church, apparently. I think she said they went for a coffee afterwards. She didn't say much about their work; I'm not convinced she was taking it all that seriously. That was also something we changed the following year; only those studying for a Master's were allowed to take part.'

Fredrika tried to remember Rebecca's diary. Surely, the abbreviation 'VL' had appeared more than twice?

'Did you ever speak to Valter Lund? About his experiences as a mentor, I mean.'

'I never spoke to him personally. We ran an evaluation session with the mentors, but he wasn't here. Actually, now I come to think of it, he decided to leave the programme after the first year.'

'He hasn't been involved since then?'

'No. He's incredibly busy, of course. Several others left for the same reason.'

But none of the others had been working with a student who was murdered.

Fredrika ended the call with a vague feeling of unease in the pit of her stomach. She searched through the material from the original investigation and discovered that Valter Lund had been interviewed only once.

*Why?*

She found her copy of the lists Peder had given her showing the results of Ellen's check on all the main characters who came up in the original investigation. There was no mention of Valter Lund. She was surprised, and sent an email to Ellen asking her to check Valter against police records like all the others.

From the tabloid press, Fredrika knew that Lund was one of the city's most eligible bachelors. Could he have been Rebecca's new love? That would explain all the secrecy surrounding both the relationship and the pregnancy.

The pregnancy that had frightened Rebecca, because she suspected that the father would want to keep the child. Would Valter Lund have expressed such a view? Would he have wanted to have a child with a student who was only half his age? And if he had, would he have been so upset over her decision to terminate the pregnancy that he killed her? Because Rebecca herself had probably not known who the child's father was; perhaps she had thought it was Valter Lund.

*Murdered, dismembered and buried.*

Fredrika rested her head in her hands. The killer's MO had to be taken into account. They couldn't disregard the fact that the body had been dismembered; there had to be an explanation. The thoughts that had kept her awake at night were back. The person who had lifted a chainsaw above Rebecca's dead body and sliced it in two could not possibly have been a first-time killer. It was out of the question. An inexperienced killer made mistakes, dumped the body where it could be found, left evidence behind, was spotted by witnesses. People didn't disappear from a built-up area in the middle of Östermalm, only to have their dismembered body turn up two years later. Things like that happened in only the most evil tales.

# CHAPTER 18

As usual, there was no sound from the old lady's room when Malena Bremberg knocked. She pushed the door open and saw that the lamp on the bedside table was on.

'Are you reading, Thea?'

She moved quietly towards the bed, almost as if she were afraid of being seen. Thea lowered the book she was holding, looked at Malena then went back to her reading.

Malena wasn't sure what to do next. She picked up an apple core that Thea had left beside the bed, along with some papers. She threw the rubbish in the bin and came back to the bed. She looked at the old lady, who was ignoring her completely. According to the information the care home had received, Thea hadn't spoken since 1981. Malena had no idea what had provoked this self-imposed silence. In a way, she could see certain advantages in not needing to communicate with those around you, not being expected to join in all the time. But at the same time, she could see the high price Thea paid for her silence.

Thea was regarded as unhealthily antisocial. She

never took part in the group activities that were organised at the home, and she always ate in her room. At the beginning, her divergent behaviour had caused serious concern for the staff, who had consulted a doctor on Thea's behalf. The doctor offered to prescribe antidepressants, but when he heard about the background he changed his mind. Someone who had chosen not to speak for almost thirty years was unlikely to start playing bingo with other pensioners all of a sudden, simply because he or she was being fed antidepressants. He left his card with Thea and said that she was welcome to contact him at any time. Malena had sneaked a look in the drawer of Thea's desk and seen that the card was still there.

In the end, Malena moved one of the visitors' chairs over to Thea's bed and sat down. She didn't say anything; she simply gazed at the old woman in silence. After a while, Thea lost patience and lowered her book again, resting it against her chest. The expression in the pale blue eyes looking at Malena was razor sharp.

*Don't think I'm stupid just because I choose not to speak.*

Malena swallowed several times.

'I need your help,' she said.

Thea stared at her.

'If you don't want to speak, then you have to help me in some other way,' Malena whispered.

She broke off, trying to choose her words with care.

'You know what I want to talk about; you've been following the news too over the past few days.'

Thea turned her head away and closed her eyes.

'Rebecca Trolle,' Malena said. 'You have to tell me what you know.'

# CHAPTER 19

Peder Rydh breathed in the cool afternoon air through the half-open car window. The interior smelled unpleasant as a result of too much use and too little cleaning. His colleague in the passenger seat looked frozen, but said nothing. Peder kept his eyes fixed on the doorway of Gustav Sjöö's apartment block on Mariatorget.

They had rung the bell, but no one had answered. Peder had shouted through the letterbox without success. There was a risk that Sjöö might be at his summer cottage in Nyköping; Peder had contacted the local police and asked them to send a patrol car to his address. They reported that the house was in darkness, and seemed to be empty.

Peder slid down in his seat. A man like Gustav Sjöö didn't suddenly decide to live rough. He was out there somewhere, and soon he would come home.

Ylva called, reminding him of what was important in life. A cosy Friday evening with the boys – he hadn't forgotten, had he? He assured her that he hadn't, but explained that he would be late.

'Very late?'

191

'I'll ring you if that's the case.'

This new routine they had established was amazing. Ylva's tolerance for his working hours evoked a feeling of guilt that he didn't recognise. In the past he had been too busy defending his choices in life to have any room for guilt. If they hadn't ended up quarrelling, he had reacted by feeling unhappy. He didn't really understand the logic of it all.

His colleague tapped him on the shoulder.

'Isn't that him?'

Peder wasn't sure. The court case and recent upheaval must have taken more of a toll on Sjöö than Peder had realised. The man was pale and looked old, very different from the pictures Peder had seen in his file.

They got out of the car and stood behind Sjöö as he was about to open the door of the apartment block.

'Gustav Sjöö?'

It was lucky that he was holding onto the door handle. Every trace of colour drained from his face; even his lips went pale and his eyes widened as Peder and his colleagues held up their ID.

'What the hell do you want now?'

The interview with Gustav Sjöö began at four o'clock in the afternoon. Peder found it difficult to summon up a great deal of enthusiasm. Håkan Nilsson had left HQ just a few hours ago, and now Peder was about to embark on his second interview of the day. He was working with a female officer, Cecilia Torsson. She was a new experience for Peder; he had heard that Fredrika had complained about her to Alex, but obviously she hadn't got very far, because Cecilia was still here. In his former life as the Casanova of HQ, he would have been interested and would have asked her out for a drink afterwards. Now he barely looked in her direction, focusing instead on Sjöö.

'You seem to be finding things rather difficult at the moment?'

He looked at Sjöö, who chose to keep his eyes fixed on the table.

'You could say that.'

His voice sounded as if it was used too infrequently; it was hoarse and rough. His shoulders sloped with the weight of the burden that had been placed upon them. Gustav Sjöö looked exhausted, like a man who has used up all his strength and given up hope of ever regaining it.

'Rebecca Trolle,' said Cecilia. 'Do you remember her?'

Sjöö nodded. 'She disappeared.'

'As I'm sure you've heard on the news, we've found her.'

Sjöö looked up, his expression simultaneously sad and surprised.

'You've found her?'

Peder stared at him.

'I'm sorry, but where have you been for the last few days?'

'At my summer cottage. I'd just come back when you picked me up.'

'And you have no contact with the outside world when you're there?'

'No, that's the whole point of going there, so that I can be alone. I had no idea that you'd found Rebecca. Where was she?'

Cecilia replied, 'Buried on the outskirts of Midsommarkransen. A dog owner found her.'

Gustav Sjöö's voice was an almost inaudible whisper: 'Alive?'

'Sorry?'

'Had she been buried alive?'

The question made both Peder and Cecilia stiffen. Being buried alive was possibly the only thing worse than being dismembered and buried in bin bags.

'No,' said Cecilia. 'She was dead when she was buried. Why do you ask?'

Sjöö shuffled, wrung his hands.

'I probably just misunderstood what you said.'

Peder straightened the notepad in front of him.

'You seem to have a tendency to misunderstand things, Gustav. For example, you misunderstood your girlfriend when you thought she wanted to have sex with you.'

Sjöö looked at Peder with distaste.

'If that's what you want to talk about, I'd like my solicitor present.'

Peder held up his hands.

'Let's go back to Rebecca. When did you last see her?'

Sjöö gawped at him.

'Pardon me for pointing this out, but you've already asked that question. Two years ago, when she went missing.'

'And now we're asking it again.'

Sjöö rested his chin on one hand, his elbows on the table.

'I can hardly remember. We had a supervision session a few days before she disappeared.'

'How did it go?'

'Fine, as far as I recall.'

'No disagreements?'

'Not that I can remember.'

Cecilia broke in.

'Did you and Rebecca meet privately?'

'Privately?'

'Outside the university.'

Peder could see that Sjöö was genuinely bewildered.

'No, never.'

'Did you try it on with her?'

'What the fuck are you . . .?'

'Answer the question!' Peder roared.

He was risking everything on the turn of one card as he slammed his fist down on the table. Sjöö was clearly shaken.

'No, I did not.'

'Other female students have claimed that they had problems with you.'

'Thank you, I'm aware of that. I'm telling you what I've told all the other police officers: they're lying.'

Of course they are, Peder thought grimly.

There were times when he hated his job, when he thought he'd like to do something else. Why the hell did they never get a bloody confession? Why did no one ever hold their hands up and say, 'Yes, you're right, I did it'? That would have made life easier. Too easy, perhaps.

'Was Rebecca happy with your supervision?' Peder asked.

Gustav Sjöö sighed.

'No, I don't think she was. I found it difficult to cope with the amount of energy she was prepared to put into her dissertation. She went back over it, reformulated the whole thrust of the piece, rewrote the questions. I thought it lacked gravitas.'

'You thought the fact that she had energy meant her work lacked gravitas?'

'No, of course not. But . . . The whole hypothesis was flawed; it was starting to resemble a police investigation. That was when I pointed out that she was actually studying literature, not criminology.'

'What do you mean, it resembled a police investigation?' Cecilia asked.

'She was writing about Thea Aldrin, the children's author who was sent to prison for the murder of her ex-husband, and who was also accused of having written violent pornography under a pseudonym. Rebecca became obsessed with Thea Aldrin, and started digging up all kinds of old stuff that had nothing whatsoever to do with the topic of her dissertation. In the end, she was convinced that Thea had neither murdered her ex, nor written the pornographic books.'

So, Rebecca had been a conscientious student. Peder found it difficult to believe that this could have provided a motive for murder.

'How did she reach the conclusion that this Thea Aldrin was innocent?' Cecilia asked.

'Women's intuition or something,' Sjöö said. 'She said all her sources were confidential, that she couldn't reveal where the information came from. We had some lengthy discussions on that particular issue.'

Cecilia smiled.

'Do you own a chainsaw?'

'What? No. Yes.'

'Yes or no?'

'Yes, I do. There's one at my summer cottage.'

'Do you use it often?'

'No, I can't say I do.'

He paused.

'Listen, you checked me out two years ago. I had an alibi for the evening in question. Can't we just finish this off so I can go home?'

Peder slid a piece of paper from under his notepad: the timetable for the conference Sjöö had been attending in Västerås the evening Rebecca disappeared.

'We've taken a closer look at your alibi, Gustav. And it's far from watertight. See for yourself.'

He pushed the timetable across the table.

'This shows that you were free from 16.00 until 19.00, when pre-dinner drinks were served before the meal at 20.00.'

Sjöö looked at him.

'Yes?'

'Nobody would have missed you if you'd nipped back to Stockholm, dealt with Rebecca, then turned up late for dinner. It's just over a hundred kilometres from Västerås to Stockholm. If you put your foot down, it doesn't take too long.'

'From a purely hypothetical point of view, I agree with you. But you're wrong. I didn't leave Västerås.'

'And how can we be sure of that?'

Gustav Sjöö leaned back wearily on his chair.

'That's your problem, not mine. I went to my room for a nap before dinner. During the pre-dinner drinks party I chatted to a colleague from Uppsala University who can confirm that I was there.'

'What was the name of this colleague?'

Sjöö remained silent for a moment, then he said, 'Professor Spencer Lagergren.'

# CHAPTER 20

They still hadn't been able to dismiss the allegation that Rebecca had been selling sex over the internet. Peder had asked the technical team to look into the website where Håkan Nilsson claimed to have seen her; he had kept all the information, including the date when he had seen her and the alias she had been using.

A feeling of restlessness was gnawing away at Fredrika's body. She didn't want to go home until she had made some progress in the investigation. Peder was interviewing Rebecca's supervisor, and wouldn't have time to ring the techies before Fredrika went home for the weekend. Her hand hovered over the telephone as she gazed out of the window. The sun was tempting; it made the brown metal on the building opposite shimmer in countless different shades. Why didn't she go home?

They answered straight away.

'I'm calling about the website "Dreams Come True".' How stupid did that sound?

'The job we got this morning?'

'I'm just calling on the off chance, I know you haven't had enough time yet, but . . .'

'We've got quite a long way. As far as we can, actually. The website is still there, and it looks pretty bloody kinky. Several of the girls on there are definitely under fifteen.'

'What kind of website is it?'

Her voice was hesitant; she didn't really want to know.

'The principle is the same as for ordinary Internet dating, although in this case it's only girls who upload their profiles, and it's exclusively for sex. Imagine sex as an extreme sport. I mean, nobody would visit this site to find the woman he'd want to spend the rest of his life with.'

Sex as an extreme sport – the twenty-first century's distorted view of what constituted good sex.

'Did you manage to find Rebecca's profile?'

'We didn't think it would be possible at first, but we managed to identify the website's administrator.'

Fredrika was surprised.

'How come?'

'All websites have an administrator. This one is run by a guy who owns a porn shop in the Söder district. If you go and speak to him, he should be able to help; you've got her alias. Just because you take pictures down from a website, that doesn't mean they're gone forever. He'll have kept them, guaranteed. Push him hard; as I said, there are some very young girls on that website.'

Fredrika took down the name and address. Stared at the piece of paper, gazed out of the

200

window. Looked back at the address. She wanted to know more. More, more, more. She took out her mobile to call Spencer.

Spencer. Whose name was written in red ink in a brochure that had been in the possession of the murder victim.

She called home, pressing the telephone close to her ear when she heard his wary voice. An hour. That was all she needed to fit in a visit to Söder, then she would hurry home. She must find time to play her violin for a little while this evening. To dispel those thoughts, to drive away the anxiety and the distraction.

The man's groaning and moaning grew louder and louder; he could be heard throughout virtually the entire shop. He was out of sight behind a paper-thin closed door, but there wasn't much doubt what he was up to. Fredrika glanced at the male colleague she had brought with her to the porn shop; he seemed to be finding the whole thing extremely entertaining. He was looking around at the shelves, taking in the rows of dildos and sex toys.

The shop was located in a basement, with the same paucity of light as the garage Fredrika had visited. She peered through the gloom, searching for the owner of the shop and, hopefully, the person responsible for 'Dreams Come True'. She wanted to get this out of the way and head home as soon as possible.

The door to the small booth accommodating the groaning man flew open and he emerged. He caught Fredrika's eye. And smiled. She felt her cheeks flush bright red, and looked away. Why didn't he want the ground to swallow him up? How could he walk out with his head held high when he'd just been masturbating in front of a porn film?

'Can I help you?'

She couldn't see where the voice was coming from; she turned and saw a young man who had suddenly appeared behind the counter. She took two firm steps towards him, then stopped, unable to bring herself to move any closer. He smiled at her uncertainty.

She took out her ID and introduced herself and her colleague.

'It's about a website.'

The man raised one eyebrow, his expression quizzical.

'Oh?'

'Are you the person who started "Dreams Come True"?'

'Yep. There's nothing illegal in that.'

Pictures of young girls, on their way to adult life via the internet. How could it be legal to hold the gates of hell wide open for underage girls?

'We're looking for a profile that was taken down from the website about two years ago.'

The man burst out laughing and moved over to the till.

'Two years ago? In that case I can't help you, unfortunately. Much as I would like to, of course.'

The look in his eyes was so crafty that it took Fredrika's breath away. Her colleague stepped in.

'Listen to me, you slimy little bastard. Your website is smack bang in the middle of an investigation into the murder of a woman whose body was dismembered, and if you know what's good for you and your shop, you will answer my colleague's questions!'

The man blinked, his pupils dilated.

'I'm not involved in any murder!'

'Prove it by helping us!'

The officer's fist whistled through the air and slammed down on the glass counter. The shop owner stared at the cracked glass and turned to his computer.

'What was her name?'

'Rebecca Trolle.'

'That's no use to me; what was her alias?'

'Miss Miracle.'

Just uttering the words made Rebecca feel ill.

'Her profile has been taken down.'

'We know that, but we think you've kept a copy.'

'Absolutely not, I can assure you that I never . . .'

Her colleague moved so fast that Fredrika barely had time to react. In less than a second he had the shop owner pressed up against the wall. Fredrika had heard Peder holding forth when the question of the use of excessive violence by the police arose.

'We have to speak the language the bastards understand,' he always used to say.

She looked at her colleague's back view, the shop owner's face just visible over his shoulder.

'We don't want your fucking assurances because they're not worth jack shit to us. We want the pictures, get it?'

But what if he hasn't got any pictures, Fredrika thought, her heart racing.

Her colleague let go of the man, who sank down onto the floor. The shop was full of fear, as palpable as a bad smell.

'OK, OK.'

To her surprise she saw the owner pick himself up and return to his computer.

'Oh, yes, now I realise I can call up her history. But it'll take a minute, all right?'

That was fine, as long as it was only a minute. The feeling that something wasn't as it should be grew as Fredrika waited for the result. Her colleague stood behind the owner, glowering at the screen. Fredrika tried to remember if she'd ever been in a similar place before; she didn't think so. Maybe once when she was a student, just for fun. But it hadn't been like this, in a basement so cut off from reality that there could be no perception of the beautiful day outside.

'Got it,' said the owner. 'The person who uploaded this girl's profile then took it down did a rubbish job. It hasn't been removed, it's just been temporarily shut down.'

'How come?'

'Perhaps she didn't know how it worked. She must have thought she'd removed the profile, when in fact she'd just suspended things temporarily.'

'She? Who's she?'

'The girl who uploaded the profile in the first place.'

'How do you know it was a girl?'

The man looked at Fredrika as if she was stupid.

'The person in these pictures looks very much like a girl to me.'

Fredrika suppressed a groan of frustration.

'We have reason to believe that the girl in these pictures didn't set up the profile herself.'

The answer came instantly.

'That's not my problem.'

Fredrika ignored him.

'Can you tell who uploaded the profile in the first place?'

'Possibly; I think I kept the emails. When someone joins the website they have to accept the terms and conditions via email.'

'And those terms and conditions state that you have the right to use the pictures again, presumably?'

The shop owner shrugged.

'It's their choice. Nobody makes them do it.'

*Nobody makes them do it.*

Fredrika felt nothing but revulsion. And despair. Where was the choice in a place like this?

'I can give you a name and the IP number of

the computer that sent the email. The name is probably false, but you should be able to get somewhere with the IP number.'

Fredrika waited as he wrote; he passed her a grubby scrap of paper folded in half.

'Thank you,' she said. 'And now I'd like to see the pictures.'

The man stepped aside to make room in front of the computer. A click of the mouse and Rebecca Trolle filled the screen. The pictures were not what Fredrika had expected. Rebecca was lying on her side in bed, naked. She appeared to be asleep; it looked completely natural, not as if she had been drugged.

Fredrika leaned closer to the screen.

'It's impossible to tell where they were taken,' she murmured.

The images revealed nothing apart from an ordinary bed and white walls. A small number of photographs above the bed suggested that the room was in someone's home.

'When was the profile uploaded?' she asked.

The man pointed, and Fredrika could see that it was just under two weeks after Rebecca went missing. Why would someone do such a thing if they had nothing to do with the murder? She stared at the screen, desperate to spot some detail that would reveal more about the background to the pictures.

She pointed at Rebecca's head.

'Look at the length of her hair; it's quite short.

When she disappeared, it was down to her shoulders.'

'So it's an old picture. It wasn't taken by someone who was keeping her prisoner.'

Fredrika turned to the shop owner.

'I want electronic copies of all the pictures.'

He said nothing, but dug out a CD and burned all the material he had onto it.

Fredrika took the CD and turned to leave. The shop door opened and a new customer came in. Fredrika avoided looking at the man and moved away.

'We'll be back if we need any more help,' she said to the owner.

'Let's hope that won't be necessary,' he replied, glancing at her colleague.

Fredrika was clutching the CD as they walked out into the fresh air. She wanted to get home as quickly as possible, to hold Saga in her arms and protect her from all the repulsive elements of the adult world.

'I'll check out the IP number and the name this afternoon,' her colleague said as Fredrika passed him the scrap of paper with the details.

She shivered in the cool spring weather. There was something in the pictures of Rebecca Trolle that was niggling away at her. Something that would reveal where they had been taken. And by whom.

# CHAPTER 21

Alex and Peder were sitting in silence on opposite sides of the desk in Alex's office. 'I don't think Sjöö did it,' said Peder.
'Me neither.'
'Rebecca seems to have chosen an interesting storyteller for her dissertation. A perverted killer, by the sound of it.'
Alex seemed to be far away.
'We'd better have a look at the chainsaw anyway,' said Peder.
He looked downhearted.
Alex opened the file in front of him. Rebecca Trolle's life and death between two pieces of cardboard. A pile of photographs lay uppermost.
'Håkan Nilsson,' said Alex, placing a picture of Håkan in front of Peder. 'A rather persistent friend who seems to be completely divorced from reality when asked to describe his relationship with Rebecca. He has also slept with her, and was the father of the child she was expecting.'
He placed a picture of Gustav Sjöö next to the one of Håkan.
'Gustav Sjöö, the supervisor who was subsequently

accused by several female students of being a dirty old man, and who was also reported for attempted rape. He was obviously another repellent man who was in Rebecca's circle of acquaintances when she died.'

Alex took a deep breath.

'In addition, there are indications that Rebecca may have been selling sex over the Internet, which gives us God knows how many potential perpetrators. And then there was the volatile ex-girlfriend.'

Peder picked up both photographs.

'I heard Fredrika was following up the Internet lead; she was going to visit a porn shop over in the Söder district.'

'Do you believe in that angle?' Alex asked.

His voice was tired, but his expression was alert.

'No, I don't. But on the other hand . . .'

'Yes?'

Peder hesitated.

'I don't believe that Gustav Sjöö murdered her, but I do have a feeling the solution lies in that direction.'

'In what direction?'

'Fredrika quite rightly pointed out that a significant proportion of Rebecca's life was centred on her studies and the university. We ought to speak to more of her fellow students, including those who weren't particularly close to her.'

'Fredrika has started taking a closer look at the mentoring network,' Alex pointed out.

'In that case I'll move onto Rebecca's other

activities as a student. She seems to have been working hard on her dissertation, which could well have brought her into contact with a lot of people.'

Peder got up to leave, then sat down again.

'Have we got an ID on the male victim yet?'

'Ellen gave me a list of possible names just before you arrived; I was intending to go through it now.'

Peder lowered his eyes.

'We're not going to solve this unless we find out who he is.'

'I know,' Alex said.

His promise to Diana echoed inside his head. *I'll solve this case if it's the last thing I do.*

'There must be a connection, one way or another. It's just impossible that . . .'

'I know,' Alex said again.

His tone was harsher than he would have wished, but he didn't want to hear about difficulties and obstacles. For Alex, the only way was the way forward.

Peder stood up.

'Håkan Nilsson,' Alex said. 'What are we going to do with him over the weekend?'

'I think we should keep him under surveillance for a few more days, see where he goes. What about his alibi?'

'It's valid, unfortunately, although that doesn't necessarily rule him out. He could have been working with someone else who took care of her initially.'

'And Gustav Sjöö?' Peder asked.

'I think we'll let him go for the time being. We've got nothing on him. His alibi worked out after all, didn't it?'

'Looks that way. He gave me the name of a colleague who can confirm that he didn't leave the conference in Västerås; I'll follow it up on Monday.'

Peder went back to his office, and Alex settled down with the list of possible missing persons who could be the man they had found buried not far from Rebecca's body. They were all men who had been reported missing in the Stockholm area twenty-five to thirty years ago. There was only one who was as tall as their victim, and he was considerably older. Damn.

Alex moved onto the next list, which covered men reported missing throughout the whole of Sweden. He went through the names carefully; one had been circled by Ellen. *Possible?* she had written in the margin.

Henrik Bondesson. A man who had disappeared in Norrköping two weeks before his forty-sixth birthday, and had never been found. Why not?

Alex went to see Ellen and asked her to contact the local police.

'I'd like them to bring up his file and fill me in on the background.'

He went back to his office with renewed vigour. Perhaps he was on the way to providing another family with a grave to visit.

★   ★   ★

211

She was like a fairy tale, a saga. That was the way Fredrika Bergman thought of her daughter, and that was why she had chosen the name Saga. Simple and logical, like so many other things.

Saga was asleep when Fredrika got home from work. Spencer was in the library, reading a book. The light from the window caught his hair, making it shine like silver. Fredrika stopped in the doorway.

'Sorry I'm so late.'

Spencer looked up and raised one eyebrow.

'As you know, I've never been very good at keeping an eye on the clock either.'

She went over to him and perched on the arm of the chair. She gave him a hug, enjoying the feeling of closeness to a man she didn't think she could ever stop loving.

'What are you reading?'

'A book that a colleague of mine co-wrote. It's pretty boring, to be honest.'

*Yes, you should be honest.*

She trembled as she breathed out. Should she bring up the issue of Rebecca Trolle with him right now?

'How was work?' he asked.

'Stressful. How was your day?'

'Saga and I went to the swings; we had a lovely walk in the sunshine.'

He fell silent.

'Have you heard any more from the university?'

Spencer stiffened.

'About that student who was complaining about your supervision,' Fredrika clarified.

Spencer grunted and got to his feet. He grabbed his stick and went over to the window.

'No, I haven't heard a thing.'

He seemed tired and downcast. Fredrika didn't know what to say.

'Are you enjoying being at home with Saga? It's not too tiring for you, is it? Because if it is . . .'

Her voice died away. What would happen if it was all too much for Spencer? Would she give up work?

'It's absolutely fine.'

Fredrika watched him as he stood by the window. All of a sudden he seemed out of reach, lost in problems he wasn't prepared to share with her.

'Rebecca Trolle,' she heard herself say, and Spencer turned to face her.

'The woman whose body was found in Midsommarkransen?'

'Yes.'

She hesitated. But she had to know.

'Did you know her?'

'No, of course not; why do you ask?'

*Because I saw your name among her papers, Spencer, and now I'm wondering how the hell you were connected with her.*

She shrugged.

'No particular reason. I just thought you might have bumped into one another at a seminar or something; she was studying the history of literature after all.'

Spencer was looking at her as if she had lost her mind.

'I have no recollection of ever meeting her.'

So that was that. The matter was resolved.

Saga woke up, and Fredrika hurried into the nursery.

'Hello, angel,' she said as she picked her up.

Saga wriggled in her arms; she wanted cuddles, and rubbed her forehead against the base of Fredrika's throat.

'Did you miss Mummy today?' Fredrika said, kissing the top of the child's head. 'Did you?'

Saga hurled her dummy onto the floor and attempted to follow it. Fredrika crouched down and let her daughter crawl away. In many ways she envied the child, who had the privilege of being able to regard the world as exciting and genuinely uncomplicated. Every day promised new discoveries that made her chortle with joy. It was as if she never experienced the tedium of everyday life, but was constantly on the way towards a new adventure.

Saga crawled towards Fredrika, clutching a big piece of Lego in her hand. She grabbed her mother's legs and pulled herself up, beaming with delight.

'She'll be walking any day now.'

Spencer was standing in the doorway.

'It certainly looks that way,' Fredrika replied.

The joy of being a mother suffused her entire body; work was far, far away.

Until her mobile rang.

It was the colleague who had accompanied her to the porn shop in Söder. Fredrika avoided looking at Spencer as she answered; she didn't really want to tell him about her trip to the depths of sexual behaviour.

'The IP number belongs to the university,' her colleague said. 'And the name didn't get us anywhere.'

'Rebecca's profile was uploaded from a computer at the university?'

'Yes – one of the student computers that anyone can book.'

A fresh hope sprang up.

'We had a similar situation when we were working on the murder of the Ahlbins last year,' she said. 'Check with the university to see if they keep their booking records. If they do, we can see who booked that particular computer and . . .'

'I've already called them. They don't keep any records.'

'Damn.'

She was about to hang up, feeling crestfallen, when something occurred to her.

'Can you send the pictures on the CD to my private email address?'

Her colleague hesitated.

'What for?'

'I want to look at them again; I thought some-thing rang a bell in one of them.'

Her colleague promised to send them over.

'Are you working this weekend?' Spencer asked when she had finished speaking.

There was nothing accusatory in his tone; it was a simple enquiry. She shook her head firmly.

'This weekend is our time.'

She had left the carrier bag full of Rebecca's papers in her office. She thought of the floppy disks; she had forgotten to go through them. They could wait.

They looked at one another, and Fredrika smiled. She could play her violin later.

'Would you like to do something special, Professor?'


It would soon be evening; the colours in the sky left no doubt. Alex Recht looked at his watch: it was almost half-past six, and the department was almost deserted.

His reluctance to go home was almost insurmountable. The children had questioned his decision to stay on alone in the house in Vaxholm; shouldn't he move closer to the city, try living in an apartment?

He didn't want to think about that too much. Alex and Lena had always planned to move into a city apartment when they got older, but now he was alone, and the project had completely lost its appeal. If he moved out of the house, he would no longer know who he was. His daughter understood better than his son.

'It's a house, for God's sake. Sell the bloody thing.'

It had been impossible to reason with his son when he returned from South America. His girlfriend had found it difficult to obtain a residence permit, and he had cursed Swedish bureaucracy. He picked quarrels with Alex, telling him the hours he worked were just ridiculous. He cursed his mother for not getting better, and he hated his sister who was in a serious relationship with a man the rest of the family found slightly odd.

'Stop fighting with the rest of us and focus on your own life instead,' Lena had said to her son the day she died. 'It's not our fault you've found it difficult to grow up.'

Her words had brought about a change. There were fewer arguments, and when the family gathered in church for Lena's memorial service, Alex felt that their son was at peace.

The very thought of the service made him want to cry.

He turned to the computer and read through the log that had been set up to record the progress of the case. No leads on the person who had published pictures of Rebecca Trolle after her disappearance on a website aimed at those looking to buy sexual services. But Fredrika had asked for copies of the pictures to be sent to her home email: Why?

He thought about the profile. Could Rebecca have been kept prisoner as a sex slave and sold to the highest bidder, then murdered and buried? He didn't think so. The profile had been taken down after a few weeks, and had not reappeared.

Alex read on. Several interviews had been conducted with Rebecca's friends and fellow students, but nothing new had emerged. A few hastily written lines caught his eye. One of the students had remembered that Rebecca had been so dissatisfied with her supervisor that she had secretly contacted another researcher at the University of Uppsala to ask for help. The student wasn't sure if Rebecca had managed to establish regular contact with this new supervisor, but she thought they had spoken on the phone. She couldn't remember his name.

Alex took out the copy of Rebecca's diary and leafed through it. The abbreviations that had not yet been identified had been circled in red:

**HH**
**UA**
**SL**
**TR**

Could one of these be the new supervisor? If Alex had been younger he would have gone to the home page of the Department of the History of Literature at the University of Uppsala, to check if any of the academic staff had the initials HH, UA, SL or TR. But instead, he wrote an email to Ellen Lind, asking her to check when she came in on Monday. It seemed rather foolish to suspect every male employee at a Swedish university, but then again . . .

He was determined to leave no stone unturned.

His mobile rang just as he was about to pack up

and go home to dig out his old fishing equipment ready for Sunday's outing with Torbjörn Ross.

It was the officer at the grave site who had begged for more manpower. It was becoming impossible to keep the journalists at bay. They were bombarding the police with questions: why were they still digging? What were they expecting to find?

*No bloody idea.*

'Sorry to disturb you on a Friday evening,' his colleague said. It sounded as if he thought Alex was at home.

'No problem.'

'I just wanted to let you know that we're going to take a break from digging until Sunday or Monday. The lads are worn out, and I haven't had the relief team I asked for.'

No relief team? Was there really another case that had been given a higher priority? Alex doubted it.

'It's fine,' he said. 'I know you're doing your best. Go home and rest; just make sure someone stays there to guard the site.'

Otherwise, the graves would be turned into a sandpit overnight. It wasn't only the journalists who were curious; a number of private individuals were also keen to see what was going on. They would come tiptoeing along, watching the police from a safe distance, expectant and desperate for excitement. It was as if the trees and the ground had been transformed into a magical place over the past few days.

The day they buried Lena, Alex had seen several people he didn't recognise in the church.

The priest had explained, 'There are always those who don't belong, but come to join in.'

'But why?'

'Because they're lonely. Because they have nothing better to do. Because they couldn't bear it if they weren't able to share in the misery of others. Someone else's grief gives them a perspective on life.'

Alex had been astounded. And slightly annoyed. If there were people who wanted to prey on his grief, they could at least ask permission first.

Slowly, he got ready to go home. The days when he had been eager to leave work were long gone. The house that was waiting for him was silent and empty and full of memories. Fridays were the worst. Sunday evenings were the best.

When he finally got to his feet he decided to drive past the site of the graves in Midsommarkransen. He somehow felt that he wasn't grounded in this case; he was fumbling among the different lines of inquiry. There were too many of them, and they were too vague.

Countless times, he had tried to imagine the final hours of Rebecca Trolle's life. He had pictured her calling her mother, telling her about the social event with the mentors. Leaving the student hostel and walking towards the bus stop. Travelling to Radiohuset and getting off the bus.

*Why was it so difficult to work out where she had been going?*

Feeling frustrated, Alex closed the door of his office and locked it.

A colleague from Nyköping called: they had picked up Gustav Sjöö's chainsaw from his summer cottage. SKL, the National Forensics Lab, would attempt to match the chain with the surfaces of the bones in Rebecca's skeleton where the body had been cut in half. He sounded optimistic; if they got a match, it would mean they had identified the tool that had been used to dismember the body.

True, Alex thought. But we won't get a match. Because it isn't Gustav Sjöö we're looking for.

# CHAPTER 22

The apartment had become a prison. Håkan Nilsson looked out of the window, making sure he was standing to one side and not right in the middle. They were sitting down there in the car, he was absolutely sure of it. He had seen them when he left for work this morning, and when he came back from the police station this afternoon. Surveillance. Watching his every move.

Håkan guessed that they had started listening in to his telephone calls as well, which was why he kept his mobile switched off in his jacket pocket and had unplugged the landline. This didn't really affect his life – he had very few friends, and they wouldn't react if they couldn't get hold of him for a few days. His mother might be a bit anxious. She worried about everything, and seemed to have developed an actual need to be nervous.

He hoped she wouldn't realise who the newspapers were writing about. The headlines were mercifully vague: '*Suspected killer is friend of Rebecca Trolle*'. He avoided watching the parts of the news broadcasts that related to him. He wished that the whole circus would come to an end, that they would leave him in peace.

There were words within the general hubbub of news that hit him so hard he couldn't catch his breath. Her body had been in plastic bin bags. Dismembered. He almost threw up. She had been desecrated before she was laid to rest. If only he had known where she was during the two years he had been without her. If only he had had a place to go where he could feel her presence.

Håkan started to cry, and moved away from the window, sticking close to the walls to make himself invisible in his own apartment. He went into the bedroom and lay down. The photo album was under his pillow; he rolled over onto his stomach and slid it out. He opened it with trembling hands, gazed at the many photographs.

The first class photo, taken when they started secondary school. All those expectant faces looking into the camera. Their naivety made him feel sick again. The others in the class had seemed younger than him, immature. But not Rebecca, who always smiled when he was talking to her, who lit up his world.

'Don't get bogged down in all that boring stuff,' she used to say. 'You're letting yourself down more than anyone when you refuse to have some fun.'

He had learned to listen, to follow her advice and take note of her ideas. He had tried to be around her as much as possible, to feel her energy and lust for life rubbing off on him. He loved to see her

223

face light up when he appeared, welcoming him into her circle.

The problem was that he could never get her alone. Håkan leafed through the album. Pictures of his father, which Rebecca had encouraged him to keep. He had wanted to chuck the lot, get rid of everything his father had ever touched. He hated him for his betrayal, for the fact that he hadn't thought Håkan was enough, and had taken his own life. And had let Håkan find him.

Håkan was left alone with his mother; how he had hated life in those days. His mother drank more than ever, and smoked forty cigarettes a day. Håkan stank. The smoke got everywhere, into his freshly washed clothes and his newly showered hair. The stench betrayed the fact that his home life was in a state of collapse, and he had to start seeing a counsellor – a complete idiot who hadn't a clue how things really were for Håkan.

But Rebecca knew. She listened when he talked, sat close to him even though he smelled horrible. Sometimes he would go back to her house after school and have tea with her mother and brother. They were a proper family, and Håkan loved being a part of it. When he and Rebecca did their home-work together, he wanted to be at her house rather than in the library. There were photos of those occasions in the album, taken by Rebecca's mother Diana. Håkan ran his finger over Rebecca's face; she was gazing steadily into the camera. She was such a strong person compared to him.

More pictures, this time from the weeks before their final school exams. Their first crisis. Håkan sighed. All good relationships have to go through a crisis in order to define their parameters. The problem was that Rebecca had blown their crisis out of all proportion. She had said she couldn't breathe, that he was suffocating her, that he was always in exactly the same place as she was, and that it was too much. She wanted to see her other friends, and he was getting in the way.

*How could that possibly be true?*

They had a perfect relationship, and gave each other everything they needed. Rebecca kept saying they had to give each other space, that Håkan mustn't misinterpret what they had together.

A new page in the album, and Håkan felt a surge of irritation as usual. After the student pictures, there was a gap of a whole year in the time line. The year when Rebecca went to study in France. He found out a week before she left. His rage had threatened to boil over. He had kept out of the way ever since the exams, giving her every opportunity to understand the importance of their relationship. And she had responded by asking for more time.

He clenched his fist, slammed it down on the bed. It was lucky for Rebecca that Håkan was such a patient and generous person. He congratulated himself on his own magnanimity as he turned to the final page in the album. Few people would have show their beloved such tenderness and tolerance.

The tears began to flow as he looked at the very last picture.

A blurred, black-and-white image. An ultrasound image.

Håkan and Rebecca's child, twelve weeks old.

He sat up on the bed, breathing heavily as he gazed at the scan.

'Why did you have to destroy everything?' he whispered.

# CHAPTER 23

The balcony was bathed in evening sunshine. There was a cool breeze, but it was very pleasant sitting outside with a cardigan around their shoulders. Peder and Ylva sat in silence at the table, drinking wine. They caught each other's eye and burst out laughing.

'Bloody hell, we're sitting here like two pensioners,' Peder said.

'You mean like two worn-out parents!'

Ylva's voice, always husky but never less than strong. A smile so wide that it had made Peder go weak at the knees the first time they met.

'Do you want more children?'

He hardly knew why he had asked the question.

'No, I don't. Do you?'

'I don't think so.'

*God knows, we had enough problems last time, didn't we?*

She followed his movements without saying anything as he drank a little more wine then put down the glass.

'Why do you ask?'

He twisted in his chair, trying to get the sun on his face.

'I don't really know; I was just thinking about it.'

'About what?'

'Kids. How many people should have, how many people can cope with.'

Ylva tilted her head on one side so that she could see his face properly.

'I don't think you and I can cope with any more than we have at the moment.'

There was no hint of accusation in her words; it was more a statement of fact. A pleasant contrast to the way they used to speak to each other, shouting and crying, furious and hurt. Looking back, he couldn't understand how they'd ever ended up in that state.

'I agree,' Peder said.

He thought back to another time when he had lied to her and deceived her; how he had despised himself in those days.

'You have to forgive yourself,' the therapist had said. 'You have to find the courage to believe that you deserve your wonderful family and a good life with them.'

It had taken time, days and nights of his thoughts going round and round. But now he knew that he had reached safe harbour. He felt contented. Calm and secure.

'By the way, Jimmy rang again,' Ylva said.

'It's because I haven't had time to ring him all week. I'll give him a call tomorrow.'

'No need. He's coming over for a meal. Just try to be here.'

Peder raised an eyebrow.

'Of course I'll be here. Where else would I be?'

'At work?'

He shook his head.

'Not this weekend.'

She shivered, pulling her cardigan a little tighter.

'Do you want to go inside?'

'No, I'm fine.'

She took a sip of her wine.

'Tell me about your new case.'

He pulled a face.

'Not tonight. It's too revolting to talk about.'

'But I want to hear. It keeps coming on the news.'

Where should he begin? What could he tell her? What words could describe the case facing Alex and his team? A girl who had disappeared in Östermalm and been found by a man out walking his sister's dog. Two years later. The colour drained from Ylva's face when he told her about the bin bags and the chainsaw. About Rebecca's peculiar friend Håkan and her repulsive supervisor. About the false sex profile that had appeared on the internet after her death, and about all the dead ends they had come up against so far.

'Who would do a thing like that?' Ylva said thoughtfully, referring to Rebecca's photo on the website.

'A sick bastard,' Peder said.

'Are you sure about that?'

He looked up. 'What do you mean?'

'I'm not sure it was a sick bastard, as you put it. You said the profile appeared two weeks after she went missing. That means nobody knew what had happened to her; some people probably thought she'd just gone off of her own free will.'

Peder considered what she had said.

'You mean someone uploaded the profile because he or she was angry?'

'Exactly. Or because they felt hurt or betrayed. That could explain why it was taken down again.'

'When the person in question realised that there was something not quite right about Rebecca's disappearance after all,' Peder said.

Ylva took another sip of wine.

'It was just a thought.'

Their neighbour appeared on his balcony; Peder and Ylva waved and he sat down with a beer.

'And what about the man?' Ylva asked.

'The body that was found near Rebecca's? No idea. Alex thought he might have found out who he was, but I'm not sure.'

'How terrible for his family.'

'Not knowing?'

'Yes, not having that closure.'

Peder swallowed.

'How long do you think a person could wait?'

Ylva frowned.

'What do you mean?'

'How long would you wait before you gave up?

If a friend or a member of the family disappeared and was missing for decades . . .'

His voice died away.

'Sooner or later you have to move on,' Ylva said. 'Is that what you mean?'

'Yes.'

She tucked a strand of hair behind one ear.

'That doesn't mean you'd ever stop wondering what happened.'

Peder looked over at the neighbour's house and down at the street where they lived. The man who had been buried must have had a family who missed him and agonised over what had happened to him. The question was whether the police would be able to find them and provide the answers they had been waiting for.

The trees cast long shadows over Alex. He was standing alone in the forest glade, aware of his colleagues standing guard a short distance away. The crater in the ground lay at his feet; he could see that the process of digging had been difficult. Rocks and tree roots had got in the way of the police team's spades and had needed to be moved out of the way.

Alex crouched down, staring at the ground. On at least two occasions, a murderer had dragged a dead body here. Or he might have killed his victims on the spot. They couldn't be sure, but every instinct told Alex that the murders had taken place elsewhere.

*You dragged or carried your victims to this place. I can feel it: you moved through the trees like the angel of death.*

He tried to reconstruct the course of events. Someone drove to the car park where he had just left his own car. Opened the boot, picked up the body and began to walk. It must have been dark. And he must have been there before. You don't head off into a dark forest unless you know the way, know exactly where you're going.

The grave must have been prepared before the perpetrator arrived. He could hardly have carried both the victim and a spade. Unless of course, he went back and forth to the car. Alex closed his eyes, trying to picture the scene. Had the murderer stood on this very spot holding a spade? Had he driven it into the ground, over and over again, until the grave was deep enough for the victim of his crime to disappear?

*You were careless.*

Alex opened his eyes. They would never have found the dead man if they hadn't been digging. And they wouldn't have been digging if they hadn't found Rebecca first. Why had the killer made such an error? How come he had buried Rebecca so close to the surface that a dog had managed to dig her up?

Everything pointed to the fact that the killer had been stronger when the first murder was committed, which made sense. The first time, between twenty-five and thirty years ago, he had been strong

232

enough to dig a grave almost two metres deep. He had also managed to carry his victim all the way here. The second time, things were very different. He wasn't capable of digging such a deep grave, and he had dismembered the body so that he could carry it. And to make identification more difficult. However, if the only purpose of dismembering the body had been to make sure Rebecca couldn't be identified, then the killer would have contented himself with removing the hands and head, rather than chopping the body in half.

There could be other reasons behind the dismemberment: sadism and sexually motivated murder sprang to mind. But Alex no longer believed this was the case. The perpetrator was a pragmatist. It was entirely possible that he had carried out the murder and chopped up the body without the slightest feeling of guilt or angst; Alex knew nothing about that. However, these were not the actions of a psychopath, in Alex's opinion.

He straightened up. He was doing his best to push the thought aside, but the fact remained: they *could* be dealing with two different killers. Who were working together. Or perhaps one took over when the first couldn't cope any more.

Whatever the situation might be, it was no co-incidence that Rebecca and the male victim had been buried in the same place. And it would be difficult, if not impossible, to solve one murder without solving the other at the same time.

The ringtone from his mobile was so loud that Alex almost fell head first into the grave. He dug the phone out of his pocket, fumbling as he answered.

'Alex Recht.'

'It's Diana Trolle. I'm sorry to keep ringing you.'

He took a step back from the edge.

'No problem. How are things?'

She hesitated. 'Not so good.'

'I can understand that.'

There was a brief silence; Alex waited.

'I feel as if I'm going mad. I'm trying to remember all kinds of things that would help you with the case, but it's as if my brain is completely empty. I can't remember a single thing she said that would have told me she was in trouble. I'm such a bad mother, Alex.'

He tried to calm her down. No one had asked her to start digging through painful memories, or trying to re-interpret things her daughter had said that didn't mean anything.

'But I should have realised,' Diana said. 'Done something to help her. How could she have been pregnant and not told me?'

That thought had occurred to Alex several times. How could Rebecca have been pregnant for several months without telling a single person? With the exception of the child's father, in all probability. Håkan Nilsson.

*But had she known?*

Alex held his breath. With the help of DNA

234

testing, the police had been able to establish the identity of the father. But had Rebecca been certain? There was much to suggest that she had believed it was Håkan's child, but there was also a chance she had thought it might be someone else's.

'Children don't tell their parents everything,' he said.

'Rebecca did.'

*Not everything, Diana. Definitely not.*

'Would you like to come over for a glass of wine?'

Alex stiffened.

'Sorry?'

'No, I'm the one who should apologise, it was a stupid idea. I just wanted . . . I feel so desperately lonely.'

*Me too.*

'It wasn't a stupid idea, but . . . Perhaps we should wait.'

He looked around the forest. Wait for what? For the sky to fall, for Rebecca to come back from the dead, or for a week with two Sundays in it to come along?

'That sounds sensible. Let's wait.'

*Sod it.*

'I can be with you in an hour. But I'm driving, so I'm afraid I'll have to pass on the wine.'

'You're very welcome in any case.'

He thought she was smiling.

He could feel the ground quivering beneath his feet, almost as if it was sighing loudly because of all the secrets buried there. He walked quickly back to his car. A thought struck him when he had almost reached it:

Would he have been able to cover the same distance carrying a dead man?

# SATURDAY

# CHAPTER 24

Yet another night of no peace. The thought was upsetting. Fredrika didn't have time for sleepless nights. Spencer was breathing deeply by her side, enjoying the sleep Fredrika needed. She suppressed the urge to reach out and stroke his hair. There was no reason to wake him. He seemed to have enough troubles of his own, as far as she could tell.

At one o'clock she got out of bed, passing Saga's room on her way to the kitchen. The little girl always slept well. Her head was resting on the pillow with an air of self-assurance that sometimes made Fredrika go weak at the knees. Saga was not a temporary visitor in their lives; she was a permanent fixture, and Fredrika was expected to love and care for her in the decades to come – a commitment that would not be possible without all the love only a parent can feel for a child.

The shadows in the library were calling to her. She tiptoed into the room without switching on the overhead light, and sank down in the armchair where Spencer had been sitting when she got home from work. She could smell him on the blanket

239

draped over the arm of the chair and pulled it closer.

Spencer had no recollection of meeting Rebecca Trolle through his work, or in any other context. But in that case, why had she made a note of his name? Had Rebecca been planning to ring him, but disappeared before she got around to it? That must be the answer. Rebecca hadn't been happy with her supervisor, and no doubt she had wanted to consult someone else.

*That must be the answer.*

Fredrika gazed at the silent spines of the books lining the shelves. Spencer's books interspersed with her own; it was only natural, now that they shared so much. In spite of the hour, the room wasn't completely dark. The light from the street lamps reached Fredrika through the window, giving her a welcome sense that she was part of a living context rather than a vacuum. Her fingers itched with the desire to pick up her violin and play. Few things made her feel better.

It had once been written in the stars that Fredrika would have a career as a violinist, but an accident had put paid to her plans. Her mother had wept when Fredrika told her that at long last she had begun to play again in her spare time.

'What a gift for Saga,' she had said.

Fredrika wasn't too sure about that. Her daughter showed little interest when her mother played, and was an uninspired listener. Perhaps things would change as she got older. Perhaps she would begin to play an instrument of her own? A burst of envy flared briefly within Fredrika, but quickly died away. She would never begrudge Saga such joy. Just because she had been forced to dedicate her life to a profession that rarely matched up to what her expectations had once been, she would never feel bitter if her daughter was given the opportunity to live a different life.

*A life that I would rather have – but it wasn't to be.*

Was that still true? Did she really want a different life? Wasn't she satisfied with what she had? With Spencer and Saga? Her love for them both had changed so many things that she could no longer count them. As far as her job was concerned, it wasn't perfect, but things had got better. Much better, in fact.

She curled up in the armchair with her legs tucked underneath her. The computer was on the table beside her. She glanced at it, well aware that she shouldn't open it up. She shouldn't start working in the middle of the night. Once she got the job in her system, she would never sleep. Curiosity won, and she lifted the laptop onto her knee. It sounded like a purring cat as the fan came to life.

Her colleague had done as she asked and sent over the photographs of Rebecca Trolle. She opened them one by one, feeling revulsion at the fact that she was sitting here in the middle of the night looking at photographs of a naked Rebecca.

241

What was it she had recognised but been unable to place?

She looked at them again, searching for the detail that had triggered her memory. Rebecca lying on her side on a wide bed. The white sheet against her body. Her hair falling over her cheek, her mouth half open. Such a betrayal, to take photographs of a person who was sleeping. One arm outstretched, one leg drawn up. Fredrika had seen other pictures on the website, and these photographs of Rebecca just didn't fit in. They were simply too tasteful. Too discreet.

And there it was.

Fredrika leaned closer to the screen, clicking to zoom in on the detail that had caught her attention. A single framed photograph on the otherwise bare wall behind the bed where Rebecca lay. A face filling the entire picture, a young boy with a stern expression, staring directly into the camera. When the image was sufficiently enlarged, Fredrika knew exactly where she had seen him before.

In Rebecca's ex-girlfriend's apartment. He was Daniella's dead brother.

Fredrika looked at Rebecca. There wasn't a trace of anxiety in her face. She had felt safe in that bed. Safe enough to sleep naked. She wasn't to know that she would be secretly photographed, and that the pictures would be kept for future use.

Daniella must have been furious when Rebecca disappeared, believing that she had been abandoned. Fredrika thought about ringing Alex right away, but decided it could wait until the following day. After all, there was no reason to think that the case was keeping anyone else awake at night.

He was bound to be asleep.


'I never loved him.'

Alex was surprised.

'No?'

'No,' said Diana. 'Not really. Not the way you talk about your wife.'

Alex shuffled.

'But love isn't the same for everyone. We're all looking for different things, we have different needs.'

Diana smiled at him.

'And what needs do you have?'

'Is that a fair question?'

She shrugged.

'Why not?'

Because it's embarrassing the person you're asking, he wanted to reply. Instead he said:

'I have pretty simple needs, I think. I hate being alone, I like having someone to live with.'

Would he ever have that again? Would any other woman stand a chance with Alex, after all those good years he and Lena had shared?

His children had warned him about this, told him that he mustn't let his marriage stand in the way of future relationships. They had insisted it was perfectly natural that he would meet someone else.

'You're not even sixty, Dad.'

The very idea terrified him. He felt a heavy weight on his chest, making it difficult to breathe. He had no idea of how to approach a woman; he hadn't courted anyone for over thirty years.

Diana put her wine glass down on the coffee table. She was half-lying on the sofa, and had made herself comfortable with cushions. Tiredness covered her face like a veil, and grief lurked beneath her skin like an abomination. She had only wept once since he arrived, which had made him regret his decision for a few moments. What the hell had he been thinking of, visiting the victim of a crime on a Friday night?

Then came a sense of calm. Coming to see Diana had been a good decision. They had a lot to talk about, and an unexpected number of common denominators. Above all, they shared the experience of having lost someone close, someone they hadn't thought they could live without.

'And yet we're still alive. Strange, isn't it?' she had said.

They were indeed still alive. Living hour by hour, day by day. She had been missing her daughter for more than two years, knowing that she was dead even though no one had been able to tell her for sure. Alex realised that at least he had had the privilege of being a part of it all when his wife passed away.

'You were there,' Diana said. 'All the way through. You should regard that as a gift.'

If anyone else had said that, he would have

lashed out. But when it was Diana who spoke those words, he couldn't fight back; he had to admit that she was right. Another person's grief couldn't lessen his own, but at least he could see that there were degrees of torture.

It was almost half past one, several hours later than the time Alex had been expecting to leave.

'I really ought to make a move.'

'I think you ought to stay.'

He was taken aback; he felt her words rebound off his chest and disappear into nothingness.

'It's best if I go.'

But he didn't get up; he couldn't bring himself to leave the armchair.

'I'll be working for a while tomorrow. You know you can call me at any time if you think of something?'

She nodded.

'As I keep saying, Alex – I don't remember anything.'

'That's because you're trying too hard.'

Her hand clenched into a fist and she pressed it against her forehead.

'We had an argument a few days before she disappeared.'

'I remember that. For a while, we thought she wanted to wreak some kind of revenge on you, and had simply gone off somewhere.'

Diana closed her eyes, squeezing them tightly until they were no more than narrow lines. As if the pain was making the muscles contract.

'I couldn't work out what was wrong. She just wasn't herself. She kept yelling and screaming, slamming doors the way she used to do when she was fourteen and thought I was stupid.'

She opened her eyes.

'She said she hated me. The next day, she rang and said she was sorry. But I never saw her again.'

The tears welled up, and she made no attempt to hold them back.

'You couldn't have known that was the last time you'd see her,' Alex said.

'I know. But that doesn't change anything. It hurts so much.'

He wanted to get up, go over to her and put his arms around her. But he stayed where he was. An indefinable fear held him back. The fear of what would happen if he took her in his arms.

*I would do what she wanted and stay all night.*

'How could she not have told me she was pregnant?'

'Perhaps she was embarrassed?'

Diana sat up straight.

'I can't make any sense of it. Why didn't she have an abortion if she didn't want to keep the child?'

'We have reason to believe that she was intending to have a termination.'

'But when? She was four months gone.'

Alex realised he didn't have an answer to that question.

'We've spoken to her supervisor,' he said.

Diana raised her eyebrows and dried her tears.

'The man we talked about on the phone?'

'Yes.'

'She definitely wasn't happy with him.'

'We're aware of that.'

'Do you think he killed her?'

'No. For one thing, he has a watertight alibi, and for another, we can't come up with a motive.'

Diana settled down among her cushions again.

'She was obsessed with her dissertation.'

'Wasn't that because she wanted to carry on and do some research work?'

'It was the topic itself that absorbed her so completely. She wanted to clear Thea Aldrin's name at any price.'

Alex tried to recall the story of Thea Aldrin.

'She was convicted of the murder of her ex-husband, wasn't she?'

Diana nodded, gazing sorrowfully at the empty wine bottle.

'It sounds a bit ambitious for a university dissertation, attempting to clear up a murder that was committed thirty years ago where the perpetrator has already been convicted, served her sentence and been released.'

He was smiling as he spoke; he didn't want to appear condescending.

Diana gave a wan smile.

'That's what I thought. But Rebecca just said I was like all the rest of them, that I didn't realise Thea Aldrin was the real victim, who had lost her husband, her reputation and her career. And her son.'

'Sounds fairly typical of the way young people think; they want to see the best in everyone.'

Diana took a deep breath.

'That was how the quarrel started.'

'You argued about Thea Aldrin?'

'About the fact that I said exactly the same as you: young people always want to pardon every sinner. She went mad. Told me that Thea Aldrin had been the subject of one of the worst examples of character assassination in modern Swedish history, and that it would never have happened if she hadn't been a single woman.'

Alex leaned back in the armchair. He ought to go home. Right now.

'What's that got to do with anything? The fact that she was a single woman? As far as I understand it, the evidence was overwhelming.'

Diana spread her hands wide. Neat, feminine hands that would feel warm in his own, Alex thought.

'Rebecca was talking about everything that had happened previously: the story of Thea Aldrin's involvement in the publication of two books, *Mercury* and *Asteroid*. Well, I say books; they were more like crazed descriptions of disgusting murders in the form of short novels.'

She pulled a face. Alex glanced at his watch again, aware that he wasn't really up to speed on the story of Thea Aldrin. But he remembered hearing that Rebecca had spent a huge amount of time on her dissertation.

'I'm afraid I haven't read *Pluto* or *Venus*, and I really do have to go home now.'

Diana laughed quietly.

'*Mercury* and *Asteroid*. And the fact that you haven't read them is a point in your favour.'

Her eyes sought his.

'Are you sure you have to go?'

'Yes.'

Her expression was serious now.

'Perhaps you'll stay some other time?'

He swallowed.

'Perhaps.'

She walked with him to the door.

'You have to find him, Alex.'

Her proximity made him want to pull back, run away.

'Of course. You won't have to wait many days before you find out who did this.'

His body felt heavy as he got into the car. The promise he had made to Diana weighed down on his shoulders like a yoke. He turned the key and reversed out into the street.

It was almost two o'clock; it would soon be morning.

Thank God.

# CHAPTER 25

The care assistant refused to be quiet. In spite of the fact that it was morning, she was making more noise than a normal teenager. Her voice was so loud that Thea was afraid the wallpaper would come away from the walls and roll up into fat sausages just below the ceiling. She closed her eyes and tried to distance herself from the racket.

'Goodness me, you're tired!' she heard the assistant say. 'And I'm nattering on and on!'

Without being asked she started to plump up Thea's pillow.

'There now, is that better?'

She looked at Thea.

'I think it's really sad that you don't want to talk. You've lived such an exciting life; there must be such a lot you could share with the other residents.'

Thea doubted that very much. The parts of her life that had been interesting were completely overshadowed by the fact that she had been sentenced to life imprisonment for the murder of her ex-husband, and that her son had been missing for almost thirty years. She knew what the rumours said: that she had murdered him too and buried his body somewhere.

One of the detectives who had been involved in the search for her son still came to see her. He wanted to get a confession out of her. Sometimes he would sit in silence, gazing at her. Sometimes he would sit very close, talking to her in his calm, steady voice. Asking her to confide in him. Surely, she wanted to be at peace with herself before she died? There was still a chance to put everything right.

Thea had never asked him to come and see her. If he had done his job properly, things would have been very different. Thea would have been free. Alive. She would have been able to carry on being a mother. And her reputation as an author would have been restored.

There was no point in brooding about it all. At the same time, she had nothing better to do. Malena Bremberg's visit had frightened her more than she wanted to admit. How could a girl like her have been drawn into the drama that had raged around Thea for decades?

She had seen the fear in Malena's eyes, heard the tension in her voice. Malena had been asking questions about the girl they had found in Midsommarkransen, Rebecca Trolle. She had somehow discovered that Rebecca had visited Thea in the home, and now that Rebecca had been found dead, Malena wanted to know what she had asked Thea about.

Thea closed her eyes tightly and wished everyone would leave her alone. Wasn't her long silence a clear enough signal that she didn't want to discuss what had happened? She remembered making the decision, right in the middle of an interview with the police shortly after she had been sent to prison.

'Your son,' the officer had said. 'We think you killed him. Just as you killed his father. Where is he?'

Her heart had burst, disintegrated into a collection of atoms in her chest. They thought she had killed her own son. Had they completely lost their minds?

Sometimes she had forced herself to see things from their point of view. She was a convicted killer who was supposed to have stabbed a man to death in her own garage. According to persistent rumours, she was also the author behind *Mercury* and *Asteroid,* two books that caused a furore in both the cultural sections of the newspapers and in a number of other circles when they were published. They had evoked hatred and condemnation, they had been burned and spat upon. It was hard to think of any other publication in recent times that had caused so much fuss.

With a background like that, it was hardly surprising that the police suspected Thea of murdering her son. It was obvious that she was both a sadist and a psychopath.

The door of her room opened again, and the same care assistant bustled in.

'Your flowers have arrived. Every Saturday, regular as clockwork.'

With brisk movements she removed the vase containing last week's flowers and came back with the fresh ones. She placed them on the bedside table, turning the vase so that Thea could read the card. She smiled at the scrawled message, which was always exactly the same: 'Thanks'.

Don't thank me, Thea thought. I owe you far more than you could ever imagine.

There had been a time before everything was destroyed. A good time. Her first book for children had been published towards the end of the 1950s. She had been very young, and in those days it was still possible for a best-selling author to live a quiet, anonymous life. Thea's public appearances had been few and far between. She liked meeting her young readers, but had never regarded herself as being particularly fond of children. Her sporadic contact with her readers had been widely misunderstood; the newspapers said she was shy, which made her even more popular. When her stories about Dysia the angel began to sell abroad, the critics were beside themselves.

The books were described as unique, both in form and content. Dysia the angel was a different kind of fairytale heroine from the ones people were used to reading about in children's literature. She was strong and independent. Honest. She was actually very much ahead of her time. During the '50s and '60s, women who fought for independence were still regarded as somewhat radical. Thea never commented on the issue of equality in the public debate, so instead people tried to work out her political views by examining her books.

They also examined her lifestyle. At the time when she still had her life under control, a small number of disparaging articles were written about her. At the age of twenty-five, she was unmarried and childless; a few years later, she was a single mother. Certain sections of society condemned her, others saw her as a role model. Several cultural commentators suggested that Thea's choices in life characterised the modern woman.

There was only one person who knew the truth, and that was Thea herself. The fact was that she loathed her life as a single parent. And choice had never come into it.

She had given everything to the man she loved. And he had responded by committing the most serious crime of all.

# INTERVIEW WITH FREDRIKA BERGMAN, 03-05-2009,
## 08.30 (tape recording)

Present: Urban S, Roger M (interrogators one and two). Fredrika Bergman (witness).

Urban: Let's summarise the state of play in the investigation when you went home for the weekend on that Friday: 1) You didn't believe that Håkan Nilsson was the murderer; 2) Nor did you believe that it was Gustav Sjöö, Rebecca's supervisor; 3) You didn't believe the photographs on the website had anything to do with the murderer. Have I understood you correctly?

Fredrika: We had to abandon the lines of inquiry that were deemed unproductive.

Roger: What was the status of Spencer Lagergren at this point?

Fredrika: I don't understand the question.

Roger: In the investigation, I mean. Was he regarded as a suspect?

Fredrika: No, he was not.

Urban: Why not?

Fredrika: We had nothing linking him to the victim.

Urban: I would like to suggest that you most certainly did. You actually had several concrete links between him and the victim. *Both* victims.

(Silence.)

Fredrika: Not on the Friday.

Roger: But you had found the brochure in which Rebecca had made a note of his name in red ink. That must have made you think.

Fredrika: Not really.

Urban: I see. But the fact that he was also the only person who could provide Gustav Sjöö with an alibi must have made you raise your eyebrows?

Fredrika: I hadn't checked the investigation log when I went home; I didn't know that Sjöö had named him.

Roger: Interesting. But you were up to speed on developments with regard to the pictures of Rebecca on the internet?

Fredrika: We had information to follow up on that aspect of the case. When it came to other aspects, it didn't seem as if we had.

Urban: Aspects such as Spencer, for example.

(Silence.)

Roger: What conclusions did you reach about the pictures?

Fredrika: That Rebecca's ex-girlfriend, Daniella, must have taken them. And uploaded them to the website.

Urban: Did that make her more or less of a suspect, in your eyes?

Fredrika: Less. I assumed she had done it because she was angry and felt betrayed.

Roger: What did Peder think?

Fredrika: I didn't have the opportunity to discuss

the matter with him over the weekend. I just rang Alex on the Saturday and told him what I had worked out.

Urban: How did he seem?

Fredrika: He sounded tired, but I think he was OK. He was going fishing with Torbjörn Ross.

Roger: And then a new working week began. What happened next?

Fredrika: We had a call from the team who were digging up the grave area. They thought they had found . . . something.

Roger: Another body?

Fredrika: They didn't say what it was.

# SUNDAY

# CHAPTER 26

The men's movements were soundless. They were sitting in the boat in silence, gazing at their floats, bobbing on the surface of the water. One rod was made of plastic, the other of sarkanda reed. They had been in the boat for quite some time.

'I'm really glad you came,' said Torbjörn Ross.

He had already said it once, but thought it was worth repeating.

'Sonja and I are very pleased to see you. You're welcome to join us any time.'

'Thanks, much appreciated,' said Alex.

He hadn't actually realised how much he needed to get out of the city. He had thought that nature and its quietness would stress him out, make him feel restless, desperate to get back home. The effect had been the direct opposite. The cloudless sky and fresh air gave him renewed energy.

But he was embarrassed because he had arrived so late the previous evening. Torbjörn and his wife had assured Alex that there was no harm done, that they had been looking forward to seeing him and were happy to have a late dinner. They had asked if he had been held up because of work, and he had given an evasive answer. Under normal circumstances, he preferred to stick to the truth, but somehow it didn't seem appropriate in this case.

He hadn't got home until almost three o'clock on Saturday morning, because he had been sitting in Diana Trolle's living room watching her drink wine. He had slept until midday, and hadn't got anything done until the afternoon. Which was why he was late.

'Do you think he had a place like this?' Torbjörn asked. 'The man who killed Rebecca Trolle, I mean.'

Alex looked around. The shining surface of the lake, surrounded by tall trees. The odd summer cottage or chalet where the trees had been felled to allow for building.

'It's possible.'

'The dismemberment itself provides quite a lot of information, in spite of the gruesome nature of the act.'

'We've thought about that. And we've questioned suspects for that very reason. But I can't get away from the fact that she was buried close to another body that had been lying there for almost thirty years. There has to be a connection. Somehow.'

'You still haven't identified him?'

Alex jerked his fishing rod, reeled in the line and checked that the bait was firmly attached, which it was.

'I was hoping he might be a man who went

missing in Norrköping just under thirty years ago – Henrik Bondesson. But it wasn't him. Bondesson had broken a leg when he was a teenager, and our body didn't have any injuries of that nature.'

'I recognise the name,' Torbjörn said. 'I think I remember the case.'

Alex looked at him in surprise.

'So will you, if you think about it,' Torbjörn said. 'He disappeared just after that bank robbery in Norrköping. He was a divorced father of two who had been fired from a firm of architects. Up to his ears in debt.'

'You're absolutely right. I'd forgotten that his name was Henrik Bondesson. He was the main suspect in the bank robbery, wasn't he?'

'Exactly. But there wasn't any proof.'

'Strange that he's never turned up. I mean, the statute of limitations for that particular crime is long gone.'

Torbjörn shrugged.

'People do the strangest things.'

Alex reached for his coffee, took a swig and put down the plastic cup.

'Top up?'

Sonja had sent them off with coffee and sandwiches. Lena would not have done the same if he had asked her, which he definitely wouldn't have done. They had opted for a more modern relationship; if they wanted to make a thoughtful gesture, there were other ways.

'Do you think you're going to solve this case?' Torbjörn asked.

Alex almost dropped his fishing rod.

'Of course I'm going to bloody well solve it.'

'I didn't mean to be rude. I'm just saying it's an incredibly difficult case.'

'It's virtually crawling with suspects. We'll find the person who did it.'

Torbjörn put down his rod and unwrapped a sandwich.

'You discover some interesting stuff when you start digging into the relationships between different people,' he said. 'Other people don't realise what you stumble on when you're investigating a murder. Regardless of which social class a person belongs to, there are always friends or acquaintances with a record for violent crime or some other shit. Always.'

'It's particularly frustrating when a case involves younger people,' Alex said. 'Take Rebecca Trolle, for example. The church choir, the mentoring network, swimming lessons for babies, and her university studies. I just don't understand how they fit it all in.'

'That means there'll be plenty of leads to follow up.'

'Each more bizarre than the previous one. Diana, her mother, told me Rebecca was almost obsessed with her dissertation about an old children's author who killed her husband and spent about ten years in prison.'

'Eleven,' Torbjörn said. 'Not nearly long enough, if you ask me. They should have thrown away the key.'

He put down his sandwich. 'So she was doing her dissertation on Thea Aldrin?'

Alex looked blankly at his colleague.

'Yes.'

'When you say she was obsessed, what do you mean?'

'Her supervisor said the dissertation was almost like a police investigation.'

Alex tried to sound light-hearted, but Torbjörn looked so serious that he decided to drop that particular approach.

'She thought Thea was innocent?'

'Something like that.'

Torbjörn shook his head and picked up the sandwich.

'It was my first murder,' he said. 'And believe me, she was guilty.'

He took a bite, chewed and swallowed.

'I'd been in the force for a few years and was brought in as an additional resource on the investigation side; I was allowed to go out with the big boys on a murder case. Thea Aldrin's neighbour called the police after hearing terrible screams from Thea's garage – one male, one female voice. We went straight there, assuming she'd been beaten up. But we were wrong. We knocked on the door, but no one answered. We walked around the house, looked in all the windows. She was sitting in the garage when we broke in; the knife was in her hand and the man lay dead on the floor.'

'She'd stabbed him to death?'

'With at least ten blows. Completely crazed. There was blood everywhere. The carotid artery had been severed. She was just sitting there, staring into space; she was obviously in shock. She was covered in his blood.'

'Why did she kill him?'

'We never managed to get a sensible explanation. She said it was self-defence, but the violence to which he had been subjected didn't fit in with that at all. He had left her and her son before the boy was even born. The prosecutor cited that as a motive – the fact that she hadn't forgiven him for deserting her.'

'Bloody hell. What happened to the son?'

Torbjörn wiped his hands on his trouser legs.

'You obviously don't remember this at all. The papers went mad – they filled page after page.'

'Hang on,' Alex said. 'I do remember. The son had already disappeared, hadn't he?'

'The previous year. Thea Aldrin, the famous author, travelled all over the country searching for her lost son. But believe me, Alex, she knew exactly where he was. She did everything that was expected of her, but you could see that she wasn't particularly worried.'

Alex blinked.

'You thought she'd murdered him as well?'

'The others thought it – I knew. Or to put it more accurately, I know. There were plenty of people who said how difficult she had found her son throughout his life. I think she blamed him for the fact that his father had cleared off, and in the end she took her revenge on both of them.'

The boat bobbed in the water as a gentle puff of wind rippled the surface.

'There was something else about Thea Aldrin that was bloody terrifying, but it never made the papers.'

Alex reluctantly admitted to himself that his curiosity had been aroused by his colleague's words.

'The police confiscated a film when they raided a porn club called Ladies' Night in 1981.'

'What film?'

'It was the sickest thing we'd ever seen. It was nothing like any other porn film you can think of. Actually, it wasn't even a porno. It was pure violence, just insane. It had been recorded using a home video camera, with terrible lighting. It lasted just a few minutes. We played it on an old projector I dug out from the cellar at home.'

'What was it about?'

'There was no plot. It showed a young woman being murdered in a room where all the walls appeared to be made of glass, covered with sheets. Then it ended. It was obviously supposed to look like a snuff movie.'

Alex looked sceptically at Torbjörn.

'A snuff movie?'

'Yes – you know. A film that claims to show a real murder. There are sick bastards who get off on that kind of thing.'

'And you thought this film was genuine – that the murder had really taken place?'

'To begin with, yes. Then we weren't sure. There are so many myths about films like that; why should we have found a real one?'

'But what did all this have to do with Thea Aldrin?'

'A few years previously, she had been accused of being the author behind two books that were published under a pseudonym; they contained a number of descriptions of bestial murders, interspersed with violent pornography. The film we saw was an exact copy of something that happened in one of the books.'

Torbjörn waited for a reaction, but Alex remained silent.

'Don't you understand? She must have been heavily involved in the production of the film. She's one sick woman.'

He spat into the water.

'Was she questioned about the film?' Alex asked.

'Yes, but she refused to admit anything. And we didn't have any proof that she was involved.'

'And the son – she didn't confess to murdering him?'

'No, but I haven't given up hope yet.'

Alex frowned.

'What do you mean?'

'I mean exactly what I say. I'm going to find that boy; he deserves a better fate than to be missing for ever.'

When Alex didn't speak, Torbjörn went on:

'You know what they say: every police officer has a case he can never let go. The disappearance of Thea Aldrin's son is mine. I still visit her regularly, try to get her to talk.'

'Have you got permission to keep the investigation going?' Alex asked.

'I don't need permission. I know I'm right. Believe me, one of these days she'll start talking.

# MONDAY

# CHAPTER 27

Spencer Lagergren was more worried than he was prepared to admit. All weekend this business with Tova Eriksson had been playing on his mind, wearing him down. Fredrika had noticed the change, but said nothing. Perhaps she was too busy making up for all the hours she had been away from Saga during the week.

He knew he ought to talk to her, tell her what had happened. Instead he kept quiet, hoping it would all blow over soon, and then he would be able to give her a less dramatic version of the whole story. This was beginning to seem more unrealistic with every passing day.

He had called the police in Uppsala on Saturday morning while Fredrika was in the shower, and his worst fears had been confirmed. A formal complaint had been made. The prosecutor had not yet decided whether to instigate a preliminary investigation, but the complaint in itself brought Spencer out in a cold sweat, and he had immediately decided to contact his solicitor on Monday.

It was Monday now, and Fredrika had gone to work. Saga had fallen asleep after breakfast, and the apartment felt silent and empty. Spencer was sitting alone at the kitchen table with the telephone in his hand. His solicitor, who was also a childhood friend, had been very helpful during the divorce proceedings. He thought he had done a good job of extricating himself from his former life, and Uno, his solicitor, had agreed.

To hell with it, he needed help and Uno was the only person he could turn to. His friend answered almost immediately, and was pleased to hear Spencer's voice.

'It's been a long time – how's life now you're a dad?'

He was laughing as he spoke; Uno was one of the few people who had had no hesitation in telling Spencer what he thought of the new life he had chosen.

'You're going to have a child? At the age of sixty? With a woman who's thirty-five? You're out of your bloody mind.'

Spencer had appreciated his honesty, and had wished that more people were like Uno. Honesty was beyond price in any relationship. He hoped Uno would be straight with him now.

In a voice thick with emotion, he explained that fatherhood was wonderful, but that other parts of his life weren't going quite so well. Uno remained silent as Spencer told him what had happened. When Spencer stopped speaking, his solicitor remained worryingly quiet for a moment.

'Spencer, between you and me, is there any truth whatsoever in her accusations?'

Was there? He wavered, thinking about that damned hug.

'No,' he said firmly. 'Absolutely none.'

'That's even more worrying, in a way. What does she want? Is there any chance that you've upset her without realising it?'

Spencer hesitated. Remembered the day she brought a cake in and he went for coffee.

'I think I might have rejected her without being aware of it at the time.'

'So you suspect she was interested in you?'

'I didn't see it at the time, but with hindsight I think that was probably the case.'

Uno didn't reply; it sounded as if he was tapping away at his computer keyboard.

'What do you think?' Spencer asked eventually.

'I think you've got problems. Big problems.'


The Lions' Den was available for the Monday-morning briefing, which meant that order was restored. At least for Fredrika Bergman: she liked routine, and had taken a dislike to the temporary meeting room.

Alex looked brighter and fresher than he had done for a long time. Fredrika remembered her promise to keep an eye on him; so far he hadn't shown any sign of putting a foot wrong.

Fredrika herself wasn't sure how she felt about being back at work. The weekend with Saga had made her question her decision to return – she missed being with her daughter.

'Let's make a start,' Alex said, interrupting her thoughts.

He nodded to Peder to close the door. Peder also looked rested. Both men must have had a quiet weekend. For his part, Alex confirmed this when he spoke.

'I did a few hours' work on Saturday, then I was away for the rest of the weekend. I know that some of you were busy conducting interviews and monitoring Håkan Nilsson's phone calls; anything to report?'

One of the additional investigators who had been brought in spoke up.

'Only that Nilsson's phone is bloody quiet.'

'What do you mean?'

'There's virtually nothing going on; there are no calls to monitor. Either he knows we're listening, or he hasn't got any friends.'

'Or both,' said Peder.

'What about the surveillance?' Alex asked.

'He left his apartment once during the weekend, and that was to do some shopping.'

Alex looked at his team.

'Remind me why we don't believe Håkan Nilsson is our killer.'

Peder and Fredrika began to speak at the same time, and Alex nodded to Peder to continue.

'First of all, there's the MO. Because he was so fond of Rebecca, it seems unlikely that he would do such terrible things to her body after killing her. Second, he has an alibi. We've spoken to other people who attended the mentors' event, and they confirm that they saw him during the course of the evening. Several of them recall that he was the one who contacted the police to report Rebecca missing.'

'The mentors' event was held not far from the place where we assume she disappeared,' Alex reminded them. 'If he was gone for an hour, it would have given him enough time to deal with Rebecca. I mean, he didn't necessarily have to do everything at the same time.'

'You mean she was kidnapped first, then murdered later? That's a possibility, of course.'

Alex scratched his forehead.

'Did Håkan have a mentor? If not, why was he at the party?'

'He was there to help out,' Peder replied. 'He didn't have a mentor.'

'That's right, I remember now,' Alex said.

'And who backs up his alibi?' Fredrika wanted to know.

'Countless students and other people who were at the party. Håkan had a number of duties that evening; among other things he was responsible for the technology, making sure the business representatives could give their presentations.'

Peder rested his elbows on the table, supporting his head on his hands.

'I think we have to accept that Håkan Nilsson is out of the picture,' he said.

'I think you're right,' Alex agreed. 'Unless of course, someone was helping him, but that doesn't sound credible.'

'I checked the records from the previous investigation,' Fredrika said. 'When Rebecca disappeared, you interviewed Valter Lund, her mentor, only once. Why was that?'

'Because we had no reason to speak to him again. Why do you ask?'

'I don't think he was paid very much attention, under the circumstances. And you don't seem to have asked any questions about his relationship with Rebecca.'

Peder turned to face her.

'Are you suggesting Valter Lund could have been her boyfriend?'

'Well, we don't know, do we? On Friday, I spoke to the president of the students' union who used to run the mentoring programme. He said that Rebecca had told him she saw Valter Lund only on the odd occasion, but according to the notes in her diary, they saw each other rather more often. I've asked Ellen to run the same checks on Valter Lund as she's already run on everyone else in the previous investigation; I'm hoping to hear back from her this morning.'

She could see that her comments had riled Alex.

'There was nothing to indicate that they were in a relationship. Nothing.'

She could also see that the thought alarmed him.

Could the murderer have been right there under their noses from day one?

'Is there anything else apart from the fact that they seem to have met up more frequently than they told other people?' Peder asked, looking extremely sceptical.

'At the moment, nothing at all,' Fredrika said. 'But it won't do any harm to check. The union president said that Valter Lund is religious, and that he went along to see Rebecca's church choir. If she thought he was the father of her child, she might have been afraid that he would want to keep the child – that he would be totally opposed to abortion.'

Alex looked at his scarred hands, recalling why he had sustained serious burns.

'We all remember the Lilian Sebastiansson case in the summer of 2007. Are we dealing with the same thing this time? Unwanted children?'

'No chance,' said Peder. 'Absolutely not.'

'I agree,' said Fredrika. 'But that could be one element in the case.'

'So what about the man?' Peder said. 'The man who was buried thirty years ago? Who the hell is he?'

Alex looked despondent.

'I've spoken to the pathologist and a number of other people. We're beginning to wonder whether he might have been a foreign national, or someone who was never reported missing in Sweden for other reasons.'

'A homeless person?' Fredrika suggested.

'That's one possibility. There must be a reason why he isn't on our database of missing persons. No man of his age and height who has disappeared in the last twenty-five to thirty years fits.'

'If he is a homeless person who was chosen at random by our perpetrator, then we're looking for a really sick bastard,' Peder said. 'That means Rebecca's murder could also be completely random.'

Fredrika's lips narrowed to a thin line.

'There's a connection,' she said. 'There's no chance that these murders aren't linked in some way.'

'I agree with you,' said Alex. 'How old is Valter Lund, by the way?'

'About forty-five.'

'So from a purely theoretical point of view, he could have killed both of them.'

'I didn't see anything about his alibi; was he at the mentors' party too?'

'I can't remember; check it out.'

Alex looked at his watch.

'Let's move on. Fredrika, report back when you've heard from Ellen. Look into Lund's background. Find out where he grew up and what he was doing before he embarked on his career.'

He turned to Peder.

'Can you check on Gustav Sjöö's alibi, once and for all? I'm going to try and find out who Rebecca turned to when she got tired of Sjöö and was looking for a new supervisor. She seems to have been very committed to her dissertation; both her mother and Sjöö have made that point. Sjöö even said it was more like a police investigation.'

Fredrika looked up from her notebook.

'I've collected all the material relating to Rebecca's dissertation that was in her aunt's garage, and I'm happy to go through it, but I've got one more thing to take care of this morning, if you remember.'

Alex smiled.

'Daniella, the ex-girlfriend. Go and see her right away.'

Peder was curious.

'What's going on with the ex?'

'We think she was the one who uploaded the pictures of Rebecca onto that website.'

The sun was in the sky and spring was in the air. Fredrika stopped on the pavement outside HQ and turned her face up to the warmth. She stood there drinking it in for several minutes before she walked over to the car. She was alone this time; she didn't see any need to take a colleague with her.

She called home. She wanted to hear that everything was all right, but she sensed a fresh underlying tension in Spencer's voice.

They ended the conversation with mutual reassurances that everything was fine. Fredrika felt a knot in her stomach, an unease that she couldn't shake off. Her face was tight after her spell in the sun, and her scalp itched.

*Talk to me, tell me what's happened.*

When she arrived at Daniella's apartment block she was in a bad mood before she even got out of the car. She hurtled up the stairs and hammered on the door.

She heard shuffling steps on the other side of the door; she wanted it to open immediately. Which it did.

'You again?'

The voice was weary, but her eyes sharpened when she saw Fredrika's determined expression.

'May I come in?' said Fredrika, stepping over the threshold.

As before, Daniella made her way into the kitchen. Fredrika followed, stopping to look at the photographs of Daniella's brother. She was absolutely certain. It was the same boy she had recognised in the pictures of Rebecca.

They sat down at the kitchen table. Fredrika opened her handbag and took out the nude pictures of Rebecca. Without saying a word, she placed them in front of Daniella, who looked at them and recoiled.

'Where did you get these?'

'On the Internet. On a website called "Dreams Come True".'

Daniella swallowed.

'You took them, didn't you?'

'Yes.'

Daniella picked up the printouts, gazing at them one by one. She cleared her throat.

'She didn't know I had them. I took them when she was asleep.'

'So I see.'

Her tone was more acidic than she had intended.

'I didn't mean any harm. She looked so beautiful lying there; I just wanted a picture of her.'

'And how did they end up on the Internet?'

'I don't know.'

'Oh, come on!'

Daniella was distraught.

'It's true! I don't know!'

'You're not seriously telling me that someone got into your apartment, stole these photos and put them on a sex website? Do me a favour.'

She raised her voice, feeling the surge of adrenalin. Daniella had chosen the wrong day to mess with Fredrika. But Daniella stood her ground, her voice thick with tears.

'I'm telling you, I don't know how they got there. I took them, but I would never have done such a thing. Why would I?'

'I think you were furious, Daniella. I think you were absolutely bloody livid. That makes a person do stupid things – me included. When Rebecca didn't get in touch, you thought she'd just decided to go away. So in order to get your revenge, you uploaded a profile on the Internet. Then you realised something must have happened, and you felt guilty and took them down.'

Daniella was shaking; her chin had begun to quiver.

'You don't understand jack shit, do you?'

Fredrika took a deep breath and tried to gather her thoughts. She was getting nowhere fast.

'OK, help me out here. Who else had the photos?'

'Nobody!'

'In which case, you have to understand that . . .'

'Hang on, Håkan Nilsson had them.'

Fredrika was taken aback.

'Håkan Nilsson?'

Daniella looked down at the table.

'Rebecca was so sick of him following her around. And he hated me. Said horrible things to me when I turned up at parties and he was there. I sent the pictures to him to get my revenge.'

'When was this?'

'The week she disappeared; a day or two beforehand.'

Daniella started to cry.

'I wanted to make him jealous, I wanted him to see that she was happier with me than with him.'

Bloody hell. Håkan Nilsson again.

'Have you still got the email, Daniella?'

Daniella went and fetched her laptop; she came back and opened it up. The sun was reflected in the screen. She turned it around so that Fredrika could see, then opened the email program and searched for the message she had sent to Håkan.

'Here.'

And there it was, a short message:

'Have a good look, Håkan. Have you ever seen Rebecca as relaxed as this when she's been with you? I thought not. And guess what? She never will be. Never.'

# CHAPTER 28

He had actually intended to leave during the night, but the darkness frightened him and he was far too tired to make the effort to go. Håkan fell asleep on top of the bedclothes, his arms wrapped around the photograph album. He didn't wake until seven, when he heard the noise of the bin wagon out in the street.

Those fucking nude pictures.

How he hated the fat cow who had sent them to him. Not because he had had to look at them, but because she had taken them. Violated his lovely Rebecca as she slept.

He stayed away from the windows, certain that the police were out there keeping him under surveillance. He put the television on while he had breakfast and got dressed: kids' programmes, devoid of both meaning and content.

He remembered being alone at home with his father once when he was a little boy. They had eaten ice cream and watched TV for hours. Håkan had been allowed to sit on his father's knee, and they had ordered pizza. When his mother got home, she ruined everything. Called Håkan's

286

father irresponsible, screamed that he was spoiling their son.

'You make me look worthless,' she had said.

Not true, Håkan had thought. His mother could do that perfectly well all by herself.

He had spent less and less time with his father, who was away for long periods and could not be contacted. Håkan would stand at the kitchen window looking out for him for hours and hours. Sooner or later he would turn up, with a deep furrow in his brow, but always pleased to see his son.

As Håkan grew up he began to understand how serious the situation was. His mother was in the process of driving his father away forever. Håkan couldn't think of anything worse. The days in school were endless. When they were finally over, he would run all the way home.

And one day everything was over.

His father was hanging from the ceiling hook in the hallway. With his strong hands he had relieved the light of its duties as a source of illumination, and had hanged himself with a rope attached to the hook. Håkan saw him the second he opened the door. He had never screamed more loudly in his entire life.

*What would he have done without Rebecca then, when he lost his reason and wanted to kill his mother?*

Håkan placed the album in his bag with the rest of the things he had decided to take and fastened the bag carefully. If he went out the back way, the police wouldn't see him leaving the building.

# CHAPTER 29

The woman on the switchboard at the University of Uppsala informed Peder Rydh that Professor Spencer Lagergren was on leave for an unspecified period of time, and could therefore not be reached by telephone at the moment. She did not have access to the professor's mobile number, but there was a possibility that he would still be checking his emails.

Peder typed a short message and sent it to the email address he had been given. Almost immediately he received an automatic reply informing him that Spencer Lagergren was unavailable, and that it might be some time before he was able to respond to the message.

He had more success through directory enquiries. He found a Spencer Lagergren who lived in Uppsala, and made a note of his mobile number. Less than a minute later he was able to speak to him.

Peder introduced himself and explained why he was calling.

'I'm currently working on the investigation into the death of Rebecca Trolle. Do you have time for a brief chat?'

He could hear the hesitation in the other man's voice.

'I suppose so. What's this about?'

'It's to do with a conference that took place in Västerås in the spring of 2007. I would really like to meet up with you, but as I understand it you live in Uppsala. I don't suppose you happen to be coming into Stockholm either today or tomorrow?'

Silence.

'I'm on paternity leave at the moment; I'd really prefer to clear this up over the phone.'

Paternity leave. Peder struggled to hide his surprise. He hadn't checked on Spencer Lagergren's age yet, but thought he sounded too old to be at home with a baby. On the other hand, Fredrika Bergman had somehow persuaded her other half to stay at home with their daughter, and he was getting on a bit.

'I understand,' Peder replied. 'In that case I'll run through my questions now, and if anything else comes up I'll be in touch again.'

'Fine.'

Peder peered at his notes.

'So we're looking at a conference in Västerås at the end of March 2007. Do you remember whether you were there?'

He heard the professor clear his throat.

'Yes, I do remember. I gave a talk.'

'Interesting,' Peder said, without meaning it. 'Do you remember roughly how the conference programme looked?'

Spencer Lagergren laughed.

'Yes and no. One conference is much like another. Were you thinking of anything in particular?'

Peder suddenly felt unsure of himself. Was this really something that should be dealt with over the phone?

*Sod it, Gustav Sjöö is of no interest in our investigation anyway.*

'Do you remember whether you met a man by the name of Gustav Sjöö?'

'Gustav Sjöö? From the University of Stockholm?'

'Exactly.'

'I definitely remember him. He gave a very good lecture on the contribution of modern crime fiction to Swedish literature as a whole.'

'Did you speak to him during the course of the evening?'

He was trying to sound relaxed, but the reason behind his question was all too apparent.

'I'm sorry, but what is this about?'

'It's about the fact that Gustav Sjöö has stated that you can confirm that he did not leave the conference in Västerås once the working day was over, and that you and he chatted before dinner.'

He could hear the professor breathing at the other end of the line.

'Now you come to mention it, I do remember us having quite a long chat during pre-dinner drinks. I usually try to avoid that kind of thing, but Sjöö had raised several important points during his lecture, and I wanted to discuss them with him.'

'Do you remember what time this was?'

'Not off the top of my head. Between seven and eight.'

And there was the confirmation. Gustav Sjöö had been in Västerås when Rebecca disappeared, and couldn't possibly be the killer they were looking for. Now it was just a matter of checking that the distinguished Professor Lagergren wasn't hiding some terrible secret, but that seemed unlikely. At the end of the day, the professor was just a university lecturer on paternity leave.

Alex was lost in thought when the phone rang.

Diana.

Her voice aroused so many conflicting emotions that Alex considered putting the phone down immediately. He ought to say something, explain that he didn't have time to talk. Which was true.

But he wanted to.

Her tone was apologetic. She didn't want to be a nuisance, but she was wondering how the investigation was going. Had anything new happened over the weekend?

He tried to be evasive; he didn't want to make any promises.

'Valter Lund,' he said in spite of himself.

'Her mentor?'

'Do you remember if they met up often?'

'No, I don't think they did.'

He knew she was curious: Why was Alex asking about Valter Lund? Was he involved? Then again, he had asked about so many different people by this stage that it was difficult for her to follow the way the police were thinking.

'Thanks for Friday, by the way.'

He said it so abruptly that he almost interrupted her mid-sentence.

'No, thank you – I'm glad you came.'

*Me too.*

He hesitated, unsure of what to say next.

'You know you can ring me any time.'

'Will you come over again soon?'

A knock on the open door of his office made Alex look up. Fredrika was standing there with her coat on. Her cheeks were rosy, her expression eager.

'Unfortunately, I have to speak to a colleague right now; I'll be in touch.'

Not a lie, but cowardly all the same. Had he always been like that?

'What is it?' he said to Fredrika.

'It wasn't Daniella who uploaded those pictures of Rebecca. It was Håkan Nilsson. I'm absolutely certain.'

'Well I'll be . . .'

Peder appeared behind Fredrika.

'In that case, let's bring him in. For real, this time. He's lied his way throughout the whole bloody case; he's given us nothing. Enough is enough.'

Alex nodded.

'I'll speak to the prosecutor, then we'll ask surveillance to pick him up.'

Fredrika was still standing there, looking unsure of herself.

'What are you thinking about?'

'Håkan Nilsson. And the case. A few hours ago, we were convinced it wasn't him. And now . . .'

'And now we still don't think it was him. But we think he might have been involved. That he's withholding further information.'

'In that case, I agree,' Fredrika said. 'We need to search his apartment too.'

'Of course. I'll mention it to the prosecutor.'

Fredrika went to her office, and just as Alex picked up the phone to call the prosecutor, Ellen Lind appeared.

'I checked out those initials you sent me on Friday.'

Alex looked slightly puzzled.

'You asked me to find out whether any of the staff in the Department of the History of Literature at Uppsala University had the same initials as the people we hadn't managed to identify in Rebecca's diary.'

'Oh, yes.'

'I got a match with SL. There's a Spencer Lagergren in the department, but he's on leave at the moment.'

Alex put down the phone.

'Spencer Lagergren. Why do I recognise that name?'

'He's already in the investigation log,' Ellen said. 'When Gustav Sjöö was interviewed, he said that Spencer Lagergren could confirm his alibi.'

'Which means that Spencer Lagergren also has an alibi for the night Rebecca went missing,'

'Have a word with Peder,' Ellen said. 'I think he was intending to ring Spencer Lagergren this morning.'

'I'll just give the prosecutor a call first.'

The only negative point about the good weather was that it destroyed Peder's focus when it came to his job. Police work was best carried out in the fog or rain. A beautiful sunny day took away his sharpness.

Fredrika had returned from her visit to Rebecca Trolle's ex-girlfriend with some interesting news, which meant that Håkan Nilsson was once again relevant to the investigation. He was an unlikely perpetrator, but he didn't appear to be entirely innocent either.

The surveillance team reported that Håkan had not been seen leaving his apartment that morning. Because they were monitoring his phone, they had heard him ring work and call in sick. Peder couldn't explain why, but he felt uneasy. Håkan had any number of good reasons to call in sick, but Peder still thought something else was going on.

He shook off his misgivings and moved on to a routine check on Spencer Lagergren. He opened the police address database and entered the professor's name. If he could get a personal ID number the check would only take a couple of minutes, and he wouldn't need to ask Ellen for help.

There was only one Spencer Lagergren, but contrary to what directory enquiries had told him, this Spencer Lagergren was registered at an address in Vasastan in Stockholm, not in Uppsala. Peder frowned and made a note of his ID number.

*I would really like to meet up with you, but as I understand it you live in Uppsala. I don't suppose you happen to be coming into Stockholm either today or tomorrow?*

Why hadn't he said that he lived in Stockholm? Perhaps he was lying about the child as well. The database showed that this wasn't the case: Spencer Lagergren did indeed have a child – a daughter just under one year old, by the name of Saga.

Peder stared at the screen. Saga. Like Fredrika's daughter. He took a deep breath. Clicked on the child's name. Mother and legal guardian: Fredrika Bergman. Father and legal guardian: Spencer Lagergren.

His heart was pounding, his pulse rate increasing.

What the hell was going on here? Why hadn't Fredrika said anything?

He stopped himself.

She hadn't known. Nobody in the team had actually mentioned Spencer Lagergren's name.

Peder buried his face in his hands, overcome with embarrassment. Admittedly it was very odd that nobody on the team knew the name of the man Fredrika was living with, but it was even more odd that Peder had called Spencer without checking on his background in advance. Sloppy. Spencer must have wondered what the hell Fredrika's colleagues were up to.

'Bloody unprofessional,' Peder muttered to himself.

His mobile rang, and Peder was relieved to see that it was Jimmy.

'You answered!'

It was very easy to win Brownie points in Jimmy's limited world, where his brother Peder was king, and beyond reproach. Even when he let Jimmy down.

'Of course I answered – you called me, didn't you?'

Jimmy's clear laugh echoed down the phone.

They talked for a while. Jimmy had been out for a walk with someone who had a dog. They had made biscuits in the assisted living complex, and Jimmy had taken one of the biscuits for the dog.

Peder felt a stab of sorrow. In just a few years, his own sons would have passed their uncle in terms of development.

'The weekend was good,' Jimmy said.

He was referring to Saturday, which he had spent with Peder and his family. It had been more than just dinner; Jimmy had wanted to be picked up at lunchtime.

'It was,' Peder replied.

'Can we do it again next weekend?'

'Maybe. If not, I'll see you soon.'

When Jimmy had rung off, Peder felt the emptiness grow in his breast. The therapist had told him he had to accept Jimmy as a source of joy; he couldn't go on grieving for everything his brother was missing out on. He couldn't spend his life feeling guilty because he had become an adult while Jimmy remained a child.

It didn't matter how many times Peder heard those words; he would always feel a pang of guilt.

Alex walked in and interrupted his brooding.

'Spencer Lagergren,' he said.

Peder groaned.

'Look, I'm really sorry I stuffed up, Alex. I had no idea he was Fredrika's . . . boyfriend.'

'I'm sorry?'

Alex closed the door.

'What did you say? What are you talking about?'

'He's Fredrika's partner. The father of her child.'

He pointed to the computer.

'Unless I've mixed him up with another Spencer, but I really don't think I have. I just called him. *Before* I checked who he was. He must think we're a right load of clowns.'

Alex sat down.

'I knew I recognised the name Spencer,' he said. 'The thing is, Fredrika isn't as open as the rest of us. She doesn't even have a photograph of him on her desk. Which isn't all that strange, when you think about it. After all, he was married to another woman, more or less right up until Fredrika gave birth to their child. And she hasn't been in work since then. All I knew was that he was a professor.'

He looked at Peder.

'Rebecca contacted Spencer Lagergren when she wasn't happy with Gustav Sjöö.'

'Was he her new supervisor?' Peder asked, sounding surprised.

'So it seems.'

Peder shuffled uncomfortably.

'Perhaps that's not so strange. Sjöö knew Lagergren; perhaps he recommended him.'

'In which case he should have mentioned that when we interviewed him.'

'He did say that Lagergren could confirm his alibi. And it doesn't really matter whether Rebecca found Lagergren herself, or through Sjöö.'

'According to Spencer Lagergren's profile on the university website, the main focus of his research has been prominent Swedish women writers who have been active during the past fifty years.'

'Like the subject of Rebecca's dissertation – Thea Aldrin.'

'Exactly.'

Alex bit his lip.

'Bloody hell, why does he have to be Fredrika's partner? Then again, that's irrelevant as far as the case goes. If we need his help, we have to ask for it.'

'What do you want to talk to him about?'

'I want to know whether he and Rebecca ever

met, if he noticed anything he would like to share with us. The same questions we've asked everybody else who had any contact with Rebecca during the last part of her life.'

Peder looked out of the window.

'Shouldn't be a problem.'

Alex smoothed down the crease in his trousers.

'No. We'll inform Fredrika that her partner has cropped up in the investigation.'

He fell silent, and Peder sensed there was something else on his mind.

'I'm just wondering why he didn't come forward in the first place. Rebecca's name has been all over the news since Wednesday. He must have realised that the police would want to speak to him. That we would have wanted to speak to him when she disappeared two years ago, in fact.'

There was another pause. Peder scratched his arm.

'Perhaps they never met, in which case there was nothing to tell.'

'He was in her diary, Peder.'

'I know, but that doesn't necessarily mean anything. She might have had her eye on him as a possible replacement for Gustav Sjöö, but then she disappeared before they started working together – so there's nothing he feels he ought to pass on to the police.'

Alex spread his arms wide.

'I'm sure you're right. But we still need to talk to him. I assume there's nothing on him in our records?'

'I haven't had time to check yet,' Peder admitted. 'I'll do it right now.'

Alex stayed where he was as Peder opened the police intranet and did a multiple search of all records. There was a match in criminal records; Spencer had several fines for speeding.

'Nothing serious,' Peder murmured.

Alex stood up and looked at Peder's screen over his shoulder.

There was a match in the database of those currently under suspicion of a criminal offence.

They both saw it at the same time.

The colour drained from their faces as they read the complaint.

'Fuck,' Alex whispered. 'I'll ring the Uppsala police straight away.'

# CHAPTER 30

**P**eder's door slammed, and a second later, Fredrika saw Alex walk quickly past her office. He kept his eyes fixed firmly on the ground and didn't look in her direction. Had something happened?

She wondered whether to go and ask Peder, but dismissed the idea. To her relief, he hadn't got annoyed when she followed up Rebecca's appearance on the website, and then Rebecca's dissertation. They were working well together; a situation which would have been unthinkable when she first joined the team.

Valter Lund, the businessman who had been Rebecca's mentor, would have to be looked at. And then there was the material relating to Rebecca's dissertation, which Fredrika had brought from the aunt's garage. She decided to tackle that first.

Fredrika didn't quite know where to begin. Both Diana Trolle and Gustav Sjöö had made it clear that Rebecca had spent too much time on her dissertation, and had got far too involved in her topic in the end. In fact, she didn't get it finished. The dissertation should have been handed in in January

2007, but Rebecca wasn't satisfied, and was aiming to submit it later, during the spring term.

How come? The subject had been the life and work of a writer who was almost seventy years old. Thea Aldrin hadn't been a hot topic of conversation for decades. And even when her case had been in the news, no one had really been talking in terms of guilt or innocence. Thea Aldrin was guilty of the crimes for which she had been convicted; the evidence was almost ridiculously convincing.

But Rebecca had thought differently, according to her mother and her supervisor. She had insisted that Thea was innocent of the murder of her ex-husband. How could she have reached such a conclusion?

Fredrika started to go through the articles Rebecca had photocopied, trying to familiarise herself with Thea Aldrin's background. Rebecca had been meticulous, seeking out older articles as well. Virtually every newspaper in Sweden had followed Thea's trial, telling her story over and over again.

The court case formed a kind of bizarre finale to years of remarkable episodes in Thea's life, Fredrika discovered. It began when she gained success as an author. Some people were horrified by her status as a single mother, because no one seemed to know who the child's father was, and because Thea hadn't even been married. Should parents really be giving their children books by a woman like this?

The answer to the question was clearly yes – Thea's books had sold in large numbers, not only in Sweden but also on the international market. Some cynics maintained that Thea should have had more sense, and published her books under a pseudonym instead so that her private life wouldn't have affected her success.

Rebecca had gathered together a large collection of articles. A person who was unfamiliar with the topic would have found it difficult to produce a time line, but Fredrika had a certain amount of basic knowledge to help her. She knew that there were certain critics who never gave up in their efforts to destroy once and for all the image of Thea Aldrin as an independent woman with a child and a career.

In 1976, just such an opportunity arose. A small and relatively new publisher brought out the books *Mercury* and *Asteroid*, two short works with the sole aim of provoking debate, apparently. Extremely heated debate. In more recent times, only Brett Easton Ellis had aroused a similar outcry with *American Psycho*. The stories in *Mercury* and *Asteroid* contained sequences of exaggerated and violent pornography which always ended in murder. They also contained deeply unpleasant murders of women in a variety of sexual contexts.

Fredrika hadn't read the books herself, but she had always wondered why it was rumoured that Thea Aldrin had written them. The publisher behind the books, Box, refused to comment.

The rumours about Thea's involvement might well have died away, but for the fact that her son disappeared in 1980.

The boy seemed to have been something of a sore point in Thea's life even when he was a child. She had given very few interviews, and had consistently refused to discuss her private life. She protected her son as fiercely as a lioness. There was only one photograph of the boy when he was little, taken at the premiere of a British film in Stockholm, according to the article. The year was 1969, and the boy was five years old. His hands were pushed deep in his pockets, and he was staring into the camera with a defiant expression. Fredrika leaned forward to look more closely at the picture. It was a poor copy, and the image wasn't very sharp. It looked as if Thea and the boy were standing in the foyer of the cinema, with people crowding around them. She read:

'Thea Aldrin is a rare guest at film premieres, but this evening she has brought her son Johan along. The author has a keen interest in film, and is a member of the exclusive film club known as The Guardian Angels, which meets on a regular basis to watch and discuss both new and old films.'

*The Guardian Angels.*

Fredrika immediately thought of the floppy disks she had found in the garage. One of them had been labelled with those very words: The Guardian Angels. She must remember to hand them over to the IT boys.

She concentrated on the article again. The slightly blurred caption below the picture read:

'Thea and Johan Aldrin. Morgan Axberger, who is also a member of The Guardian Angels, can be seen in the background.'

Morgan Axberger, former vice president of Axbergers, where Valter Lund worked, and now chairman of the board. She could picture Morgan Axberger today – he was a man who personified the concept of power in every way. Tall and imposing, exuding authority. He had inherited his father's empire in the 1970s, and had ruled it with an iron hand ever since. In spite of the fact that he had recently celebrated his seventieth birthday, no one was expecting him to retire. Nor was it clear who would take over from him in the future, because there were no heirs.

Rebecca must have wanted to meet Morgan Axberger to talk about the film club. Fredrika dug out the copy of Rebecca's diary that Peder had given her; she leafed through it without coming across Axberger's name. However, he was one of the most influential people in Swedish industry, so it would probably have been difficult to arrange a meeting with him. Then again, with Valter Lund as her mentor, it shouldn't have been impossible. Feeling frustrated, Fredrika put the question to the back of her mind and decided to take a break.

She found the floppy disks she had brought from the garage and headed for the IT department. In the corridor, she met Peder, who gave a start when he caught sight of her.

'Hi, there.'

She laughed.

'Hi there.'

He stopped.

'What is it?'

'Nothing – it's just the way you said, "Hi, there." It's not your usual greeting.'

Peder shrugged, looking as if he was forcing himself to smile at her. Then he walked away.

Something was wrong, she could feel it, but curiosity with regard to what she might find on the disks overshadowed everything else.

The IT department was almost empty; the only person available to help her was one of the admin staff.

'So you want to know what's on these disks?'

'Please. And if there isn't too much on there, I'd like a printout straight away.'

'OK, let's see what we can do.'

Fredrika hurried back to her office. Her intention was to try to work fewer hours per day than she had done in the first week – if that was possible while she was working on the Rebecca Trolle case.

Alex and Peder were in Alex's office when she went past. They were talking quietly, their expressions tense. She stopped in the doorway, wondering what was going on. Alex saw her first.

'We've heard from surveillance. About Håkan Nilsson.'

She waited. 'Oh?'

Peder couldn't look at her; he appeared to be reading the sheet of paper in his hand with immense concentration.

'He's disappeared. They rang the bell several times, and eventually they went in. The apartment was empty.'

'He got away even though we had surveillance outside his door?'

'So it seems. There's a door at the back of the building; apparently we weren't watching that one.'

Fredrika could see that Alex was annoyed and stressed. But there was something else. Peder still hadn't looked up from his sheet of paper.

'I'll follow up that other point we discussed,' he said, and left the room.

Fredrika watched him go.

'What do we do now?'

'We'll put out a call for him. The prosecutor has given us permission to search his apartment; Peder's going over there as soon as he's dealt with another matter.'

Another matter. Fredrika felt as if she had been pushed aside for no good reason.

'What are you working on?' Alex asked.

'I'm reading through Rebecca's dissertation notes and trying to get an idea of what she found out that . . .'

'Excellent,' Alex interrupted her.

He went and sat behind his desk, turning his attention to the computer screen.

'Was there anything else?'

The tone of voice was new. Not unpleasant, but not exactly inviting.

'No, I don't think so. Oh, yes.'

He looked at her.

'Valter Lund, Rebecca's mentor. I still haven't heard back from Ellen.'

'Did you look him up on the electoral register?'

She had completely forgotten about that.

'No, but I'll do it straight away.'

He gave a brief nod, focused on the screen once more. As she was leaving the room, she heard him say:

'Would you mind closing the door behind you? I've got a few calls to make.'

The situation that had arisen was completely alien to Alex. Spencer Lagergren's unexpected appearance in the investigation was delicate to say the least. And unwelcome. Alex had made an initial decision not to pass on the information to anyone at all.

'Anything we find out stays between you and me,' he had said to Peder. 'If it's obvious that Lagergren has nothing to do with the case, then I want to establish that as soon as possible. Don't make any notes in the general log for the time being. I'll take the responsibility for making sure the right people upstairs are informed if necessary.'

Peder hadn't raised any objections, but Alex could see that he was less than comfortable with the arrangement.

The telephone rang. It was the officer in charge of excavating the site in Midsommarkransen.

'We've found something.'

His voice was hoarse with tension, as if he'd known all along that there was something else waiting to be discovered in that accursed plot. Alex clutched the receiver tightly.

'Male or female?'

'Neither. Some objects. A gold watch. And an axe and a knife.'

'Bloody hell.'

'We think there's an inscription on the back of the watch, but we can't make out what it says.'

Alex swallowed.

'Send it straight over to forensics. It might help us to identify the man we found last week.'

Last week.

After more days than Alex had the strength to count, they still had no idea who the dead man was, in spite of the fact that Alex had set himself the goal of identifying the body before the weekend was over.

'We've already sent the watch. And the axe and the knife.'

Alex thanked his colleague for the information, wondering what the new discoveries might mean. He couldn't explain why, but he was convinced that the watch was linked to the unidentified man rather than to Rebecca. It should take them a step closer to solving the case. And a step further away from the grave. It was almost a week since Rebecca had been found, and the police were still digging. If they didn't find anything else, they would stop the following evening.

Journalists from all over the country were breathing down their necks. Why were they still digging? Alex had finally judged that the situation was untenable, and had accepted that the police needed to issue a statement. He didn't want to hold a press conference until they had something to say, but a few lines were required to settle their curiosity. And to avoid encouraging the ghost stories that were growing in the shadow of the continued silence on the part of the police.

He glanced at the headlines in today's papers:

POLICE FEAR MASS GRAVE

ENDLESS NIGHTMARE: DESPERATE POLICE CONTINUE TO DIG

One of the articles speculated that the area around the grave was cursed, and that people had gone out into the forest, never to return. There were no concrete examples, merely wild rumours and allegations.

Rubbish, to put it simply.

There was a knock on his door.

'Come in.'

The door opened and Peder slid in. Closed the door behind him. This was something new for both of them. The only person who liked to work with her door closed was Fredrika, and at the moment it was wide open.

'Have you spoken to the police in Uppsala yet?'

310

Alex shook his head.

'I haven't had time. Other things keep getting in the way.'

He told Peder about the new discoveries, and Peder listened with keen interest.

'An axe and a knife. I wonder what they were used for?'

'If it hadn't been for the chainsaw, I might have had a suggestion.' Alex said.

Peder let out a guffaw, but fell silent when he realised it wasn't really appropriate to burst out laughing.

'I called Spencer Lagergren's head of department,' he said. 'I wanted to get the university's point of view. He promised everything would remain confidential.'

'Did you tell him why you were calling?'

'I kept it vague to say the least; I didn't want to tell him the real reason.'

'Good. What did he say?'

'What we already knew. That a student had reported Lagergren for sexual harassment, and that she had decided to go to the police.'

'But why? I thought that kind of thing would be sorted out within the university.'

'The girl who reported him had produced incriminating emails that Lagergren had allegedly sent her. They contained indirect threats, and it was these threats that made the university authorities react.'

Alex sighed, gazing towards the window. Another

311

lovely day. Not that he would get much chance to appreciate it.

'Did the head of department think Lagergren was guilty?'

'He wished the emails hadn't existed; they made it more difficult to explain things away. The university was accustomed to angry students, but this was something different. In his opinion.'

'Could anyone else have sent the emails?'

Peder leafed through his notebook.

'From a purely theoretical point of view, yes. But he didn't think that was the case.'

Peder took a deep breath.

'The fact that Spencer Lagergren is now living with one of his former students doesn't exactly help.'

Alex was annoyed.

'Bollocks. It's ridiculous to regard his relationship with Fredrika as something frivolous.'

'I totally agree,' Peder said. 'But to be honest, I had no idea they'd been together for such a long time. Over ten years, according to the head of department. Apparently, she used to attend conferences with Lagergren. He was married then, Alex. I'm not casting aspersions on Fredrika, but how do we know if she was the only one he was seeing?'

'Would it matter if there were others?'

'Not if they were all happy with the situation. But he might have exploited his position in order to seduce female students in the past. And taken it badly if they turned him down.'

Alex's eyes were itching, as if listening to what Peder had to say had produced an allergic reaction.

'Go and search Håkan Nilsson's place, then I'd like you to drive over to Uppsala. Turn over a few stones, have a chat with the local police. Get a feel for the situation and report back to me before the end of the day. In the meantime I'll try to find out if there's any reason to think that Spencer Lagergren ever met Rebecca. Then we'll decide how to proceed.'

'OK.'

Peder would have to move fast in order to get everything done. As he was about to leave the room, Alex said:

'I still want to keep this between the two of us, Peder. For Fredrika's sake.'

# CHAPTER 31

This wasn't going to end well. The certainty covered her skin like a painful sheen. Malena Bremberg had switched off her mobile, hoping that would keep her persecutor at bay. And yet the gesture seemed pointless. There was nothing she could do to make her life good once more.

She could hardly remember how it had all begun. It was as if all her problems appeared overnight, as if she had had no control over them right from the start. She had believed they had met by chance; it was only with hindsight that she realised that was not the case. Nothing that had happened between them was chance; everything had been planned.

He often came back to the assertion that they needed one another. For different reasons, admittedly, but the important thing was their mutual dependency. She had defied him only once. That was enough for her to learn the lesson that his rules took precedence. And that was when he had made the film.

*The film.*

Waves of terror washed over her, made her want

to climb the walls of her apartment. He had hinted that he watched it occasionally. That he enjoyed it. She hated him for that. Hated and feared him, two concepts that lay very close to one another, as she had learned.

Malena didn't know how she was going to pass the time. She had already worked several extra shifts, and her supervisor at the care home had explained, very kindly, that she didn't want her working more than necessary.

'I mean, you've got to find time for your studies as well.'

How could she explain? She hadn't been to a single lecture since Rebecca Trolle was found. And she wasn't going to sit the exam on Friday. What did it matter if she did it next term instead? She already had far more serious problems.

She remembered the moment when she first realised things weren't right. She was staying over at his place; they had just turned off the lights and were settling down to go to sleep.

'Thea Aldrin – she's a patient in the care home where you work, isn't she?'

She wasn't really allowed to give out that kind of information, but it sounded as if he already knew that the notorious writer was a resident at the home, so she saw no reason to deny it.

'Yes, she's been there for a few years now.'

'Is she nice?'

'I don't know. Nobody knows whether she's nice or not.'

'So she's still not speaking?'

At that point, she had hesitated. Should she be talking about Thea's silence?

'Yes, she hasn't said a word in ages.'

He had turned to face her, gazing at her in the darkness.

'Does she get many visitors?'

That was the line she couldn't cross. She didn't say anything.

'Well?'

'I can't tell you that. I'm not allowed to discuss the affairs of individual residents with outsiders.'

She had heard the sound of his heavy breathing. Felt him stiffen, then relax.

'Think twice before you defy me, Malena. Just so you know.'

Then he had fallen silent and turned his back on her in bed. She hadn't slept a wink that night. And she had never stayed the night with him again. It was as if she suddenly sobered up and saw him for what he was from then on. He wasn't an exciting fling, just a considerably older man who helped himself to parts of her life that she would rather give to someone else.

But by then it was already too late.

What annoyed her was the fact that she still didn't get it. Why was a man like him interested in Thea Aldrin's visitors?

# CHAPTER 32

There was no real indication that Håkan Nilsson was intending to be away for long. He had left food in the fridge, and hadn't taken out the rubbish. The bed was made, the blinds open. An unwashed coffee cup stood on the kitchen table.

Peder and his colleagues went through the whole apartment systematically. They opened drawers and cupboards, spread newspaper on the floor and tipped out the rubbish. Any information about where he might have gone would have been welcome. There was nothing to suggest that he had been forced to leave.

'Do we have any idea what time he took off?' Peder asked.

'No, unfortunately.'

Nobody actually said it, but they all felt embarrassed that Håkan Nilsson had simply managed to walk out of his apartment when there was a surveillance team sitting in a car outside. When they had known that there was a back door, but hadn't put an officer there.

'He hasn't exactly emptied his wardrobe,' a colleague called out from the bedroom.

'No?'

'It doesn't look that way.'

Peder passed a notice board in the hallway, which also seemed to function as a work station. There were letters from his bank and his insurance company, and a number of bills. Håkan had dated the bills in ink, presumably to indicate when they had been paid. He was an orderly person. Peder leafed through the papers, unsure what he was looking for. One of the bills was for a newspaper subscription, another for books he had ordered. A third was for insurance on a boat.

Peder frowned. Interesting – Håkan Nilsson had access to a boat.

'How do you find out if someone owns a boat, and if so where it's moored?' he asked a colleague who happened to have a boat himself.

'The insurance company should be able to confirm ownership, but they probably won't know where it's kept. You'd have to ring around various boat clubs and ask.'

He glanced at the bill in Peder's hand.

'That tells you what type it is.'

He pointed. Ryds hajen. Five metres long. Evinrude outboard motor, fifty horsepower.

'Not exactly a luxury yacht,' Peder said. 'What the hell is a Ryds hajen?'

'A real diamond,' his colleague replied. 'A

318

seventies model, I should think. Hard top and a cockpit. Two berths.'

'So you can sleep on board?'

'Absolutely.'

But not at the moment, Peder thought. It was still below minus ten at night. You didn't go and sleep on a little pleasure boat when it was that cold. Unless you were desperate, of course. Which they could assume that Håkan was.

'Has the season already started?'

'No. The clubs usually start putting their boats in the water from the first of May onwards.'

'So we can assume that this boat is still ashore somewhere?'

His colleague shook his head.

'We can't assume anything. He might have put it in the water himself, even if it's against the rules of his club. If he even belongs to a boat club, of course.'

Håkan's desk was small, surrounded by tall bookshelves. Peder examined the spines of the books and discovered a row of files towards the bottom, neatly marked with the year: 1998, onwards. Peder pulled out the current file: 2009.

Håkan was well organised, and the contents were filed under different headings, separated by coloured dividers: 'Telephone', 'Apartment', 'Internet', 'Guarantees'. And right at the back: 'Boat'.

Peder quickly turned to the relevant section, and found all the information he could have wished for. The boat belonged to St Erik's boat club, which was opposite Karlberg. As far as Peder could tell, Håkan had recently paid for another year's membership.

Feeling stressed, he closed the file. Alex would have to ask someone else to follow up that particular lead; he needed to get to Uppsala.

Every fibre of Alex's being wanted to walk down the corridor and knock on Fredrika's door, sit down opposite her and explain what had happened, so that she was fully informed and up to speed with everything that he and Peder knew. From a purely emotional point of view, he felt it was the right thing to do. But reason was saying something else. There was a minute risk that Spencer Lagergren could be mixed up in the murder of Rebecca Trolle. And there was an even smaller risk that Fredrika knew about her partner's involvement and had decided to keep quiet. This meant that Fredrika had to be kept out of the loop when it came to the lead Alex and Peder were currently following up, so that no one could come along afterwards and claim that the matter had not been handled correctly.

Alex had gone back to the material from the original investigation, looking for traces of Spencer. He had discovered that Rebecca had called the switchboard at Uppsala University on several occasions; the last time was the day before she disappeared. And according to her diary, she had a preliminary meeting booked in with Spencer two days later. Or at least the initials 'SL' appeared in the diary, with 'unconfirmed' after them. Alex was almost certain this was Spencer Lagergren.

The diary was a dubious source of information. There was always a danger that they were misinterpreting the brief notes. And who knew how many other meetings Rebecca might have had, without jotting them down in her diary? Or which meetings she might have cancelled without crossing them out?

Dubious or not, it was all they had.

Alex opened the investigation log and searched for the few short lines that had led him to start looking into the issue of Rebecca's supervisor in the first place. One of her fellow students had hinted that Rebecca was so dissatisfied with Gustav Sjöö that she had turned to a new supervisor. At Uppsala.

He called her; he didn't bother with the formalities. All he wanted was the answer to a few simple questions.

'Frida.'

'It's Alex Recht from the police. Am I disturbing you?'

No, he wasn't. He could tell from her voice that the call had made her nervous. He quickly explained that he knew she had spoken to one of his colleagues last week, and hoped she wouldn't mind answering one or two more questions. She hesitated; she had already told the police everything she could remember.

'This other supervisor that Rebecca contacted – you still don't remember his name?'

'No, unfortunately. I'm really sorry I can't be of more help.'

'That's fine.'

*But you could at least try. Everyone remembers something.*

'Do you remember whether Rebecca mentioned this person by name?'

He could hear Frida breathing at the other end of the line. He wondered why people breathed differently when they were thinking hard about something.

'I think so. But I don't know what his name was, just that it was a bit odd. Gilbert, something like that.'

'Spencer?'

'Yes!'

Relief in her voice; at last she remembered and could help.

'His name was Spencer, and his surname ended with "gren".'

Alex looked at the picture of Spencer Lagergren that he had printed off from the university website. Strong, distinctive features. Thick, silver-grey hair. Eyes as sharp as an eagle's. Was this what a murderer who dismembered his victim looked like?

'Do you know if they met up?'

'I'm sorry, I don't. I know she wanted to see him because she needed help with her dissertation, but I'm not sure if they managed to arrange it. I do remember something else, although I've no idea if it's relevant to your investigation.'

Alex felt his expectations increase.

'Tell me.'

'She'd come across the professor's name in a different context while she was working on her dissertation.'

'Oh?'

'I'm not sure how, but she was hoping he'd be doubly useful.'

Alex thanked her for the information, cursing the fact that they didn't seem able to establish whether Spencer and Rebecca had met without asking Spencer himself. He wanted to avoid a formal interview with him at all costs, because that would mean informing Fredrika.

She had to be told in any case. Not telling her that Spencer now figured in the investigation was untenable. And morally wrong. And illegal. If Spencer Lagergren emerged as a possible suspect, Fredrika would have to be removed from the case.

*She would never accept that under any circumstances.*

He felt a surge of sorrow and rage. The weekend's fishing trip seemed light years away, and it had been tainted by Torbjörn's account of his obsession with the Thea Aldrin case. He was still visiting a woman who was over seventy years old, waiting for her to confess to the murder of her son. That had to be against the rules.

He stood up and marched along to see Ellen Lind.

'Have you got a list of Håkan Nilsson's relatives?'

323

'Here.'

She handed him a list that contained fewer names than the fingers on one hand.

'Is this a joke?'

'His father is dead, and so are both sets of grandparents. His only living relatives are his mother, a maternal aunt and two cousins.'

The list was too sad to comment on. How could a young man in his prime have so few close relatives?

'By the way, I called the university to ask about Håkan Nilsson's studies.'

'Yes?'

'That girl who came in with her mother, the one you interviewed about who started the rumours about Rebecca Trolle? She said he'd found the website when he was writing his dissertation on the new laws regarding prostitution.'

'Correct,' said Alex.

'Well, she was lying. Or Håkan was lying.'

Alex looked at her.

'Lying about what?'

'It was probably him. He never wrote a dissertation; he dropped out when he still had a year to go.'

'He never graduated?'

'No.'

How was this possible? Alex wondered. How could someone who had been a central figure in the case from day one still manage to surprise them? Over and over again? Without being the guilty party?

★   ★   ★

With a sense that time was running out for her, Fredrika carried on ploughing through Rebecca's notes. The fact that she didn't have a copy of the dissertation to refer to made the work difficult; she hoped it was a temporary problem, and that the IT team would be able to provide her with the material she so badly needed by the end of the day.

Thea Aldrin's life was never the same after the two scandalous books were published in 1976. There were constant rumours. In spite of the fact that no one knew for certain, the rumour became the truth as far as the general public were concerned: Thea had written those disgusting books, proving once and for all what a disturbed person she was. The books were the reason why she had chosen to live an isolated life, and why she didn't want to meet her readers.

'That's why she can't look children in the eye,' one article stated in 1977, a year after publication.

Someone reported the matter to the police, but it led nowhere.

Obviously.

Fredrika dug out the picture of Thea and her son Johan at the film premiere. He had disappeared in 1980: He had never been found, and no one had heard from him. Where had he gone? If he hadn't been so young at the time, Fredrika might have thought he was the one sharing a grave with Rebecca in Midsommarkransen.

Rebecca had also gathered articles relating to the search for Johan, which had covered the length and breadth of the country. To begin with, everyone was behind their favourite writer, but when a fresh rumour began to circulate, they took a step back. Thea had killed the boy. Still more press coverage followed in the wake of this vicious rumour. Once again, there was speculation as to why Thea Aldrin had chosen to live alone. What secret was she hiding that meant she wouldn't let any man get near her? Something must be weighing so heavily on her conscience that it had driven her to insanity.

Fredrika was getting more and more annoyed. Where did all this gossip come from? First of all about *Mercury* and *Asteroid*, then about the disappearance of her son. The relentless hate campaign seemed to have pushed Thea over the edge, because a year later she stabbed her ex-boyfriend to death – he was the man she claimed was the father of her child. The newspapers inaccurately referred to him as her ex-husband, even though they hadn't been married.

There was nothing to explain why he had suddenly turned up on Thea's doorstep. No one and nothing spoke up in her defence. She chose not to appeal against her life sentence, and allowed herself to be taken to prison in handcuffs as the TV cameras rolled.

It wasn't difficult to see why Rebecca had become interested in Thea's life. But a large piece of the puzzle was missing, the piece that would explain how interest had turned into obsession.

How Rebecca had come to the conclusion that Thea was innocent of the murder of her ex.

*What did you find out, that I can't see, Rebecca?*

A call from IT informed her that the printouts from the floppy disks were ready. Fredrika almost ran to collect them.

She was surprised and disappointed when she was given a pile of paper that was significantly smaller than she had expected.

'That's all there was,' the girl explained.

Fredrika flicked through the sheets.

'Which pages came from which disk?'

'The top three came from the one labelled "The Guardian Angels", and the rest from the one labelled "Dissertation".'

It looked like a half-finished outline. Better than nothing, Fredrika told herself.

On the way back, Alex called her into his office.

'We need to speak to Håkan Nilsson's relatives about where he might have gone. There aren't many of them, unfortunately; could you possibly ring his mother and one of his cousins? I've asked Cecilia Torsson to call the other two.'

He handed Fredrika a note with the details on it. His thoughts were elsewhere, and he didn't even look at her as she left.

Fredrika sat down at her desk and decided to satisfy her immediate curiosity by looking at the printouts from 'The Guardian Angels' disk. The three pages consisted of a description of the composition of the group, and why it had once been the subject of considerable interest. The number of members had always been limited, as if to intensify the air of mystery that already surrounded the little group.

Thea Aldrin was the only woman.

Morgan Axberger.

A man Fredrika had never heard of.

And – later, when one of the others left the group – Spencer Lagergren.

*It couldn't be true. It mustn't be true.*

Fredrika felt the colour drain from her face. In 1972, a new member joined the film club known as The Guardian Angels: Spencer Lagergren, a young PhD student and specialist in the history of literature.

Spencer. Again.

Fuck.

She forced herself to think clearly, trying to see a logical explanation for the fact that he had once again been mentioned in Rebecca's notes. The police had obviously missed something when Rebecca disappeared. She hadn't seen Spencer's name anywhere until she picked up the material from the garage.

Fredrika was about to push the document to one side when she noticed a word that Rebecca had jotted down right at the bottom of the last page, followed by a question mark. She read the word over and over again, feeling her blood pressure drop.

Just one word, but it was enough to make her heart stop.

S n u f f ?

# CHAPTER 33

The one thing with which Diana Trolle was unable to come to terms was her daughter's pregnancy. She thought she would be able to live with the rest of it in time, to reconcile herself.

But she couldn't deal with the thought that she had misjudged the level of trust Rebecca had had in her. Diana had been under the illusion that she and her daughter had shared everything. Things had always been different with her son; he chose to confide in his father. Diana had never questioned this; she had simply accepted it as the natural order.

She and the children's father had realised at an early stage that they were not meant for one another. While other couples gradually grew apart, Diana and her ex-husband discovered that they had never really been close enough. The split was far from dramatic: one day her ex-husband moved out and took their son with him. He rented a place not far away and lived there until the children started high school, then he moved to Gothenburg. They saw each other less and less often.

Rebecca had always occupied a special place in Diana's heart. Not a better place than the one reserved for her son, but somehow more important. People say that every parent has a particularly strong bond with their first-born, and for Diana, this was an absolute truth. The daughter she had once carried was special, a perfect mosaic of qualities and characteristics inherited from her parents, mixed with her own unique personality. This applied to both the physical and the spiritual elements.

The night she was born, Diana and Rebecca's father had stood gazing at the child as she slept.

'She looks like both of us,' Diana had said.

'She's an individual.'

'It doesn't do any harm to have an inheritance.'

How those words had hurt her over the past two years, when Diana suddenly discovered that was all she had left. During the first twenty-four hours of the search, she had managed to remain calm. She had phoned her ex and explained what had happened, told him there was no need to come to Stockholm. Rebecca would soon be back.

The following morning he was on her doorstep. He stayed for ninety days. Slept on her sofa and wept in her arms when the pain got too much for him.

Ninety days. That was how long the search for their daughter had remained active. After that, there was a change. When Diana went to see Alex Recht at police HQ, she could feel that things were different. There were fewer officers still searching. Far fewer. Alex placed his big hands on her shoulders and said:

'We'll never stop looking. But we have to accept that the chances of finding her alive are now minimal. At least the police have to take that view.'

The consequences of his comments were implicit: he had to re-prioritise the deployment of his staff. He would be leading a new team.

'I don't care whether you find her alive; I just want to know what's happened to her,' Diana said.

After that, her ex-husband had gone back to Gothenburg. His new wife couldn't cope without him any longer. It was summer, and it had rained every single day. Diana was glued to the television when six-year-old Lilian Sebastiansson vanished from a train. She felt for the child's mother, who was a single mum, and wished her well. By the time the summer drew to a close, Diana had fallen apart. For the first time in her life, she didn't know how she could ever be whole again. She didn't want to be whole again. As long as her daughter was missing, she had no reason to feel at peace.

With the autumn came a return to everyday life. The knowledge that her daughter would have wanted her mother to go on living carried Diana through the days. She began painting more, spending time with her son. The memory of Rebecca didn't fade for a second. Her face was the last thing Diana saw when she closed her eyes and fell asleep at night, and the first thing she saw when she woke up in the morning. The child she had given life to might have disappeared, but the memories remained, as Diana and her son frequently reminded one another.

*She's here, even though we can't see her.*

Rebecca was dead. Diana had known that when that hellish summer with all its rain came along. The only thing she couldn't understand was why her daughter couldn't be found. Where was she?

In the ground.

Someone had given Rebecca a grave without telling her family. Diana wanted to go there, to Midsommarkransen. Stand at the edge of the grave and look down into the hole that some unknown person had dug. Alex had advised her against it, told her it would be best to wait until the police had finished their work.

Alex.

Who had led the search for her daughter and identified her with the help of a piece of jewellery. She liked him. She had liked him two years ago, when Rebecca went missing. She knew he had sorrows of his own. It didn't feel right to compare her pain with his; she could see that he was suffering, but didn't know how to ease his torment.

Or how he might be able to help her.

Diana burst into tears. How could her daughter have been pregnant, and never said a word? For several months!

*I thought we had no secrets from one another.*

Alex wasn't saying much about the way the police were thinking. Rebecca's pregnancy was one of several important lines of inquiry. Diana couldn't understand how there could be a number of different leads.

She called her son, hoping she wasn't disturbing him.

'Of course not, Mum.'

She had to smile.

'That's what the police say when I ring them.'

Her eyes filled with tears.

'Was there something in particular, or did you just want a chat?'

He was so like his father, always wanting to know how things stood.

'Both.'

She hesitated before going on.

'I want you to be absolutely straight with me. Are you sure you didn't know Rebecca was pregnant?'

'For God's sake, Mum, you've asked me that a hundred times, and every time I tell you . . .'

'. . . that you didn't know. I'm sorry to keep asking, it's just that I'm finding it so difficult – *so* difficult – to cope with the thought that she never mentioned it to either of us.'

Damn, she couldn't stop herself from crying.

'Sorry,' she whispered. 'I'm so sorry.'

'You have to accept that she had secrets, Mum.'

'But why keep that a secret?'

'I suppose she was intending to have a termination.'

'All the more reason to tell me. I wouldn't have judged her, she knew that.'

Her son said nothing; he couldn't deal with his mother's grief as well as his own.

'What about that Valter Lund?' he said eventually.

'Her mentor?'

Diana could hear the surprise in her voice.

'But he was much older than her. Are you saying he might have been the father?'

'There was something odd about all that, Mum. He came to church once to hear her sing.'

'Wasn't he religious?'

'What's that got to do with anything? He was there, Mum. He sat right at the front, staring at her.'

'You were there too?'

'Yes, and I know what I saw.'

Diana allowed her son's words to sink in. Alex wasn't prepared to say whether the police had found the father of Rebecca's child. Could it be Valter Lund? That would explain Rebecca's silence. And Alex's.

# CHAPTER 34

At first, it looked as if Valter Lund had never existed. The high-flying financier who shot across the company directors' sky like a comet had no past.

'Why does it look like this?' Fredrika asked Ellen as they attempted to map out his life together.

'Because he didn't come to Sweden until 1986. He's been a Swedish citizen since the beginning of the nineties; started his first company the year he arrived.'

Fascinated, Fredrika carried on leafing through the documents.

'What an amazing story. It looks as if what people say about him really is true; he came from nowhere and broke through with a force that would have frightened Thor himself.'

'Who?'

Fredrika smiled.

'Thor, the Norse god. The guy with the hammer.'

Ellen laughed.

'Is he in our records?'

'I'm afraid not.'

'Shame.'

Ellen bit her lower lip.

'I don't know if this is of any interest, but . . .'

Fredrika turned to look at Ellen, the papers sliding out of her hands.

'What?'

'Carl, my partner, he works with Valter Lund occasionally. And he's told me a bit about his life. His private life, I mean.'

'Go on.'

Ellen sat down. Fredrika noticed that she was wearing a loose top yet again. Was she pregnant? It wasn't out of the question; Ellen was under forty.

'Well, Carl said that Valter Lund always attended functions and work-related events alone. Without exception. And of course that led to a certain amount of speculation about his sexual orientation.'

Fredrika's hopes began to fade. If Valter Lund was gay, he was hardly likely to have had a relationship with Rebecca. But Ellen hadn't finished.

'But then he turned up at one dinner with a much younger woman on his arm. It only happened once, but it was enough to start a fresh rumour. People said he was only interested in women half his age.'

'If it only happened once, it seems a bit rash to draw such a conclusion,' Fredrika said. 'Perhaps the girl was his niece, or some other relative?'

Ellen shook her head decisively.

'That was the whole point. She wasn't a relative; he introduced her as "a young woman who has yet to find her true path in life".'

'And you think this might have been Rebecca Trolle?'

'When Valter Lund's name cropped up in the investigation, I remembered Carl telling me about that girl. I mentioned it to him, and he's absolutely certain it was Rebecca.'

Fredrika took out her copy of Rebecca's diary.

'Does he remember the date?'

'Not the exact date, but it was around the beginning of February 2007.'

Fredrika flicked through week after week in the relevant month. Plenty of meetings, but nothing with the initials 'VL'.

'Maybe there's nothing odd about it,' she said. 'After all, he was her mentor; perhaps he was just being kind and inviting her to a dinner. We'll ask Diana; she might have heard Rebecca mention it even though it isn't in her diary.'

Ellen pursed her lips.

'Feel free to speak to her mother, but I'm absolutely certain there was something dodgy about it.'

'Because?'

'Because the dinner was in Copenhagen. How many other mentors invited their students to spend a weekend in a luxury hotel in Denmark's capital city?'

The gold watch that had been dug up in Midsommarkransen gleamed in Alex's hand.

*'Carry me. Your Helena'*

He had read the inscription on the back of the

337

watch several times. Simple words, worth their weight in gold.

How many watches like this could there be? Not many. It should have been all they needed to identify the man in the grave. Who was he, this man who had lain in the ground for decades without being missed by anyone?

It just couldn't be true.

No one disappears without being missed by a single person. No one.

Alex held on tightly to the watch. He had asked one of his colleagues to try to trace its origins, as far back as possible.

'Try jewellers and specialist watch makers. Find out when it was made, where it might have been bought.'

The officer in question was given a series of pictures to take with him; Alex hoped he would be back soon. If the watch couldn't help them, he had already decided to turn to the media. He would publish pictures of the watch and pray that someone recognised it. Preferably this afternoon.

Forensics called about the axe and the knife; there were very old traces of blood on both. It was unlikely that the blood had come from either Rebecca Trolle or the unidentified man, but it was impossible be sure. Alex shuddered at the thought of having yet another dead person to deal with.

He glanced at his watch. Peder should be in Uppsala by now; he was going to speak to the

338

local police to find out what they knew. He was also intending to visit Spencer Lagergren's ex-wife, who still lived in Uppsala; Lagergren had been living with her when Rebecca disappeared.

Alex went back to the lists of Rebecca Trolle's telephone activity, which didn't directly link her to Lagergren; all they had were the calls to the university switchboard. Which proved absolutely nothing.

Nor had it been possible to trace any emails from Rebecca to Spencer, at least not from her account. That was no guarantee that messages hadn't been sent, of course, just that they hadn't been traced.

But if they had spoken on the phone only infrequently, and hadn't exchanged emails, how had they been in touch? The conclusion could well be that they hadn't been in touch, and that Spencer Lagergren had no place in the investigation.

Alex sent up a silent prayer that this would turn out to be the case.

The image of Gustav Sjöö emerged from the shadows of his mind: the supervisor who had named Spencer Lagergren as the witness who could confirm that he had not left the conference in Västerås, and who therefore could not be involved in the murder of Rebecca Trolle. A witness who was now accused of having sexually harassed a female student, just like Sjöö.

*What if they knew one another?*

The thought was intriguing. What if the two of

them had worked together, each providing the other with an alibi to protect them? Their profiles were very similar: two men in their sixties, recently divorced, subsequently finding it difficult to maintain appropriate relationships with young women.

Peder called.

'I've spoken to our Uppsala colleagues about Lagergren.'

His voice was tense; it sounded as if he was making the call outdoors.

'What did they say?'

'That a Tova Eriksson has made the accusation. She claims that Lagergren used his position of power as her supervisor to force her to provide sexual favours. And when he didn't get what he wanted, she says he scuppered her dissertation.'

'Fuck.'

'I wouldn't be too sure that everything is as it seems, Alex.'

Peder sounded anxious, his voice peppered with uncertainty.

'This isn't like the accusations against Gustav Sjöö.'

'No?'

'The women who complained about Sjöö had attended lectures given by him on a small number of occasions. They had no real "relationship" with him. In Lagergren's case, the girl was in a position of dependency, in a way. The accusations come from a young student who was given a poor grade by her supervisor. She didn't make any kind of complaint before he failed her dissertation.'

'So you think she made the whole thing up?'

'I'm saying that she might well have a reason to make up something like this so that she would appear in a better light. If you see what I mean.'

Alex could see exactly what he meant. Spencer Lagergren had made the mistake of rejecting a student who had hoped to gain a better grade by getting close to her supervisor.

'She was the one who came on to him, rather than the other way around,' Alex said.

'That's what I think,' Peder said. 'That's what it sounds like to me.'

Alex sensed trouble ahead.

'So we should be able to eliminate him from our inquiries?'

'Definitely. But Lagergren is still going to have serious problems.'

'How come?'

'Tova Eriksson's father was the local councillor in Uppsala; he died a few years ago. Apparently, he was a close friend of the local chief of police, and Tova Eriksson took her complaint straight to the top. He's taken a personal interest in the case; he sees it as an opportunity to raise his profile in equality issues. Unless Lagergren can come up with a bloody good explanation for all this, he doesn't stand a cat in hell's chance.'

Alex heard what Peder said, and understood all too well how things were likely to go for Spencer

Lagergren. However, it wasn't their problem. If the opportunity arose, he would try to have a word with Fredrika.

'So your conclusion is that we don't think this has anything to do with Rebecca?' Alex said.

'Correct. But I thought I might as well have word with Lagergren's ex-wife anyway, since I'm here. I forgot to look up her address: Could you do that for me?'

'Of course, hang on a second.'

Alex put down the phone and opened the internal address database. He couldn't remember the name of the ex-wife, so he looked up Spencer Lagergren. He was currently registered at an address in Vasastan in Stockholm, and before that. . .

At an address in Östermalm.

A few more clicks of the mouse. He could hear Peder's voice on the other end of the phone, but ignored it.

Eventually, he picked up the receiver.

'Listen to this. Until April last year, Lagergren was registered at an address in Uppsala, where he lived with his wife. Do you know where he moved to after that?'

'No – he was in hospital, wasn't he? After that car accident Fredrika told us about.'

'He was indeed, but his first change of address was a place in Östermalm. On Ulrikagatan. Close to Radiohuset, which was the last place where Rebecca was seen. Just a few streets away from Gustav Sjöö.'

'What's that got to do with anything?' Peder asked.

'Rebecca had already been missing for a year by then.'

'He's owned the apartment for several years. It used to belong to his father.'

Peder was lost for words. Alex waited for his reaction.

'Bloody Radiohuset,' Peder said eventually. 'It just keeps on coming up.'

'And here we are again. But we do know that Rebecca was looking for a new supervisor. One of her fellow students has confirmed that she had decided to get in touch with Professor Spencer Lagergren. And that same Spencer Lagergren lived very close to the spot where she was last seen. It's not in Spencer's favour that he didn't correct you on the phone when you referred to the fact that he lived in Uppsala. And he never got in touch with the police while Rebecca was missing, even though he must have realised that we wanted to speak to everyone who had been in contact with her.'

'But had he been in contact with her?' said Peder, who still had his doubts. 'We don't know that.'

'Not for certain, but there's a great deal to suggest that he had. Rebecca called Uppsala several times, and she has no other links to the university. She had written "SL" in her diary. And she had mentioned him to a friend, said she was going to get in touch with him.'

He heard Peder sigh.

'There's no way round it – we need to speak to him.'

'You're right. But have a chat with his ex-wife first of all. Her name is Eva.'

It took Peder less than ten minutes to drive from police HQ in Uppsala to the address where Spencer Lagergren had lived with his wife. It was an attractive house not far from Luthagsesplanaden. Only after he had rung the bell did it occur to him that Eva Lagergren might not be at home.

He rang once, twice. Ylva would have loved this house. She was keener on the idea of a garden than he was. She wanted to watch things grow, pick her own fruit and flowers. Peder couldn't see how that would be possible. As long as they stayed in the apartment they could afford to live in central Stockholm, but if they bought a house they would have to move further out, to the suburbs. Over Peder's dead body.

The door opened; Peder was stunned. Had Fredrika met her partner's ex? If Ylva was half as beautiful at sixty, Peder would be thanking his lucky stars.

Eva Lagergren was strikingly attractive. There was nothing artificial about her appearance. She was well preserved, no more and no less. And beautifully dressed.

'Yes?'

She smiled as she spoke, no doubt aware of the effect she had on men.

Peder smiled back.

'Peder Rydh, police. I'd like to talk to you about a couple of things.'

She stepped aside to let him in. He had left his jacket and sweater in the car; he liked to feel the caress of the spring sunshine on his arms. As he walked into Eva Lagergren's home, the fact that he was wearing a short-sleeved shirt felt completely wrong. She wasn't just well dressed, she was dressed up. As if she were expecting a visitor. He asked the question as she showed him into a spacious lounge.

'Am I disturbing you? Are you expecting visitors?'

'No, no. I usually work at home in the mornings, then I go into the office after lunch. It's a routine I've developed since I've been alone.'

For the past year, Peder thought.

They sat down and she asked if he would like something to drink. He declined; he wanted to keep the meeting as brief as possible. He found it difficult to find the words to explain what he wanted.

'I'm here to ask a few questions about a matter that concerns your ex-husband, Spencer. And I would appreciate it if anything I say remains between the two of us.'

He couldn't interpret her expression; her face gave away nothing. It frightened him. They couldn't afford to make any mistakes in this case.

'You're here to talk about Spencer? Do go on. This should be interesting.'

There was no trace of irony in her voice. He cleared his throat.

'Two years ago, a girl called Rebecca Trolle went missing.'

'The one whose body you've just found?'

'That's right. We were wondering if she had had any contact with Spencer. Does that ring any bells with you?'

*Why the hell would it?*

As the words left his mouth he could hear how ridiculous they sounded.

'Spencer and I never discussed who we were seeing.'

He stared at her, unable to grasp what she had said.

'No . . . but . . .'

'Listen to me, my friend. Spencer and I had a clear agreement which allowed us considerable freedom within our marriage. But for obvious reasons we never discussed the way in which we chose to use that freedom.'

It was a long time since Peder had felt so stupid.

'I think we might have crossed wires here,' he said. 'I wanted to know whether Spencer had acted as her supervisor, or as a sounding board.'

'How should I know? You'll have to ask his colleagues about that.'

'Of course,' Peder said hurriedly. 'But I wondered if he had ever mentioned Rebecca's name at home, or . . .'

'Never.'

Peder looked up as a movement at the window behind Eva Lagergren caught his eye.

'There's a man in your garden.'

'He's a friend. He can wait.'

She gave a wry smile that made him blush.

A friend? Who was younger than Peder?

One thing was perfectly clear: neither Spencer nor Eva Lagergren went for partners of their own age.

'Do you remember a conference in Västerås in 2007? It was held in the spring, in March.'

She frowned, thinking back.

'Not off the top of my head. We both did an unusual amount of travelling that spring. Spencer had a lot of conferences to attend; I don't remember all of them.'

Peder smiled and got to his feet.

'In that case, I won't keep you any longer.'

'No problem.'

They walked towards the door. All the walls were painted white, and were adorned with large works of art.

'Just one more thing,' he said.

She was listening.

'During all the years you were married to Spencer, did you ever hear of any problems between him and his female students?'

'Are you talking about sexual harassment on his part?'

Peder was embarrassed yet again.

She shook her head firmly.

'Never. Spencer wouldn't do such a thing. He doesn't need to, neither to maintain his position of power nor to boost his ego.'

Straight answers were liberating. Peder thanked her for her time and reminded her not to mention his visit to anyone else.

As he was reversing out of the drive he saw the young man who had been standing in the garden walk up to the door and ring the bell. He was carrying a bunch of flowers. Peder couldn't help feeling a stab of envy.

# CHAPTER 35

The textbook lay open in front of Malena Bremberg, but she couldn't see a word. She just wanted the day to pass quickly, wanted the week that lay ahead to disappear. She didn't want to do this any more. Life had lost its lustre since he called. She didn't know what he wanted, and she hated Thea Aldrin, who understood perfectly but refused to say what she knew. If he called again Malena would force Thea to speak. Whatever it took.

The phone rang after lunch. It had rung in the morning as well, just after she had switched it back on, but she hadn't been able to bring herself to pick up. If it was him this time, calling from an unfamiliar number, she would hang up. But it wasn't him. It was a wrong number.

A wrong number. And yet her heart was pounding as if she'd run ten kilometres.

She closed her eyes, resting her head in her hands. How much longer could she carry on? How much longer could she go on behaving in such a peculiar way before her friends started asking if she was OK? Before her family reacted?

Her father's gaze was always the most difficult when it came to defending herself. He always wanted to know how she was feeling, if everything was as it should be. There had been many times when she had been at rock bottom; broken years lay piled up behind her, and she hated the thought that she might be heading down a blind alley, in spite of the fact that she had fought so hard and come so far.

*Fuck, fuck, fuck.*

If it all went wrong this time, she would be lost. She would never have the strength to start all over again.

# CHAPTER 36

It was almost three o'clock, and Spencer Lagergren was desperate for Fredrika to walk through the door. Saga had a temperature, and had been grizzling all day. His hip and leg were aching more than usual, and when Saga fell asleep after lunch, he went for a lie down. The double bed felt horribly empty without Fredrika by his side. What would happen when he had to retire? He wouldn't go willingly, but one of these days they would force him out. Would he end up spending all day alone? Waiting for Saga to come home from school, for Fredrika to come home from work?

His solicitor had advised him to wait; the police might not decide to proceed with Tova Eriksson's accusations. But Spencer's gut feeling was telling him something different. He was facing a problem that could spell professional ruin. Everything he had worked for could easily be destroyed. The very thought filled Spencer with panic.

The solicitor had read his mind.

'Under no circumstances are you to contact the girl who reported you.'

'But I have to speak to her; I have to find out why she's so angry.'

'We already know that. You rejected her, and she couldn't deal with it.'

'Do we know that for sure?'

'Trust me, there's not a shadow of doubt.'

All this brooding was driving him mad. He had to tell Fredrika soon, or he wouldn't be able to cope.

His thoughts turned to the conversation he had had with one of Fredrika's colleagues earlier that day. A very odd conversation indeed. Didn't her colleagues know who she lived with? Didn't she have any photographs of her family? Didn't she talk about him and Saga? He should have offered to go down to the station, but he just couldn't do it. The direction the call had taken had also made him nervous. Fredrika had asked if he knew Rebecca Trolle, the student whose dismembered body had been found recently. And Spencer had said no. Then her colleague rang in relation to the same case, but with a different question. Gustav Sjöö had stated that Spencer could confirm his alibi, which was correct. But why hadn't Gustav called to warn him that the police would be in touch?

Spencer knew about Gustav's position. The accusations had come as no surprise. After Gustav's wife left him, he had developed a deep contempt for women. He couldn't bear to see women in positions of power, women making decisions. That kind of sickness got into your soul. Spencer knew that, which was why he was keen to avoid ending up in a similar situation.

He had just fallen asleep when the telephone rang.

The voice on the other end was the one he knew best of all, but he realised he hadn't heard it for many months.

'Hello, Spencer; it's Eva.'

Eva. A warm feeling spread through his chest, and he could do nothing about it. Her voice had always made him go weak at the knees, through all those years. Melodious and strong. Feminine, but never powerless.

'How are things?'

He sat on the edge of the bed, misery surging through his body.

Bad. Things were bad. Even worse than the last time he had spoken to her.

'Fine. I'm on paternity leave.'

He heard her laughing quietly.

'I tried you at work and they said you were at home with your daughter. Unbelievable.'

He had to smile in the midst of all the gloom. From her perspective he was of course a lunatic who had become a parent just as he was approaching retirement age. At the same time, he felt anxious. He didn't like the fact that she had called him at work.

'Why did you want to speak to me?'

She stopped laughing, as the rain stops pitter-pattering on the surface of a puddle.

'The police were here today.'

He closed his eyes.

'Eva, listen to me. All that business about the student who made a complaint against me is groundless. Entirely groundless.'

Why the hell had they gone to see his ex-wife? To find out about his bad points?

'A student has made a complaint against you?'

Her tone of voice was light; she had never taken things too seriously. Not until the day she realised he was intending to move out.

'That certainly explains a few things.'

Confusion was making his head spin.

'Wasn't that why the police came to see you?'

'No, it wasn't.'

He could hear something rattling; he thought it might be the English tea trolley she had bought when they were living in London. It was her most prized possession.

'They were asking questions about that girl whose body was found in Stockholm. Rebecca Trolle.'

Spencer held his breath.

*Rebecca Trolle. Again.*

'What?'

'Peder Rydh, the detective who was here, asked if I'd ever heard you mention Rebecca Trolle.'

'And what did you say?'

'I said no, of course. What did you think I'd say?'

She sounded annoyed; she was always quick to take offence. She went on:

354

'Anyway, he was talking about a conference in Västerås.'

'Back in 2007.'

'Exactly. I told him I didn't remember it.'

But Spencer did.

It had been excellent in every way. At first, he had intended to ask Fredrika to go with him, but then he had decided against it. He had felt it was unnecessary to cajole her into going to conferences with him, making their relationship stronger than it was.

Sjöö. That was why the police had called – to check Sjöö's alibi.

'Did he ask about anything else?'

'Whether you'd ever had any problems with female students. I said you hadn't.'

Spencer lay down on the bed, staring up at the ceiling.

'Are you still there?' Eva asked.

'Yes, I'm here.'

His heart was beating fast, pounding against his ribs as if it was trying to escape from his body. Now more than ever, he regretted the fact that he hadn't talked to Fredrika right from the start. He had thought that the police had contacted Eva to talk about Tova Eriksson's complaint, but this was much worse.

He was a suspect in a murder case.

There wasn't much to report back to Alex. Fredrika had spoken to Håkan Nilsson's mother and cousin, but neither of them had heard from him, and they had no idea where he was.

'He can't have vanished off the face of the earth,' Alex said. 'He's hiding somewhere.'

Earlier, he had asked Cecilia Torsson to check up on Håkan's boat. She came to see him while Fredrika was in his office. The two women exchanged a look, acknowledged each other silently. They weren't exactly best friends, but as long as they could work together Alex didn't care. He had two murders on his desk, which meant he had far more important things to think about.

'Håkan Nilsson emailed the chairman of the boat club over the weekend,' Cecilia said. 'He asked for permission to put his boat in the water earlier than the other members; he said he was thinking of selling it, so he wanted it in the water.'

'Her,' Alex said.

'Sorry?'

'You don't say "it" when you're referring to boats, you say "she" or "her".'

Cecilia looked at him without speaking.

'Could he have slipped out of his apartment over the weekend without our knowing about it?' Fredrika wondered.

'I've no idea,' said Alex. 'I wish I could say no, but for obvious reasons, I can't.'

'The boat club chairman visited the yard on Sunday, and Håkan's boat was still ashore then.'

Alex let out a whistle.

'In which case he must have put her in the water today. Call the coastguard right away.'

'Why the coastguard?' Fredrika said. 'Isn't it more likely that he's still on Lake Mälaren? Call the harbourmaster's office instead; they're bound to remember if they've seen a small boat heading out to sea this early in the year.'

Alex asked Cecilia to check.

'I don't understand Håkan Nilsson,' he said when Cecilia had gone. 'He's been here no fewer than three times, and not once has he voluntarily offered us any information; we've had to drag it out of him. The fact that he'd had sex with Rebecca. That he was the one who spread the rumour about Rebecca selling sex over the Internet.'

'And that he was the one who uploaded her profile onto the website,' Fredrika added. 'Although it's hardly surprising that he didn't tell us any of those things – not if he's actually involved in the murder.'

'And that's where we come unstuck. Because we don't think he's the killer who dismembered her body with a chainsaw.'

Fredrika sat down. Her boss looked less tired; still far from rested, but a little bit brighter.

'So what do we think?'

Alex leaned back in his chair, gazing up at the ceiling.

'We think he's hiding something.'

He straightened up.

'Why do we keep seeing Håkan, and not the

killer? Time and time again he pops up like a
bloody Jack-in-the-box. And always when we've
just decided that he's of no interest.'

Fredrika crossed her legs.

'His alibi,' she said.

'Watertight.'

There was a draught from the open window.
Alex got up and closed it, then sat down and
leaned across the desk.

'By the way, what did you find among Rebecca's
stuff in the garage? Anything interesting?'

Fredrika felt herself stiffen.

*Spencer. I found the father of my child.*

'Yes and no. I found her dissertation, or parts of
it. And tons of material about Thea Aldrin. What
they say is true: Rebecca seems to have spent an
enormous amount of time on her dissertation.'

'But does it have anything to do with the murder?'

'I don't know yet,' Fredrika replied. 'But I found
a link to Morgan Axberger, the man who runs
Axbergers.'

'Oh?'

'Morgan Axberger used to spend time with Thea
Aldrin. They were both members of the same film
club, The Guardian Angels.'

'Were they indeed!'

Fredrika nodded.

'Axberger's name is one of the first you come
across if you start digging in Thea's past. Rebecca
might have met up with him, even though we
don't know anything about it.'

Alex's expression was clouded with doubt.

'Morgan Axberger is a seventy-year-old billionaire, Fredrika. In what way would he be of interest in a case like this?'

She looked down at the floor first of all, then out of the window. The final word in Rebecca Trolle's notes echoed through her mind.

*Snuff.*

'You were the one who said we had to keep all lines of inquiry open,' she countered. 'Morgan Axberger is one of a small number of people with a solid link to Thea, and Rebecca had a connection with him via Lund. I don't think he's involved, but he could be interesting for other reasons. Regardless of the fact that he's one of Sweden's leading businessmen. Even if he never met Rebecca, he might be able to help us understand the mystery of Thea Aldrin.'

It was obvious that Alex had his doubts.

'It's not that I'm afraid to take him on,' he said. 'But we have to prioritise.'

'I agree. And I'm certainly not saying that he's our most important lead. Valter Lund, on the other hand . . . I really think we should bring him in.'

Alex looked as if he wanted to laugh. The media would go mad if the police picked up both Valter Lund and Morgan Axberger.

'I just want to go over a few basic facts that we need to bear in mind,' Fredrika said.

She told Alex what Ellen had said: that Valter Lund had taken Rebecca to a dinner in Copenhagen.

359

Alex held up his hand.

'We need to speak to Diana Trolle about this; I'm sure she'll remember if her daughter went away for a weekend with her mentor.'

'Would you like me to ring her?'

Alex coughed and looked down at the desk.

'No, I'll call her myself.'

He looked up again. Fredrika could see that her words had made him think. She didn't really want any more questions about all this, but Alex asked anyway.

'Who else was a member of this film club?'

*My Spencer.*

'Nobody whose name I recognised. But I'll look into it, as well as following up everything else.'

She paused and looked at Alex.

'And what about you? Have you and Peder come up with anything new?'

Alex hesitated for such a long time that she thought he wasn't going to answer.

'No, nothing,' he said eventually.

She had a feeling that he was lying too.

# CHAPTER 37

The decision was made before Alex had even finished thinking the thought. He would ring Diana Trolle and see where the conversation led.

'There's something we need to discuss,' he said.

'Is it about Rebecca?'

Wasn't everything? Alex was surprised; wondering if she thought he'd rung for some other reason.

'Yes, and people we think might have been around her before she disappeared.'

Why did he always put it that way? He always said, 'before she disappeared' rather than 'before she died'. Because it was the most accurate? The pathologist had been unable to say how long she had lived – if she had lived – after the evening when she went missing. Perhaps the murderer had killed her immediately. But he could just as easily have kept her prisoner for several days. Or weeks. They didn't know for sure. And unless the murderer told them himself, they would never know.

'Would you like to come over?'

*No I bloody wouldn't*

Her gentle voice aroused a forbidden longing.

361

'Yes, if that's OK.'

'If you're here at six thirty I can offer you dinner.'

A pulse throbbed at his temple. His gaze fell on the pictures of Lena.

It's too soon, he thought. I can't.

'It's just dinner, Alex.'

As if she could read his mind.

He hurried along to Peder's office when he had ended the call and decided to accept Diana's invitation.

'You haven't said anything to Fredrika about Lagergren, have you?'

'No, of course not,' said Peder. 'How did it go with Håkan Nilsson?'

'He hasn't passed through the lock, so he's still on Lake Mälaren. We've put out a call, so let's hope we hear something tomorrow. The fine weather is very tempting; a lot of people have decided to put their boats in the water a little earlier than usual this year. He might be difficult to find.'

Alex looked searchingly at Peder when he had finished speaking.

'Isn't it time you went home?'

'I won't be long; I've still got one or two things left to do. What about you?'

'I'm going soon. I'm just waiting to hear about that gold watch that was found in the grave.'

He heard a voice behind him:

'I'm back.'

He turned around and saw the officer he had sent to visit various jewellers and watchmakers.

He felt like glancing at the time, making the point that it had taken too long to find the answers.

'This model was introduced on the Swedish market in 1979; it was known as "The Father" when it came out. It never caught on, and was sold in only a small number of shops in Stockholm and the rest of the country.'

Alex was disappointed.

'Is that all you've got?'

'Not quite.'

His colleague looked triumphant, as if he were celebrating a major success.

'I must have visited twenty shops, but there were only two where the owner had been in the game long enough to recognise the model. And one of them was absolutely certain that he had sold this particular watch once upon a time.'

'Seriously?'

Peder looked dubious.

The other officer nodded firmly.

'He had no doubts whatsoever. It's the inscription on the back; he remembers it well. The name Helena struck a chord because his wife is also called Helena.'

Alex was very interested.

'What else did he say?'

'He sold the watch to a woman towards the end of 1979; it was the year he and his wife had a child. She brought it back three days later, because it had stopped working. The watchmaker repaired it, and by way of recompense he took it round to her apartment in person when it was ready.'

It took a second before Alex and Peder grasped the significance of what he was saying.

'She lived on Sturegatan, next door to the watchmaker.'

He handed over his notes to Alex.

'We don't have a surname for this woman?'

'No, but since we have an address and a first name, it shouldn't be difficult to find her. Unless of course she's left the country, or died.'

Alex clutched the piece of paper.

'We'll find her.'

He wasn't himself at all. Fredrika could see the change, but she couldn't understand it. Eventually, she had to put her fears into words.

'It's nothing,' Spencer said. 'I've just been feeling a bit under the weather this last week or so.'

Fredrika shook her head slowly.

'You're lying to me.'

A simple statement of fact.

He looked at her.

'I have never lied to you. If you're referring to my past, I didn't lie.'

'You're lying now, Spencer. This is not about you feeling under the weather for the past week; this is about something else altogether.'

He was unable to absorb the calmness in her voice. He became restless and couldn't remain sitting on the sofa beside her. When he got up, she could see that he was finding it difficult to stand.

'Is your leg worse? Or is it your hip?'

'Neither, I'm just a bit stiff.'

Another lie. And she knew she didn't want to hear any more.

'We're not going to bed until you tell me what's happened.'

They rarely raised their voices when they had a disagreement, but this time a combination of frustration and sorrow meant she couldn't help it.

'You haven't told me the real reason why you wanted to start your paternity leave so suddenly.'

He looked at her, his eyes full of something that resembled sorrow and anger.

'You haven't told me everything either.'

Fredrika recoiled as the accusation flew at her.

'Me? Darling Spencer, I have nothing to tell you that you don't already know.'

She saw that he didn't know what to think. What the hell was going on?

'Eva called me today.'

He tried to sound nonchalant, but failed.

'Is this about Eva?'

'She sends best wishes.'

She could feel his rage filling the room, but had no idea where it was coming from.

'How nice. Is she OK?'

He snorted and turned away. He moved over to the window, leaning on his stick, and stood there with his back to her.

'What did she want?'

He didn't reply.

Fredrika tried to remain calm, tried to remember

if they had ever had an argument like this before. But there was nothing to remember. Their relationship wouldn't have survived so many years if they hadn't been able to talk to each other. They had always sensed which words the other person needed to hear, which phrases fitted a particular situation.

But this was something new and alien. It was obvious that Spencer was facing some kind of crisis, and that something had happened during the day to exacerbate things. And yet he chose to remain silent, to shut her out. As if he were beyond redemption.

She felt a mixture of fear and despair.

'You have to tell me, Spencer. What's going on?'

He half turned and she could see every facial muscle tense, his jaws working.

'Nothing,' he said. 'Not a bloody thing.'

Peder stayed on at work for a while. It appeared that Fredrika had inadvertently saved her partner by arousing interest in Valter Lund.

First of all, he read through the log; then, Alex's notes.

Unlikely though it seemed, there were certain indications to suggest that Rebecca and Lund might have had a deeper relationship than the team had originally realised. Than anyone had realised. Alex had said he was going to speak to Rebecca's mother that evening. Peder had thought that sounded odd, but hadn't said anything. Why would Alex be ringing Diana Trolle during the evening? Did they know each other outside work?

He glanced at his watch, aware that he ought to go home.

Jimmy called, and was thrilled that Peder had actually answered the phone twice in one day.

His voice brought Peder peace of mind, temporarily at least. Nobody was better than Jimmy at making a difficult situation seem simple. When Peder heard him speak, he could see his brother the way he had been as a child: strong and stubborn, with Peder always one step behind, frightened and unsure of himself. The memories of his brother's accident would never completely leave him. At any point during the day, he could summon up the image of Jimmy swinging higher and higher until it looked as if the swing might loop right around the frame, and Jimmy suddenly slipped and was flying through the air. Like a bird, Peder had thought. Until Jimmy's body crashed to the ground, his head making contact with the hard surface of a rock.

Perhaps it was this experience that had sent him off balance when Ylva became depressed. It was as if he were programmed to believe that there was only one possible outcome to a serious illness, and so he had let her down, abused her trust.

But she had taken him back. He would never leave her again.

Jimmy lowered his voice.

'There's somebody standing outside,' he said.

Peder wasn't really listening.

'Well, you'd better let him in. Or her.'

'It's a man. He's looking in through the window.'

Peder put down the document he was reading.

'He's looking in through your window?'

'No, somebody else's.'

Should he take this seriously? Sometimes Jimmy's perception of what was happening around him was less reliable than that of a child. He saw what he wanted to see, and drew conclusions that amused him.

'What does he look like, this man who's looking in through the window?'

'I don't know; he's got his back to me.'

Peder knew the layout where Jimmy lived: there were several low buildings in an enclosed area, with a beautiful park at the back. Mångården assisted-living complex shared the facilities with the care home, and Jimmy's window looked out onto one of the blocks that belonged to the care home. Peder tried to work out what his brother might be seeing. Some lovesick old man trying to catch a glimpse of a lady he'd fallen for during a game of bingo?

'Does he look old?'

'Not really.'

Peder had had reservations about the assisted living complex when Jimmy moved there after leaving school. He hadn't wanted his brother living next door to some old people's home. But their parents had insisted: it was good for Jimmy to live in a calm environment, without lots of hustle and bustle.

'It doesn't matter how much you want it to happen,' his mother had said. 'Jimmy is never going to be like you. He doesn't fit in in the city, and that's the end of the matter.'

As time went by, Peder realised that Jimmy was in exactly the right place. The world over there was small enough to allow Jimmy to feel big, and that was worth a great deal.

'He's turned around,' Jimmy whispered.

Fear in his voice.

'He's looking at me.'

The fear spread to Peder.

'For God's sake Jimmy, get away from the window. Now!'

He heard Jimmy's running footsteps, then the voice of a woman in the background, one of the care assistants at the complex.

'What are you up to now, Jimmy?'

Peder sighed. Another storm in a teacup. He ended the call and put down the phone.

He turned his attention back to the investigation. Fredrika had highlighted a link between Morgan Axberger and Thea Aldrin, through a film club that had been active since the 1970s. If it hadn't been for the fact that Valter Lund worked for Axbergers, Morgan Axberger would have been of no interest whatsoever.

And perhaps that was still the case.

Peder didn't really think the film club was of

any significance, but it was still worth checking out. Fredrika had said it was big news at the time, so it must be possible to find it on the Internet. He typed in the name of the club, The Guardian Angels, and got far too many hits. He tried The Guardian Angels and Thea Aldrin; fewer hits this time. He found both articles and pictures; he wouldn't have time to go through them all. After a quick overview of the available material, he looked at some of the photographs. Like Fredrika, he recognised neither names nor faces, apart from Thea Aldrin and Morgan Axberger.

One last click, one last picture.

And there was something completely unexpected.

A photograph of Spencer Lagergren, with his name in the caption underneath. Linked to both Thea Aldrin and Morgan Axberger.

Peder sat in front of his computer for a long time, trying to digest what he had seen. One thought kept coming back:

There wasn't a cat in hell's chance that Fredrika hadn't found the same information.

# INTERVIEW WITH ALEX RECHT,
## 03-05-2009,
### 10.00 (tape recording)

Present: Urban S, Roger M (interrogators one and two). Alex Recht (witness).

Urban: So you sent Peder Rydh to see Spencer Lagergren's ex-wife in Uppsala?

Alex: Yes.

Urban: Was that a wise move?

Alex: At the time, I decided that the most important thing was to establish whether or not Spencer Lagergren had any place in the investigation. That was why we contacted his ex-wife.

Roger: Is it normal for a murderer to confide in his nearest and dearest that he's planning to kill someone?

Alex: I refuse to answer questions of that nature.

Roger: You are required to answer all our questions.

(Silence.)

Urban: Why wasn't Fredrika Bergman informed immediately?

Alex: We felt it was completely unnecessary to drag her into things before we knew what we were dealing with.

Roger: And Diana Trolle?

Alex: What's she got to do with Spencer Lagergren?

Roger: I'm not talking about a connection between Spencer and Diana, I'm talking about your relationship with her.

Alex: I have no intention of making any bloody comment whatsoever about Diana. That's not why I'm here.

Urban: You're absolutely right, Recht. You're here because you were in charge of an investigation that ended in disaster. And our job is to try to understand how that happened. OK?

(Silence.)

Roger: We realise that it must have been very difficult for you, Alex. Rebecca Trolle was your first serious case after Lena's death.

Alex: Don't you dare bring Lena into this.

Urban: We are merely stating facts. Trying to help you. You had more suspects than you could shake a stick at, and suddenly the partner of one of your colleagues pops up in the investigation. Just when you'd found the solicitor's watch. Of course you were under pressure.

Alex: We didn't know it was the solicitor's watch at that stage.

Roger: What did you actually know?

Alex: We knew that Rebecca was pregnant when she died. That she didn't disappear voluntarily. That she was murdered and her body was dismembered by someone who had murdered thirty years ago.

Roger: So what happened next?

Alex: I had another call from the grave site. I thought they were ringing to tell me they were going to stop digging, but they had other news.

# TUESDAY

# CHAPTER 38

Monday slipped into Tuesday, and Alex was still at Diana's. The situation was the same as the last time: he was sober, sitting on the sofa, and she was reclining in the armchair after a couple of glasses of wine. When Peder called and told him that Spencer had cropped up in the investigation yet again, Alex's first thought was that he must go home. Or back to work. He couldn't think clearly while he was with Diana. And if Fredrika was keeping important information from her colleagues, he really did need to think clearly.

Diana had objected, saying he couldn't leave her when he'd been there for less than an hour. After all, they hadn't even had dinner. Veal casserole with rice and tomatoes.

Alex found himself unable to say no. He didn't *want* to say no, he wanted to stay. They had dinner, including pudding. He drank one glass of wine, then stuck to mineral water. Diana drank two glasses of wine, then showed him a new painting she was working on.

'It's beautiful,' Alex said.

377

They went for a walk and hardly said a word. At one point she slipped her warm hand into his. Stole a glance at his face, trying to work out whether he objected. He didn't, and the hand stayed where it was.

When they got back they had coffee with Italian biscotti in front of the TV in the living room. And now it was gone midnight, and they were still sitting here.

'Valter Lund,' Alex said.

Diana sat up straight. Her expression was suddenly different. Darker, sharper.

'Yes?'

'What do you remember about his relationship with Rebecca?'

Sometimes memory was a misleading source. After the event, people had a tendency to recall things that had never happened, to add or erase details in a way that rendered their testimony worthless.

'I know Rebecca was pleased when she got him as her mentor; she admired his work in the developing countries.'

Diana pursed her lips as she reached for her glass.

'Although I could never really see the point of the mentoring programme. Rebecca had nothing in common with a businessman; she should have been allocated a mentor with some kind of cultural background.'

'How often did they meet up?'

Diana took a sip of her wine.

'Just a few times. At least that's what she told me.'

Alex considered her words. Was Diana hinting that Rebecca might have said something different to someone else?

'Do you think she might have been lying? That she actually saw him more frequently?'

'I don't know; it was just a feeling I had. Rebecca's brother had the same feeling.'

There was a tension in the air that Alex couldn't explain. The mention of Valter Lund's name had set in motion something he didn't understand.

Diana went on: 'Valter Lund came to the church once when Rebecca was singing. Did you know that?'

Alex nodded.

'We didn't think anything of it. Valter Lund has been involved with the church for years, and Rebecca was in the choir. If they were going to meet up anywhere outside the university, it was likely to be there.'

Diana slammed down her glass.

'And why did they have to meet up outside the university? That's what I don't understand.'

'To get to know each other better?' Alex suggested. 'Mentoring is based on trust and respect. Doesn't it seem reasonable for them to see each other under less formal circumstances?'

But that didn't include a weekend in Copenhagen. Alex hesitated; should he tell Diana about the trip?

He cleared his throat.

'Do you know if they ever saw each other outside Stockholm?'

'I don't think so. Why do you ask?'

He shrugged. 'I'm just trying to get a picture of their relationship. Perhaps he took her on business trips?'

'Not that I know of.'

The fact that Diana obviously hadn't known about the weekend in Copenhagen gave Alex pause for thought. How much did his own children keep from him? His son had been living in South America for several years, and his daughter was tight-lipped when it came to information about her family life. Or was it just that he didn't listen? Didn't show any interest?

Diana slid down in the armchair; she was starting to look tired.

I need to go home, Alex thought. I can't risk ending up sitting here all night.

'I just find it so incredibly difficult to accept that she didn't tell me she was pregnant.'

Tears glittered in Diana's eyes, making her more fragile than she already was.

'Perhaps she had good reason to keep it to herself?'

The tears began to fall.

'Like what?'

Good question – what reason would there be to keep quiet about such a thing? Alex had been asking himself the same question ever since they found out about the pregnancy. It occupied an indefinable place in the investigation – sometimes it seemed crucial, at other times insignificant.

'Do you think Valter Lund was the father?' Diana asked.

'No,' said Alex. 'We don't.'

But he didn't tell her that they knew it was Håkan Nilsson. Or that Håkan had disappeared. He made a move; time to go home. Diana stopped crying, dried her eyes and walked with him to the door. He caught himself wishing she would ask him if he wanted to stay, but she didn't. Alex was too insecure to suggest it himself.

# CHAPTER 39

Fresh information had leaked from the police overnight. Thea was watching the news while eating her breakfast. A knife and an axe had been found in the grave and sent to the National Forensics Lab, where they would try to establish whether the traces of blood on the weapons had come from the unidentified man or Rebecca Trolle.

*Neither of them.*

Thea forced herself to eat some of her breakfast. Otherwise, they would start wondering if she was feeling unwell; they would ring the doctor and cause all kinds of problems. A knife and an axe. Thea didn't need to know any more to realise who else was waiting to be dug up by the police.

She felt a stab of anxiety. They mustn't give up, they must carry on digging until all the dirt that had been hidden came to light.

There was a knock on the door, and the new nurse who didn't know how to behave came bustling in.

'Good morning,' she said.

Her voice was shrill enough to crack the window panes.

'You've got a visitor, Thea.'

She stepped aside and a tall figure was visible behind her.

'Good morning,' said Torbjörn Ross. 'I must apologise for disturbing you in the middle of your breakfast.'

He smiled at the nurse as she left the room.

She couldn't believe that he was still pursuing this with such determination. Or that he had the authority. But in fact, she didn't think he had official permission at all. Torbjörn Ross was sick; Thea had realised that a long time ago. His recurring visits had been torture at first, but over the years she had learned that the best thing was simply to ignore him.

As usual, he pulled up a chair and sat down beside her. Too close. As if it wasn't enough that she could hear him; he wanted her to feel his presence as well.

Thea stared at the television and carried on eating.

'I see you're following the Rebecca Trolle story,' Ross said. 'I can understand that.'

He sat there like a king on his chair, his hands in his pockets.

'I'm sure my colleagues will be coming to see you. They know that you and Rebecca Trolle met. It was in her diary.'

Thea remembered the visit, the eager questions.

'I think you can be free again,' the girl had said. 'Clear your name. It's not right for you to be sitting here alone and forgotten.'

She had no idea how Rebecca Trolle had found out everything she knew; it was a mystery. Even though she didn't know everything, she knew enough.

'The nurse said you had a terrible cough last week,' said Torbjörn Ross. He seemed concerned. 'You're no spring chicken; you need to look after yourself.'

He stank of snuff; it made her want to hold her breath.

'This business of not speaking, Thea. You're losing so much.'

He shook his head, looking sympathetic.

'If you could only get this off your chest. We'd all be ready to listen, to help you.'

She would have liked to turn her head and stare at him at this point, but she forced herself to carry on eating her breakfast. Who were 'all' these people who would be ready to help her? During all these years, no one but Torbjörn Ross had continued to visit her. The other police officers didn't care; they had moved on. The case of her missing son was regarded as insoluble, and under the circumstances she was deemed innocent. By everyone except Torbjörn Ross, who wasn't prepared to give her the benefit of the doubt. His obsession with the case terrified her.

She remembered their first meeting. She had immediately been aware that the look in his eyes was somehow different. Cloudy, unclear. Evil in a way that she was sure few people perceived. He had been young then, eager to learn, impatient when other officers wanted to take a break during interrogation. His role had been to sit and listen, to observe his more experienced colleagues.

She had watched him in silence. Seen the contempt that radiated from him behind the backs of his colleagues. He sat by the wall, behind the others, his arms folded, anger emanating from him and filling the entire room.

The first visit was to her cell. She had been afraid at first, thinking that he had come to hurt her. But he had just wanted to talk.

'I know that you know,' he had said. 'And if it takes a lifetime, I will get you to talk so that the rest of us will know too. The boy will have justice. Whatever it costs.'

Many times, she wondered whether she ought to recognise him. Was he an old acquaintance, someone whose path she had crossed? If not, why the hell did he still care? Why did her son mean so much to this one policeman?

After three decades of visits, she thought she knew the answer to that question. Torbjörn Ross was crazy. If Thea wasn't careful, her already wretched life could get even worse.

# CHAPTER 40

Fredrika Bergman was tired. Yet another night when she was unable to settle and get to sleep. Yet another night filled with speculation. Her brain was slow, unwilling to co-operate. Her heart was beating desperately, pumping oxygenated blood around a body that wanted only to rest.

A report from Kripos, the Norwegian National Crime Investigation Service, had been faxed through during the morning and was waiting for her when she got to work. A report on Valter Lund. She hadn't been satisfied with the information that Lund was an immigrant from Norway; she wanted to know more, and had asked her colleagues in Kripos for help. What was his background with regard to education and training? Had he been married? Did he still have family in Norway?

The report was brief. Valter Lund was born in 1962, and grew up in Gol in Norway. His parents were both dead, no siblings. No living grandparents. The only living relative was an uncle who still lived in Gol.

Gol. Fredrika had been there once. It was about

two hundred kilometres from Oslo, a charmless dump not far from the inviting ski slopes of Hemsedal. Low-rise buildings scattered in the middle of nowhere, with a railway line slicing the community in two. Was that where Valter Lund, one of Sweden's most prominent businessmen, had grown up?

According to Kripos, Lund had spent two years at grammar school, and had not fulfilled his compulsory military service. He had a criminal record, and had been punished for a number of minor offences by the age of twenty. His father was heavily involved in criminal activities, and there was a suspicion that his mother had turned to prostitution. The Norwegian tax office had no income details for Valter Lund after 1979. At that point, Valter had declared a minimal income paid out by a shipping company based in Bergen.

Fredrika read through the report again. She didn't know what to think. She tried to remember what she had read about Valter Lund in the past, how he himself usually described his background. Hadn't he said he had a degree in Business Administration? Or was that something she had taken for granted?

She logged onto the Internet, searching for information on Valter Lund. She found plenty of interviews, countless articles, but nothing about his education. Valter Lund, smiling at the camera. Sitting at a desk, standing on a podium, in the back seat of a car. He looked friendly rather than over-confident. He was thinking about those who would be looking at the pictures; he wanted to convey the sense that he was a person who could be trusted. Fredrika met Valter's gaze on the screen, let him get under her skin.

He had taken a different approach when it came to building his brand. He had taken responsibility, acknowledged the fact when he made mistakes. For two years in a row, he had given more than half of his bonus to technological support projects in Africa, south of the Sahara. His visits to places where these projects were running were documented in detail by the press. Valter Lund without a jacket or tie, his sleeves rolled up, his face creased with concern.

Fredrika recalled seeing the articles when they came out. She had admired Valter Lund's generosity and his willingness to make a stand; she knew that he had fallen out with many colleagues in industry who felt that Valter's contributions to development and security put others who gave less in a bad light.

Morgan Axberger had been less keen to open his wallet. In interviews, he naturally made positive comments about Valter Lund's efforts, but he also maintained that the solution to global poverty was not to be found through providing support.

Therefore, while Valter Lund was regarded as warm and generous, Morgan Axberger came across as cynical and hard. Lund was the kid from Norway who had built his own success from nothing; Axberger was the man who had inherited both his position and his wealth. Valter Lund was often heard to say that there should be more women on the boards of major companies, while Axberger would smile with the authority of age when the question arose; in his opinion, the women destined for such a role were already in situ.

Fredrika thought back to the way Alex had almost burst out laughing when she suggested they should interview both Axberger and Lund. She herself found it difficult to see the funny side of the situation. After all, wasn't everyone equal before the law?

For the first time, Peder and Alex were holding a private morning briefing in the Lions' Den, with the door closed and the curtains drawn. None of the other team members had been informed.

'What the hell do we do?' Peder said.

Alex had been thinking about that very question almost all night. He had got home far too late and far too wide awake after visiting Diana. It was rare for those who were grieving to pass on energy to another person, but Diana did.

'This is what I've decided: I'll speak to Fredrika; then you go and pick up Spencer Lagergren. Unless anything else has emerged that changes the situation, in your opinion.'

Peder shook his head sorrowfully.

'I don't understand how she could have kept this information from the team.'

'I do,' Alex said drily. 'She wanted to look into Spencer's involvement herself, rather than bringing in the rest of us, because she's convinced he's innocent. To be honest . . . we would have done the same.'

Peder didn't really want to think about that; he chose to carry on feeling annoyed.

'Did you manage to find out any more about that film club?' Alex asked.

'A bit,' said Peder. 'It seems to have been a grade A gathering for snobs, if you ask me. Very few members with a very low turnover. The first time they were noticed was in 1960, when the four of them turned up at a premiere here in Stockholm, then slated the film in a review in *Dagens Nyheter* the following day.'

'1960? It sounds as if they were active for a long time.'

'Almost fifteen years. And there were never more than four members. Thea Aldrin was there from the start, as was Morgan Axberger. Thea was twenty-four at the time, and Axberger was twenty-one. Did you know that he defied his father for the first few years after his military service, and spent all his time writing poetry?'

Alex was surprised. Morgan Axberger's father had founded the empire his son now headed; Alex had no idea the regime change had been preceded by some kind of rebellion.

Peder noticed his reaction.

'I know, I was surprised too. Anyway, Morgan Axberger had his first collection of poetry published after completing his military service, and it attracted a considerable amount of attention and some very good reviews.'

'And that's how he became a member of The Guardian Angels,' Alex concluded.

He could imagine that Axberger's rebellion would have made an impression on someone like Thea Aldrin, paving the way for all kinds of things.

'Who were the other members?'

Peder took out a sheet of paper with a poor copy of a black and white photograph taken at a film premiere.

'Thea Aldrin and Morgan Axberger.'

He pointed, and Alex followed his finger.

'And this guy on the left, can you guess who he is?'

'Haven't a clue.'

'That's Thea Aldrin's ex, the man she later stabbed to death in her garage.'

Alex let out a whistle.

'He's bloody tall.'

'And she's bloody short. Did you know that he acknowledged paternity of her son?'

Memories of his fishing trip with Torbjörn Ross came back to Alex. The weekend at his colleague's summer cottage had left an increasingly bitter aftertaste. Alex had seen a new side of Ross – a side he didn't like. A side that suggested things weren't quite right.

'So I've heard,' he murmured in reply to Peder's question. 'What was his name, Thea's ex?'

'Manfred Svensson. Apparently, there was a real

scandal over the fact that they were expecting a child and had no intention of getting married.'

Alex looked at the picture again.

'And who's the fourth man?'

'A literary critic who died of a heart attack in 1972. Not exactly a celebrity. He was the one Lagergren replaced, by the way.'

'Do we know how Lagergren became a member?'

'No,' Peder replied. 'No idea. We can ask him when we interview him.'

The unpleasant feeling returned. Interviewing the partner of a colleague was something to be avoided, if possible. Suspecting that a colleague had withheld information during an investigation was even worse.

Alex broke the silence.

'So who replaced Thea's ex when he left the film club after they split up?'

'That's the only person I haven't been able to identify. Some other high flyer, no doubt.'

'And the film club kept going until Thea ended up in prison?'

'Apparently not. For some unknown reason, it was dissolved a few years after Lagergren joined. I don't know why.'

What was the connection between a film club and the disappearance and death of a twenty-three-year-old woman? Why did these odd characters keep on coming up in the investigation, over and over again?

'We started with a bitter ex-girlfriend and a male friend who had a somewhat skewed view of reality, to say the least. We looked into the rumour that Rebecca was selling sex over the Internet; that turned out to be fabricated, but we still don't know why. Then we found a supervisor who got into all kinds of trouble after Rebecca's disappearance, and that led us to Spencer Lagergren. And now the cast has been increased with the addition of one of the country's most noted businessmen. Two, if we include Morgan Axberger.'

Peder considered Alex's summary, and added:

'And in the middle of the spider's web we have a silent writer who was convicted for the murder of her ex, and whose son is missing.'

A thought drifted through his mind; Alex only just managed to catch it.

'Actually, it's Thea Aldrin who links this whole mess together.'

He frowned.

'According to her diary, Rebecca went to see Thea. You have to wonder why; her silence isn't exactly a secret.'

'We ought to go and see her as well,' Peder suggested.

'Later. We're not going to try to interview a woman who has remained silent for several decades until we know exactly what we want to find out.'

'Where does she live?'

'I haven't checked yet; a care home, I think.'

'Isn't she too young to be in a home?'

'Yes, but she had a severe stroke during her last

year in prison, and I don't think she can look after herself.'

There was a knock on the door. Fredrika walked in, catching them red-handed. Alex caught himself hunching his shoulders as if he were ashamed.

Fredrika's face, full of questions. Unease in her dark eyes. Far too intelligent to be easily deceived.

'Hello, there!'

Alex's voice grated as he spoke; he grinned nervously. And 'hello there' – what was that about?

'Hi.'

Her expression was non-committal.

'Am I disturbing you?'

'No, no, come on in.'

She sat down at the table. She was carrying a sheaf of papers; it looked as if she wanted to discuss something important.

'What did Diana say when you spoke to her?'

Alex didn't know what to say. Diana? How did Fredrika . . .

'You were going to ask her about Valter Lund and the trip to Copenhagen,' Fredrika clarified.

The relief was so great that he almost burst out laughing.

'As I understood it she had no knowledge of the trip, but she had actually found it strange that Lund came to listen to Rebecca sing in church.'

'There are a number of strange things about Valter Lund,' Fredrika said.

She told them what she had found out from their colleagues in Norway.

'We ought to interview him,' she said. 'And Morgan Axberger. I want to find out more about this film club, and everything that happened around Thea during those years.'

Alex and Peder exchanged a glance, reaching silent agreement.

'We'll wait until we find the woman who bought the gold watch,' Alex said slowly. 'Let's get together after lunch and see where we stand.'

Fredrika was suddenly alert.

'Has something happened?' she asked.

'We'll discuss it after lunch,' Alex insisted.

There was another knock on the door, and Ellen came in.

Pale and shaken.

She said the words no one wanted to hear:

'They've just called from the grave site. They've found another body.'

# CHAPTER 41

If the sun hadn't been shining during the day, Håkan Nilsson wasn't sure if he could have coped with staying on the boat. The night had been chilly, and the dampness on board had made his skin feel clammy. He hadn't bothered to repair the cockpit in the past, and the cool night air soon found its way inside.

He had never thought about living on the boat. Not even as a joke. He had bought it a few summers ago with a friend. The plan had been to impress Rebecca; he knew that she loved the lake and the sea. But she hadn't been all that interested, and after only one season his friend had changed his mind. Håkan bought him out and kept the boat. He chugged slowly through the Karlberg canal, seeing Stockholm from a completely fresh perspective. He enjoyed the fresh air, loved the sense of freedom.

He felt safe on the boat, and the club members valued him for his commitment. Håkan was always ready to volunteer; he painted the jetties and varnished the floor of the clubhouse veranda.

He had hoped that Rebecca would want to share

the experience with him, but she stayed away, didn't want to know when he was making his plans for a summer on the boat.

'We don't have that kind of relationship, Håkan,' she had said.

That was the summer before everything happened, the summer before she went missing. Autumn came, then winter. And suddenly she was pregnant.

*With his child.*

He had found the ultrasound scan by accident when he was visiting her in the student hostel. He had wondered what it was, asked where it had come from. She had snatched the picture from him, said it was nothing to do with him.

It hurt to remember his fury. How he had completely lost it, yelling over and over again:

'Is it mine? Is it? Answer me, for fuck's sake!'

And she had replied that she didn't know.

Håkan covered his ears with his hands, trying to shut out the sound of her voice which seemed to echo out across the lake.

*I don't know who the father is.*

He sat down, resting one foot on the reserve tank of petrol in the stern. How long would he have to stay away? How long would it be before they realised he had a boat? If the police found out what he had said to Rebecca that night when he found the ultrasound image of the child, they would lock him up and throw away the key. He would never be able to convince them of his innocence.

*But it wasn't my fault.*

Lake Mälaren was vast, with plenty of places to hide. At the same time he didn't want to go too far away, to become so isolated that he might start to feel forgotten. He had anchored up in Alviken. At first he had thought of mooring off the island of Ekerö, but then he carried on past both Ekerö and Stenhamra. He wanted to put a reassuring distance between himself and all the terrible things that were going on.

Håkan heaved himself up from the floor and lay down on the short, cushioned seat. The boat was quite a good place to sleep, even if it wasn't nearly as comfortable as home. He had brought plenty of food and drink; he should be able to stay away for a week at any rate.

A week.

That was quite a short amount of time, really. He had no idea what he would do after that.

A fresh wave of despair washed over him. Everything was irretrievably ruined. His father would never come back, and neither would Rebecca. The child she had been expecting was gone too.

Håkan curled up on his cushion. He had to make a decision. Because at the end of the day, did it really matter if he disappeared as well?

# CHAPTER 42

For the third time in a week, Alex Recht was driving from police HQ in Kungsholmen to the grave site in Midsommarkransen. It was warm and sunny to a degree that seemed incomprehensible for the time of year.

The news that yet another body had been found in the grave had upended all their plans. Fredrika was told to carry on looking for the woman who had bought the gold watch, while Peder accompanied Alex to Midsommarkransen.

'I've got a bad feeling about this,' Peder said in the car.

'Me too, but I don't see how I could have prioritised things any other way,' Alex said.

Peder glanced at him.

'It's not about prioritising, it's about this whole bloody case. For example, what do we do with Lagergren now?'

'He can wait,' Alex replied.

It was a real effort not to add: We've got all the time in the world.

Because that was how it felt. As if the new horrors that had been unearthed altered the landscape, creating a sense that everything had changed. Even though they didn't understand how or why.

Eventually, Peder commented: 'You seem to be taking this very calmly.'

Alex wasn't sure whether he could find the words to describe his intuitive thoughts properly, but he made an attempt.

'I've got a feeling that we shouldn't regard this new victim as a setback. I think it might explain a great deal, fill in the gaps in the story.'

Peder's expression was sceptical as his boss parked the car.

'Fill in the gaps?'

'Come on,' Alex said, opening the door.

The ground was silent beneath their feet, while the trees towered above them as magnificently as before. They walked the four hundred metres from the car to the site. The same route the perpetrator must have taken. Not once, not twice, but three times. With a dead body in his arms. Or on his back. Or in two black bin bags.

They stopped at the edge of the crater, amazed at the extent of the area that had been excavated.

'This is the end of the road,' said the DI who was in charge of the dig. 'We'd already made the decision before we found the body; we're not going any further than the police tape over there.' He pointed. 'Beyond that, the ground is full of stones and roots; there's no chance that anyone has been digging there.'

'How are you coping with the press?' Alex asked.

'Not too well. The reporters are starting to lose both patience and respect; they're pushing and pushing to find out what we're doing. I've had to use several officers to guard the area, which is why the digging process has been so slow.'

Alex gazed out across the crater. Earth had been dug out, sifted through and piled up around the edge, creating high ramparts that provided a natural defence against curious onlookers.

'We meet again.'

The voice of the forensic pathologist came from down in the crater. He nodded to Alex, then clambered up the ladder, brushing the dirt from his knees.

'What can you tell us?' Alex asked.

The pathologist squinted at Alex, then moved so that the sun wasn't in his eyes.

'Next to nothing. I'll have to get back to you when I've had the chance to take a closer look at the body in the lab.'

The air that found its way into Alex's lungs as he breathed in was almost warm enough for summer. Birds flitted playfully among the trees.

'Is it a man or a woman?'

'I don't think you understood what I said, Alex. Go down and have a look at the body for yourself before we take it away.'

Alex's legs refused to move; he didn't know if he wanted to see what had been revealed down in that hell hole.

'I can have a look,' Peder offered.

'I'll go first,' Alex said.

He grabbed hold of the ladder and began to make his way down. He felt it sink slightly into the ground and wondered if it might tip over and dump him on top of the corpse.

'The body is a few metres behind you,' the pathologist said.

Alex reached the bottom and turned around. He saw a tarpaulin that was being used as a temporary cover for the body. He went over and crouched down. He could feel the eyes of his colleagues on his back as he lifted the plastic to see what it was hiding.

He couldn't stop himself from recoiling.

He heard the pathologist's voice behind him:

'Now do you understand?'

Peder arrived and looked over his shoulder.

'Bloody hell.'

Alex rearranged the tarpaulin and got to his feet. A skeleton, nothing more.

'How long has he or she been here?'

'Hard to say exactly. All I can tell you is that it's a very old body. It's been in the ground for decades. Even longer than the man we found last week.'

The pathologist used the word 'we' as if he were a part of the team investigating the case. And in a way he was. Alex liked his approach; he was in favour of including all the relevant parties in the investigation.

They clambered out of the crater.

'So this is the last day of digging?' Alex said to the DI in charge.

'Everyone agrees that we won't find anything in the rocky areas.'

'That's not what I asked.'

'The answer is yes, this is the last day of digging.'

A breeze ruffled the tops of the trees, sending up a faint cloud of dust from the piles of earth. Alex felt as if evil were burning beneath his feet.

'Fine,' he said.

He nodded to Peder to indicate that it was time to head back to the car. He had no desire whatsoever to stay here.


Fredrika fingered the gold watch in her hands. The gold watch that had been found in the grave, and would hopefully give them the name of the unidentified man.

'Carry me. Your Helena.'

A beautiful, ambiguous inscription.

Carry me.

Would Fredrika have said something like that to another person? She didn't think so.

'That's lovely,' Ellen said when she came into Fredrika's office and saw the watch.

'Classic,' said Fredrika, stroking the watch, which had stopped long ago.

Ellen sat down.

'I checked the address we got from the watchmaker against the property database, but it's impossible to see who used to live there. And there's no Helena at that address today.'

She handed Fredrika a Post-it note.

'But this is the phone number of the chair of the residents' association. He ought to be able to find her in their records. Do you want me to call, or would you prefer to do it?'

Fredrika shrugged; she was feeling unsettled after finding Alex and Peder closeted in the den.

Something had happened. And they weren't telling her what it was.

'I can do it.'

After a brief hesitation, she asked:

'Ellen, do you know if anything in particular has happened over the last few days?'

She could see that Ellen didn't understand the badly phrased question.

'To do with the case, I mean.'

Ellen looked unsure of herself.

'I don't think so.'

Was she lying? Fredrika didn't know for certain; she felt as if time was running through her fingers like sand, and she was fighting against become paranoid. There had been another body in the grave, carelessly tossed into a hole by strong arms that ruled over life and death with utter ruthlessness.

Who are you? Fredrika thought. Who are you, creeping through the forest time after time, decade after decade, with your silenced victims?

*Spencer?*

The thought could not be allowed to take shape; it was obliterated before it even existed.

What possible motivation could there be behind such deeds? Fredrika was afraid there might be more victims. She pictured a body under every tree in the forest. Reason told her that couldn't possibly be the case, but at the same time reason was notable by its absence in the investigation she was working on.

Spencer.

Whom Rebecca Trolle had tried to get in touch with. Who had been a member of the same film club as Thea Aldrin. Who wouldn't say why he was so tense and unhappy. Fredrika didn't really believe for a moment that Spencer was involved, but she hated constantly stumbling over leads connected to him. Her sense of frustration grew, and she could feel the tears threatening.

*I am bloody well not going to be the kind of person who sits at her desk crying.*

She looked at the note with the phone number of the residents' association and picked up the phone. She raised her hand to key in the number, but keyed in a different number altogether. She called the switchboard at the University of Uppsala and asked to be put through to Erland Malm, Spencer's Head of Department.

Spencer would never forgive her. But she had to know. She had never exchanged confidences with Erland Malm in the past, but as someone close to Spencer, she surely had the right to call and ask what had happened. At least that was what she told herself.

Erland's voice was as deep as ever when he answered. Only Spencer's was deeper. And only

Spencer was more popular than Erland, more successful. It was fortunate for Erland that Spencer had never wanted the kind of power and influence that went with the role of head of department.

'Hello, Erland, it's Fredrika Bergman.'

How many times had she and Erland met? Quite a few. From an early stage Erland had been aware of her relationship with Spencer, and had accepted the fact that she would turn up like an extra piece of luggage at various conferences. He had always been polite, never condescending like some others, who knew the situation and despised her. As the Other Woman, she was regarded as a loser, while Spencer was seen as cock of the walk.

She tried to put her anxiety into words, hesitant at first, then with increasing assurance.

'What's happened? I don't recognise him these days.'

A lump formed in her throat; she swallowed to get rid of it. She felt she ought to end the call, but was struck by Erland's silence.

'The thing is, Fredrika, I can't really discuss this matter. You must realise that. You need to speak to Spencer.'

'I'm afraid I don't even know what I'm supposed to realise. And I *have* spoken to Spencer. Several times. He won't tell me anything; he just freezes me out.'

The words turned into a physical pain in her chest. She didn't want to be pushed away when she had exposed herself like this.

406

*Help me, for God's sake.*

Erland's voice was full of hesitation when he spoke.

'We've found ourselves in a rather tricky situation, to say the least. Last autumn Spencer was supervising a young woman, Tova Eriksson. Has he mentioned her?'

'In passing. He said she wasn't happy.'

Erland laughed wearily.

'That's one way of putting it, I suppose. No, she wasn't happy. She's accused him of sexual harassment, Fredrika. And of having used his position of power to obtain sexual services.'

Fredrika was dumbstruck.

Empty.

'What? This has to be a misunderstanding.'

Erland's tone became harsh.

'The department cannot express a view on the issue of culpability; we have to . . .'

'Of course you bloody can!' Fredrika yelled.

'She's reported him to the police. We have no choice but to await the results of the police investigation.'

Police. Sexual services. Spencer's sudden desire to take his paternity leave.

'Has he been sacked?'

'Originally, he was encouraged to take some time off, but as soon as Tova Eriksson reported him to the police he was formally suspended.'

There was nothing more to say. Fredrika ended the call, felt the fight go out of her. What else had

Spencer lied about? In Fredrika's mind there had never been any secrets between them. Cards on the table, all the way; that was what had carried their relationship forward.

Should she go home? Interrupt her working day to grab hold of him, shake him, curse him for keeping quiet about all this?

*Rebecca Trolle.*

Fredrika knew instinctively that Spencer had nothing to do with the case. The fact that he had been a member of the film club was irrelevant, it had nothing to do with Rebecca's death. But what about this other student, the one who had reported him to the police? Was there even a grain of truth in her story?

There couldn't be.

There *mustn't* be.

Fredrika knew that she was off balance, that she wouldn't be able to handle a confrontation with Spencer while her disappointment over the fact that he had kept his problems from her was bubbling away inside her.

She picked up the Post-it note Ellen had given her and keyed in the telephone number. The chair of the residents' association answered almost immediately. He listened to her explanation, then said:

'I know which apartment you mean. It was sold two years ago. The name of the previous owner is Helena Hjort.'

# CHAPTER 43

I t was still early in the morning when Spencer Lagergren presented himself at the passport office in the police station on Kungsholmsgatan. He glanced at Saga in her buggy, thinking that they were close to Fredrika. He had no intention of calling in to see her. The call from her colleague, combined with the fact that the same colleague had been to see Eva, frightened him. From being suspected of sexual harassment and the abuse of power, he now appeared to be a suspect in a murder investigation. Why else would they ask about that bloody conference, which was an alibi in a way?

Perhaps he was even suspected of *several* murders.

There were unconfirmed rumours all over the radio and television, suggesting that yet another body had been found in Midsommarkransen. It seemed unlikely that the police would suspect him of one murder, and not the other. Spencer didn't know what to think; he just wished the whole sorry mess was a bad dream, and that he would soon wake up.

There were four numbers ahead of him in the queue; with a bit of luck he would be seen before Saga woke up.

His whole body was aching with anxiety; the feeling that he was genuinely miserable was growing stronger with every passing day. He knew he should have spoken to Fredrika. Right from the start. Had confidence in her, trusted that she would believe him.

The anxiety turned to anger. Because Spencer wasn't the only one who should have revealed his secrets. She had asked him straight out if he had known Rebecca Trolle, then turned away, pretended that there was no particular reason for her question.

It didn't make any sense.

How could she trust him at home alone with her child all day if she secretly suspected that he had murdered several people? Hacked a young woman's body to pieces, carried those pieces through a forest, dropped them into a hole in the ground and walked away?

*We don't know each other at all, do we?*

He loved to remember their first meeting, at a time when they were both somehow more undamaged, their relationship undemanding. They saw each other when they had the time, the desire, the opportunity. The relationship had been both innocent and sinful: innocent because it was characterised by a rare honesty, and sinful because he was married.

They had had so much in common. Interests and values. On those rare occasions when they fell out, love quickly mended what was broken.

Their mutual dependency, their need, bound them closer and closer, and they began to meet with increasing frequency. They had taken risks, put Spencer's colleagues in a difficult situation when Fredrika discreetly arrived at conferences, creeping into his room and sharing his bed.

It was almost two years since she had turned everything upside down by telling him how much she longed for a baby. She had talked about adopting a child from China, bringing it up without a father on the scene. Without him. Once he got over the shock, he had made himself clear: he would like to give her a child, if that was what she wanted.

Give. Like a bunch of flowers.

He had sounded like someone from another century, and yet she had said yes. Said there was no one she would rather have as the father of her child. As if she had several candidates to choose from.

Spencer was woken from his reverie by the fact that it was his turn. He had requested an urgent meeting with his solicitor, and had explained the situation in which he believed he now found himself. Uno, his solicitor, had gone pale and said: 'How the hell did you end up in this mess, Spencer?'

The answer was that he didn't have a clue. And his friend had no advice to offer. Spencer would just have to wait; if the police seriously suspected him of murder, he would be brought in for questioning and presumably held in custody if they

411

believed he was dangerous. Which they really ought to do, given the crimes of which he was suspected.

He had no trouble in deciding on a course of action. After leaving the solicitor's office, Spencer went straight home and dug out his passport. He had had enough of all the crap; if things got worse he wanted to be able to leave the country quickly. Temporarily. For the sake of his own peace of mind.

But his passport was only a few months from its expiry date, which limited the number of countries to which he could travel. Therefore, like the lost soul he had become, he marched straight down to the passport office to apply for a new one.

As a last resort.

If it should become necessary.

Back at HQ, Alex and Peder swept down the corridor and disappeared into their respective offices. Peder switched on his computer and checked his messages. Fredrika walked in, her face rigid, her eyes full of sorrow. In a way, Peder felt as if he had foregone his right to ask her what had happened, since he was preparing to question her partner.

'Helena Hjort,' Fredrika said.

She sank down on a chair, tiredness etched on her face.

Peder felt a burst of renewed energy.

'Is she the person who bought the gold watch?'

Fredrika nodded.

'I managed to identify her with the help of the

chairman of the residents' association, and I've got her current address. She lives in the Söder district, at Vita bergen.'

Peder leaned forward eagerly, keen to hear more.

'Have you called her?'

'I thought I might go over there.'

A brief hesitation, as if she was considering whether to add something.

'Would you like to come with me?'

They had worked together for two years, and never once had she asked him to go anywhere with her.

'Of course,' he said. 'Absolutely.'

He finished what he was doing and popped into Alex's office to tell him where they were going.

'I thought you and I had something else to take care of.'

*Spencer Lagergren.*

'Couldn't we do that later?'

Alex didn't raise any objections. He was just as loath as Peder to tackle the thorny issue of Spencer Lagergren.

'What was that all about?' Fredrika asked as they were walking to the car.

Peder hated playing the role of Judas; he felt the lie stick in his throat as he spoke.

'Nothing in particular.'

Fredrika could probably make a living as a mind-reader if she left the police; Peder could feel her eyes burning into his back, and he knew she didn't believe him.

He had to smooth over his sin, hide it. He turned to face her.

'Honestly, it was nothing.'

'Right.'

The silence in the car was dense. Buildings lined the road, the sky was a clear blue with so much sunshine it almost felt unreal. The car sped across Västerbron and cut through Södermalm.

'I don't want to go via Slussen,' he said. 'Too much bloody traffic.'

Fredrika said nothing; she didn't care which way he went.

He glanced at her profile, trying to work out what she was thinking. He wanted to apologise, but he didn't know how or for what. He pulled up outside the block where Helena Hjort allegedly lived. According to the records, she was single and childless. She had been married, but not since 1980, and her ex-husband had emigrated the following year.

Emigrated. Both Peder and Fredrika had reacted to that piece of information, as if they had expected it to say 'buried'. If people really did think he had emigrated, and if he had no other ties to Sweden, it was less surprising that no one had reported him missing.

'We need the names of friends and acquaintances,' Fredrika said as they made their way up the stairs. 'We must be able to trace him somehow.'

'You don't think it's his body we found?'

'I think we might have found his watch. If Helena

bought the watch for him in the first place. But it seems odd that a man who emigrated could lie dead for thirty years without anyone missing him.'

Peder's jaw muscles tensed; he would have liked to run up the rest of the stairs.

Helena Hjort was an old woman, almost eighty. There was a distinct possibility that she wouldn't be as much help as they might have wished.

Lonely, Peder thought as they rang the bell. She must be incredibly lonely.

The door opened and an elderly woman appeared. She was the epitome of a Bohemian singleton who had survived the winter. Her clothes were so colourful they were almost painful to look at.

Peder allowed Fredrika to take the lead; she introduced them and explained why they were there.

'We wondered whether you've seen this before.'

The gold watch on Fredrika's open palm made Helena Hjort take a step backwards.

'Where did you find that?'

'Perhaps we could come inside?'

The apartment was enchanting. The ceilings were almost four metres high, wonderful stucco work, white walls and freshly polished floorboards. Discreet works of art on the walls, with only a small number of personal photographs on display. The curtains would have made Peder's mother green with envy, as would the authentic rugs on the floor.

Helena Hjort showed them into the living room, indicating that they should sit down on the large sofa facing the window. She sat down on one of the armchairs opposite.

Fredrika passed her the watch, observing Helena as she examined it.

'We found it in an area that was being excavated in Midsommarkransen,' she said.

Helena raised her eyebrows.

'Excavated?'

'I'm sure you've heard about it on the news,' Peder said. 'The body of a young woman was found there at the beginning of last week. Her name was Rebecca Trolle.'

Helena leaned back in her chair.

'You found a man's body too.'

'Yes, and unfortunately we haven't been able to identify him so far,' Peder said. 'But we found this watch a short distance away from him, and we believe it was buried at the same time.'

He spoke quietly and in a matter-of-fact tone.

'And you think the watch might have belonged to this man?'

'Yes,' Fredrika said.

Helena Hjort weighed the watch in her hand; she seemed to disappear to a place where she was no longer accessible. The watch had brought back memories, and Peder no longer had any doubt that she was the one who had bought it.

'I bought it in 1979,' she said. 'For my husband, Elias Hjort. It was a present for his fiftieth birthday. We had a big party in our apartment; lots of people came.'

Helena got up and fetched a photograph album. Peder watched the way she moved; she was a lot more supple than most of the eighty-year-olds he had met.

She put down the album in front of Peder and Fredrika, showing them a picture of her husband Elias on his fiftieth birthday. A tall, imposing man with a forbidding expression. The watch was on his wrist.

'Elias was always a melancholy soul, all the way through our marriage. Perhaps it was the fact that we didn't have children, but I think he suffered from depression as well. In those days, things were very different when it came to psychiatry; you didn't seek help because you were feeling low. You just gritted your teeth and carried on.'

Peder looked at the photograph of Elias Hjort; he felt as if he recognised him.

'What did he do?'

'He was a solicitor.'

It looked as if Helena had intended to say something else, but decided to keep quiet.

'Where is he living now?' Peder asked.

Helena gazed at the watch, still in her hand.

'He moved to Switzerland in 1981, the year after our divorce went through.'

She raised her head and looked Peder straight in the eye.

'But you think it's his body you've found in Midsommarkransen, don't you?'

'We think so, but we're not sure. Now we have

a name for the recipient of the watch, we hope to be able to confirm his identity with the help of dental records.'

Helena put down the watch, a thoughtful expression on her face. She didn't seem upset: Had she already had an idea that he had never emigrated at all?

'Did you have any contact after he moved to Switzerland?' Fredrika asked, as if she could read Peder's mind.

'No,' said Helena. 'No, we didn't. We didn't have any contact at all, in fact.'

'When was the last time you saw him?'

'February 1981. He came to see me in our old apartment and told me he was moving abroad.'

'Did that surprise you?'

'Of course it did. He'd never even mentioned it before.'

'Did he say why he was moving?'

A smile flitted across Helena's face, disappearing so quickly that Peder wasn't sure if he'd really seen it.

'No, he didn't. And we had no contact after that, as I said.'

Fredrika straightened up, rested her hands on her knees and reflected in silence on what she had learned about the couple's marriage from the police database.

'Isn't that a little odd? I mean, you were married for over twenty years, after all. Did he never come back to Stockholm? Didn't you write to one another?'

Helena grew pensive.

'I'm not sure I find it acceptable that I should have to defend the fact that I had no contact with my ex-husband after he left the country. We didn't have all that much contact after the divorce, while he was still living in Stockholm. I think we both felt we needed a clean break.'

But why did a couple who had been married for over twenty years suddenly decide to get a divorce? What could cause such a split that there was no further communication? Peder thought of Ylva and their temporary separation. If it hadn't been for the boys, would they have broken off all contact? He didn't think so.

'Why did you divorce?' he asked, hoping the question was neither too direct nor insensitive.

'For several reasons. We no longer had any common interests or shared values.' She hesitated. 'Over the years he developed a lifestyle and an attitude to life that I didn't wish to be a part of.'

'Were you the one who instigated the divorce?' Fredrika asked.

'Yes.'

Peder sensed that Helena was getting impatient; she had had enough of their personal questions. He changed direction.

'Did Elias have any enemies?'

Helena brushed a hair from the leg of her trousers.

'None that I know of.'

'We're asking because he was a solicitor,'

Fredrika explained. 'Perhaps he upset one of his clients?'

'Who killed him and buried him in Midsommarkransen?'

Fredrika didn't respond.

'No,' Helena said. 'I don't think he had any enemies like that.'

'Was he part of a larger firm, or did he have his own practice?'

'He worked on his own; he had no colleagues.'

'Did you have any mutual friends who might have been in touch with him after he left Stockholm?'

Helena shook her head.

'I couldn't say. Our mutual friends turned out to be his friends after the divorce,' she said drily. 'But while we were married, he was something of a recluse; perhaps our mutual friends weren't really friends at all.'

Peder saw Fredrika make a note on the pad she always carried with her. They had only one question left.

'Rebecca Trolle,' he said. 'Have you ever met her?'

For the first time he got a reaction from Helena.

'The girl who was found dead? No, definitely not.'

'Are you quite sure?' Fredrika asked.

'Quite sure.'

There was no hesitation in either the tone of her voice or her choice of words, unfortunately.

Something was niggling away at Peder; he couldn't for the life of him think why he recognised Elias Hjort.

'In that case, we won't disturb you any longer,' he said. 'Could we possibly take one of these pictures of Elias with us?'

When they got back to HQ, Fredrika headed for her office while Peder went to see Alex. He wanted to discuss Spencer Lagergren, to find out how they were going to divide up the rest of the working day. Fredrika saw where he was going and followed him.

'I was just going to discuss something with Alex,' Peder said. He stopped, not wanting her to go with him.

He saw the change in her expression. She had looked tired and worried before they went to see Helena; but during their visit, she had brightened up considerably. But now, that brightness faded once more. Peder knew she must be wondering about all these meetings that were suddenly taking place behind closed doors.

'What?'

'Just something we talked about earlier.'

Peder felt under so much pressure that fear almost spilled over into irritation. It was a reflex defence mechanism, and his therapist had told him he must work to stop it happening.

'Something that I and the rest of the team are not allowed to share?'

421

Peder didn't know what to say.

Fredrika's eyes suddenly shone with tears. She had had enough.

'Is it to do with Spencer?'

Peder stiffened. He raised his head and met her gaze.

Alex had heard their voices and came out into the corridor. He looked from one to the other.

'Has something happened?'

'That's exactly what I'm wondering,' Fredrika said.

In the tense silence that followed, Peder finally realised where he had seen Elias Hjort before.

'Elias Hjort was a member of Thea Aldrin's film club.'

# CHAPTER 44

It could of course be a figment of her imagination, but Thea had the distinct feeling that she was being watched. She peered discreetly out of the window, trying to see who was moving around out there. It could be one of the young people from the assisted living project across the garden. If that was the case, she would feel much calmer.

The memory of Torbjörn Ross's visit still lingered, almost as palpable as a smell. He had changed; he was more driven than he used to be. It was as if everything had been ramped up several notches, become more of a strain.

*Why couldn't he just let go, leave everything alone?*

Thea had never understood how Rebecca Trolle had managed to get so far with her research. She had, of course, not managed to go all the way, but she had got close enough. At first she had just talked about *Mercury* and *Asteroid*, about Box, the firm responsible for their publication, and about the film club. She would have been able to read up on all that in old newspapers.

But then she had begun to talk about the

423

unmentionable. About the film and the police investigation. About Elias Hjort. And that was when Thea had realised the girl was in trouble.

Elias Hjort, the stupid solicitor who hadn't done a single thing right in his entire life. Who had not carried out the task with which Thea had entrusted him, but had tried to use it to his own advantage instead. Thea was certain it was his body the police had found in Midsommarkransen. They should have identified him by now, worked out who he was and what role he had played in the drama that was still claiming its victims thirty years on. Her thoughts turned to Helena, Elias's wife, who deserved better. They could have been good friends, Thea and Helena, if only Helena hadn't l listened to gossip and started to imagine things.

The film club had been Morgan Axberger's idea, in spite of the fact that the media claimed at an early stage that it had been Thea's. He was right in the middle of his delayed teenage rebellion, and was more eccentric than all the rest of them put together. Thea recalled that her first impression of him had been positive. He was one of the few who didn't condemn the fact that Thea and Manfred wanted nothing to do with the institution of marriage, and that they intended to bring a child into the world without getting married.

'What's important to one person is of no importance to another,' Morgan had said.

It was Morgan who recruited Elias into the film club. And then Spencer Lagergren. Spencer had always been too young, in Thea's opinion. He wasn't rich enough to catch up with the others. He was bright – sometimes brilliant – but far too inexperienced to bring anything of value to their discussions. Besides which, Morgan and Elias thought he drank too little.

Thea sighed, wishing all those old memories would go away.

She got up and switched on the TV; she wanted to watch the lunchtime news. The police had confirmed the rumours: another body had been discovered. They were not prepared to give any details regarding age or gender. Thea followed the story, wide-eyed. How long would it take before they worked out how everything hung together?

She felt sick as she thought about the latest body that had been dug up. If she had been younger she would have felt embarrassment and revulsion over what would now be revealed about her past, but she was over seventy, and couldn't have cared less. The only thing that bothered her was her son.

However, if they hadn't managed to find him in thirty years, there was no reason to believe they would find him now.

# CHAPTER 45

They couldn't deal with everything at once, even if that would have been desirable. The realisation was painful, and Alex was finding it almost impossible to prioritise. In the end, he decided it was high time to prepare to question Valter Lund, but first he wanted Spencer Lagergren brought in so that they could find out once and for all what the man knew, and eliminate him from their inquiries. Now that they had found another body and identified the man with the gold watch, Spencer was no longer so interesting. In spite of his connection with the film club, he was too young; he hadn't been a member for long enough. However, he still had to be questioned.

Alex had a serious conversation with Fredrika on the matter.

'You withheld information,' he said. 'That's professional misconduct. I could have you out of here like that.'

He clicked his fingers.

'I didn't withhold anything,' she said. 'I chose to save us from following yet another lead, if Spencer had nothing to do with all this.'

'And how were you planning on finding out whether he had anything to do with it or not?'

Fredrika hadn't been able to come up with an answer to that question, so their conversation was quite short.

'What are you going to do?' she asked.

Her expression was anxious; no doubt she was terrified of losing her job.

'I ought to report you,' Alex said. 'But unfortunately, I can't afford to lose a member of the team who is more or less brilliant the rest of the time.'

That had come from the heart, and his words went straight to Fredrika's heart in turn. She was, however, removed from any further contact with Spencer Lagergren as far as the investigation was concerned.

'You are not to call home and tell him about this,' Alex said, stressing every word. 'You carry on working on your other tasks, and Peder and I will take care of Spencer as soon as possible.'

'Saga,' Fredrika said.

'I'll let you know when we're going to bring him in,' Alex said. 'You can go home and look after her for as long as necessary.'

That had been Alex's intention before lunch, when he still believed that time was on his side. But as two o'clock approached and they started trying to track down Spencer Lagergren to ask him to come to the police station straight away, it proved impossible to get hold of him. His mobile was switched off, and no one answered the door when they sent a patrol car to Fredrika and Spencer's apartment.

For some reason, Spencer's silence worried Alex. He couldn't shake off the feeling that he had missed something obvious, and he couldn't settle. He didn't really want to ask Fredrika if she knew where Spencer might have gone.

Peder came into Alex's office.

'Shall we move on to Valter Lund, since we can't find Lagergren?'

Alex's mouth narrowed to a thin line.

'Call and make an appointment to see Valter Lund to begin with,' he said. 'Say we'd like to see him today, if possible. In the evening, if necessary.'

Peder swallowed.

'The press will go crazy.'

Alex suppressed a sigh.

'We no longer have a choice. And besides, we're only questioning him in order to obtain information, remember that.'

The sense of impotence was eating away at Fredrika Bergman from inside and out. Her colleagues were on their way to pick up her partner so that they could question him about several murders, while she was expected to sit in her office and carry on working. As if nothing had happened.

The fear had an almost anaesthetising effect. What would remain of her relationship with Spencer when all this was over? And what about the accusation that had been made against him in Uppsala? The very idea that he might have forced himself on a female student made her feel sick.

It couldn't possibly be true.

*It mustn't be true.*

She gazed at her desk, trying to put together all the little pieces of the jigsaw to form a picture that made sense. A coherent picture.

A young female student, four months pregnant, thrown into a grave alongside a solicitor aged about fifty, who had already been lying there for almost thirty years. One single common denominator: Thea Aldrin, a children's writer who had been sentenced to life imprisonment, and who was now growing old in self-imposed silence in a care home.

If it hadn't been for the fact that Thea didn't communicate with the outside world, Fredrika would have already been on her way to the home to insist on questioning her.

Someone knocked on Fredrika's door, interrupting her thoughts as if bursting a bubble. Torbjörn Ross was standing there.

'Am I disturbing you?'

He was smiling warmly.

'Not at all,' Fredrika replied.

Alex had told her about their colleague's involvement in the original Thea Aldrin case, and had mentioned that Ross was still visiting the old lady in the hope that she would one day confess to the murder of her son. Fredrika found this somewhat repugnant, but welcomed him with a smile anyway.

Her cheeks felt tight, as if her face was trying not to co-operate. She had no reason to smile. She had no *time* to smile.

Torbjörn Ross walked in and sat down opposite her.

'I heard a rumour that you'd identified the man in the grave,' he said.

'We think we have,' said Fredrika. 'But we haven't yet received confirmation.'

'Who is he?'

'His name is Elias Hjort.'

Torbjörn stared at her with such intensity that it was painful to meet his gaze.

'Elias Hjort?' he repeated.

She nodded. 'Does the name mean anything to you?'

'Too bloody right it does.'

His voice was hoarse with tension. Fredrika dropped the pen she was holding, heard it land on the desk.

'Have you heard of two books entitled *Mercury* and *Asteroid*?' he asked.

His eyes were burning, dark as a winter's night.

'The books Thea Aldrin was accused of having written under a pseudonym. But nothing was ever proved.'

Torbjörn let out a harsh laugh, devoid of pleasure.

'We followed the money trail, which is the way

the real person behind a pseudonym has always been exposed,' he said.

He leaned back in his chair and ran a hand over his face.

'We forced the publisher, Box, to tell us who received the royalties for the books.'

Fredrika frowned.

'Why did you do that? The books were hardly illegal, after all.'

Torbjörn ignored her comment.

'The money was paid to Elias Hjort. Not in the capacity of author, but as the legal representative of the author. But when we went looking for him to find out exactly who he was representing, he had already left the country. And we never managed to track him down.'

He laughed again.

'Hardly surprising, if he was buried in Midsommarkransen all along.'

'Why did you want to find out who'd written the books?' Fredrika asked again.

'Because of the film.'

The film?

Her mobile rang, a loud, shrill tone. She automatically grabbed it; she didn't recognise the number.

'Fredrika Bergman.'

Silence. Then Spencer's voice.

'You have to come to Uppsala.'

She heard the hesitation.

'They've arrested me.'

★  ★  ★

At first, Alex didn't understand what could possibly have gone wrong. Why had the Uppsala police decided to arrest Spencer Lagergren? And how could this have happened in Stockholm without Alex being informed?

'They'd blocked his passport,' Peder explained when he was reporting back to Alex later. 'So that they'd know if he tried to leave the country.'

'And why the hell would he do that? He's only been accused of sexual harassment, for God's sake!'

'Because yesterday, the girl who reported him came back with fresh information. She's raised the stakes significantly; now she's accusing him of rape.'

Alex was lost for words.

'Rape?'

Peder nodded.

'The police in Uppsala suspected that Lagergren would be afraid of this new information coming out; they thought he might try to leave the country and stay away until it had all blown over.'

'And when he applied for a new passport . . .'

'. . . that gave them a reason to arrest him.'

Alex locked his hands behind his head.

'I really didn't think he was guilty.'

'But in that case we don't know why he applied for a new passport,' Peder said.

'Why else would he have done it?'

'Because he needed one?'

Alex shook his head slowly.

'Something else is going on here, Peder.'

Their deliberations were interrupted by a gentle tap on the door.

'Sorry to disturb you,' said Torbjörn Ross. 'But I think I have some important information that you need to know.'

The sound of his voice made Alex stiffen, taking him back to the case involving the death of Rebecca Trolle.

'Come in,' he heard himself say.

And he immediately had the feeling that he was making a terrible mistake by letting his friend and colleague into the investigation.

# CHAPTER 46

Jimmy Rydh knew he was stupid. There was something wrong with his brain; he had hit his head on a rock, and it didn't work properly. He also knew that was why he couldn't live on his own, like Peder did. Although, of course, Peder didn't really live on his own; his whole family lived in Peder's apartment. Jimmy was a part of that family; Peder had said so, over and over again.

But now and again, Jimmy still found life diffi-cult. When it came down to it, he didn't live with his brother and his family, but with his friends in the assisted living complex. He got fed up of them sometimes; he couldn't cope with all their silly chatter in the kitchen or the common room. He was very glad he had a room of his own, where he could be alone with his thoughts.

And with his observations.

Jimmy was standing motionless by the window, staring out across the lawn that filled the space between his own building and the one opposite. The man was looking into that old lady's room again. Jimmy knew there was an old lady in that particular room, because he saw her almost every day. Sometimes she sat inside, but sometimes, even in the middle of winter, she would sit outside on her little patio. Where the man was now standing. Jimmy wondered if the lady could see the man who was looking in through her window. She ought to be able to see him, even though it was obvious that the man was creeping up on her. As if it were a game.

It was the second time Jimmy had seen the man, and although he didn't know why, the man made him feel frightened. That was why he hoped the old lady hadn't seen the man, because then she would be frightened too.

Suddenly the man moved. Towards the open patio door. And went inside. Jimmy inhaled sharply. What if the man was going to hurt the old lady?

Jimmy picked up his mobile; he would ring Peder. But Peder hadn't wanted to listen last time, Jimmy recalled. Perhaps one of the staff could help him?

He couldn't see the man any longer. Jimmy had a pain in his tummy. There was no time to think. He had to do something.

He opened his own patio door and went outside. He wasn't wearing any shoes, but it was so warm that it probably didn't matter. He had his socks on, after all.

It took him less than a minute to reach the old lady's room and suddenly Jimmy didn't know what to do. Should he knock on the door, call out and say hello? Intuitively, he knew that wasn't a good

435

idea. Instead he pressed himself against the wall, right by the window. He could hear the man talking.

'If you've kept quiet for thirty years, you can keep quiet until you die,' the man said. 'Do you understand what I'm saying?'

The lady probably didn't understand, Jimmy thought, because she didn't speak.

'I know why you've kept quiet,' the man went on, lowering his voice. 'And you know that I know, Thea. It's to protect that boy of yours, and I have every sympathy with that.'

The man paused.

'But if I go down, I will take him with me. I will crush him, if it's the last thing I do. Do you hear me?'

At first, there was complete silence, then Jimmy heard the lady, who apparently was called Thea, say in a hoarse voice:

'If you threaten my son once more, you're a dead man.'

The words reached Jimmy outside the window. He couldn't stop himself from calling out:

'No, no, no!'

Then he stopped speaking and stood there rooted to the spot as the man inside slowly came closer.

# CHAPTER 47

The outside world had ceased to exist. Fredrika Bergman was making a huge effort to understand what the police officer opposite her was saying, but she was finding it impossible to process his words. Spencer had been arrested. He had put Saga in her buggy and walked to police HQ, where Fredrika worked, in order to apply for a new passport. In spite of the fact that his current passport was still valid for a few months.

'We're convinced he was intending to leave the country,' the officer said.

'That's just ridiculous,' Fredrika said.

'I don't think so. He knew we were onto him, so he decided to make a run for it.'

'He's innocent.'

'Believe me, I know it's difficult for you to sit and listen to this. But you have to face facts. Spencer Lagergren is not the man you thought he was. He's a rapist. And men like that can have many different faces, as you well know.'

She was so angry that her fury threatened to consume her.

'I've known him for over ten years.'

The police officer leaned back.

'Interesting. And for how many of those years was he married to someone else?'

The rage was red, almost blinding her.

'That's totally irrelevant.'

'To you, but not to me.'

She got up and left. Picked up her child and walked out of the room. Asked to speak to Spencer. She was informed that this was not possible under the circumstances.

'We're going to charge him,' the officer behind her said.

'You'll regret it if you do,' she replied.

The shock debilitated her. Hugging Saga tightly, and with tears pouring down her face, she left the police station. There wasn't a single part of her that doubted Spencer's innocence with regard to the student who had made an accusation against him. She obviously wanted to destroy his life, or at least his career. But Fredrika had no intention of allowing that to happen.

*Over my dead body.*

Her mobile rang in her pocket; her hand was shaking as she answered. The sound of Alex's calm voice reached her.

'Where are you?'

'I've just left the police station.'

Saga dropped her dummy and began to whimper. Fredrika reacted automatically, replacing the dummy and settling the child in her buggy. She set off, walking quickly so that her daughter would be distracted by her surroundings as they whizzed by, and with a bit of luck would forget that she was no longer being carried.

'Don't do anything stupid, Fredrika,' Alex said.

'I won't.'

'I'm serious. You run the risk of making Spencer's situation, and your own, even worse if you start acting on your own initiative.'

He must have realised that she wasn't listening to a word he said, because he carried on with his exhortations until she excused herself and ended the call. She increased her speed and set off in a different direction. Along Luthagsesplanaden and off towards Rackarberget. She would go and see that bloody girl, pin her up against the wall. Make her understand what she was doing.

Her years as a student in Uppsala had been among the best of Fredrika's life, and yet they felt so far away. Every street, every district held the memory of a particular event that meant something to her. Under normal circumstances she enjoyed walking around the city, but not today. A rage that was fierce enough to cloud her vision held her soul in an iron grip, and she knew it wasn't about to let go. Her life had turned into a nightmare, and she had no idea how she was going to escape from it.

It was almost six o'clock, and Peder wanted to go home. The working day was over; they would carry on tomorrow.

'Valter Lund,' Alex said. 'He's coming in tomorrow, not today.'

'Spencer Lagergren,' Peder said.

Alex nodded pensively. The discovery of a third body had changed things.

'Go over to Uppsala tomorrow, and ask if you can question him on our case. Get it out of the way. He doesn't belong in this investigation, but he might be able to help fill in the background to everything that's happened. Ask him about the film club, and Thea Aldrin. And our friend Elias Hjort.'

They were sitting alone in the Lions' Den, finishing off a working day that had brought more twists and turns than they could count.

'What's your take on the information Torbjörn Ross gave us?' Peder asked.

Alex stiffened.

'I think we need to handle it with extreme care,' he said slowly.

With a certain amount of hesitation, he told Peder what had happened during the fishing trip, and about their colleague's clearly unhealthy interest in Thea Aldrin. Peder was horrified.

'He's still visiting her? After all these years?'

'He seems to be obsessed with the idea of finding her son, and holding her responsible for his death.'

'But if he's dead, surely the crime is beyond the statute of limitations by now?'

'Which just makes the whole thing even more

peculiar, but apparently that makes no difference to Ross.'

Peder massaged his temples.

The story Torbjörn Ross had told them covered the whole case like a wet blanket. Elias Hjort had acted as the legal representative of the author who wrote *Mercury* and *Asteroid*. According to Ross, the books had been turned into a so-called snuff movie, which had been seized by the police during a raid on a strip club. Ross also maintained that it was Thea Aldrin who had written the infamous books; this, he claimed, was a clear indication that she was insane.

As far as Peder was concerned, it made no difference whether Thea Aldrin was insane or not, because that was hardly a crime. Nor was writing tasteless books. And when it came to the film, Peder couldn't understand what Ross was driving at. Ross and his colleagues had concluded that the film was a fake – not a snuff movie at all, in fact – and as far as Peder could tell, no new information had emerged to change that judgement.

'There was something about that case,' Ross had said. 'Something that was never cleared up at the time.'

Peder felt sure that Alex wouldn't take any notice of such far-fetched nonsense. However, both Alex and Peder were aware that it was no longer possible to disregard Thea Aldrin in their investigation. The fact that she couldn't talk was irrelevant. They would have to go and see her, try to communicate with her in some other way. If they could make her understand that their errand was important, then hopefully, she would co-operate.

Alex's voice interrupted Peder's thoughts.

'Tomorrow we'll start off by interviewing Valter Lund. The press will go mad, but that can't be helped. We need to find out what was going on there – whether Rebecca and Valter had a relationship.'

Something else occurred to Peder.

'What about Håkan Nilsson? Have we found him?'

'No, but it's only a question of time. Lake Mälaren is large, admittedly, but not large enough for a person to disappear completely.'

What linked a young man fleeing on his boat to a silent woman in a care home and one of Sweden's most influential industrialists? Peder couldn't see it; he couldn't even begin to imagine what it might be.

'I'm going home,' he said. 'I'll take some of Fredrika's stuff on Rebecca Trolle's dissertation with me.'

'Good idea,' Alex said. 'I won't be far behind you.'

An edge of tiredness in his voice made Peder doubt that. Alex was lonely, rootless. Why go home when he might just as well stay at work?

'By the way, have we heard anything from forensics on the latest body?'

'Only that it's probably a woman,' Alex replied. 'Around one metre sixty-five tall. Young. Hadn't given birth. Difficult to say how long she'd been down there, but around forty years.'

'How did she die?'

'The pathologist wasn't willing to commit himself, but he could see that she had sustained a number of stab wounds. He wasn't sure if that was the actual cause of death.'

Peder was taken aback.

'Stab wounds?'

'Yes, there was evidence of damage to the ribs. And there were also blows to the head. He observed a deep groove in the skull that can't be explained in any other way.'

The evening sun pouring in through the window fell on Alex's face, casting shadows over the lines.

'Are you thinking the same as I am?' Peder said. 'The axe and the knife that had been buried?'

'Yes, that did occur to me.'

'Perhaps we'll find out more tomorrow – if they match as murder weapons, I mean.'

'I'm sure we will,' Alex said.

Peder got up, keen to get home to Ylva and the boys.

'It looks as if you've got something on your mind,' he said, pausing by the door.

Alex looked worried.

'Fredrika,' he said. 'I'm just hoping she's not doing something she'll regret in Uppsala.'

*  *  *

It was several hours before Tova Eriksson came home. Meanwhile, Fredrika sat waiting with Saga on a bench outside her apartment block. Fredrika recognised Tova from the university's website, which had featured a picture of her.

Tova's fair hair stood out around her head like a ragged halo. Big blue eyes, well-defined eyebrows. Skin already tanned. Long legs, short skirt, a jacket slung over one arm. She didn't notice Fredrika until they were standing just a few metres apart, face to face.

'Do you know who I am?' Fredrika asked.

The girl shook her head.

'Sorry, no. I don't think we've met.'

Fredrika took a step closer. She left the buggy by the bench, not wishing to taint her daughter with Tova's presence.

'My name is Fredrika Bergman. And I live with Spencer Lagergren.'

Tova's face changed instantly from open to closed, from relaxed to horrified. She quickly tried to walk around Fredrika, but Fredrika barred her way.

'Forget it,' Fredrika said. 'You're not going anywhere until you and I have finished talking.'

The sun was in Tova's eyes, and she blinked.

'I've got nothing to say to you.'

She stuck her nose in the air, trying to look tough.

But Fredrika was tougher; she had considerably more to lose than her reputation.

'But I have something to say to you,' she said. 'You are in the process of destroying Spencer's life completely. And mine. And his daughter's. You're wrecking an entire family, Tova.'

She tried to catch Tova's eye; she wanted to see her expression change.

'You have to put a stop to this while you still can.'

It might have been because of the sun, but Tova's eyes were filled with tears.

'It's not my fault if you're living with a sick bastard. Or that you chose such a monster as the father of your child.'

'He's a wonderful partner and a wonderful person,' Fredrika said, feeling her voice break. 'I have no doubt that he's capable of hurting others, but you're playing with very high stakes, Tova. Tell me what makes you so angry.'

Tova was transformed before Fredrika's eyes. She became smaller, more pathetic. And it struck Fredrika that she hadn't thought through her actions. She hoped she hadn't managed to create even bigger problems for herself.

'Was he a poor supervisor?'

It was a bit thin, but it was the closest she could get to a reasonable guess. Tova remained silent, refusing to answer Fredrika's question.

'Or was it because he didn't want you? In spite of the fact that you wanted him?'

Fredrika had also experienced the unique embarrassment that follows a rejection; it burned a hole in the soul. She knew that humiliation could lead to insanity, but not in the way that it appeared to have affected Tova.

'You're going to regret coming to see me!'

The voice was rough with unshed tears, the eyes shining with concentration.

'And you're going to regret trying to destroy my life,' Fredrika said when Tova had walked away.

She knew those were empty words, however. There was very little that could be done about the situation in which Spencer now found himself. All they could do was pray for a miracle. And an assessment of the so-called evidence that would stand up to the scrutiny of due process.

# CHAPTER 48

This was the third evening in less than a week, and Alex could no longer deny, to himself or anyone else, that there was something going on here. Nor could he deny his feelings.

Lust. Longing. And sorrow.

Another evening at Diana's.

It was too early to start a new relationship – less than a year since Lena's death.

*Or was it?*

What would the children say? And his superiors? As long as he was working on Rebecca's murder, it was patently irresponsible to embark on a relationship with her mother.

But he wanted to. And that desire cast immense shadows over his doubts.

She knew exactly how he was feeling, knew exactly why she was sitting alone on the sofa while he sat opposite, with the coffee table between them. He thought she could cope with waiting for him.

'You still love her,' Diana said, taking a sip of her wine.

'I'll always love her.'

Diana lowered her gaze.

'That doesn't mean you couldn't love another woman. As well as Lena.'

Alex was overwhelmed by her generosity.

'Perhaps.'

His embarrassment made her smile.

'How about a late night stroll?'

'I ought to go home.'

'It's only an hour since you had a glass of wine.'

'I still ought to go home.'

And he smiled.

She got up, came around the table and took his hand.

'My dear detective inspector, I'm absolutely certain that a breath of fresh air would do us both good.'

There was no point in trying to resist. He wanted nothing more than to stay, he wanted nothing more than to go home. A walk seemed like a good compromise.

They strolled through the area where Diana lived, and she took him on a guided tour of her life. She pointed out the park where her children used to play when they were little, and she wept as they came to a tree Rebecca had loved to climb. The tears stopped, and with a wobbly smile she showed him where the children's father had lived following their separation.

'We tried to keep things as civilised as possible,' she said. 'We both thought it would be terrible if the children suffered.'

Alex told her about his own family. About his son, who was something of a lost soul, but who seemed to have grown up after his mother's death. About his daughter, who was now a mother herself, and had made him a grandfather. Diana began to cry again, and Alex apologised.

'Forgive me; that was a stupid topic of conversation to choose.'

She shook her head.

'I'm the one who should be apologising. Because I can't let go. Because I can't get it out of my head that my little girl was pregnant when she died.'

Alex swallowed; he didn't really want to discuss Rebecca's death with Diana. He squeezed her hand.

'We don't know our children as well as we would wish. We just don't.'

He could see that she didn't agree, but she didn't say anything. She wiped away her tears once more, and pointed out another landmark.

'When Rebecca was a baby I used to bring her here in her pram,' she said, pointing to an overgrown patch of grass between a play area and a large house. 'It was my little oasis. I would sit on the grass and read while she slept.'

Where had he gone with the children when they were little? Alex had no similar memories. Nor had he needed an oasis; he had always had his work, after all. While Lena took care of everything at home. What the hell had they been thinking?

449

His thoughts turned to his daughter; he hoped she wouldn't repeat the mistakes her parents had made. Even a man like Spencer Lagergren could see the point of taking paternity leave. The basis for a good relationship with children was laid when they were little, not when they had grown up. You only got one stab at some things, and the childhood of a human being was one of them.

Although, when it came to Spencer Lagergren, Alex had his doubts. His decision to take paternity leave had more to do with running away from his problems than a genuine interest in his daughter. As Alex considered Spencer's motives for spending time at home, it occurred to him that he hadn't heard from Fredrika since he had called her when she was in Uppsala. A feeling of unease over what she might do in order to sort out her life made him suddenly stiffen.

'What are you thinking about?'

'Nothing,' he said. 'Just a friend who's having a few problems at the moment.'

They set off back towards Diana's house. Where had all these warm spring evenings come from? The roof formed a black shape against the gathering darkness. The door was a gateway to the unknown. To a place he dare not go. Not yet.

'Are you staying?'

He wanted to. But he couldn't.

*But he wanted to.*

He wanted it more than he had wanted anything for a very long time. The need to refuse was so painful. He struggled to find the right words, but when he opened his mouth, they simply came.

'I can't.'

They said good night by his car. She did what she had done last time; she leaned over and kissed his cheek. He opened the door and got in the car. Drove a hundred metres down the street before he changed his mind. Stopped the car and reversed back to her house. Got out of the car and rang her doorbell.

He wanted to. And he could.

There was something deeply moving about seeing small children asleep, thought Peder Rydh as he gazed at his sleeping sons. The peace and security in their faces was all the evidence he needed to tell him he was getting it right. Coming home from work at a reasonable time. Behaving like an adult rather than a panic-stricken teenager. Taking responsibility, showing respect.

Ylva appeared behind him. Slipped her slender arms around his waist and rested her head against his back. He loved feeling her closeness.

They left the children's room and sat down on the balcony, where Peder's papers from work were strewn all over the table. Ylva settled down with her novel, and Peder carried on reading an article on Thea Aldrin. Things really had gone crazy. A writer and a dead man. A film club and an amazing career as an author. A dead solicitor and rumours of a dead son.

It's the film club and the writer that link this whole mess, Peder thought. It's only because we can't see how that we keep on trying other avenues.

He thought about Valter Lund, who might have had a relationship with Rebecca Trolle, and about Morgan Axberger, who was Lund's boss, and also a member of The Guardian Angels. They were intending to bring Lund in for questioning the following day, which made Peder feel slightly better. He tried to imagine what information Rebecca Trolle had stumbled upon that had cost her her life. He leafed through the pages relating to her dissertation, asking himself whether the key to this wretched case might be there.

*How had the person who killed her found out what she knew?*

Peder read through Fredrika's notes. Unlike all the other minor figures in the investigation, Håkan Nilsson had no connection with either Thea Aldrin or any members of the film club. His only connection was with Rebecca and the child she had been expecting. If Håkan was the killer, then the dissertation was totally irrelevant.

Peder looked at a picture of Håkan Nilsson and asked himself how they were going to get him to talk. How could they get through to him, make him understand that they had his best interests at heart? The fact that Rebecca had not been alone in her grave was actually all the proof they needed that Håkan was innocent, because Håkan couldn't possibly have murdered Elias Hjort as well.

452

*And there has to be a connection.*

Torbjörn Ross claimed that the police had been looking for Elias Hjort because of a film that might have been based on books that might have been written by Thea Aldrin. Books for which Elias Hjort had received royalties. But the film was of little value unless it was genuine, unless it was a recording of an actual murder. A snuff movie. Peder didn't know much about that kind of film, but as far as he knew, the genuine article had never been found. His colleagues with the National CID would probably know more about that kind of thing; he would check with them tomorrow.

The telephone rang and Ylva went indoors to answer it. She sounded agitated; she seemed to be walking towards him.

'Peder,' she said.

He turned to face her; he would never forget how she looked that evening. The telephone in her hand, her face pale, eyes wide open.

'Apparently, Jimmy has gone missing.'

# INTERVIEW WITH ALEX RECHT,
## 03-05-2009,
### 15.00 (tape recording)

Present: Urban S, Roger M (interrogators one and two). Alex Recht (witness).

Urban: So, another body.
  Alex: Yes.
  Roger: That must have been depressing.
  Alex: No, actually. I felt as if that last discovery somehow made things easier.
  Roger: Interesting. Could you explain that in a little more detail?
  Alex: It was just a feeling I had.
  Urban: Elias Hjort. The solicitor with the gold watch. What was your next move with regard to him?
  Alex: Through Peder's work, we were able to link him to the film club. At that stage, we began to sense how everything hung together, but . . .
  (Silence.)
  Alex: . . . we were a long way from the truth.
  Roger: And Fredrika Bergman?
  Alex: Yes?
  Roger: What happened with her partner, Spencer Lagergren?
  Alex: We decided we needed to question him,

but by that time the Uppsala police had already picked him up.

Urban: And how did you deal with the fact that she had withheld important information from the rest of the team?

Alex: I discussed the matter with her and concluded that her actions had had no impact on the investigation.

Urban: No impact? How the hell do you work that out? She withheld crucial information!

Alex: That information was insignificant. We were able to eliminate Lagergren from our inquiries.

Roger: But you couldn't possibly have known that from the beginning, could you? And what about Peder's brother? Had he been reported missing at that stage?

Alex: It all happened at the same time. There was absolute bloody chaos. Jimmy had called Peder earlier and told him that he'd seen someone peering in through the window of the building opposite.

Roger: And how did Peder react to that?

Alex: He didn't. Jimmy is . . . I mean, he was just the way he was. He had certain difficulties. When he said someone was standing in the flowerbed spying on one of the neighbours, Peder didn't take it seriously.

Urban: Until you realised who the neighbour was.
(Silence.)

Roger: Was Peder still adopting a balanced approach at this stage?

455

Alex: He remained calm and professional throughout the entire investigation.

Urban: Except at the end. I mean, that's why we're sitting here now.

Alex: Like hell we are. We're sitting here because you haven't got enough to do, so you go after decent coppers.

# WEDNESDAY

# CHAPTER 49

In the world of fairy tales, the bond between brothers was sacred. Peder Rydh's mother had never let him forget that. His childhood was enveloped in warm memories of Peder and Jimmy sitting on her knee while she read them story after story about young boys battling everything from dragons to illness. Only when Peder was older did he realise that her words of wisdom were meant for him. It was Peder, not Jimmy, who would grow up and become the stronger one. The one who protected, took responsibility.

The evening when Peder heard that his brother was missing, everything came crashing down. Not during the first few hours, but later. As time passed, as darkness fell over the city, as it became clear that Jimmy hadn't just gone off on one of his usual tours of the complex and happened to end up in the wrong block. When everyone realised that Jimmy was actually missing, the ground beneath Peder's feet opened up and he plunged into an abyss he hadn't even known existed.

He didn't realise what had happened to him until later, when it was all over and nothing could be undone. Ylva saw it right from the start, and did everything in her power to save him. Without success. She had never been more powerless in her entire life.

After the initial call from the assisted-living complex, Ylva rang her mother and asked her to come and look after the boys. She and Peder went over to the complex and searched the area, along with the staff and Peder's parents. They called Jimmy's name over and over again. Peder felt as if their shouts were embedded in his brain, a recurring echo that just wouldn't go away. Then he called the police and reported his brother missing.

Peder knew all too well how this worked. Police resources were not unlimited; it was always a question of priorities. When someone rang and said that his brother, an adult with learning difficulties, was missing from a gated complex on the outskirts of town, other cases would be regarded as more urgent. That was how he would have reacted, and that was how his colleagues reacted.

'We'll find him before the night is over,' said the officer who was first on the scene.

How could he have known right from the start? Peder asked himself later. How come his heart had been screaming with fear all the time, even though Jimmy had gone missing before, and always turned up safe and sound?

'Is he in the habit of going off on his own?' his colleague asked.

Not often. It did happen, but it was rare. On one

particularly harrowing occasion, Jimmy had managed to catch a bus into the city centre, and had been found on Sergels torg, where he was happily smoking a cigarette that a group of junkies had given him.

Peder had nearly blown it that time; the anxiety that had been building up during the hours while Jimmy was missing had culminated in a blind rage, and he had beaten up one of the junkies. He would never have survived an investigation by internal affairs if the guy had reported him. But he hadn't, and after a few months the memory of the incident began to fade.

When morning came, Jimmy was still missing. The sunlight hurt Peder's eyes. In the darkness, he had felt protected, but now there was nothing but pure fear.

'We need to go home and sleep for a few hours,' Ylva said as they drove back into the car park at the Mångården complex after driving around, up and down one street after another, searching for Jimmy. Their eyes had scanned the area like laser beams, desperate for Jimmy to appear.

She stroked Peder's back, but he pulled away.

'I'm not going anywhere.'

'We're no use right now,' she said. 'We're both completely exhausted. It's better to let the police keep looking.'

'I am the police, in case you've forgotten.'

Ylva didn't say anything.

'We'll find him, you know. It's only a question of time before he turns up.'

But other images filled Peder's head. Some people disappeared and never came back. Rebecca Trolle. Elias Hjort. The unknown woman who had lain in the ground for forty years. He felt as if his chest would explode with panic. The mere thought of life without Jimmy was unbearable.

*Please God, give me a grave to visit.*

Ylva shifted by his side.

'I have to go home. Get some sleep. I'll call work and tell them I won't be in today.'

Peder looked out of the car window.

'I think it would be best if you stayed at home,' he said. 'Jimmy might decide to go round to our place, and there has to be someone there that he knows.'

They both knew it was impossible for Jimmy to get to their apartment under his own steam. But hope is the last thing we give up, so Ylva raised no objections to Peder's suggestion.

'Will you be back later?'

'I'll call you.'

His tone was brusque, his gaze fixed on some distant point. She gently caressed his cheek. Peder hardly felt it. Nothing existed but the search for his brother.

The bed had never felt as big as it did now. Fredrika woke with the feeling that she hadn't slept a wink. Her body felt heavy and weary. She rolled over, stroking the empty space where Spencer ought to be. The hot tears were unstoppable. She suddenly thought back to her encounter with Tova Eriksson, and pulled the covers up over her head. Had she irrevocably destroyed something by going to see the girl who was literally responsible for having Spencer locked up? She remembered Alex's words and warnings; she knew she had been wrong to ignore them.

She raised her head from the pillow and wiped away the tears. There was no room for a mental collapse right now. She had to keep going, for the sake of Saga and Spencer if nothing else.

It was six o'clock. The day lay before her like a deserted motorway. Should she go to work? Or – to put it more accurately – could she bear to stay at home? The answer to that question was no. She had to go back to work, keep an eye on the efforts that were being made to ascertain whether Spencer had a part to play in a murder investigation. And she had to do her best to get the Uppsala police to release him.

But why the hell had he applied for a new passport?

When Spencer was arrested, he had been unaware that Tova had raised the stakes and accused him of rape. So why did he need a passport?

He must have realised that he figured in the murder investigation Fredrika was working on. That was the only conclusion that made sense. What was less easy to understand was why he had decided not to confide in Fredrika. Why hadn't he mentioned it to her? And why hadn't she talked to him?

Or had she? Fredrika thought back to the times when she had confronted Spencer over the past week. About his problems at work, about how he knew Rebecca Trolle. He hadn't said a word about any of it. She felt the tears threatening once more. Had they lost the most important ingredient in their relationship, the ability to talk about anything?

*If we have, it's all over.*

Fredrika got out of bed and fetched her bag. She had brought some work home. She got back into bed and sat cross-legged. She re-read the short piece Rebecca Trolle had put together about the film club known as The Guardian Angels – the group that provided yet another link between Spencer and the investigation. Alex had told her that according to one of Rebecca's fellow-students, Rebecca had approached Spencer for more than one reason. She wanted him to act as her supervisor, but his name had also come up in her research.

Because of the film club, Fredrika thought.

She read the last word on the page.

Snuff.

The word did not occur anywhere else, and no explanation was given. Just before Spencer's phone call from Uppsala, Torbjörn Ross had mentioned just such a film. Or at least he had talked about the filming of the books Thea Aldrin had allegedly written.

Fredrika went into the library and found one of Spencer's film lexicons. As far as she knew, the idea that there had ever been genuine snuff movies was a myth, as was the belief that there had ever been a demand for them. The expression 'snuff movie' was first used in the early 1970s, based on the English expression 'to snuff it', or die. According to legend, violent films were secretly produced, recording real murders and rapes; these films were then sold for vast sums of money. The victims were often homeless prostitutes, and the purchasers of the finished product were rich and influential individuals with perverted tendencies.

According to the lexicon, no police authority had ever reported the discovery of a genuine snuff movie – in every suspected case the film had turned out to be a clever fake, which meant that the victim had not died, but had survived. The closest approximation was murderers who filmed their own crimes so that they could watch them over and over again, but in those cases the murder itself was more important than the recording, and the films were not made with the intention of selling them.

Fredrika replaced the book on the shelf. Why did the word come up in Rebecca's notes at all? Had she made the same link as Torbjörn Ross had done between Thea Aldrin and *Mercury* and *Asteroid*? Although how could that be? There had never been anything in the press about the film Ross had referred to.

Fredrika glanced through the piece on The Guardian Angels again. There was no indication as to why Rebecca thought the group might be associated with snuff movies. Admittedly several of the members fulfilled the criteria for the type of person who was allegedly interested in that kind of thing, but Fredrika found it difficult to see how Rebecca could have established such a connection.

Fragments of conversations and all the information she had acquired during the past week drifted through her weary mind. Rebecca's supervisor had compared her dissertation to a police investigation. Her mother had said something similar, but Fredrika could see no evidence that Rebecca had been in touch with the police to discuss Thea Aldrin's case. At least Rebecca hadn't made a note of any such contact.

Or had she? Had they missed it? Fredrika dug out her copy of Rebecca's diary and the list of unidentified initials:

HH, UA, SL and TR.

*TR?*

Torbjörn Ross. It couldn't be anyone else.

Fredrika scrabbled through her papers, searching for the lists of phone calls. Had anyone noticed that Rebecca had called the police? She couldn't remember it being mentioned, but on the other hand it wouldn't have seemed particularly noteworthy. People called the police all the time, for a wide variety of reasons.

The more she thought about it, the more convinced she became: Rebecca Trolle must have been in touch with Torbjörn Ross. In which case, why hadn't Ross said anything, either when Rebecca originally went missing, or when she was found dead? Torbjörn Ross, who still visited Thea Aldrin on a regular basis, with the aim of getting her to confess to a murder no one even knew for sure had been committed. Torbjörn Ross, who believed Thea had written some of the most controversial literary works in the whole of the twentieth century. And who thought it was possible to link Thea Aldrin to a violent film his colleagues believed was a fake. What was he actually hiding?

When Alex woke up, he had no idea where he was at first. The long, thin white curtains were unfamiliar, as were the white sheets and the pale striped wallpaper. The memories came flooding back as he turned his head and saw Diana lying beside him, sleeping on her stomach and facing away from him.

Instinctively, he sat up, running a hand through his hair, peppered with grey. The sensation spreading through his body was both pleasant and frightening. He had made love with a woman other than Lena. Should he be apologising to someone?

The idea almost made him let out a high-pitched, nervous laugh. The children certainly wouldn't be interested in an apology; they wanted nothing more than for him to move on. They might be surprised that things had happened so quickly, but on the other hand, they didn't need to know right away.

He lay down again, taken aback by thoughts and feelings he didn't recognise. Not everything that had happened during the night was a good idea. He had gone to bed with the mother of a murder victim whose death he was in charge of investigating. The police weren't in the habit of turning a blind eye to that kind of behaviour. He could be in big trouble if anyone found out what he was up to.

*But he hadn't been able to stop himself.*

That was his one recurring thought. And it was liberating.

It was also liberating, and calming, to wake up next to a person he knew he wanted to see again. Many of his friends and colleagues had found themselves alone following a bereavement or divorce, and had embarked on a constant search for a woman who didn't exist – who *couldn't* exist – making it impossible for them to sustain a new relationship.

Alex had promised himself he would never be one of them.

At the same time, the grief was overwhelming. He could never find what he had had with Lena with another woman. There would be no more children, no new family. Everything that lay ahead of him would forever be incomplete, damaged.

His mobile rang; Diana stirred as he answered.

'Jimmy's gone missing,' Peder said.

'Missing?'

'They rang from the assisted living complex yesterday. Ylva and I have been out looking for him all night. It's as if the ground has swallowed him up.'

Peder's voice was thin and high, full of an anxiety that made Alex forget everything else.

'I presume the police are involved?'

'Of course. But they can't find him either.'

'Right, listen to me. If you've been out all night, you need to go home and get some sleep. I don't bloody want you . . .'

'I'm not going anywhere until we find him.'

There's nothing quite as irrational as a person who has been deprived of sleep; Alex knew that only too well.

'In that case, you will be jeopardising the inquiry,' he said.

A little more brusque than necessary, perhaps, but he was hoping to make Peder see reason. At the same time he could see his team falling apart. Fredrika's partner had been arrested; Peder's brother was missing.

He would have to request additional resources, that was all there was to it.

Peder said something in a subdued voice.

'Sorry?'

'I said I don't know what I'll do if we don't find him. I think I could fucking kill the person who takes Jimmy away from me.'

'There's nothing to suggest that he's dead,' Alex said. 'Nothing at all.'

He was trying to reassure Peder, but he could tell that his colleague wasn't listening.

'He called me,' Peder said.

'Jimmy?'

'He called to tell me that someone was standing outside looking in through a window. Someone who frightened him.'

Alex was confused.

'Someone was looking in through Jimmy's window?'

'No, through another window. And Jimmy saw him and he was scared. That's what he said when he rang me. "It's a man. He's looking in through the window. He's got his back to me".'

# CHAPTER 50

The ground gave way beneath Malena Bremberg's feet as she ran. She could feel her pulse pounding in her body as she forced it on, kilometre after kilometre. Two years ago, she had been like any other student. She had finally decided what she wanted to do at university, and had managed to find student accommodation and a part time job at Mångården care home.

It had taken time for Malena to get her life on the right track; there had been many diversions. Her high school years were a fog of binge drinking, countless love affairs and poor marks. She hated thinking back to that time; she didn't want to dwell on the life she had lived in those days. After leaving school, she had spent several years working abroad. As an au pair. As an undernourished model. As a holiday rep.

She came home feeling emptier than ever.

'Your life belongs to you and you alone,' her father had said. 'You're the one who chooses how you're going to live. But if you choose not to live your life at all, that will make me very sad.'

She enrolled on adult education courses that

same autumn. Started working in a clothes shop. Carefully built herself a new life, made new friends. Friends who were very different from the ones with whom she had surrounded herself in the past. She didn't have a boyfriend; for the first time, she didn't need one.

She celebrated the most important day of her life when she was finally accepted to study law at the University of Stockholm. Success gave her the taste for more. She knew what it had cost her to gain that place, and now she was determined to make progress, to forge ahead. If you were over thirty it was high time you knew what you wanted to be when you grew up.

At first, she had believed they had met by chance, at an opening event for a new, unusual restaurant on Stureplan. Suddenly he had appeared by her side, standing just a little too close. It had bothered her to begin with, but the feeling didn't last long. She had allowed herself to be flattered by his compliments and his presence – all too easily.

And his voice. That deep, almost hypnotic voice had made her blush, and however much she wanted to, she just couldn't stop listening. Helpless. That was how she had felt.

She remembered that her friends had seen them together and wondered what she was playing at. He was so much older than her. Admittedly he was a man with power and wealth, but above all he was older. She had dismissed their words as nothing more than envy.

Warning bells had rung at an early stage, when he had started asking questions about Thea Aldrin. She hadn't made the connection immediately, hadn't realised that he had known all along where she worked, and that was why she was interesting.

With hindsight, she felt nothing but embarrassment and revulsion. She had allowed herself to be seduced and led astray by a man with an agenda that could only be described as sick. Because it had seemed so exciting, because there was a part of her that would never be like everyone else, that would never be a good girl. The desire had come from nowhere, the desire to do what was dangerous, what was taboo. She had played with fire, and she had almost been consumed by it. While he documented the whole thing on film.

# CHAPTER 51

It was half-past eight by the time Fredrika got to work. Alex was surprised to see her.

'I thought you'd be staying at home with your daughter today.'

'My mum's looking after her. I can't just stay at home. I have to keep busy.'

Alex didn't question Fredrika's reasoning. However, he did make it clear that she couldn't be involved in their dealings with Spencer.

'I've sent another officer over to Uppsala to carry out a formal interrogation,' he said. 'I assume that will put an end to the matter from our point of view. But I'd like to hear what he has to say about the film club and its members; he might also be able to tell us something about Thea Aldrin.'

Fredrika nodded.

'Why isn't Peder interviewing him?' she asked.

Alex went pale as he told her about Peder's brother. Fredrika's eyes filled with tears, and she sat down on one of the chairs in Alex's office.

'What the hell is wrong with you two?' Alex said when he saw her reaction. 'We're bound to find him. He's probably gone for a walk and got lost.

I'm sure that kind of thing can happen with someone like Jimmy.'

Fredrika could see that Alex believed what he was saying, and she admired him for that. Personally, she was up to her eyes in crap, and couldn't manage one single positive thought.

'Is he coming in later?' she asked.

'Maybe. We'll see.'

Fredrika opened her bag.

'With regard to the film club,' she said. 'Something occurred to me this morning. Something that has nothing to do with Spencer.'

Alex watched as she took out her papers. She glanced over at him; there was something unfamiliar about his face, as if it had acquired a patina of tranquillity that had not been there before.

She lost focus for a moment, and had to think about what she had been going to tell him. Then she remembered. Alex looked sceptical.

'So you think that Torbjörn Ross, who has been a colleague of mine since the 1980s, was in touch with Rebecca Trolle before she died? And that he then withheld this information from the investigating team?'

Fredrika swallowed. The sleepless night had taken its toll.

'I think it's possible, yes.'

She pushed Rebecca's notes across the desk. Pointed to the word at the bottom. Snuff.

'It's just a word,' Alex said.

'It's *his* word,' Fredrika replied. 'He's the one who thinks the books were filmed.'

Alex thought for a moment.

'Ask Ellen to go through the list of calls,' he said. 'Check whether Rebecca called the police, either via the switchboard or to a direct line. We might have missed it, thinking she'd contacted the police for a completely different reason.'

Fredrika got to her feet.

'I'll do that right away.'

'And if Peder doesn't come in, I'd like you to sit in on the interview with Valter Lund. He'll be here in an hour.'

'And Thea Aldrin?' Fredrika asked.

'What about her?'

'Aren't we going to speak to her as well?'

'Find out where she's living these days, and we'll go and see her later. Not that I think it'll make much difference, if she never speaks anyway.'

Fredrika had one more question.

'What's our thinking on Morgan Axberger? Don't we need to talk to him too?'

Alex suppressed a sigh.

'We'll hang fire on that. Let's tackle one thing at a time.'

Fredrika hurried to her office, then went to see Ellen, who promised to check Rebecca's phone records as soon as possible.

'By the way, you've had several faxes from the Norwegian police about Valter Lund,' Ellen said.

More paper, more work.

Fredrika went back to her office and read through what her Norwegian colleagues had to say. They had done quite a bit of digging. Among other things, they informed her that Valter Lund's uncle had reported him missing at the beginning of the 1980s, when he signed on as a crew member on a car ferry, and was never heard of again. According to the police, this uncle still turned up at the local station in Gol on a regular basis, year after year, to ask if they'd found out anything about his nephew.

But why? Valter Lund was known all over northern Europe, and was frequently featured in the Scandinavian press. Didn't the old man realise that the successful man who now lived in Stockholm was his missing nephew?

Fredrika frowned. Could there have been a mix-up? Was there more than one Valter Lund who had emigrated from Norway to Sweden in the same year?

Probably not.

She took out a picture of Valter Lund and stared at it. Why hadn't he been in touch with his only remaining relative in Norway? And, even more to the point, why hadn't his own uncle recognised him?

The night had been interminable. All the unfamiliar sounds, smells and impressions pierced Spencer Lagergren's skin like needles, forcing him to stay awake. As the lonely hours passed, a new certainty formed in his mind. Even if they let him go, the life he had lived before was gone forever.

477

He would only ever be remembered as the man who raped his female students. Who showed such contempt for women that he felt compelled to subject them to physical violence.

There was no margin for error when it came to sexual offences, Spencer knew that. Nobody wanted to be the one who had been wrong after the event, the one who had given the benefit of the doubt. So in the end it didn't matter if Spencer was cleared of the crimes which Tova claimed he had committed; the verdict of his colleagues and the outside world would still be the heaviest burden to bear.

No smoke without fire. Not when it came to sexual offences.

And as if that wasn't enough, his partner's colleagues suspected him of being involved in a murder. With hindsight, he bitterly regretted not having told Fredrika what was going on from the start. To a certain extent, he blamed this obvious error of judgement on his problems with Tova. There hadn't been room for two situations of such gravity; he could only deal with one at a time. In addition, he had only recently become aware that he was a suspect in a murder case – far too late for him to be able to work out how to behave. There had been just one thought in his head, and that had been born out of a state of sheer panic.

He needed a passport so that he was ready to leave the country.

He hardly dared to think about what that mistake

478

had cost him, and it wasn't much of a defence to state that he had applied for a new passport because he was suspected of a completely different crime: murder.

It was after nine o'clock when he was taken to an interview room. The custody officer informed him that it was the Stockholm police rather than Uppsala who wanted to speak to him. Spencer was only too well aware of the reason for this.

The officer from Stockholm introduced herself as Cecilia Torsson. A colleague from Uppsala was also present. Spencer felt that Cecilia Torsson came over as almost a caricature copper. The handshake was a parody of a normal handshake: far too firm, far too long. If her plan was to gain respect, she was distinctly wide of the mark. Her voice was loud, and she emphasised every word as if she thought he had severe hearing difficulties. In a different context her behaviour would have made Spencer smile. Now he just found it upsetting.

'Rebecca Trolle,' said Cecilia Torsson. 'How did you know her?'

'I didn't know her at all.'

'Are you sure?'

Spencer breathed in, then out. Was he sure?

His memories of the spring when Rebecca Trolle went missing were relatively clear. He had had quite a lot to do as far as work was concerned, and he and Fredrika were seeing each other with increasing frequency. At home, the silence had been dense, the distance between him and Eva

479

immense. As a consequence he had spent more and more time at work, more and more time away from home, even more evenings in the apartment in Östermalm with Fredrika.

That spring might well have been one of the best in his adult life.

But did Rebecca Trolle fit in somewhere? Had she passed through his life that spring, so fleetingly that he didn't remember it when he looked back? He searched his memory, feeling that there were events he ought to be able to recall.

'She called me once.'

He was surprised to hear his own voice.

'She called you once?'

Cecilia Torsson leaned forward across the desk. Spencer nodded; it was all coming back to him now.

'I had a message from the switchboard saying that a girl by that name had tried to get hold of me, but she didn't ring again. That must have been in March or April.'

'Didn't you react when she disappeared?'

'Why would I do that? I mean, I remember the newspapers ran stories about her disappearance, but to be honest I wasn't sure if it was the same girl who had called me, even if the name was a little unusual.'

Cecilia Torsson looked as if she accepted his argument.

'She didn't leave a message asking you to call her back?'

'No, I was just told that she had rung, and that she would try again. It was to do with a dissertation she was working on.'

More memories came to the surface.

'I remember thinking I didn't really have time for her. It's not unusual for students to ring up asking for help.'

Spencer shrugged.

'But I rarely have the time. Unfortunately.'

'I understand,' Cecilia said.

She turned the page in her notebook.

'The Guardian Angels,' she said.

The words were as much of a shock as if the ceiling had collapsed. He hadn't heard those words for a long, long time.

'Yes,' he said.

'You were a member of that particular film club?'

'I was.'

Spencer was on full alert; he had no idea where the conversation was going.

'Could you tell me a little more about it?'

Spencer folded his arms, trying hard to think back to a time that was so many years ago. What was there to tell? Four adults, three men and one woman, who regularly got together to watch films, then went for something to eat and drink and wrote poisonous reviews.

'What do you want to know?'

'Everything.'

'Why? What have The Guardian Angels got to do with all this?'

'We think there might be a connection between the film club and the murder of Rebecca Trolle.'

The laughter came from nowhere. Spencer pulled himself up short when he saw the expression on Cecilia Torsson's face.

'But for goodness' sake, that film club has been defunct for over thirty years. You must see how unreasonable it would be for . . .'

'If you could just answer my questions, we'll both get out of here a lot sooner. Unfortunately, I am not at liberty to explain why the film club is of interest to us, but we would be very grateful for any information you can provide.'

Her tone was almost pleading by the end, as if she was hoping that Spencer would produce a magic wand and transform the entire investigation in a trice.

'I'm afraid I have to disappoint you,' he said, hoping he sounded honest. 'I was the last person to be chosen as a member of the group before it was dissolved. Morgan Axberger and I knew each other from an evening class in French that we had both attended in the mid-'60s. That was before he became a high-flyer; he spent all his time smoking, drinking and writing poetry.'

The memory made him smile.

'After that, things moved quickly for Morgan. He became a different person when he realised he could shoot up the corporate ladder in record time. But he still had an interest in film, and in the early '70s we bumped into one another at an

art exhibition. He told me about the film club –
I'd already seen articles about it in the newspapers,
of course – and hinted that there was an opening
if I wanted to join. Naturally, I said yes.'

'Tell me about the other members. Are you still
in touch with them?'

'No, not at all,' Spencer replied. 'After Thea
Aldrin ended up in prison and Elias Hjort moved
abroad, that left just Morgan and me. And we had
very little in common, I must say. It was only
natural that we stopped seeing each other.'

Spencer thought for a moment.

'The film club was dissolved around 1975–6. I
never really understood why, but that's what
happened. By the time Thea Aldrin was charged
with murder, the film club hadn't met for several
years.'

Cecilia Torsson looked interested.

'Could there have been disagreements you were
unaware of?'

'It's possible, of course, but I don't know what
they could have been about. If you speak to
Morgan Axberger or Elias Hjort, I'm sure they'll
be able to tell you more. Thea could tell you plenty
as well, of course, but if what it says in the papers
is true, she hasn't spoken since she went to prison.'

'How did the other members of the group react?
To the fact that she'd murdered her husband, I
mean?'

Not at all, Spencer thought. He hadn't seen Morgan
or Elias after Thea was arrested. He remembered

ringing Morgan to talk it over. Morgan, who had known Thea's ex, had been shocked and refused to discuss what had happened.

'We had virtually no contact at all by then,' Spencer said. 'I was the youngest of the four, and I hadn't been a member from the start. I didn't know Thea's ex, or anything about their relationship. But obviously I was horrified when I found out what she'd done.'

'So you never questioned her guilt?'

Spencer shrugged.

'She confessed.'

The air in the room was stale, the walls grubby. How much longer would he have to sit here talking about things he hadn't done, hadn't been involved in?

'There were rumours that Thea Aldrin was the author of *Mercury* and *Asteroid*. Was that the case?'

'Not as far as I knew. We discussed the matter, of course, but not in any detail. It was just a piece of particularly nasty gossip, nothing else.'

He felt a sudden spurt of anger at all the attempts that had been made to ruin Thea's reputation. It had been sheer persecution, as if some powerful force was secretly working to destroy everything she had achieved. Spencer hadn't understood the background at the time, and he didn't understand it now.

'Her son went missing,' Cecilia said. 'Do you remember anything about that?'

'Of course,' Spencer replied. 'You could say that

was the beginning of the end for her. She never got over the loss, and who can blame her? Although by that time the film club had already broken up, and I hardly ever saw her.'

'But there were more rumours; people said she'd killed her son as well.'

Spencer shook his head.

'It was absolutely bloody ridiculous. The boy disappeared and didn't come back. I have no idea what happened to him, of course, but I think I can say with some certainty that his own mother didn't kill him.'

The watch on Cecilia Torsson's wrist flashed as it caught the light on the ceiling.

'So what do you think happened to him?'

Spencer no longer needed to make an effort to recall the events of all those years ago. He remembered exactly what he had thought when the boy went missing.

'Thea rarely mentioned her son or her relationship with him, but I know they quarrelled quite a lot. He kept asking where his father had gone, and he didn't treat her with the respect she wanted from him.'

The words stuck in his throat; for some reason, they were more difficult to get out than they had been at the time.

'OK, they quarrelled,' Cecilia said. 'And?'

'And I think he ran away from home. That's what I've always thought. He was a very enterprising young man.'

'You think he ran away and had some kind of accident, which is why he's never been found?'

'No,' said Spencer. 'I think he left with the intention of never coming back. And I think he's still alive.'

# CHAPTER 52

The place was crawling with police. Thea Aldrin sat in her room watching them from her window, struck dumb with horror. *How could it have happened again?* How could the events that had taken place in the '60s still be claiming victims? Because Thea had no doubt about the fate that had befallen the boy who had been standing in the flowerbed outside her window. Nor had she been capable of preventing it.

Boy wasn't really the right word. He was a man, but it was obvious almost straight away that there was something not quite right about him. The look in his eyes would haunt Thea for the rest of her life: a grotesque mixture of pleading and incomprehension that almost made her stop breathing.

There was a time when she had believed she would enjoy a rich and happy life. A time when she and Manfred had fallen in love, when they made their co-habitation into a political issue and refused to get married, even when she became pregnant. She had never felt that Manfred found it difficult to cope with her success. Quite the opposite, in fact: he had praised her to the skies with deep sincerity.

But none of the things she had taken for granted had been true, and none of the things she had held sacred had remained untouched. She could still recall the fear that had made her chew her own tongue as she watched the images flickering on the screen. And the powerlessness that followed when she confronted him.

'It's not real, for fuck's sake!' he had bellowed.

As far as Thea was concerned, that was of minor importance. She didn't want to be anywhere near a man with desires of that kind. Nor did she want him anywhere near her unborn child.

He had been so easy to drive away, and she had always taken that as an indication that the film was in fact genuine. That a murder really had been committed. In her parents' summerhouse, which she had visited countless times. With fear clutching at her throat, she had tried to find proof of what had happened there. She found nothing. And yet she knew that they had been there, that they had destroyed everything. Manfred and someone else, someone who was holding the camera. It wasn't until several years later she found out who that someone was.

If only she hadn't given up the film on the night he moved out. That was the price she had to pay: Manfred refused to leave without the film.

'I don't trust you,' he had said. 'If you're sick enough to believe the film is real, then I don't know what to think of you any more.'

So she had given him the film and assumed she had seen the last of him. Perhaps she should have realised what a terrible error of judgement that was. Everything that followed was undoubtedly a consequence of the first catastrophe. But she couldn't have known how badly things would turn out. If she had had any idea, she would have acted differently a long time ago.

Many things frightened her as she sat there alone in self-imposed silence. Had anyone heard what had happened in her room yesterday evening? Had anyone seen the boy disappear? And, almost more significantly, had anyone heard Thea speak?

# CHAPTER 53

There was no time for rest or recuperation. Peder Rydh decided not to go home and sleep as Alex had suggested. Instead he drove around the streets yet again, then went back to the assisted living complex.

He remembered his brother's earlier phone call with absolute clarity.

*It's a man. He's looking in through the window. He's got his back to me.*

The police had already left when Peder got back to the complex; there was no reason for them to stay. He went to see the manageress and asked to her to let him into Jimmy's room. She couldn't stop apologising.

'I don't understand how this could have happened,' she said as she led the way down the corridor.

She looked and sounded as if she had been crying. Peder didn't care. He didn't understand why she was apologising; she hadn't been on duty when Jimmy disappeared.

'One minute he was here, the next he was gone.'

Peder didn't answer; he just walked past her into Jimmy's room. Everything was as it should be, just as it had been when Peder was there in the morning. The bed with the quilt their grandmother had made, the bookshelves full of cars, pictures and books.

The staff had called Peder and his parents as soon as they realised Jimmy was missing. It was hard to know how long he had been gone; no one had seen him since the afternoon. There was nothing particularly unusual about that; Jimmy liked spending time on his own. Sometimes he didn't bother coming to supper, but stayed in his room instead.

'We found out he wasn't there when we knocked to see if he'd started getting ready for bed. Otherwise, he stays up till all hours, as you know.'

Peder knew. It had been impossible to get Jimmy to bed even when he was a little boy. He wanted to be awake all the time; he was afraid he might miss some fun if he went to bed before everybody else.

The manageress carried on talking, telling Peder things he had already heard the previous evening.

'The only thing missing was his jacket. And the patio door was open when we came in, so we think he must have gone out that way.'

Peder could understand that, but he just couldn't work out where his brother had gone. He could count on the fingers of one hand the times when Jimmy had gone off on his own.

A missing jacket, an open door.

*Where did you go, Jimmy?*

Peder looked out of the window.

'Who lives in the building opposite?' he asked.

He thought back once again to what Jimmy had said; he had seen a man looking in through someone's window.

'That's part of the care home,' the manageress said.

'Is it private?'

'Yes, they just take a few elderly residents each year. I've heard there's a long waiting list to get in.'

Peder looked at the row of small patios on the other side of the lawn. Where could the man Jimmy had seen have been standing? An elderly woman caught Peder's eye. She was so pale and unremarkable that he almost didn't notice her. It looked as if she was gazing straight into Jimmy's room, straight at Peder.

There was something familiar about her.

'Who's she?' Peder asked, pointing at the woman.

'She's one of the more eccentric residents,' said the manageress. 'She used to write children's books. Her name is Thea Aldrin. Have you heard of her?'

Valter Lund was waiting in reception at the appointed time. In his dark suit and white shirt he looked just like any other businessman. Fredrika observed him through the glass door before she went out to collect him. She looked at his open, confident expression, his friendly smile. Shoulders relaxed, legs crossed, hands resting in his lap.

*Was it you who murdered Rebecca, dismembered her body and put it in bags, then carried her through the forest?*

He had no legal representative with him, which surprised Fredrika. His handshake was warm, his voice deep as he said hello. In another time, another life, Fredrika would have found him attractive.

Alex joined her for the interview; he and Fredrika sat down opposite Valter Lund. The time was approximately half-past nine.

'Thank you for taking the time to come in,' Alex began.

Almost suggesting that attendance at a police interview was voluntary.

'Naturally, I want to help in any way I can.'

'Rebecca Trolle,' Alex said.

'Yes?'

'You knew her.'

'I was her mentor.'

'Was that your only connection or relationship with her?'

Fredrika hoped her surprise at Alex's direct approach so early in the proceedings didn't show in her face.

'I don't think I understand the question.'

'We're wondering whether you spent time together for any other reason, apart from the fact that you were her mentor.'

'We did, yes.'

The interview was stopped in its tracks before it had even got going. Fredrika knew she wasn't the only one who was stunned by Valter Lund's honesty; Alex was also surprised.He couldn't hold back a wry smile.

'Could you tell us more?'

Valter Lund ran his hand over the surface of the desk.

'Absolutely. But I would like an assurance that any information I give you will be dealt with discreetly.'

'It's very difficult to give such an assurance when I don't know what you're going to say.'

'I understand.'

Fredrika cleared her throat.

'As long as what you tell us has no relevance as far as our inquiry is concerned, then of course we can ensure that it is not made public along with the documentation relating to the preliminary investigation.'

That seemed to satisfy Valter Lund.

'We had a brief relationship,' he said.

'You and Rebecca?' Fredrika asked.

'We realised almost immediately that there was a mutual attraction. One thing led to another, and in December 2006, I asked her out. We carried on meeting discreetly until the beginning of January, when I decided that we couldn't carry on.'

'So it really was a brief relationship.'

'Indeed.'

'You took her to Copenhagen,' Alex said.

'That's true. That was after we'd broken up. We slept in separate rooms at the hotel, and took different flights to Kastrup. Unfortunately, I realised that Rebecca thought the trip was an attempt to rekindle the relationship on my part. She was terribly disappointed when I explained that wasn't the case.'

Valter Lund's voice filled the room, and his entire being radiated calm stability. He owned the interview in a way Fredrika found fascinating.

'It's hardly surprising that she misunderstood an invitation of that kind,' Alex said. 'My God, a romantic weekend in Copenhagen could make anyone go weak at the knees.'

Lund had to smile.

'Naturally, I realised I had made a mistake. I knew she was upset because I'd finished with her, and I wanted to prove that I still took my role as mentor very seriously. It was stupid of me to think she would understand the difference from the way I behaved.'

'What happened after Copenhagen?'

'Not much. She called me a few times and we decided we would meet up one evening, but it never happened.'

'Because she went missing?'

'Yes.'

Alex looked down at his scarred hands, then glanced over at Fredrika.

'You were considerably older than Rebecca,' he said.

Over twenty years, Fredrika worked out. The same as the age difference between her and Spencer.

'And that was definitely a contributory factor in my decision to stop seeing her. We had nothing in common.'

He spoke as if this was something simple and self-evident, but Fredrika knew that Rebecca must have seen things very differently, and fallen apart.

*That's what I would have done.*

'Did you tell anyone about your affair?' Alex said.

'No.'

'Did she?' Fredrika asked.

'Not as far as I know.'

'Did you know she was pregnant?'

Alex's question remained hanging in the air. For the first time Fredrika could see that they had said something that had not been part of Valter Lund's calculations from the start.

'Pregnant?'

He whispered the word. He quickly passed a hand over his forehead, then lowered it again.

'My God.'

'You didn't know?'

'No. No, definitely not.'

'But the child could have been yours?'

They knew this wasn't the case, but Fredrika asked anyway.

'I doubt it. She said she was on the pill.'

Valter Lund suddenly looked smaller, and genuinely upset.

'She was so very young,' he said quietly.

Alex gave him a moment to recover.

'Did you discuss her dissertation?' he said eventually.

'No.'

Lund quickly recovered his composure; gone was the grief and the shock.

'Really?'

'Yes. Well, obviously I knew what she was working on, but I didn't feel I had anything to offer when it came to that particular topic.'

'We have reason to believe that she may have wanted to talk to Morgan Axberger about her dissertation. Did she ask you for help in arranging a meeting with him?'

'No.'

'Are you absolutely sure about that?'

'One hundred per cent. I would have remembered.'

'Did you ever discuss Axberger with Rebecca?'

'Only superficially. She wasn't really interested in my work.'

Alex broke in.

'Did you attend the mentors' event that took place on the night she disappeared?'

'Yes.'

For the first time, Valter Lund looked genuinely concerned.

'Were you surprised when Rebecca didn't turn up?'

'Of course. I was there mainly for her sake, after all.'

Lund thought for a long time; he looked as if he were considering whether or not to say more.

'The thing is,' he began, 'something happened that day, but I didn't mention before. Or to put it more accurately, something I didn't think was of any significance.'

He ran his hand over the surface of the desk once more.

'Bearing in mind your interest in Morgan Axberger: I was just about to leave for the mentors' dinner and I went along to Morgan's office to speak to him. He was standing there talking to someone on his mobile. As I drew closer I heard him say something along the lines of, "Make sure you're there at quarter to eight, and I'll meet you at the bus stop. I know a place nearby where we can talk".'

Valter Lund spread his hands wide.

'I'm not at all sure this is relevant; I mean, he could have been speaking to anyone. About anything. But . . . deep down, I've always been afraid that Rebecca was on the other end of the phone, just because the time he mentioned fitted in perfectly with the time she went missing. I'm sorry I didn't say anything before.'

Fredrika tried to work out the significance of what she had just heard. Had Morgan Axberger called Rebecca before the dinner and arranged a meeting? There had been an unidentified call on the list. Someone had rung Rebecca just before she left home.

*Was that person Morgan Axberger?*

If that was the case, then Rebecca must have tried to get in touch with him without involving Valter Lund. How had she managed that?

They brought the interview to a close. They would check on what Lund had told them, but Fredrika didn't expect to find any inconsistencies. It was obvious that he had agreed to speak to the police in order to eliminate himself from their inquiries, and Fredrika thought he had succeeded in his aim. Morgan Axberger, on the other hand . . . Fredrika wanted to talk to him right away.

They said goodbye at the glass doors leading to reception.

'Just one more question,' Fredrika said.

He turned back.

'Your uncle,' she said. 'Your mother's brother. Do you see much of him?'

He looked blank.

'My uncle? I don't have an uncle. My mother was an only child.'

Clouds in the sky, no sunshine. Suddenly the night seemed far away, almost completely overshadowed by the events of the morning. Alex felt at peace, grateful to have put some distance between himself and what had happened. He was convinced that it had all happened too fast. One look at Lena's photograph, and he was plagued by a guilty conscience.

*I'll always love you, I'll never leave you.*

Ellen came in and confirmed that Rebecca Trolle had been in touch with the police in the weeks leading up to her disappearance. Because her calls had come via the switchboard, it was impossible to say who she had spoken to. But Alex thought he knew anyway.

Torbjörn Ross.

The question was, where had she got his name from? Ross had been a young man at the time of Thea Aldrin's trial, a peripheral figure in a major police investigation. Rebecca must have gone to the archive department, asked to see the original case notes and found Ross's name among the rest. Perhaps she had made a list of all the officers involved in the case; perhaps Ross was the only one who was still a serving officer.

Or perhaps she had got the name when she went to see Thea Aldrin, since Ross was still visiting her in the hope that he would be able to solve another crime. But who would have told her? Thea Aldrin never spoke, and why would Rebecca have asked the staff about the old woman's visitors?

'There's some material missing,' Fredrika said.

Alex gave a start when he heard her voice.

'What do you mean?'

'Rebecca was very meticulous when it came to making notes on anything to do with her dissertation. But I can't find a single bloody word about either her visit to Thea Aldrin or her contact with the police. And I think we can safely say she had been in touch with the police, because I've gone through all her material over and over again, and there is absolutely no mention of the snuff movie. She got that information from elsewhere.'

Her voice was so strained that Alex had to make a real effort to hear what she was saying.

'How are you feeling?' he asked.

'Bloody awful. If you'll pardon my language.'

Alex had to smile. Fredrika sat down.

'I don't know what to do with myself.'

'It'll all work out.'

He didn't know that, of course, but he thought everything would be fine. Spencer Lagergren wouldn't be convicted of rape if the only evidence was a statement by a disgruntled student. If that really was the only evidence. He hoped it was.

'He's more fragile than you might think,' Fredrika said. 'I don't know how much longer he can cope with being locked up.'

'They'll let him go by tomorrow at the latest,' Alex reassured her. 'They can't justify holding him for any longer than that.'

'The passport.'

'The passport is irrelevant, because he went to get a new one for a completely different reason, didn't he?'

Fredrika managed a wan smile.

'Yes, but it wasn't exactly a better reason.'

'Doesn't matter. We have to take some of the blame for that; we didn't handle that part of the inquiry particularly well.'

Alex changed the subject.

'Rebecca Trolle. You thought she'd been in touch with the police, and the list of calls confirms that.'

'And I also think someone has removed papers from among Rebecca's belongings. Information she got from the police.'

Alex linked his hands behind his head.

'Let's assume you're right. What kind of notes do you end up with when you interview a woman who refuses to speak?'

'Nothing much, I'd say. But I'm sure she would have jotted down a line or two.'

Fredrika was probably right. Alex decided to get to the bottom of this once and for all.

'Morgan Axberger,' he said.

A small smile played around Fredrika's lips.

'He could have been involved. At least he could have been the reason why she got on the wrong bus. If it was Rebecca he was speaking to on the phone, of course.'

'We need to talk to him,' Alex said. 'Sort this out.'

The sound of the telephone interrupted them, and Alex answered. Peder's voice was hoarse.

'Where have you been? I've called several times.'

'Interviewing Valter Lund. Has something happened?'

What a question. Peder's brother was missing, and Alex had just asked him if something had happened.

'Do you know who lives opposite Jimmy?'

'Haven't a clue.'

'Thea Aldrin.'

Alex stared blankly at Fredrika, who was frowning.

'Thea Aldrin is your brother Jimmy's neighbour?'

'She lives in the building opposite. On the ground floor. She has a small patio that faces Jimmy's room. Do you remember what I told you this morning?'

The tone of his voice frightened Alex.

'That Jimmy saw a man looking in through someone else's window.'

502

'Exactly. And whose window do you think that might have been?'

'Peder, listen to me.'

'I'm already on my way over there to give the old bag a good shake.'

Alex slammed his hand down on the desk with such force that Fredrika jumped.

'You will do no such thing. She is one of the key figures in a major murder inquiry. You will not go over there in your present state. Do you hear me?'

Peder was breathing heavily at the other end of the line.

'In that case you need to send Fredrika over here, or someone else. If they're not here within the hour, I'll speak to her myself.'

With a click he was gone.

'Fuck.'

Alex put the phone down and turned to Fredrika.

'I need you to go and speak to Thea Aldrin right away.'

He outlined the background.

'But how could Jimmy's disappearance have any connection with Thea Aldrin? It has to be a coincidence.'

'I think so too, but Peder has been out looking for him all night, and he isn't thinking clearly. I want you to go over to Mångården care home and set up an interview so that the whole thing doesn't go pear-shaped.'

A memory from a few years ago flashed through his mind: a time when Fredrika was new to the job, and Alex didn't know how to handle her. To be honest, he hadn't believed he would ever come to value her, let alone trust her. Not the way he did now.

'And Torbjörn Ross?' she said.

'I'll confront him with what we've got. If he didn't discuss Thea Aldrin with Rebecca, he might know whether someone else did.'

Fredrika got to her feet.

'Are we going to bring in Morgan Axberger? I think we need to speak to him as a matter of urgency.'

'I'll get on it right away.'

'OK,' Fredrika said. 'And then we can think about why Valter Lund lied to us.'

Alex raised his eyebrows.

'You think he lied?'

Fredrika told him what had happened as they were saying goodbye.

'Give our Norwegian colleagues a call and ask to see a passport photo of their Valter Lund so that we know we're talking about the same person,' Alex suggested. 'And get hold of the uncle's contact details.'

'Already in hand,' Fredrika replied.

Alex's phone rang again. It was one of the officers who had been involved in the search for Håkan Nilsson on Lake Mälaren. The boat had been found. And Håkan Nilsson was missing.

# CHAPTER 54

It started to rain just as Fredrika drove into the car park at Mångården. She hadn't been there before, and was surprised at how much greenery there was. Low buildings separated by lawns, deserted in the rain.

There was no actual barrier separating the assisted living complex from the care home, but the difference was clear to Fredrika. The windows of the assisted living complex had bright, colourful curtains with pot plants on the sills, and a young girl was gazing out from one of the rooms. On the other side, where the elderly residents lived, the windows lacked any sign of life. They almost acted as the opening to a peep-show in the complex, but revealed nothing whatsoever about the aged inhabitants of the care home.

She met Peder outside Jimmy's block. She placed a hand on his shoulder, and felt him pull away impatiently. He showed her Jimmy's room.

'This is where he was standing when he spoke to me on the phone, I'm sure of it. And that's what he could see.'

He pointed to the building across the lawn.

'Is that where she lives?' Fredrika asked.

Peder nodded. The sinews in his neck were strained; his eyes were dull with exhaustion.

'We'll go straight over there,' he said.

They followed the path around the edge of the lawn and went into the care home through the main entrance on the other side of the building.

'Peder Rydh, police.'

He showed his ID, and the care assistant immediately stopped what she was doing and showed them to Thea Aldrin's room. The corridor smelled fresh, not stale and unpleasant like some other care homes Fredrika had visited.

The assistant stopped outside one of the anonymous white wooden doors and knocked firmly before walking in.

'You know she doesn't talk?'

'Yes.'

They found themselves in a small hallway, then moved into the room itself; it was light, quite large, and simply furnished.

Thea Aldrin was sitting in an armchair facing the window. She didn't move a muscle. She gave no indication that she had heard them come in.

'You have visitors, Thea.'

Still no reaction. Peder quickly walked around the armchair and stood directly in her line of vision.

'My name is Peder Rydh. Police.'

Fredrika moved to his side and introduced herself in a slightly less stressed tone of voice. She pulled up a chair and sat down; Peder did the same.

'We're here to ask you one or two questions relating to an investigation we're working on,' Fredrika explained. 'Do you remember Rebecca Trolle?'

No reply, no reaction.

Thea didn't appear to have aged significantly since the last pictures of her were published when she was released from prison. Grey hair, cut in a simple bob. Dark eyebrows, a pointed nose. She looked ordinary, like any other pensioner.

Fredrika took out a photograph of Rebecca and held it up in front of Thea.

'We know she came to visit you on one occasion,' Peder said. 'We know she wanted to talk about your past.'

'About the murder of your ex-boyfriend,' Fredrika clarified.

'And the disappearance of your son,' Peder added.

The silence was so dense that Fredrika felt as if she could touch it if she just reached out. Peder's jaws were working. He wouldn't give Thea many more chances to speak before he exploded.

'The film club,' Fredrika said. 'Do you remember the film club?'

It was just possible to sense the hint of a smile, but it vanished so quickly that Fredrika wasn't sure if she had seen it after all.

'To be perfectly honest, we're really confused right now,' she said. 'We've found several bodies on the site where Rebecca's body was dug up, but we don't understand the connections. The only thing we know for certain is that whichever way we look at this story, it leads straight back to you, Thea.'

The old woman went pale, but still she said nothing. She leaned back in the chair and closed her eyes, trying to shut them out in every possible way.

'There was a man in the grave: Elias Hjort. Do you remember him?'

Peder's voice was sharp, quivering with suppressed irritation.

He went on: 'There's an assisted living complex just across the lawn. Do you know any of the residents?'

He leaned forward.

'One of them went missing last night. Are you aware of that?'

Thea stiffened and her eyelids trembled. There was no doubt that she could hear what they were saying, so why the hell did she persist in remaining silent?

'A young man who's good at some things, not so good at others. Did you see him, Thea? He's tall, with dark hair. He nearly always wears blue.'

He sounded as if he was on the point of bursting into tears.

Fredrika gently placed a hand on his arm and caught his eye. She shook her head.

*We're not getting anywhere, we have to drop this.*

Then she saw that Thea had begun to cry. The tears made transparent tracks down her cheeks. Her eyes were still closed.

Peder slid off his chair and crouched down in front of her.

'You have to talk to us,' he said.

His voice was filled with such pleading that Fredrika didn't know what to do with herself.

'If you saw something, anything at all, you have to tell us. Or if someone is threatening you – you can talk to us about that too.'

Thea wiped away the tears with the back of her hand. Fredrika didn't know what to think. The old woman was straight-backed and indomitable, yet clearly marked by the life she had led. Once upon a time, she had had everything anyone could wish for; now she sat alone in a care home, stripped of all that had been written in the stars for her.

Thea got up and lay down on the bed with her back to her visitors. Fredrika and Peder stood up.

'We'll be back,' he said. 'Do you hear me? We're not letting this go just because you refuse to co-operate.'

As they left the room a few minutes later, Thea was still lying in exactly the same position.

'Old bitch,' Peder said when they were out in the corridor.

Fredrika ignored him and went in search of a member of staff. She spotted a young woman who was reading what appeared to be a patient's file.

'Excuse me.'

The woman looked up with the most hunted expression Fredrika had ever seen; her face was pale and weary. Fredrika hesitated.

'Excuse me,' she said again. 'Could I possibly ask you one or two questions about Thea Aldrin?'

The young woman swallowed and attempted a smile.

'Of course. But I don't think I can be of much help; I've only just come on duty. They usually call me in at short notice.'

'Were you working yesterday?'

Relief spread across the woman's face.

'No.'

As if she really didn't want to help.

Fredrika read her name badge: Malena Bremberg. There was such a depth of anxiety in her eyes that it made Fredrika's skin crawl, and she could see that Peder had noticed it as well.

'We need to know whether Thea had any visitors yesterday,' Fredrika said.

'In that case you'll have to ask someone else,' Malena replied. 'As I said, I wasn't working yesterday.'

A colleague appeared in the corridor; she must have overheard the conversation, and took it upon herself to answer the question.

'Thea hardly ever has visitors. Yesterday was no exception.'

'Were you on duty?'

'All day. The only person who visits Thea on a regular basis is that detective. Ross, I think his name is.'

Fredrika made no comment on Torbjörn Ross and his activities. She felt embarrassed for him, and wished he would put a stop to his visits.

'He's been here so often we were almost starting to wonder whether he's the one who sends Thea flowers every Saturday.'

There. A fresh scrap of information.

'She gets flowers every Saturday?'

'She does.'

'And how long has this been going on?'

'Ever since she came here.'

Instinctively, Fredrika knew that this was important. Peder must have felt the same, because he suddenly decided to join in the conversation.

'You don't know who they're from?'

The second care assistant smiled, clearly enjoying the attention more than Malena Bremberg, who excused herself and slipped into one of the anonymous rooms further down the corridor.

'We haven't a clue. They're delivered at eleven o'clock in the morning. Always the same kind of flowers, always the same message on the card: "Thank you", that's all it says.'

So someone had a reason to be grateful to Thea Aldrin, who might have written violent pornographic novels under a pseudonym, and who had stabbed her ex-boyfriend to death.

'We'd like the name of the florist,' Peder said.

Fredrika was holding her breath. So far every road they had followed had led them back to Thea. Now at last they had found a road that led away from her. The question was – who was hiding at the other end?

★   ★   ★

While he was waiting to hear more about Håkan's disappearance and Fredrika and Peder's visit to Thea Aldrin, Alex decided to confront Torbjörn Ross.

'You've been withholding information, Torbjörn.'

A direct statement, leaving no room for denial.

Ross gazed at the papers on his desk as Alex sat down opposite him.

'You met up with her, didn't you? You helped Rebecca Trolle with the research for her dissertation.'

When Ross didn't reply, Alex went on:

'Memory sometimes lets us down, doesn't it? It only struck me today that you were involved in the investigation when Rebecca disappeared. But only during the first week, when we were questioning everyone and going through her things. Then you requested a transfer to another case, didn't you?'

Alex felt the disappointment forming a lump in his throat.

'You took material that could have been useful to us from among Rebecca's belongings. You withheld important clues from me and the others.'

At last, Ross reacted.

'Like hell, I did! You all ignored Thea Aldrin completely. You were too busy searching for the mysterious secret boyfriend. Nobody had even seen him, but you were all convinced he existed. I was the one who looked into the link with Thea Aldrin, and when it led nowhere I didn't see the point in passing on information about an irrelevant minor line of enquiry.'

'You don't believe that for one minute. You kept quiet in order to save yourself, so that you could continue your bizarre, endless investigation into the disappearance of Thea's son.'

Torbjörn Ross flushed deep red.

'She murdered her son, Alex. Surely she shouldn't be allowed to get away with that?'

Alex shook his head.

'You're the only person in the entire world who thinks that. It's unhealthy. You need help.'

Ross got up from his chair, clearly agitated.

'Thea Aldrin was right there in front of you, and you all ignored her completely.'

'At the time, yes, but not now. And you knew that.'

Last weekend. Their conversation on the boat. It was Torbjörn Ross who had first brought up Thea's name, who had pretended to be surprised that Rebecca Trolle was writing a dissertation about her. In fact, the opposite was true. Ross had merely wanted to ensure that Alex wasn't going to drop Thea Aldrin this time.

'What did you take during the original investigation?'

'A few notes, that's all.'

Ross's voice was quiet. He sat down again.

'Notes which included your own name, I presume?'

Ross said nothing.

'What else?'

Silently, Ross reached for a thin folder on the top shelf of his safe. He handed it to Alex.

A page torn from Rebecca's file block, containing notes about the investigation into the murder of Thea's ex. Dates, names. Including that of Torbjörn Ross.

'Who are the other people mentioned here?'

'Officers involved in the case. Most of them have retired by now. She contacted the police and asked to see the records from the preliminary inquiry; that was how she found me and the others.'

'So she called you?'

Ross nodded.

'We met only once, at Café Ugo on Scheelegatan. We went through the case together, and she asked some pretty banal questions. Then it was over.'

'Hang on a minute. It must have been more than some banal questions. It was you who led her to the snuff movie, wasn't it?'

Ross looked surprised.

'She'd saved some of her notes on a floppy disk, and you missed it,' Alex said, trying not to sound triumphant. 'We couldn't understand why the word "snuff" appeared, but now we think we know where she got it from.'

Ross's eyes were darting all over the room.

'I might have given her a helping hand; she was already heading in that direction.'

'Like hell she was,' Alex bellowed. 'It was you and your bloody obsession that gave her ideas. And now she's dead.'

'Exactly!'

Ross raised his voice.

'Now she's dead, and what does that tell us, Alex? It was no coincidence that she died. She must have stumbled on something that you and your colleagues missed.'

'I don't think it's a coincidence either; the question is whether we still have any chance of finding out what she came up with. Because unlike you, she believed Thea was innocent of the murder of which she had been convicted. Why do you think that was? Where did she get that idea from?'

Ross had no answer to that.

'Did she mention it to you?'

'No. When we met she didn't say anything at all about the issue of Thea Aldrin's guilt.'

Alex thought for a moment.

'Do you know what she did after that? Did she speak to anyone else who had worked on the Aldrin case in the '80s?'

Torbjörn Ross hesitated.

'I think she might have pursued the snuff movie angle after I mentioned it to her. I heard she'd spoken to Janne Bergwall; he was there when the film was found, but Janne and I have never discussed it.'

Janne Bergwall. The toughest of them all. A corrupt bastard who had a hold over God the Father himself, which was the only reason he hadn't lost his job. Now he was only a year or so away from retirement. Alex knew a lot of people who would be relieved when he finally went.

Dragging Bergwall into this investigation was the last thing he needed.

'I want to see that bloody film myself before I speak to Bergwall,' Alex said. 'Where is it?'

'In the archive. Would you like me to . . .?'

'No thank you – you've already done more than enough.'

Alex raised a hand to indicate that Ross should keep his distance from now on.

His next job would be to watch this notorious film. He wondered what it would tell him.

*Who was it who had so much to hide, Rebecca?*

# CHAPTER 55

Time was running out for Malena. When they rang from Mångården to ask if she could work an extra shift that day, the call had felt like a blessing at first, but after she had spoken to the police, that no longer seemed possible.

Now, Malena could see more clearly how everything hung together, how she had become a pawn in a game she did not understand, a game she had never asked to be a part of. And she realised that she had good reason to keep out of the way.

*Out of the way of a monster from hell.*

Malena hated Thea Aldrin. For her silence, for her refusal to take responsibility. She was at the centre of the whole thing, and yet no one grabbed hold of her, forced her to tell them what must be told so that everyone could move on. So that everyone could get their lives back.

As lunchtime approached, Malena's fear had turned to sheer terror. She hardly dared walk down the narrow corridors of the care home, and instead sought refuge in the residents' rooms. She might not be aware of the full picture, but Malena sensed that she knew far too much for her own good.

Terror sliced through her belly like a knife.

What if she died? This wasn't like the film she had made. Death was irrevocable.

*There's still so much I want to do.*

And that was the tipping point for Malena, because if there was one thing in her life that she had had more than enough of, it was being a victim. It had to stop. No more.

Without looking back, she left the care home just before midday and headed for her bicycle. The morning's clouds had dispersed, and it looked as if it was going to be another lovely spring day.

Malena took a deep breath.

This was the day when she would find peace of mind.

# INTERVIEW WITH PEDER RYDH,
## 04-05-2009,
### 14.00 (tape recording)

Present: Urban S, Roger M (interrogators one and two). Peder Rydh(suspect).

Urban: How are you, Peder?
  (Silence.)
Roger: We realise things are difficult at the moment, but it's in your best interests to co-operate with us.
Urban: You know how these things work. The people who come off worst are those who don't co-operate during an internal inquiry.
  (Silence.)
Roger: We think we have a relatively clear picture of what happened out on Storholmen, but we would very much like to hear your own version.
Peder: I don't have my own version.
Roger: OK. What does that mean?
Peder: Exactly that. I don't have something called 'my own version' of what happened. I'm the only one who was there. Therefore, the version I have given ought to stand.
Urban: We understand your thinking, but that's not how it works, as you well know.

Roger: We carried out some additional investigations after we received your original statement, and it just doesn't add up.

Peder: Doesn't it?

Roger: No. It's just not possible that you shot the suspect in self-defence. He was unarmed and defenceless, and you shot him right between the eyes.

Urban: You're a good officer, and you are also tall and strong. You had plenty of opportunities to put the suspect out of action without killing him.

Peder: I assessed the situation differently.

(Silence.)

Urban: Are you sure about that, Peder?

Peder: Am I sure about what?

Roger: How many hours' sleep did you get after Jimmy went missing?

Peder: None.

Roger: Almost forty-eight hours without sleep, and with an enormous amount of stress in your system. It's understandable that a significant number of things went wrong.

Peder: Nothing went wrong.

Urban: Everything went wrong.

(Silence.)

Peder: So what is it you actually think?

(Silence.)

Urban: We think you shot the suspect in cold blood, that's what we think. It's called manslaughter. At best. The prosecutor might even decide to call it premeditated murder.

Roger: If you have anything to tell us, it would be best to speak up now, Peder. Otherwise you risk going down for life. Do you understand?

Peder: I have nothing more to add. Not one single word.

# CHAPTER 56

The film appeared to have been made in some kind of summerhouse, because in spite of the fact that all the walls were covered with white sheets, the sunlight found its way through the fabric. Alex was running the film in one of the rooms belonging to the photographic department.

'It's been a while since you lot wanted to borrow a projector,' the technician who had helped him to set up the film had said.

Alex had asked to be left alone; his gut feeling told him that would be for the best. He switched off his mobile, disconnected his thoughts, which kept finding their way back to the night he had spent with Diana Trolle, and switched on the projector.

He realised straight away that the camera was not fixed on a tripod, but was being held by someone who remained anonymous throughout. The door of what Alex assumed was a summerhouse opened; a young woman hesitated, then came in.

She was beautiful. Youthful and unspoiled, the kind of girl Alex would have been happy to see with his son. Or the kind of girl he would have been interested in when he was a young man. Her sleeveless dress breathed summer and the 1960s. The film was in colour, and her skin was tanned. She smiled tentatively at the camera and said something that couldn't be heard: there was no sound.

The room was completely empty of furniture or anything else. An open arena for what was to come. The door opened once again, and a man walked in. Tall, well-built, masked. Armed with an axe in one hand. His appearance was timeless; he looked exactly the way evil has always looked. Alex felt sick as the woman backed away and stumbled into one of the sheets. The window stopped her from falling. The man seized her by the arm, dragged her towards the middle of the room.

Then he raised the axe and swung it at her body in a frenzied attack. She fell to the floor, and even when she was motionless he continued to hack at her body with the axe, and with a knife which he suddenly produced from somewhere. The woman's dress was covered in blood, and when the man finally straightened up, huge slashes in the fabric were clearly visible.

When the film was over, Alex sat there in stunned silence. He watched it again. And again. Then he ripped it from the projector and raced up to Torbjörn Ross's office.

'What made you think the film wasn't genuine?'

'It was just too much of a spectacle to be real. We thought it had been made in the '60s, obviously inspired by the spirit of the age. And we

523

didn't find a murder victim with injuries consistent with those sustained by the woman in the film.'

'And that was it?'

Ross shrugged.

'For a long time, I believed the film was genuine, but in the end I was convinced by the fact that we didn't have a murder victim. I mean, she would have been missed by someone. As far as I was concerned, that didn't really matter anyway. The film was sick, and the person who made it must have been equally sick.'

Alex thought about the mythology surrounding snuff movies, the contention that the victims were usually people who could easily disappear without being missed by anyone.

'Thea Aldrin. You think Thea Aldrin made this film?'

He held out the reel in his hand.

'She was definitely involved,' Ross snapped. 'The links to her disgusting, filthy books were too obvious. The scene where the woman dies in a summerhouse was in both books. There's no other explanation.'

Alex finally lost his temper.

'For fuck's sake, we don't even know if she actually wrote the bloody books! And you thought the film wasn't real!'

'We found Thea's friend Elias Hjort, we found out the royalties were paid to him. And guess what, Alex? When we went to bring him in for questioning, we were told that he'd left the country.

What's that worth today, now we know he hadn't left the country at all? He was dead.'

'Your only link to Thea Aldrin was Elias Hjort,' Alex said. 'And that bloody film club.'

'And the rumours. There's no smoke without fire; you know that as well as I do.'

Alex shook his head.

'The film is real,' he said.

The colour drained from Ross's face.

'Real?'

'I'll show it to the forensic pathologist, but I'm absolutely certain. The young woman who dies in this film is the young woman who was sharing a grave with Rebecca Trolle.'

Spencer called when Fredrika was on her way back to HQ from the care home.

'They've let me go.'

Emptiness in her soul, warmth in her breast.

*How far apart have we drifted?*

'Have they dropped the case?'

'No, but there wasn't enough evidence to suggest that I was likely to abscond for them to arrest me. They've blocked my passport; I can't apply for a new one until all this is over.'

Fredrika said nothing. The whole thing had gone beyond the point where words were even possible.

'I wasn't the only one who was keeping secrets. And your secrets were my secrets.'

She heard what he said, but was incapable of taking in the words.

She wanted to say that she hadn't been keeping any secrets at all, but she knew it was a lie. Several days had passed since Spencer's name first came up in the investigation; several days of silence.

Then again, no silence was worse than Spencer's. He had changed their life in order to hide his problems. Said he wanted to take paternity leave, when in fact he was running away from a difficult situation at work, a situation that could well cost him both his job and his future.

'I could have helped you,' Fredrika said.

'How?'

'Given you some advice.'

That wasn't true, and she knew it. There was nothing she could teach Spencer in that respect, nothing she could use to support him. All the same, she felt as if he had rejected not only her professional expertise, but her heart and her love. In his hour of need, she had not been permitted to be there for him.

And it hurt like hell.

'See you at home.'

He ended the call. Fredrika drove into the underground car park, then hurried upstairs. Peder wasn't there, of course – he had said he was going to carry on looking for Jimmy – and there was no sign of Alex either.

Ellen came to see her. Morgan Axberger had been in touch after Ellen had spoken to his secretary, at Alex's request. He had promised to call in later that afternoon.

'Since when do people decide when they'd like to be questioned?' Fredrika wanted to know.

'Since we started contacting leading figures within Swedish industry,' Ellen replied.

One of the officers who had found Håkan Nilsson's boat called; Håkan was still missing.

Fredrika felt a creeping sense of anxiety as she put the phone down. They had assumed that Nilsson had taken off in order to get away from the police, but they could have been wrong. Perhaps he thought his life was in danger, and that he had to find somewhere safe to hide? But in that case, why hadn't he spoken to the police and asked for protection?

She went over the many events of the day. The meeting with Valter Lund hadn't been as helpful as she had hoped; it had merely generated yet more confusion with regard to his identity. It was obvious that he was trying to hide something, but what? And did the fact that Valter Lund might not be the person he claimed to be actually have anything to do with the case?

A man with his roots in Gol, outside the beautiful area of Hemsedal. A man who, on paper, had had a catastrophic upbringing, and had no living relatives. Unless you counted a bewildered uncle who turned up at the local police station every year to ask if his nephew had been found. An uncle who obviously didn't recognise his nephew in pictures of Valter Lund.

Then there was the meeting with Thea Aldrin.

A woman who had chosen to live in self-imposed silence for decades; she had been convicted of premeditated murder, and since her release she had spent all her time in a care home. Could there really be a connection with Jimmy's disappearance, or was the fact that they were neighbours no more than a coincidence?

*I don't believe in coincidences any more.*

Rebecca Trolle had obviously felt the same way, because she had pursued the tip-off about the snuff movie, assumed that it was somehow relevant. Fredrika and her colleagues had yet to fully appreciate the connection with the dead bodies; they only knew that there was allegedly a link between Thea Aldrin and the snuff movie. Fredrika reminded herself that Alex was taking care of that particular line of enquiry; in fact, he was probably working on it right now.

The corridor was eerily silent. Fredrika went along to Alex's office: still empty. Everyone else seemed to be out too. She returned to her own office. There was only one way out of this mess that kept on sending them back to Thea Aldrin and her silence: the flowers that were delivered to the care home every Saturday.

The helpful assistant had quickly found the name of the supplier: Masters Flowers, a shop on Nybrogatan in Östermalm. Fredrika decided not to waste any more time on speculation, and gave them a call.

'I'm ringing about the flowers you deliver every Saturday to a lady by the name of Thea Aldrin.'

'I'm afraid we operate a policy of strict confidentiality when it comes to our clients. They have the right to rely on our discretion.'

'Obviously, we will treat any information you give us with great care, but we are in the middle of a murder inquiry, and I really do need your help.'

The shop owner was still hesitant, and Fredrika thought she was going to have to get a warrant from the prosecutor to make him talk.

'It's a standing order,' he said eventually. 'We've made the same delivery every week for more than ten years. Payment is made in cash; the client's representative comes to the shop once a month. A woman.'

'And the name of the client?'

'I don't honestly know.'

'You don't know?'

Fredrika heard a sigh at the other end of the line.

'We questioned the arrangement in the beginning, but then we asked ourselves what was the point? I mean, it was hardly likely to be some kind of criminal activity, and the payment was always made on time. Naturally, we were curious, I mean Thea Aldrin is quite well known, but . . .'

His voice died away.

Fredrika's brain kicked into gear. Someone sent flowers to Thea Aldrin every Saturday. Anonymously. Payment in cash by a third party.

'You don't have any contact details for the

client?' she asked. 'A telephone number, an email address, anything at all?'

'Just a minute.'

She heard the rustle of papers; the owner was soon back on the line.

'We do actually have a mobile number. We insisted. We have to be able to contact someone if we can't make the delivery.'

Fredrika's heart rate doubled.

'Could you possibly give me the number? That would be enormously helpful.'

# CHAPTER 57

Things would have to be done in the right order, otherwise everything would go to hell in a handcart. First of all, Alex sent the film and the projector to the forensic pathologist by courier.

'Sit down in a darkened room and watch this disgusting crap,' Alex said over the phone. 'Then call me back and tell me what you think.'

If the girl in the grave was the same girl who had died in the film, there was suddenly a clearer connection between the murders. First of all someone was killed on film, then others died so that the secret would be kept.

*But what secret?*

Alex found Janne Bergwall in his office. It was obvious that his colleague was living on borrowed time, so to speak. The walls were virtually covered with a selection of diplomas, newspaper articles and other souvenirs that Bergwall had collected over the years. Alex glanced at them; it was clear that none of the documents bore witness to some kind of impressive feat, which fitted in perfectly with his impression of Bergwall. He was a man who could fall through the ice hundreds of times during his life, and never drown or freeze to death. It was as if he sought out the spots where the ice was at its thinnest so that he would be sure of hearing that familiar crack.

But this time he had stepped onto thin ice once too often.

Alex didn't feel the need to waste time introducing himself; instead, he put his energy into explaining why he was there.

'Rebecca Trolle,' he said. 'The girl whose dismembered body we found in Midsommarkransen.'

Bergwall looked at him through narrowed eyes. 'Yes?'

'I believe she came to see you.'

'Maybe.'

Alex took a deep breath.

'No, not maybe. We're a long way past the point where you can carry on keeping quiet about this. The girl is dead, and I want to know how she ended up in a grave with two other people who had been there for decades.'

He sat down opposite Bergwall, who was looking less than happy. His face was marked by the passing of the years, marked by the problems for which no one was to blame but himself.

'Start talking. When did she come to see you, and what did you tell her?'

Bergwall closed his eyes for a second, as if he wanted to shut Alex out while he made his decision.

When he opened his eyes, his expression was unreadable.

'I didn't think the girl would come to any harm.'

*But she did, didn't she?*

Alex kept quiet.

'She came to see me after she'd spoken to Torbjörn Ross. She'd gone through the notes from the preliminary investigation relating to Thea Aldrin and the murder of her ex, and she'd found Ross's name there. I think he was probably the only one who was still on the team. Anyway, as I understood it they had discussed not only the murder, but also the dirty books the old bag was supposed to have written. The girl obviously had her doubts about whether Aldrin really was the author, and Ross mentioned that they'd been turned into a film as well. Then she found the notes from that investigation as well.'

'You mean the raid on the porn club – Ladies' Night?' Alex said.

'Exactly.'

'And what did you tell Rebecca?'

'Too much.'

Bergwall cleared his throat and folded his arms.

'I told her how we'd found the films, and that we'd tried to track down the person who'd written the books to help us establish whether the film was real. But we only got as far as Elias Hjort, who received royalties from the publisher, Box. At first we thought it was a dead end, but then we came across the film club. Elias Hjort

533

and Thea Aldrin knew each other through the club.'

Bergwall fell silent, but Alex sensed that he had more to say. After a moment he went on:

'I showed Rebecca Trolle the original case notes and went through them with her. For example, she found out who else was at the porn club on the night of the raid.'

Alex shuffled on the uncomfortable chair, wishing that his colleague would get a move on. Bergwall took a folder out of his filing cabinet, removed a sheet of paper and passed it to Alex.

A list of names. Almost exclusively men.

'The clients who were at the club that night. Anyone you recognise?'

Bergwall was wearing a supercilious smile.

Alex glanced through the list, and stopped when he reached the penultimate name:

*Morgan Axberger.*

He looked up.

'Another member of The Guardian Angels.'

'Exactly,' Bergwall said again.

Alex shrugged.

'A managing director who visits porn clubs; that's not particularly interesting.'

'If it wasn't for one nice little detail that wasn't followed up in the original investigation.' Bergwall fixed his gaze on Alex. 'It was Axberger who had the film on him.'

Alex raised his eyebrows.

'There you go,' Bergwall said. 'That surprised

you, didn't it? Me too. Unfortunately, we never found out how or why Axberger had got hold of the film; he bought his way out straight away. He paid one of the lads involved in the raid to say that the film had been found in the club's office. The truth didn't come out until several years later, when the bloody idiot – the copper, I mean – got drunk at a Christmas party and told someone what he'd done.'

He laughed drily.

'And what happened then?'

'Not a bloody thing. By that time the prosecutor had dismissed the seizure of the film as being of no interest, so we didn't bother confronting Axberger with the fresh information. After all, it's not illegal to walk around with a film in your inside pocket.'

'As long as it isn't a genuine snuff movie,' Alex said.

'Which it wasn't.'

Bergwall looked so smug that Alex felt like punching him on the nose. He clenched his fists under the desk; he was furious.

'You have no idea what your silence has cost my case. How the hell could you keep quiet about the fact that you'd given Rebecca Trolle that kind of information?'

'What do you mean, that kind of information? I'm telling you, it was irrelevant. The film was a fake and Axberger was untouchable. It was that simple.'

Alex leapt to his feet so abruptly that the chair rocked.

'I'll be back, Bergwall. Until then, you keep your mouth shut about what you know. Is that clear?'

He saw the glint in Bergwall's eye.

'Think very carefully before you threaten me, Recht.'

Alex took a step closer, leaned across the desk and hissed:

'The film was genuine, you stupid bastard. You stumbled on a secret that has led to the deaths of at least three people. If I were you, I'd keep my bloody head down.'

With those words he left Bergwall's office, slamming the door behind him. A fresh thought occurred to him as he heard the crash. What if there were more snuff movies out there? Morgan Axberger might just be able to answer that question.

Exhaustion washed over him after lunch. Peder realised he was blinking several times in order to try to clear his vision. He knew he ought to eat, even though he wasn't hungry. Ylva called him.

'Still no sign?'

Peder hardly knew how to respond. No sign, was that what people said when someone disappeared?

'No, we haven't found him yet.'

Yet. Was that too optimistic a word, under the circumstances. Was there a possibility that it was already too late?

*Don't think about the unthinkable.*

Peder's eyes filled with tears. If Jimmy was dead . . . for the first time, Peder was facing something he knew he wouldn't be able to accept. The bond with his brother was unbreakable, it would last forever. Jimmy was the eternal child, the eternal responsibility.

'What will happen to Jimmy when Dad and I aren't around any more?' Peder's mother had said a few years ago.

Peder had reacted with fury.

'Jimmy will come to me. I would never abandon him. Not for a second.'

That promise still held, even though Jimmy was missing. Peder would never abandon him, never stop searching. But why was it so bloody difficult to work out where Jimmy had gone? He couldn't explain it, but Peder knew it must have something to do with Thea Aldrin. Jimmy had seen someone standing by the window, spying on the old woman. And Peder had dismissed it as a misunderstanding, a figment of his imagination.

*What did you see, Jimmy?*

You didn't have to talk to Jimmy for long to realise that his mind wasn't that of an adult. And yet someone had felt sufficiently threatened to abduct him.

His anxiety grew into sheer terror, and Peder sat in the car with sweat pouring off him. He now felt certain that Jimmy had not simply got lost, but had been robbed of his freedom by someone who wanted him out of the way. Someone who had already committed several murders, and who definitely wouldn't hesitate to kill again.

Peder wanted to cry. He had to pull himself together, fast. He mustn't think he had lost, mustn't give up. Not yet. He had to get back to HQ and try to understand how his brother's disappearance fitted in with everything else.

There was no time for rest or food. The only thing that mattered was finding Jimmy.

Fredrika bumped into Alex as she left Ellen's office. He seemed pleased to see her, but the strain was etched on his face.

'We need to speak to Morgan Axberger as soon as possible,' he said, and filled Fredrika in on what he had found out from Janne Bergwall.

She was as shocked as Alex.

'How could Bergwall and Ross keep quiet about all this?'

'They thought it was irrelevant,' Alex said. 'They didn't think it had anything to do with Rebecca's disappearance. They should have realised that it was impossible to make that judgement without having the full picture.'

His mobile rang.

'Get the team together in the Lions' Den in fifteen minutes,' he said to Fredrika. 'I just need to take this.'

It took less than three minutes to gather everyone who wasn't out on the case. Fredrika sat down and went through the latest fax from Kripos in Norway. They had attached a passport photograph of Valter Lund at the age of eighteen.

*It's not him.*

Even though the quality of the image was poor, Fredrika could see from a distance of several metres that the man in the picture was not the Valter Lund she had interviewed earlier in the day.

Could Kripos have made a mistake? Virtually impossible.

She tried to shut out the chatter of her colleagues in the conference room. If Valter Lund had stolen another man's identity, then he must have done so at a very early age. Was that kind of thing even possible?

She looked at the man on the passport photograph. His expression was grim; he had long hair and a tattoo on the lower part of his neck, just visible above his T-shirt. How had his path crossed that of the man who was now such a well-known figure in the business world? And how had the identity switch been achieved? Murder?

Regardless of who he really was. Valter Lund was too young to have murdered the woman who had been buried the longest. He could have killed Elias Hjort, but in that case he must have known the person or persons who had murdered the woman, because otherwise he wouldn't have buried Hjort's body in the same place.

Alex walked in. Everyone straightened up and stopped talking.

'Unbelievable,' he said, dropping his mobile on the table. 'They took the guards off the grave site last night because they'd finished digging, and apparently some idiot has come along and started filling in the crater.'

He shook his head.

'Sorry?' said one of his colleagues. 'Someone turned up in the middle of the night and started shovelling the soil back into the hole?'

'Apparently,' Alex replied. 'But let's move on: we have more important things to discuss.'

Fredrika put down the fax so that she could listen properly, but a strong sense of unease had come over her. Why would someone go to the grave site in the dark and start filling the hole?

Alex updated everyone on the latest developments. He began with Valter Lund's interview, and went on to his own inquiries into the old film.

Someone let out a whistle when he had finished speaking.

'A genuine snuff movie. Bloody hell.'

Alex held up a warning finger.

'A number of points regarding the film are still unclear, including the link with the two notorious books, *Mercury* and *Asteroid*. The film was made in the '60s; whereas, the books weren't published until the '70s. This raises the question of whether the film might have inspired the person who wrote the books, rather than vice versa. And we still don't know why Rebecca Trolle made a connection between The Guardian Angels and snuff movies.'

'Does there have to be a concrete link?' Fredrika asked. 'It sounds as if she got quite a lot of information from Janne Bergwall. The snuff movie led back to both Elias Hjort and Morgan Axberger, and the fact that they were members of The Guardian Angels, along with Thea Aldrin, was no secret.'

'What about Spencer Lagergren, the fourth member?' a colleague wondered.

Fredrika looked down at the table, embarrassed.

'He's completely in the clear,' Alex replied. 'We've spoken to him purely to check our information, and he has nothing whatsoever to do with the other events.'

How many people knew that Spencer and Fredrika were a couple? It was difficult to read anything from the faces around the table, but Alex's expression clearly communicated support and reassurance. He gave Fredrika a wry smile.

'Have we heard from Morgan Axberger?' Alex asked.

'No,' said Fredrika. 'Not since this morning when he called Ellen.'

'We'll give him another hour, then we'll go to his office and pick him up.'

'Unless he's already left the country,' Fredrika said. 'If he thinks we're onto him, I mean. If he's the one we're after.'

'Is he?' Alex said.

'Maybe. Him or Valter Lund.' She explained what she had found out from Kripos.

'Valter Lund is too young,' Cecilia Torsson chipped in.

'That's what I thought,' Fredrika replied. 'But he's still living under a false identity, in spite of the risks that must involve at his level.'

She fell silent, wondering what might lie hidden in Lund's past. Images crowded her mind, images of strong arms digging in Midsommarkransen.

*It's not him.*

Her gut instinct left no room for doubt: it wasn't Valter Lund they were looking for. And yet he seemed to be an important part of the game.

'We need to speak to Lund again,' Alex said. 'I don't care if he was here just a few hours ago; let's get him back.'

'And Axberger.'

Peder's voice came out of nowhere. No one had heard him open the door of the conference room.

Fredrika swallowed when she saw him standing there in the doorway. His eyes were narrow, exhausted slits, his face was ashen. His shoulders slumped, and his hair was standing on end. There was no point in telling him to go home until they had found Jimmy.

'Obviously, we need to speak to Morgan Axberger,' Alex said gently. 'Come in and sit down, Peder.'

Peder pulled up a chair and sat down next to Fredrika.

Ellen knocked and came in.

'I know who's sending flowers to Thea Aldrin. Or at least, I know where they're coming from.'

'Who?'

'A woman called Solveig Jakobsson. When she realised why I was calling, she suddenly refused to co-operate. But then I rang the tax office and found out who her employer is. She works at Axbergers. According to the switchboard, she's Valter Lund's PA.'

# CHAPTER 58

Thea Aldrin knew that it was only a question of time until it was all over. The visit from the police indicated that the drama had entered its final act, and in just a few minutes all the actors would be called to the stage to receive the audience's appreciation.

She didn't believe she could have done anything differently. The most important thing had always been her concern for the boy, for her son. The child she had carried and given birth to all alone. The boy who had become a young man and lost his trust in everything around him the day he went up into the loft to fetch a suitcase, and found the original manuscripts for *Mercury* and *Asteroid*.

His bellowing rage had echoed in her head ever since.

'You fucking psychopath,' he had yelled. 'Everything they say is fucking true, you really are sick in the head.'

She had thought she was doing him a favour by not telling him the truth. She had thought his anger would blow over. But that hadn't happened. The following morning his bed was empty, and he didn't come back. She wasn't surprised that he had managed to stay away. He was a genuinely talented individual, and he had drive and ambition. He was also very good-looking.

That was why she never really got anxious in the way that people obviously expected. She went to the police, of course, and reported her son missing. She travelled far and wide in her quest to find him. But as the days went by and she didn't break down, she noticed a change in the attitude of the police. Why wasn't the boy's mother grieving as she should? Why was there always an element of certainty, of assurance in her eyes?

Thea moved over to the window and gazed across at the block where the missing young man lived. The fact that he had got in the way hurt her more than she could say. You only had to look at him to see how things were; he would never have been able to tell anyone what he had heard and seen in a way that made sense.

What he had heard, above all. Thea's voice. In his world, the fact that an old woman was talking was hardly sensational, but to those who knew she hadn't spoken since 1981, it was big news. According to the rumours, Thea had chosen eternal silence, but they were wrong. She practised using her voice every day. When she was sure she was completely alone. With the radio on loud. Or when she was in the shower.

Thea wept as she thought about the young man's brother. No one had told her that the detective who had come to see her with his female colleague that same afternoon was the young man's brother, but Thea could see it at once. They had many features in common: the same eyes, the same distinctive nose and chin.

And the worry. It burned fiercely in the police officer's eyes.

She dried her tears. It was unlikely that he would ever find his brother. Nor would he realise in which grave he had been laid to rest.

# CHAPTER 59

'I know who he is.'

Fredrika Bergman's chin was jutting out as it always did when she was sure she was about to be contradicted.

'So do I,' Alex replied.

'Valter Lund is Thea Aldrin's son.'

Alex had reached the same conclusion.

'Can we be sure that Thea knows who sends her flowers every week?'

'I have no doubt about that at all,' said Fredrika.

'So, mother and son. What are they hiding?'

Fredrika's mobile rang, and Alex watched as she rejected the call.

'If that's Spencer, it's absolutely fine if you want to speak to him.'

She shook her head.

'I can only think of one thing at a time right now.'

Her eyes shone like pebbles that had just been lying in water.

For God's sake, what is wrong with all my colleagues? Alex thought. Every single one of us is damaged.

Peder knocked on Alex's door; he came in and closed it behind him.

'Am I disturbing you?'

'Of course not.'

Peder's haggard appearance worried Alex. He understood Peder's agony over his missing brother only too well. The problem was that Peder failed to appreciate that his own impaired judgement could jeopardise the entire investigation. Alex couldn't afford to let that happen.

'Don't you think you should go home and rest for a few hours?'

Peder shook his head.

'It's OK, I don't feel tired.'

A lie.

Alex turned to Fredrika.

'If Valter Lund is actually Johan Aldrin, then where is the real Valter Lund? Have you spoken to his uncle?'

'Not yet. But according to the Norwegian police, who have spoken to the uncle several times, Valter signed on as a crew member on a car ferry in 1980, and was never heard of again.'

'Johan Aldrin was only young when he disappeared; he hadn't even left school. Could he have worked on the ferry as well?'

'I'll get in touch with the shipping company.'

She made a note on her pad.

Peder looked from one to the other.

'Morgan Axberger,' he said.

'We've just sent a patrol car to his office to pick him up.'

'Good.'

Peder shuffled uncomfortably.

'Do you think Rebecca Trolle found out who Valter Lund is?'

Alex stiffened.

'I mean, what if they're both equally crazy, mother and son? What if Valter Lund murdered Rebecca?'

'Their relationship,' Fredrika said. 'Rebecca knew she was pregnant, but she didn't know who the father was. She might have confronted Valter Lund, demanding that he accept the responsibility.'

'In that case, Valter Lund is a fine actor,' Alex said. 'Because I had the distinct impression that he didn't know about the pregnancy until we mentioned it.'

'We need to speak to him again,' Fredrika said. 'Scare him a bit, pretend we think he's guilty to make him start talking.'

Peder looked at them with exhausted eyes.

'What is it he's so grateful for?'

'Sorry?' Alex said.

'He always writes "Thanks" on the card that comes with the bouquet. What is he thanking his mother for?'

When Fredrika got back to her office, she was in such a hurry that she didn't notice Spencer at first.

'Busy?'

She almost let out a scream.

'God, you frightened me!'

For a moment she was at a loss. A second later, she knew exactly what to do.

'I've been so worried.'

The tears came from nowhere, and she walked straight into his arms.

She could feel his breath on her hair as he stroked her back. It sounded as if he was crying too.

'I saw your mum when I went home.'

Fredrika dried her tears.

'I asked her to look after Saga today. I couldn't stay at home doing nothing.'

Spencer moved back a step. There was still unfinished business between them. Things they would have to talk about, but not here and not now.

'I gather I'm no longer regarded as a suspect in your investigation,' he said.

'That's right.'

Fredrika swallowed hard and pushed a few stray strands of hair off her face.

'So you won't be needing a new passport after all.'

Spencer looked as if he was about to laugh, but then his face closed down again. Fredrika could feel her agitation growing.

'We need to talk, but it'll have to wait until I get home.'

'And when will that be?'

'Later. Late, in fact.'

Spencer pulled on his jacket, which he had been holding, and moved towards the door.

'I never meant to lie to you,' he said.

Fredrika felt the tears threatening once more.

'Don't do it again, Spencer.'

He shook his head slowly.

'But you lied too.'

'I didn't lie, I withheld information. And there's a big difference.'

He smiled sadly.

'Maybe.'

Then he was gone.

Fredrika stood there alone. She wrapped her arms around her body. She felt alone when she was on her own, alone when the two of them were together.

Alex walked in.

'Who was that?'

She assumed he was referring to Spencer.

'That was the father of my daughter.'

Alex looked so shocked that she burst out laughing, but the laughter was accompanied by fresh tears.

'Sorry,' she said quickly, dabbing at her eyes.

Alex placed a hand on her shoulder.

'Listen, if you need to take a break and go home for a while, that's fine.'

It was almost four o'clock; there was no time to 'take a break'.

'I'm staying until we're done,' Fredrika replied. 'How did it go with Morgan Axberger?'

'He wasn't in his office. His secretary said he'd gone to an emergency meeting.'

'Do we believe that?'

'We do at the moment, but not for much longer. We've made it very clear that we want to speak to him on an important matter, and he still chooses to stay away. Valter Lund, on the other hand, was where we expected him to be, and now he's here.'

Fredrika grabbed her notepad and pen.

'He's got a lot of explaining to do.'

'He has,' Alex agreed. 'But he'll have to wait, because first you're going to speak to someone called Malena Bremberg.'

'Malena Bremberg?'

Fredrika was surprised; she tried to place the woman's name. Wasn't she the care assistant who had been so shy when they met her at the care home?

Peder walked past the door on his way down the corridor, then turned and came back.

'I'm going out to look for Jimmy again.'

To look for the brother who had been missing for almost twenty-four hours. The brother who had vanished without a trace; it seemed as if he had disappeared without a single person having seen a thing.

Except for Thea Aldrin, who refused to speak.

The feeling of unease that had haunted Fredrika during the meeting came flooding back. It was something Alex had said. A thought that had passed through her mind so quickly that she hadn't managed to grab hold of it.

Alex's phone rang, and he answered. Peder raised a hand in farewell and set off down the corridor.

'That was one of the lads out at the grave site in Midsommarkransen,' Alex said. 'They're packing it in now. The hole has been filled in, and they'll be removing the police tape shortly.'

*There.*

The same thought once more.

An icy hand clamped itself around Fredrika's heart.

'You said someone had been there during the night and started filling in the crater,' she said.

'Some bloody idiot, no doubt,' he said. 'Short of something to do.'

'We need to open up the grave,' Fredrika said.

Alex looked at her as if she had lost her mind.

'Jimmy,' she whispered. 'I think they buried him there last night.'

# CHAPTER 60

In the dream, Jimmy was flying higher and higher on the swing. His whole face was beaming as he shouted to Peder:

'Can you see me? Can you see how high I'm going?'

Then he was falling.

Or flying through the air.

Peder usually woke up the second before Jimmy hit the ground. It was as if his mind was protecting him from the painful, inevitable outcome. Peder had seen his brother's skull and his life smashed to pieces against a stone once, and that was enough.

His mother rang while he was in the car on his way back to the assisted living complex.

'You need to go home and get some rest.'

Her voice was fractured with anxiety.

*I've already lost one son, don't make me go through that same hell all over again.*

'I'm OK, Mum.'

'We're worried about you, Peder. Can't you come home and have something to eat?'

We. That must mean his parents and Ylva. Eat? Peder couldn't remember when he last ate. Was it the previous evening, when he and Ylva were sitting on the balcony? It felt like such a long time ago.

'Where are you going?'

'To Jimmy's. To Mångården, I mean.'

'Call me soon. Promise?'

'I promise.'

He pulled into the car park a while later. He slammed the car door and marched straight into the complex, where the residents were in the middle of a meal. One of the girls who worked there got to her feet as Peder walked in.

'I can find my own way,' he said, and headed for Jimmy's room.

He closed the door behind him and stood there in the middle of the floor, searching for something out of the ordinary, some indication of where Jimmy might have gone. But nothing was missing, nothing was damaged. Nothing.

*He can't just have walked out into the night and disappeared.*

'Peder.'

The care worker's voice made him jump.

'Yes?'

He turned around and saw her standing in the doorway with one of Jimmy's friends. Had they knocked before opening the door? He couldn't be sure.

'Michael has something he wants to tell you.'

Michael. A young man Peder had met on countless occasions. He was well-built, with dark hair.

He suffered from some indefinable impairment that meant he was trapped in eternal childhood, like Jimmy. He loved Jimmy, and thought that Peder was the coolest guy in the whole of Sweden, because he was a cop.

'What is it, Micke?'

'I'm not really allowed to say.'

Peder forced a smile.

'Of course you are. I'm a cop, aren't I? I can keep a secret.'

'Jimmy said he saw a man standing out there spying.'

He pointed towards Thea Aldrin's room on the other side of the lawn.

'Was it a secret?'

Michael nodded importantly.

'Yes. That's what he said. He said it was a secret. That's why I thought I'd better not mention the other thing until now.'

'What other thing?'

'I saw Jimmy leave his room yesterday. I was looking out of my window, and I saw him go over to that lady's room and stand outside. He looked in through her window.'

Michael swallowed. Peder was fighting to maintain his composure.

'Then what happened?'

Michael hesitated, but decided to keep going.

'A man came out of the lady's room. Through the door. Onto the patio. He spoke to Jimmy, but only for a second. Then they went off.'

Peder's heart skipped a beat.

'Where, Micke? Where did they go?'

'I don't know. They went to the car park and drove off in a car. They didn't come back. I waited all night. I kept thinking he'd be really cold; he didn't have any shoes on.'

There were secrets that were just too big to keep. Secrets that couldn't be accommodated inside a normal body, a normal heart; they demanded more and more space as time went by.

Malena Bremberg looked as if she was carrying just such a secret. Her face was pale and weary as Fredrika greeted her. She refused coffee, but said she would like a cup of tea.

'What was it you wanted to tell me?'

There wasn't much time. For anything. For nothing.

Alex had sent the digger back to Midsommarkransen to open up the grave so that the dogs would be able to pick up the scent of a body.

'Let's pray that you're wrong,' he had said to Fredrika.

She felt so powerless that she wanted to scream.

And Valter Lund, or Johan Aldrin, was waiting in another interview room.

Malena Bremberg sipped her tea as she struggled to find the right words.

'I'm not sure what all this is about,' she said eventually. 'But I think I know something you ought to know too. Something about Rebecca Trolle.'

She took a deep breath and drank some more tea. Fredrika waited. Waited and listened.

'Two years ago I had a brief relationship with an older man I met in a bar. Morgan Axberger.'

Fredrika was astonished.

'But you're so much younger than him!'

Malena blushed.

'That was the point. The fact that he was forty years older than me. I know he looks boring, but he can be incredibly charming.'

Fredrika had no comment to make on that point; she had never met Morgan Axberger.

'What did he want from you?' she asked.

Malena's face lost all trace of colour.

'He wanted to know whether Thea Aldrin ever had visitors. At first I thought he was interested in me because . . . I thought he wanted a relationship with me. But that wasn't what he wanted at all. He wanted a spy inside Mångården.'

'He was just using you.'

'When I realised what he was doing, I tried to break off our relationship. I refused to co-operate. But everything went wrong.'

It was too much for Malena. Huge tears rolled down her cheeks.

'Which of Thea's visitors was he interested in?' Fredrika asked.

'All of them. But she didn't have many. There was a police officer, Torbjörn Ross, who'd been coming for years, plus the odd journalist now and again. Then suddenly Rebecca Trolle turned up.

She said she wanted to speak to Thea because she was writing a dissertation about her.'

Malena blew her nose.

'Did you tell Morgan Axberger that Rebecca had been there?'

'Yes. I happened to be on duty that day.'

Fredrika swallowed hard. Morgan Axberger appeared to have good reason to stay away from the police. In addition, he was old enough to have murdered all the victims found in Midsommarkransen.

'You said things went badly when you tried to break off your arrangement with Axberger?' Fredrika said.

Malena's tone was resigned.

'He picked me up one morning when I was on my way to a lecture. By that time, I had realised he was dangerous, and I'd kept out of his way. But it was no good. He kept me prisoner for twenty-four hours.'

'What did he do?'

Fresh tears. Then a whisper.

'He showed me a film.'

Fredrika felt uncomfortable with the direction the conversation was taking, but she had to know.

'What kind of film?'

'A film from hell. One of those silent films that only lasts a few minutes.'

Fredrika held her breath.

'At first I didn't understand what I was watching. The film had been shot in a room where all the walls were covered with sheets. A young girl came in, then a man wearing a mask . . .'

Fredrika knew. Alex had told her about the film; she had decided against watching it herself.

Malena was sobbing.

'He attacked her with an axe. Then a knife. I thought it was a sick joke. Until it was all over. Then the man bent over the girl, who was lying on the floor, and looked into the camera, at the person who was holding it. He was laughing when he took off the mask; it was just horrible. It was a really old film, but I could see the man's face clearly. He was evil personified.'

Fredrika's mouth went dry.

'Hang on, are you telling me that after the girl was dead, the man who'd killed her took off his mask?'

Time stood still in the interview room.

Malena nodded.

'I have no idea who he was. He grinned at the man who was holding the camera; he seemed really pleased with himself. When the film ended Morgan went out into the hallway, and when he came back he had an axe in his hand. I don't think I've ever screamed so loudly in my entire life.'

She shuddered, her face chalk-white.

'I ran, and he hunted me down like an animal. I tried to get out onto the balcony, but he was faster than me. He forced me down and swung the axe. It hit the floor several times, just a few centimetres from my head. I was convinced he was going to kill me. When he raised the axe for the last time, he suddenly stopped and leaned over me. Asked me whether I wanted to live or die. If I wanted to live, I had to keep my mouth shut and carry on working at the care home for as long as Thea Aldrin was alive. If I ever defied him again, he would come back. With the axe.'

Malena ran her hands through her tousled hair, and Fredrika thought that there must have been several copies of the snuff movie, including one that had been shortened in order to avoid revealing the identity of the perpetrator, and that could be shown to other people. Perhaps even sold.

'You didn't feel you could go to the police?' Fredrika said.

'Not under any circumstances. He made it very clear that the police would never be able to touch someone like him. Nobody would believe me if I said that Morgan Axberger had been in my apartment with an axe, threatening to kill me.'

True. Regrettable, but true.

Fredrika sensed that Malena had more to tell her.

'He was filming me,' Malena whispered.

'Sorry?'

'He showed me afterwards. He filmed me while I was watching the film, and when I tried to run away. How sick is that?'

Fredrika thought for a moment, giving Malena time to recover.

'You're going to have to testify against him, Malena.'

'I know.'

'One more thing.' Fredrika glanced at her notes. 'You said the killer smiled at the man behind the camera. Did you see him? The man who was holding the camera, I mean?'

'No, I didn't.'

'But you're sure it was a man?'

Malena nodded, and when she whispered her answer, Fredrika went cold.

'Morgan told me. When he raised the axe for the last time, he leaned forward and said: "Now do you realise that I was the one holding the camera?"'

# CHAPTER 61

Peder Rydh left Jimmy's room the same way as he assumed his brother had left: through the patio door. Leaving the care worker and Micke behind, he strode across the lawn to Thea Aldrin's room. Thea didn't have time to realise that he was coming to see her, otherwise she would probably have tried to lock him out.

She gave a start as he stepped inside.

'You shouldn't sit here with the door wide open, Thea.'

His voice sounded completely different from the one he normally used.

Thea was staring at him; she lowered the book she had been reading.

'There are a few things you forgot to mention to me and my colleagues. If you can't speak like a normal person, then you're going to have to write. Because I'm not leaving here until you tell me what happened to my brother Jimmy. The boy who lived across the way; he came over to your window yesterday.'

When Thea still didn't speak, Peder felt a spurt

563

of white-hot rage. He grabbed the old woman by the shoulders and hauled her to her feet.

'You. Will. Tell. Me.'

Thea made a feeble attempt to free herself, but she knew it was futile.

'*Tell me.*'

Her silence decided the matter. He looked at her for a long time, then whispered:

'We know who sends you flowers.'

The words had an immediate effect. Thea shook her head and tried once more to pull away.

But Peder held on tight.

'Oh, yes, we know. We know that Valter Lund is your missing son, Johan. The only thing we don't know, you old bitch, is what the fucker thinks he has to thank you for. Every bloody Saturday.'

She didn't cry. But she kept on shaking her head, and then she spoke.

*She spoke.*

Peder was so surprised that he let go of her.

'Please. Please.'

Her voice was hoarse and rough. Clearly under-used, but still functioning.

'You can talk.'

He cursed his words; they sounded childish, and robbed him of his authority.

'Almost everyone can,' said Thea.

Still terrified. Her legs gave way, and she had to sit down.

'You keep Johan out of this! Do you hear me?'

Peder had to sit down as well. His head was

spinning. His anxiety over Jimmy faded away for a moment. Day after day, they had followed up one lead after another. Every time those leads had pointed to Thea. Now he was sitting on her floor, and he had no idea how he was ever going to get up.

'There's just one thing I want to know.'

His heart was beating so hard it was almost chafing against his ribs.

'What happened to Jimmy?'

Thea clutched the arms of her chair.

'Johan has nothing to do with his disappearance.'

'Tell me what happened.'

He ought to call Alex and Fredrika. Tell them what he had just found out: that the great writer was perfectly capable of speaking after all. That her son was a highly sensitive issue, and that she was obviously ready to sacrifice anything for him. Even the protection that her silence had provided all these years.

She cleared her throat quietly several times, gave a dry cough. For a moment Peder thought her voice might let her down.

*In that case she was going to have to write.*

'He happened to overhear a conversation he shouldn't have heard.'

Peder could see that she was hesitating, choosing her words with great care. He raised one finger, and saw that it was trembling.

'Listen to me, Thea. Don't you dare lie. I'm warning you. Don't.'

She shook her head.

'I'm not lying. That's what happened. He was standing outside the window. We didn't hear him at first, but then he called out. As if he'd suddenly been frightened. We had quite a heated discussion.'

'We? Who's we? Who else was here?'

Her eyes filled with tears.

'I can't. Forgive me.'

'Of course you can,' he hissed, and Peder regained the upper hand.

'Was it your son Johan?'

Thea's eyes opened wide.

'No, absolutely not. He's never been here. Never.'

'So who was it, then?'

Another dramatic pause. Then the words that froze Peder's blood.

'Morgan Axberger.'

Peder slowly got to his feet. Axberger, that rich bastard who had been on the periphery of the inquiry all along, the man nobody had dared to pinpoint as a suspect.

'What happened?'

'I don't know. I just saw Morgan take your brother away. He hasn't been in touch since. I'm so very sorry.'

Sorry for what? Peder felt sick with anxiety.

'What were you talking about when Jimmy overheard?'

'The past.'

There was no time. He really wanted to hear the

wonder that public rumour assigned her to him, and that the Major's sisters in England should fancy they were about to have a sister-in-law.

Dobbin, who was thus vigorously besieged, was in the meanwhile in a state of the most odious tranquillity. He used to laugh when the young fellows of the regiment joked him about Glorvina's manifest attentions to him. 'Bah!' said he, 'she is only keeping her hand in – she practises upon me as she does upon Mrs Tozer's piano, because it's the most handy instrument in the station. I am much too battered and old for such a fine young lady as Glorvina.' And so he went on riding with her, and copying music and verses into her albums, and playing at chess with her very submissively; for it is with these simple amusements that some officers in India are accustomed to while away their leisure moments; while others of a less domestic turn hunt hogs, and shoot snipes, or gamble and smoke cheroots, and betake themselves to brandy and water. As for Sir Michael O'Dowd, though his lady and her sister both urged him to call upon the Major to explain himself, and not keep on torturing a poor innocent girl in that shameful way, the old soldier refused point-blank to have anything to do with the conspiracy. 'Faith, the Major's big enough to choose for himself,' Sir Michael said; 'he'll ask ye when he wants ye;' or else he would turn the matter off jocularly, declaring that 'Dobbin was too young to keep house, and had written home to ask lave of his mamma'. Nay, he went farther, and in private communications with his Major, would caution and rally him – crying, 'Mind your oi, Dob, my boy, them girls is bent on mischief – me Lady has just got a box of gowns from Europe, and there's a pink satin for Glorvina, which will finish ye, Dob, if it's in the power of woman or satin to move ye.'

But the truth is, neither beauty nor fashion could conquer him. Out honest friend had but one idea of a woman in his head, and that one did not in the least resemble Miss Glorvina O'Dowd in pink satin. A gentle little woman in black, with large eyes and